THE KEY
TO THE
FUTURE

ALSO BY MICHAEL BANAS

In Plain Sight
Last Words Spoken
Twelve Men in the Huddle
The Chief Resident
The Center of Excellence
Pennsylvania's Finest

THE KEY
TO THE
FUTURE

A NOVEL

BY
MICHAEL BANAS

CHAPTER ONE
DOCTOR SULLIVAN

"Mrs. Appleton, what's the earliest memory of your child-hood?"

"Excuse me, doctor? I'm having trouble hearing you."

"I said, what's your earliest recollection in life?" asked Dr. Sullivan loudly. "As a child, that is?"

"Well, that's a difficult question to answer," responded the frail patient lying in bed. "I'm ninety-four years old."

Dr. John Sullivan paused, allowing his patient to search her memory banks. Random noise from a nursing station just outside the door filtered into the room. On the patient's nightstand stood a collection of family photos.

"That's one of the two questions I ask all patients on the Alzheimer's floor," whispered Sullivan to the medical resident at his side. "The short-term memory is gone, but the long term is always there."

"Well, I can remember being a little girl and my mother running into the kitchen yelling for me to come outside," stated Mrs. Appleton.

"Yes. Go on."

"She yelled Gertrude, come outside quick, and look into the sky!"

"Interesting," said Dr. Sullivan. "What happened next?"

"I ran out to the back porch and immediately heard a strange noise overhead, a whirring sound. Then I looked up into the sky."

"Was it sunny?" asked Sullivan.

"Yes, now that you ask… it was sunny," responded the patient with a smile. "I had to squint from the afternoon sun."

"And then what?"

"I saw it."

"What, Mrs. Appleton? What did you see?"

"An airplane," said the patient while looking at her medical team. "It was painted light blue and I could see the pilot in the open seat. He flew right over the house and waved at us. Can you imagine?"

"Wonderful," said Sullivan with a clap of his hands. "You must have been thrilled."

"We were, doctor. It was rare to see an automobile in the neighborhood, let alone an airplane. We had never seen one before! I'll never forget that day. I couldn't believe my eyes. Mother even wrote a letter to Aunt Lottie in Georgia, just to tell her."

"Very good, Mrs. Appleton," concluded Dr. Sullivan as he rose from the bedside. "Tomorrow in group session, I'm going to ask you more about that day, O.K.?"

"Sure. Come to think of it, I almost tripped over my dog running out onto the porch that day."

"What was the dog's name?"

"Penny. She was all black with a spot of white under her chin."

"You see? You do have a good memory Mrs. Appleton. It just takes a little nudge to activate it."

"I hope you are right doctor. I'm trying my best."

"Tonight, as homework, I want you to think about the most memorable day of your life," said Sullivan. "A day you'll never forget…"

"The Battle of the Bulge!" yelled Mrs. Appleton.

"Excuse me?"

"The Battle of the Bulge," continued the patient. "I'll never forget it."

"The Battle of the Bulge? Why?"

"My Walter was in it."

"Your husband?"

"Yes. He sent me a long letter just before the battle, saying how dangerous it was over there. It was awful. He even told me to order a coffin in his size. That's how confident he was about dying. Oh, I sat by the radio for days waiting for news."

"The majority of patients her age will recall the war," said Sullivan to the resident. "It was the defining event of their generation."

"So many good boys died over there," continued Gertrude Appleton with a shake of her head. "A real shame. They left right after high school graduation. I can remember the train leaving the station. We were all waving and crying."

"And your husband, Mrs. Appleton, was he safe?"

"Yes, he made it. He lost all of his hearing in one ear, but compared to some other families in the neighborhood, we were darn lucky. He only described the battle to me once, then never spoke of it again."

"Very good, Mrs. Appleton," said Sullivan. "Thank you for sharing that recollection with us. Now, I want you to concentrate on those two events overnight. O.K.?"

"Yes," said Mrs. Appleton, now looking at the medical resident. "Young lady, can you please pull that afghan over me. I'm catching a chill."

"Sure I can," said Dr. Olivia Garcia while covering up the patient. "There you go, Mrs. Appleton."

The attending physician and his chief resident left the room and entered the nursing station. A dimming of the overhead lights signified quiet time on the Alzheimer's floor.

"That's a wrap, Dr. Garcia," said Sullivan. "Rounds tomorrow morning at nine o'clock."

"Great," replied Olivia Garcia. "I like the way you gave Mrs. Appleton an assignment for the night. Hopefully she'll be thinking about that airplane."

"Geriatrics can be a rewarding field," said Sullivan. "You just have to look for the little things. Be patient. That's the key to becoming a good geriatrician. Always remember my personal mantra."

"Which is?"

"I call it the 3Rs: Recall, Respect and Rejuvenate."

"Wow, that's beautiful," stated Garcia. "I'm seriously thinking of going into the field. I have to decide in less than three months. It's between geriatrics and cardiology."

"Great options. I love caring for the elderly. But then again, I'm the only geriatrician on the Philadelphia General Hospital staff. So it's not a profession in vogue."

"Sometimes you have to break from the herd," said Olivia with a smile. "Good-bye Dr. Sullivan."

"Smart girl," said the lone nurse in the station area keying data into a computer. "I like her."

"I agree, Nurse Adams," said Sullivan. "She connects well with the patients."

An awkward pause occurred between the two health care professionals, each searching for their next line. The nursing station was desolate, the Alzheimer's floor not a hotbed of activity within the hospital. The ward was located in a remote wing of the Philadelphia General.

"How's your mom?" asked Nurse Adams.

"She's hanging in there," responded Sullivan. "Thank you for asking."

"Tell her I said hello."

"I will," said Sullivan with a nod of his head. "She'll appreciate that. I'll see you tomorrow."

"Yes. Have a good night," replied Adams with a push of her glasses up her nose. "Goodnight, Dr. Sullivan."

The physician walked down the empty corridor toward the elevator, his new shoes squeaking on the tile floor. Just outside the elevator hung a sign, welcoming visitors to the floor:

Welcome to the Alzheimer's Ward
Philadelphia General Hospital
Dedicated to the Memory of Your Loved One
Director – John F. Sullivan, M.D.

Next to the sign was a picture of Sullivan, taken five years ago during the ward's dedication ceremony. It was his first year in medical practice.

The elevator ride down to the lobby stopped on the third floor, allowing Dr. Vincent Pagano to step in. At his side strolled a female physician assistant, wearing a white lab coat atop high heels. Pagano and Sullivan were medical school classmates, having graduated together ten years ago.

"Sully, how's it going up in memory lane?" asked Pagano. His assistant laughed at the comment yet did not look at Sullivan. She stood close to the orthopedic surgeon's side.

"Very good," replied Dr. Sullivan, having long grown accustomed to his colleague's crude humor. "A ninety-year old patient told me today the first time she ever saw an airplane in the sky."

"Whoa," said Pagano. "Tell me more!"

"The pilot in the open cockpit waved at her."

"How about the first time she got laid?" asked the surgeon. "Ask her if she remembers that? Maybe her husband was watching Babe Ruth on T.V."

"I'm not going to respond to that comment," said Sullivan as the doors opened into the crowded hospital lobby.

"By the way Sully, sorry to hear about the judge's decision. Demolition is in T-minus thirty days. I hope you'll be there."

The trio stepped into the crowded hospital lobby.

"The scrap heap of history," laughed Pagano as he strolled away in the opposite direction. "Sorry, Sully."

Outside the hospital Dr. Sullivan stopped at a corner food truck, picking up a salad, two hot dogs and a small gyro. He headed west toward home, his house a large double block situated between 43rd and 44th Street, just off the Philadelphia General campus. While walking up the concrete steps he noticed the front bedroom window to be open, a good sign.

"Mom, I'm home," shouted Sullivan as he walked in the door, shuffling some junk mail through his hands. A parakeet in the kitchen began to chirp excitedly.

"She's dozing," said an elderly nurse walking down the stairwell. "Had a rough day."

"How so, Ella?"

"Nauseous, bowels all clogged up. Starting to develop a cough," said the visiting nurse as she gathered her purse. "Said she wants to die."

"She's been saying that for two years. Did she take her medications?"

"Yes, but under protest," said the nurse with a grin. "She's a stubborn one."

"Thanks Ella, have a nice evening."

"You're welcome, Dr. Sullivan."

"Oh Ella, I almost forgot. Did you remember about tomorrow night? I have to give a lecture at 7 P.M."

"I remembered doctor," said the nurse as she walked out to door. "Been doing those memory exercises you taught me. I'm good until 9 P.M."

"Thank you," replied Sullivan. He walked into the kitchen and placed the salad in his mother's favorite bowl. "Mom, I've got some salad for you, extra tomatoes."

"Doctor John Sullivan," chirped the parakeet. "My son, the doctor!"

"Mom?" shouted Sullivan, now walking up the stairs with the food on a dinner tray.

He entered the front room of the home to see his mother sitting up in bed and staring out the window, a cat curled up beside her. A fresh spring breeze helped ventilate the stuffy confines. Her eyes were open but she didn't look at her son as he approached the bedside. The roar of the #42 bus shook the house as it passed by, screeching to a halt at the bottom of the hill.

"I'm ready for the bone yard," stated Martha Sullivan. "Call the grave digger."

"Ella said you had a cough. What's going on?"

"Nurse Ella is an angel, having to clean up after me day in and day out. I couldn't make it to the toilet again today... messed up the sheets."

"She's a great nurse. We're lucky to have her."

"Did you get the gyro?"

"Yes," answered Sullivan, now placing the meal before his mother, the cat suddenly alert.

"A fresh salad for you and one gyro... no onions, for Moses."

"Have you ever seen a cat that likes gyros?"

"He's your best friend Mom. Always at your side."

The trio ate dinner together in silence as a popular game show blared from the television atop a cluttered vanity. It was Mrs. Sullivan's 445th consecutive show – a streak she was quite proud of. Next to the T.V. was a framed picture of a soldier in uniform, draped with a Purple Heart.

"Somebody called to remind you about a talk tomorrow night," said Mrs. Sullivan. "He didn't need a call back."

"Must have been Fred, he's all upset about the final ruling to tear down the General Hospital's old Franklin Wing."

"What are you talking about?"

"The Philadelphia General's Franklin Wing, they're finally going to tear it down."

"The Franklin Wing... where I used to work?"

"Yep, your old wing Mom. I'm giving a historical lecture on Dr. Schmidt, whose office was in the basement of the Franklin Wing. He was quite the eccentric."

"That place is haunted. Stay out of there," stammered Mrs. Sullivan with a sudden sense of apprehension.

"Oh Mom," laughed the doctor. "That's folklore, trust me. I've been down there a bunch of times and guess what? No ghosts."

"They never found his body," said Mrs. Sullivan with a sudden clarity in her eyes. "I was a nurse on the Franklin for a long time. I remember the day Dr. Schmidt disappeared. He vanished into thin air."

"I'm just trying to document as much as possible before they implode the building. So much history will be lost. It's a real shame."

"When are they going to knock it down?"

"In a few weeks."

"He won't allow it."

"Who Mom? Who won't allow it?"

"The ghost of Zachary Schmidt," replied his mother while stroking Moses. "He won't allow his office to be destroyed. Trust me. I knew Dr. Schmidt very well."

"He's dead, Mom."

"No, he's not," retorted the octogenarian with confidence. She pulled Moses a bit closer to her side. "He kept reappearing, even after they said he was gone. He's still roaming around in that basement of his."

"Did you ever see him again?"

Mrs. Sullivan didn't respond, as if trying to remember events from long ago. Slowly she shook her head with a frown across her face.

"Mom, do you remember the first time you ever saw an airplane in the sky?"

"Oh, don't start with the memory stuff," moaned his mother with a wave of a gnarled, arthritic hand. "If there is one thing that still works in this old body – it's my memory. Now put on channel 48. The Pugs are playing."

"Sure Mom," said her son while switching channels. "Did you ever see Babe Ruth on television?" Despite his mother's love for the game, John Sullivan never cared for sports.

"Don't be silly, television wasn't invented then."

"Right, I guess not," came the reply. "Very good Mom, I'll see you during the seventh inning stretch. Call if you need anything."

Dr. Sullivan just grinned as he watched his mother now concentrate on the starting lineup introduction. She was an avid baseball fan, especially when it came to her Brookside Pugs, a minor league team located just north of the city. Moses was already fast asleep at her side, his stomach full of gyro. He quietly cleaned up the dinner plates and headed downstairs.

The doctor spent the next few hours in his study preparing for his lecture the following day. He would be addressing the West Philadelphia Historical Society, whose legal action to halt the destruction of the Franklin Wing was recently dismissed by a district judge. His topic was Dr. Zachary Schmidt, a physician who practiced at the Philadelphia General Hospital for twenty years, until he mysteriously disappeared. Sullivan had been researching Schmidt and his vast contributions to the medical community in preparation for the talk. As he scanned some old articles from the Philadelphia Chronicle it was obvious that his mother was correct in her description of Schmidt. The press depicted him as a quirky physician who at times promoted unconventional methods of care to his patients. The newspaper attached adjectives to his name such as dashing, whimsical and offbeat along with the occasional odd and erratic. A story from 1966 included a picture of Schmidt and his trademark handlebar mustache, next to a contraption attempting to take x-rays by using a magnetic field. Surrounding the physician were nurses and students in awe, a few staring at Schmidt and the others at the apparatus. The doctor wore a long white lab coat and bowtie.

"John, seventh inning stretch!" came the cry from upstairs. "Hurry!"

Sullivan bolted from his desk and ran upstairs to help his mother out of bed, her bony frame now at ninety pounds.

"Let me go," she said with a push of his hand. "I can stand alone."

Together they stood at attention as *America the Beautiful* played over the loudspeaker at Pug Stadium, a seventh inning stretch tradition at the park. Throughout the song she held a trembling hand across her heart. Immediately afterwards he helped his infirmed mother back into bed as Moses repositioned next to her.

"Pugs are up by one," said Mrs. Sullivan.

"Great. Good night, Mom."

"I hope they don't blow this one. I don't trust their bullpen."

"Good night, Mom," said Sullivan as he exited the bedroom.

"John."

"Yes, Mom."

"Stay out of that hospital basement."

"Mom, please! There are no such things as ghosts."

"Listen to your dying mother for once... and stay out of that basement. It's haunted!"

CHAPTER TWO
THE HISTORICAL SOCIETY

The West Philadelphia Historical Society met once a month in the home of their president, Attorney Frederick Mills. His home sat opposite the 40th Street Trolley Portal along the midblock of Baltimore Avenue. Mills inherited the aging homestead from his father, who like his son, struggled as a lawyer. The building was erected in 1900 and honored with a Historical Society Landmark plaque, allowing a tax break for the owner. The two front rooms of the aging construct served as office space for the attorney while the rest of the house was residential. The Historical Society gathered upstairs in a large, musty drawing room, complete with a mantle fireplace and heavy oak molding. A series of ornate chandeliers hung from a cracked ceiling, their light reflecting off a framed antique map of West Philadelphia on the wall.

"I threw everything at them," said Attorney Mills to several society members including John Sullivan. "But unfortunately in the end, the judge decided against our injunction to delay demolition."

"Money talks," said a tall, skinny member with a high-pitched voice wearing a button-down sweater. "And we know who has the money."

"The Pagano Destruction Company," said Mills with a shake of his head. "I looked it up. This judge has never decided against them over the past fifteen years." Mills was a short, portly man dressed in a crumpled long sleeve shirt with suspenders holding up his trousers. Despite not drinking beer over the past ten years, his stomach protruded grandly over his waistline. He never married and lived in the house alone. "Must be on their payroll."

"Well, what's done is done," said Dr. Sullivan. "Our job now is to try and document and preserve as much history as possible over the next three weeks."

"Yeah. You did all you could Fred," said another member with a walrus mustache and twitching left eye. "Thanks for all your hard work."

"You're welcome, Wally," replied the president.

A total of seventeen members showed up for the meeting, which began with preliminary statements from the president and treasurer. Scattered throughout the room were several worn sofas and large wing back chairs. Two older members stood in the back of the room with canes, their lumbago too severe to allow a seated position. After a brief introduction, Dr. Sullivan stood up and walked to the front of the room, facing his colleagues. He held a remote control device in his right hand, synchronized to a slide projector atop a table.

"Good evening everyone," said Sullivan. "Today's lecture is on the life and times of Dr. Zachary Wilhelm Schmidt, a colorful and controversial physician, whose office occupied the ground floor of the Philadelphia General's Franklin Wing."

"Can you please speak up?" asked one of the members standing in the back. "Us old-timers back here can't hear you."

"Sure I can, Bart," said Sullivan loudly as he advanced the first slide, delivering the picture of a young Zachary Schmidt disembarking a ship in New York Harbor.

"Zachary Schmidt was born in Stuttgart, Germany in 1930," said Sullivan. "His father was a laborer who died in a factory accident when Zachary was one year old. His mother suffered from tuberculosis and to the best of my knowledge was confined to a sanatorium when Zachary was an infant."

"What year was he born?" asked a member in the second row.

"1930," responded Sullivan.

"The great depression significantly impacted Germany," interjected the society member while looking around at his colleagues. "A worldwide economic disaster."

"Correct," said Sullivan. "With the Weimar Republic ailing and the Nazi party gaining power, a decision was made to send young Zachary to the United States with his uncle, Rickard von Steiger. This is the first known photo of Zachary Schmidt, a three-year old arriving in New York Harbor with his uncle."

The grainy photo on the screen was faded and projected a proud uncle with thick mustache and derby hat holding his nephew, bundled up against a cold November wind. Next to the travelers stood a stack of wood traveling chests, containing all their possessions. A woman in the background may have been von Steiger's wife.

"Does anybody recognize the von Steiger name?" asked Sullivan.

Silence.

"The Physics building on the University of Pennsylvania campus is named after him," said Sullivan. "Von Steiger was a well-respected physicist in Germany and confidant of all the great German scientists of his time, including Albert Einstein. He fled Nazi Germany along with Einstein in 1933. Von Steiger was warmly welcomed at Penn while Einstein of course ended up in Princeton, New Jersey."

"He was immediately accepted by the Penn Physics department?" asked Mills.

"Yes," answered Sullivan. "Solely based on his name and work in Germany. He was an all-star of the era."

"Did he help develop the atomic bomb?" asked Bart from the rear, with the assist of a gnarled oak cane.

"I'm not sure of his role in the Manhattan…"

"Does anybody remember the name of the plane that dropped the atom bomb?" interrupted the veteran.

"On Nagasaki or Hiroshima?" asked another member, the discussion starting to veer off tract. "You have to be specific with the question, Bart."

"Little Boy was the name of the A-bomb the plane dropped," countered the old codger with another shake of his cane, now stepping forward. "Not Fat Man, but Little Boy. That should give the answer away to everyone in this room."

"Gentlemen, gentlemen," said Sullivan, well aware of the group's penchant to argue over historical trivia.

"Nagasaki was the first city destroyed," said a member from the front row. "Or was it Hiroshima?"

"The Enola Gay!" yelled Bart. "The plane was named the Enola Gay!"

"I was going to say that, but you didn't give enough time!"

"It was named after the mother of the pilot," added Bart. "Enola Gay Tibbets!"

"Gentlemen please," said Attorney Mills now standing. "Today's lecture is on Dr. Schmidt and the old Franklin Wing. So please allow John to continue his discussion."

"Thank you, Fred."

Dr. Sullivan continued his presentation, describing in detail the storied career of Dr. von Steiger, who along with his wife raised young Zachary Schmidt. Von Steiger was credited with several revolutionary ideas within his field that originally appeared to be unfounded, yet ultimately withstood the test of time, including bold predictions regarding the use of computers in the future. Through a series of slides Sullivan painted the picture of a brilliant physicist, always thinking outside of the box until his untimely death in 1962.

"Untimely? How so?" asked Attorney Mills.

"An explosion in the basement of the Franklin building itself," said Sullivan. "To the best of my knowledge, von Steiger was conducting research on radioactive gases when a spark ignited a fireball, resulting in instantaneous death. The explosion so severe they never found his remains."

"How badly was the Franklin Wing damaged?"

"Several newspaper articles described major structural damage to the facility and there was discussion of razing the building, but Zachary Schmidt led a spirited charge to preserve the lab, in honor of his uncle. Schmidt relocated his office and research facilities to the basement where his uncle perished. He continued to work there until his ultimate disappearance.

"Disappearance?" asked Attorney Mills. "Schmidt disappeared?"

A low rumble of discussion began to fill the darkened room.

"Gentlemen, gentlemen, please," said Sullivan holding up both hands. "I don't want to get ahead of myself. Let me first begin with Zachary Schmidt's education and ultimate acceptance to the hospital faculty. The end of the lecture will touch upon his final days at the Philadelphia General Hospital, during which much has been written about."

Over the next twenty minutes John Sullivan outlined the story of Zachary Schmidt's life. He was a child prodigy whose intelligence landed him an academic scholarship at St. Joseph's Preparatory school in center city Philadelphia. He was high school class valedictorian and attended college and medical school at the University of Pennsylvania, graduating in 1955 with a degree in medicine. After a general medicine residency, he joined the staff at the Philadelphia General Hospital in 1959. Over the next three years he worked closely with his uncle in the Physics department at Penn, helping to develop some major medical breakthroughs in the field of radiology and infectious disease. His research greatly assisted in the development of antibiotics beyond penicillin, and ultimately set the groundwork for a polio vaccine, thus impacting the world as a whole.

"Is that him?" asked Mills while staring at a photo of the 1959 Philadelphia General Hospital medical staff. "The one with the bow tie?"

"Yes, it is," said Sullivan with a laser pointer trained on Schmidt. "He always wore a bow tie and throughout his adult life displayed a handle bar mustache."

Sullivan then advanced the slide show to bring a professional photo shot of Schmidt to the screen. He was wearing a suit coat and bow tie while staring at the camera, a subtle grin and twinkle in his eye. The photo captured his essence from mid torso upwards.

"A handsome man," said Mills. "How old was he then?"

"This was 1962," replied Sullivan. "The year of his uncle's death. So he was thirty-two. Zachary Schmidt was indeed quite the ladies' man according to several nurses who worked with him throughout his career."

"Was he married? Did he have children?"

"No, he was not married," mused Sullivan while staring at the photo. "But from my understanding, he never lacked female companionship, and that's from a reliable source."

The crowd just stared at the photo, which was a bit mesmerizing, as if Schmidt was staring directly back at them. The rumble of a trolley car passing by gently shook the chandelier.

"It was his mystique," continued Sullivan slowly. "His mystique is what defined him, not his brilliance or foresight that helped generate some of the greatest medical discoveries of his time – but the charisma of the man. His persona was said to be intoxicating to those around him. He had a presence that suggested something extraordinary, mysterious yet magical – almost mythical."

"I've got a chill down my spine," said Attorney Mills while staring at the photo.

"Well turn up the heat in this barn!" shouted Bart from the rear of the room. "I've got long johns on and my toes are still cold."

"The untimely death of his uncle greatly affected him," said Sullivan. "He suffered dearly from the loss."

"I can see why," said Mills. "Von Steiger was the father he never had."

"Dr. Schmidt continued his contributions to the medical world over the next twenty years," said Sullivan while advancing a series of house staff slides. "In the mid 1960s he helped develop laser technology instrumental in the treatment of retinal disease. In the early 1970s he helped set up a multilevel clinical trial which demonstrated that lowering cholesterol levels prevents heart disease."

"A forward thinker," quipped Mills.

"Exactly," said Sullivan. "He was always a bit ahead of the curve."

"What about the disappearance part?" asked the now impatient veteran in the rear of the room. "It's getting late and I'm about to disappear... if anybody cares."

"All was going well with Dr. Schmidt's career until about 1973," said Sullivan. "Up until that point he was well respected nationwide."

"What happened?"

"He began to make bold predictions concerning events about to affect the entire world. Quite outlandish predictions that got him in hot water and ultimately led to his bizarre demise."

"The 1970s," said Mills. "Was it a medical prediction?"

"Perhaps," said Sullivan with a smile. "Think now... the early 1970s in Philadelphia."

The congregation went into deep thought, searching their collective minds for an answer.

"The Flyers win the Stanley Cup.... the Flyers win the Stanley Cup!" yelled a member.

"Nope."

"An epidemic? Just give us a hint, John," said Mills.

"Yes, it was an epidemic of historic proportions," said the speaker.

"Disco music!" said the man with the walrus mustache. "Disco fever!" A round of laughter followed.

"No, Wally. It wasn't disco music."

"I've got it!" shouted Mills.

"Let's hear it."

"Legionnaires' Disease," said Mills with a confident nod of his head. "1976, the Bellevue-Stratford Hotel, downtown Philadelphia. Bingo!" He snapped his fingertips.

"Excellent guess... but wrong."

"Spit it out already," yelled the back row heckler. "For Christ's sake I'm eighty-seven years old. Make it fast."

"Dr. Schmidt began to predict a plague of historical proportion about to fall upon a subset of the populace, perhaps in retribution for their hedonistic ways."

Silence filled the room.

"Gentlemen, again think ahead of the curve. Schmidt was always ahead of the curve."

No one spoke.

"Alright," said Sullivan. "I'll spell it out. He spoke of a horrid curse about to befall upon the gay and homosexual community throughout the world. A menace that would become the bane of their existence."

"HIV!" yelled Miles. "Oh my god!"

"Precisely," said Sullivan while pointing a finger towards the president. "Human Immunodeficiency Virus, or AIDS."

"He used that terminology? In the 1970s?"

"Not exactly," said Sullivan. "But in retrospect he spoke eerily of a lethal blood borne disease with no cure, predominately affecting homosexuals and intravenous drug abusers. A malady that would claim the lives of millions of people before it was brought under control."

"Why?" asked Mills. "I mean... I can see why his prediction would generate outrage. But why would he talk of such nonsense back then?"

"Schmidt spoke in broad strokes," said Sullivan. "He was trying to generate an open dialogue within the medical community. He sensed the epidemic coming."

"But how?"

"I can't answer that," said Sullivan with a shake of his head. "No one can."

"Amazing."

"He began to write medical editorials making reference to the safety of the nation's blood banks. He advocated the proactive dispersal of condoms and championed safe sex practices. He even tried to open a free hypodermic needle clinic in West Philadelphia, in an attempt to protect those addicted to heroin."

"I can imagine the outrage," said Mills. "It must have been brutal."

"It was," said Sullivan. "He was immediately branded a medical heretic, a quack, a quirky physician gone off the deep edge."

"What happened next?" asked Bart.

The greater the establishment tried to squelch him, the louder he spoke. In 1975 he wrote an editorial to the Philadelphia Chronicle imploring the medical and social community to take immediate action against a pandemic about to take hold of the gay community. He called it his "medical manifesto." Sullivan then ran through a series of Chronicle articles with the name "Schmidt" commanding the headlines. One title in large bold print simply read – "Philadelphia General Physician Predicts Medical Holocaust!"

"I do remember that headline," said Mills. "I'm afraid to ask... but what came next?"

"He was warned, sanctioned and ultimately dismissed from the PGH medical staff," said Sullivan. "He then took his message to the streets and was arrested several times. Ultimately he was committed to the old Psychiatry wing at the General."

Silence again filled the room as Sullivan brought up the final slide of the lecture. It was a mug shot of Schmidt on the Psychiatry wing wearing a hospital issued white gown with a steel necklace around his neck. At the end of the necklace was a single skeleton key.

"This was his final photograph, just weeks before his disappearance. Believe it or not he was scheduled for a state mandated lobotomy the day after he went missing. The medical staff diagnosed him as a chronic paranoid schizophrenic."

"Holy cow, a lobotomy?" said Mills.

"Yes," said Sullivan. "Remember, it's the mid 1970s. Lobotomies were still being performed, albeit on a small scale."

"What's with the key?" asked the veteran from the rear.

"Good question. He always wore an old skeleton key around his neck. It was a well-known fact among the house staff. That necklace you see in the photo was pure tungsten steel, welded into a loop without a latch. It never came off his body. You would need a blow torch or hacksaw to remove it."

"Wolfram!" said the walrus man. "That's what tungsten steel is. It was part of my doctorate in college. It was recognized as a new element in about 1781, then a metal in 1783. Tungsten is a tremendously hard metal, with a density similar to gold."

"What's the significance of the key?" asked Mills.

"It was part of his odd persona," answered Sullivan. "Schmidt was once quoted in a newspaper article claiming it to be 'the key to the future.'"

"That's no ordinary key!" said the veteran from the rear.

"How so?" asked Mills.

"Gentlemen, I was raised by a locksmith and spent thousands of hours in my father's shop, learning about locks and keys. That key is from the Baroque era, early 1700s. I would guess it was from France and made of pure gold. It would be worth a pretty penny today."

"How can you tell?"

"The cut. The design. Keys from different eras rarely carried a date on them. But each era had a specific look."

"Interesting information," said Sullivan.

"So what about his disappearance?"

"Yes, yes," said Sullivan. "His disappearance. On the eve of his planned surgical procedure, Dr. Schmidt escaped from the lockdown unit he was housed in. A general alarm was sounded and a Philadelphia policeman on beat patrol spotted him just outside the hospital. Several witnesses described a surreal foot chase between the two, with Schmidt in a hospital gown and bedroom slippers, dashing down University Avenue. The two bolted into the Franklin Wing and rushed past a night shift security guard. They were last seen heading toward Schmidt's office after which, the sentry described a brief flash of bright light and a short high-pitched zoom."

"And...?" asked Mills.

"Incredibly, neither man was ever seen again," said Sullivan.

"What? That's impossible!"

"The date was July 4th, 1976."

"Our nation's bicentennial."

"Correct," said Dr. John Sullivan. "The day two Philadelphians vanished into thin air."

CHAPTER THREE
PAGANO DESTRUCTION

Tommy Pagano Jr. was the CEO of Pagano Destruction Company and went by the nickname 'Winky'." He took control of the company at the age of thirty, which at the time appeared to be a premature transition from his father. However, one week later, Tommy Pagano Sr. was gunned down in a South Philadelphia eatery while enjoying some potato gnocchi with a sprinkle of Parmesan cheese, the act so violent portions of his spleen were found on the ceiling fans. The hit was reportedly in retribution for some massive outstanding company debt. Tommy Pagano Sr. lost his life, but not the family business – a calculated transaction that Winky always respected.

Tommy Jr. was of average height and a tad overweight. He usually had an unlit cigar stub hanging from his mouth, surrounded by a rough unshaven face. Dark monochromic clothing covered his frame along with a pork pie hat. His right eye uncontrollably twitched, hence the moniker that followed him throughout his adult life. He ran Pagano Destruction for the past twenty-five years, during which time he barely kept the business afloat.

"Finally," smirked Winky. "Finally, we're going to blow that building to kingdom come. This project has been a thorn in my side for too many years." The CEO sat in a drab South

Philadelphia office at the head of the table, his inner circle in attendance. "First the bidding war with the Bloomsburg boys, then the ordinance delay at city hall, and now these Historical Society crackpots."

"You can thank the judge for that," said Winky's personal assistant, a female in her late thirties who was no stranger to the plastic surgeon's office. "The usual for the judge, Mr. Pagano?" She wore a black skirt and tight, white blouse.

"No, no. Double the judge's standard fee, Stephanie," replied Winky. "And send his wife a pearl necklace from Uncle Frank's place down on Walnut Street." Behind the company chair hung a picture of his father, taken just six months before he was sacrificed. A look of concern ran across the face of the deceased.

"Why so long a delay?" asked Rocco, the on-site foreman for Pagano Destruction. "I mean, we've been renting the equipment for months now. The machines are just collecting rust up on the lot."

"And losing thousands of dollars a month," barked CEO Pagano, his right eye flickering even faster.

"Some Historical Society was claiming the basement to be the final resting place for two men who died in the building back in the seventies, their bodies never found," said Attorney Louis Pompano. "They were represented by some legal chump from West Philly. The judge had to follow some protocol to make it look official. Therefore, the lengthy delay." Pompano was the eldest man in the room and the company's longstanding attorney.

"There's always a goddamn fly in the ointment," moaned Winky "Ain't that right, Steph?"

"Yes, Mr. Pagano," said the secretary while staring down at her cell phone. She patted her boss's hairy left hand while speaking, ignoring the ring on his stubby fourth finger.

"Gentlemen, I'd like to point out one clause in the ruling to proceed forward," said Attorney Pompano. "That being the Historical Society has access to the building subbasement area over the next four-week period. They want to document the history of the building." While saying the word "history" the attorney mockingly raised his hands in quotation mark fashion.

"What!" yelled Rocco. "I don't approve of that. We're going to be laying some heavy lines of explosives across the grid. It's dark and dangerous down there. Somebody is going to get hurt."

"I know, I know," said the attorney with a raise of his hand. "But to appear fair, the judge had to give them a concession. So, I would instruct the demo team to be aware of their presence. To my understanding the group is a bunch of old timers who meet once a month over a couple of beers. I would just let them wander around a bit, take some photos, and document their history."

"I don't like it," grumbled Rocco while stroking his massive biceps. The foreman was wearing his trademark white T-shirt with a pair of rugged work pants, imbedded with dirt.

"It's a legal decision," said Pompano. "So please respect it. I don't see a problem."

"Listen to Louie," said CEO Pagano to his burly foreman. "Just give them a safety vest and hard hat. The basement will be lit up, correct?"

"Yea," grumbled the on-site foreman. "Per city code a series of lights will be rigged up throughout the lower levels, along with the standard safety cameras."

"Wonderful," said Tommy Pagano while checking his watch. "Any other concerns, gentlemen? If not, we will meet again in two weeks to review the final schedule of events."

"What land fill should we use?" asked Pompano.

"Who offered the most?"

"The Sukas brothers down by the Naval Yard. We've used them before. They keep their mouths shut."

"Good," said Pagano. "Send the Sukas boys a box of Cuban cigars and tell them not to disappoint me." The chairman got up from his chair to leave.

"I have just one more concern," came a meek voice from the opposite end of the table.

"Yes Timmy?" asked Winky Pagano. "What now?"

"One of the city safety inspectors reported an abnormally high level of radon in the basement," said the chairman's nephew. "He wants to know how we will be managing it." Timothy Pagano was the youngest nephew of the CEO, and the son of his only living brother.

"I'd manage it with a thousand dollars of cash in his car," snapped Winky while taking a step towards the door. "Haven't I taught you anything yet, Timmy? Just ask him which car is his in the lot, tell him to leave the door open, and put the cash in the vehicle. It never fails. Any other questions?"

"He seemed really official," squeaked Timmy Pagano. "Has been calling me every day. He sounds very concerned." The youngest Pagano in the room fidgeted in his seat.

"If that doesn't work, have Rocco talk it over with him," snapped Pagano as he left the room, his secretary in tow. "Don't bother me with such nonsense, Timmy."

"The majority of these old structures have a high level of radon in the subbasements," retorted Attorney Pompano. "Especially the hospitals. They were started as clinics across the river from downtown Philly back in the late 1700s, then built over as time went on."

"Just give me the guy's name," growled an inpatient Rocco. "I'll take care of him."

"He said the levels were astronomical," said Timmy. "Never seen or heard of radon levels so high. Mentioned something about a radon belt epicenter."

"Have him measure it again," said Pompano. "There can be no more delays, or the boss will have a stroke."

"He's measured it three times, on different days, under different weather conditions. Same results. The radon levels are off the scale."

"Well then, give the inspector my name and forward the results to my office," said the firm's legal counsel. "I'll get an independent review of the numbers just in case we need a second expert opinion. We may have to get the judge involved again."

"I'm not going to listen to this crap anymore!" screamed Rocco as he got up. "Give the guy the wad of money, Timmy! For Christ's sake I feel like I'm back in college waiting for the big football game to kickoff. I just need to hit somebody! Let's implode the goddamn building!"

"Gentlemen, please calm down," said Pompano, aware of Rocco's short temper. "We only have four more weeks. Rock, I don't see a problem with these radon readings. They crop up all the time."

"No more delays!" shouted the foreman while pounding his right hand down on the table. "No more freaking delays!"

No one dare spoke as the meeting adjourned. Just outside the room Attorney Pompano ran into the CEO's favorite son, having just entered the office.

"Vincent, good morning," said Pompano. "How's my favorite orthopedic surgeon?"

"I'm good Louie. Where's pops?" asked Dr. Vincent Pagano.

"In his office with Stephanie. Make sure you knock first."

"Come on Lou, it's nine in the morning. So, are we still on track for four weeks?"

"Yes, no problems," said the attorney. "Once the demolition is done, we should have the new hospital wing up in about eighteen months."

"Great."

Without knocking Vincent walked into the office of his father. The CEO was staring at the sports page while his secretary glared down upon a cell phone, just inches from her face.

"My boy!" yelled Tommy Pagano Jr., upon seeing his youngest son stroll in. "Good morning, son."

"Hello, doctor," said Stephanie with a smile and crack of gum in her mouth.

"Good morning, Dad. Hello, Stephanie."

"We're in the home stretch, Vincent," said the CEO. "One month to detonation."

"Are the architect plans complete for the new hospital wing?"

"If you mean the Pagano Orthopedic Institute then yes, the plans are complete. I'm so proud of you, son."

"The name is definite? Are you certain?"

"Yea, yea," said Winky with a wave of his hand. "Uncle Frank is on the hospital board of trustees and flexed a little muscle to seal the deal. Look here son, the final blueprints. They just arrived yesterday."

The CEO rapidly unrolled an architect's rendition of the new building, set to occupy the former site of the Franklin Wing. While spreading the paper a broad smile came upon his face. His secretary stared adoringly at the young doctor.

"It will be the paragon for all orthopedic clinics in the United States!" exclaimed the CEO. "From top to bottom we've built a one stop shopping center for joint replacement surgery."

"Very nice, Dad. Very nice."

"It will have ample space for exam rooms, an MRI, gymnasium, therapy pool and nine brand new operating rooms," said the father while pointing at the plans. "Simply put it will be *thee* orthopedic hospital to get your hip or knee replaced in the greater Philadelphia area. We're going to blow the competition out of the water."

"A cash cow," added Vincent Pagano. "Especially with all the baby boomers limping around. Thanks Dad."

"Look here son," said the CEO while pointing to a sketch of the hospital's eastern edifice. "Look at the size of our name in relation to the building itself. A real eye catcher."

Within the blueprints, atop the hospital, sat the name of the new hospital wing in gigantic letters, – THE PAGANO ORTHOPEDIC INSTITUTE.

"Wow. I love it!"

"Everyone driving by on the Schuylkill Expressway will see it," said Tommy Pagano. "The wattage is so high that people downtown are going to have a hard time sleeping at night. We had to put in a separate generator just to power the letters. Hell, they may be able to see it over in Jersey!"

"The bigger the better," said Stephanie while tapping on her cell phone.

"Nice Dad. The Pagano Orthopedic Institute... it sure has a catchy ring to it."

"Thank you, son. Thank you for being the best son a father could have. Not like your two older brothers, wasting their time chasing tight skirts and spending my money. Mom always knew you were different."

"How's Mom? I haven't spoken to her in a while."

"Fine. Fine. She's down at the shore house for the summer. I signed her up for a few wine of the month clubs. She couldn't be happier... has a lot of friends down in L.B.I."

"The *Loveladies* section of Long Beach Island", said Stephanie with an emphasis on the word "love." She knew of the Pagano summer home in the tony Jersey shore neighborhood called Loveladies. "I just adore that word – the *Loveladies* section of L.B.I."

"Oh Dad, I almost forgot, an old med school classmate of mine belongs to the Historical Society that threw a wrench in the works. His name is Dr. John Sullivan."

"Really? A guy your age belongs to a Historical Society?"

"Yea. He is a bit of a dullard, but a nice guy. And get this, he works at the PGH. His specialty is Geriatrics."

"Geriatrics? What the hell is that?"

"A subspecialty in medicine that deals with the health and care of the elderly," said the younger Pagano. "He takes care of old folks and problems specific to their generation."

"Maybe you should see him," chimed in Stephanie with a giggle. "You know, for the little problem you have at times with 'Mr. Softie'."

"Hey, hey! Pipe it down," said the destruction boss to his secretary. "Or I'll trade you in for two twenty-year olds."

"Oh, Tommy. I was just joking! You're so sensitive."

"I think he is planning on videotaping the basement," said Vincent Pagano. "He is infatuated by some old time doctor whose office occupied the Franklin Wing."

"Well tell him to make it quick," barked Winky, now upset over his secretary's wisecrack. "Otherwise he's going to get buried in a pile of rubble."

"I already told him," replied the younger Pagano while studying the plans.

"Nobody is going to stop the Pagano Destruction Company from blowing that building to smithereens!" screamed the CEO, his right eye in a rapid twitch. "Absolutely nobody! So help me God!"

CHAPTER FOUR

THE FRANKLIN WING

"The building was named after Mister Benjamin Franklin," said Reggie Washington while staring at the camera. "Built in, oh around 1760 or so. Actually, I believe it was one of Mr. Franklin's original homes, prior to becoming a hospital."

"And Mr. Washington, how long have you been a security guard here on the Franklin Wing?" asked Sullivan with a video recorder in his right hand.

"Believe it or not since 1974," said the Philadelphian with a smile and modest laugh. "It was the first job I took out of high school. I've never left since."

"And to my understanding you were on watch the night Dr. Schmidt came racing through, with a policeman in chase. Isn't that correct?"

"That's right," said the sentry. "At this very desk. It was the evening of July 4rd, 1976.... just before the midnight hour. I remember the day well, since it was our nation's bicentennial."

"Can you describe what happened on that fateful night?"

"Sure," replied Washington. "It was a hot summer night and I was watching a late-night movie on T.V. Suddenly the double metal door down the hallway burst open and that's when I saw him." While speaking Washington pointed down a corridor to his left.

"Dr. Schmidt?"

"Yes sir, Dr. Zachary Schmidt. I hadn't seen him for several months and he looked thin. Maybe it was the hospital gown he was wearing from the psych wing that made him look so lean."

"Go ahead, Mr. Washington. What happened next?"

"The doctor was in a full sprint heading directly toward me," continued the night watchman. "His hair was flying in the breeze and he was wearing hospital slippers. He was agile, light on his feet, moving fast for his age."

"Did he acknowledge your presence or say anything to you?"

"No, he didn't speak," said Washington. "But he didn't have to. And that's what I remember most about the whole event."

"How so?"

"Well we were good friends, the Doc and me. Even though I was new to the hospital, he always took time to stop and chat with me. He was a kind and wonderful man."

"Yes, go on."

"It was his facial expression," said the guard. "Even though a city policeman was screaming for him to stop, Dr. Schmidt had a look of merriment in his eyes. A grin across his face."

"Really? I mean, you're describing to me a carefree expression on the doctor's face, despite the circumstances."

"Absolutely," said Washington with a slow shake of his head. "It was over in a few seconds but as he sped past me, he winked. I'll never forget it. He winked as if it all didn't matter, and everything was going to be alright." The sentry chuckled with a shake of his head. "Ah, old Doc Schmidt... a good man."

"Interesting. What about the city policeman?" asked Sullivan. "Can you tell me about him?"

"He was a young man. Slim and fit. The gap was closing quickly between the police officer and Dr. Schmidt. The officer's cap flew off his head as he approached my desk. As he passed…"

"Beep, beep, beep…" went the battery suddenly on the camcorder, causing Sullivan to look up in disbelief. A "low battery" warning flashed across his screen. The recorder then went dead.

"Darn this old battery," said Sullivan. "I just charged it yesterday."

"Technology," said Washington. "We're better off without it."

"It's dead. I can't believe it," growled Sullivan as he looked at the power cell. "It's my third battery this year. Must be the camcorder. Sorry Reggie, but we are going to have to continue the interview at a later date. Is that O.K.?"

"Yea, I'm not planning on going anywhere," said Washington with a smile. I'm available anytime Dr. Sullivan. You know where to find me… been here since 1974."

"It's imperative for the Historical Society to preserve your first-person account of the event, along with a description of what transpired after the two vanished down the hallway."

"You know my story doctor," said Reggie with a slow shake of his head. "It's never going to change. Those two men vanished into thin air."

"Yes, I understand, but we do need to gather as much information as possible before this old building comes down, at least for completeness sake," said Sullivan as he began to place the camcorder in a carry bag.

Mr. Washington didn't respond. He stared at the doctor with a cocked eyebrow.

"Reggie, you know my feeling on that. There are no such things as ghosts. "

"And you know mine, doctor. I know what I've seen. That's never going to change. There's no other explanation. I've gone over it in my head a million times."

"Alright, alright," said Sullivan with a wave of his hand. "Let's not get into it again. But I need you to explain what happened over the years on your watch. O.K.? Will you be willing to do that once I get this camera in functional order?"

"Sure," said Washington with a head nod. "Man, I still can't believe they're going to knock down the old wing. Where did the time go?"

"Me too. What are your plans after the demolition?"

"Retirement, Doctor Sullivan. It's time. At least that's what Mrs. Washington keeps telling me."

"A well-earned respite. You deserve it."

"Yea, I guess so. But I love working here. To tell you the truth Dr. Sullivan, I'm afraid of retirement."

"I see the corridors are lit up," said Sullivan while looking down a long hallway leading away from the guard's post. "When did that happen?"

"A few days ago. Some foreman built like Hercules came through with a bunch of laborers, cursing at them like a sailor. It took a full day to set the lights."

"Very good," said Sullivan. "That will make my job easier. Thanks for your time, Reggie."

"Where are you headed now?"

"Down to Doctor Schmidt's office. I was going to video the area but that will have to wait. Just going to check the lighting."

"It's kind of late. Be careful down there, doc."

"Reggie!"

"I know, I know. You're a man of science. There are no such things as ghosts."

Doctor Sullivan walked away from the watchman, down a long corridor toward a set of metal doors. Above the door a large sign declared "Hospital Wing Closed. No Admittance."

He swiped an ID badge attached to a lanyard through a slot, which allowed access to the hospital wing. The rusty doors gave off a loud metallic screech that echoed through the abandoned facility. Two plump rats immediately darted across his path behind a concrete stairwell. Along the stairwell were construction grade lights, strung overhead and protected by yellow plastic cages. Each light gave off enough wattage to lead Sullivan to the next level. He took the stairs to the bottom floor, four stories beneath the street. It was cool and deathly quiet as he walked into the former subterranean lair of Dr. Zachary Schmidt.

Decades ago, Dr. Schmidt had complete access to the lower floor of the Franklin Wing where he occasionally treated patients and conducted experimental work. He slept in the basement for weeks at a time, only surfacing for food and water. Sullivan had visited the basement several times over the past six months and was familiar with the layout. He headed through a series of exam rooms toward the main office of Schmidt, located in the northernmost corner of the building. The lights helped guide the way through a passage littered with fallen chunks of concrete and debris. Along the route sat an occasional wheelchair and gurney, long abandoned.

A sharp noise suddenly rang out from Dr. Schmidt's office, shattering the silence. It was the sound of wood forcefully cracking under pressure, followed by the push of an object on the gritty floor. Sullivan froze, caught off guard by the sound. His heart began to beat rapidly as he squinted into the main office space. There, directly in front of him, was the silhouette of a man, trying to push past a wooden bookcase. His back was facing Sullivan as he leaned into the shelving system, obviously trying to get behind it. The lighting in the corner was dim. Sullivan took a slow step forward, directly onto a loose metal pipe that sprang upward.

"Clank, clank," went the pipe loudly as it jackknifed.

The shadowy figure immediately turned around to face the doctor. Neither man moved for several seconds.

Absolute silence.

"Who goes there?" asked the stranger. "Identify yourself!"

"I'm Doctor John Sullivan," came the tentative reply. Sullivan's voice was weak and cracking. "Dr. Sullivan of the Philadelphia General Hospital."

The silhouetted man slowly brought up the beam of a flashlight onto Sullivan's face. The light caused Sullivan to squint and hold up his hand. The stranger began a slow, cautious approach toward the doctor, his feet crunching aloud on the floor. While still shining the light in Sullivan's eyes he stopped, just ten feet before him. Sullivan thought he saw a handlebar mustache on the stranger's face. He was about to run backward when the unknown person spoke.

"Holy crap," said the man. "You scared the hell out of me!"

The stranger lowered the flashlight beam to expose his identity. He wore a yellow hardhat and orange safety vest. His left hand grasped a rectangular box connected to a cable and sensor wand. A photo tag on his chest read "Larry Griffith, Building Inspector, City of Philadelphia".

"Wow. I thought I was alone down here," said the city worker. "My heart's beating a mile a minute. Good God!"

"Mine too," said Sullivan, relieved by the handshake extended toward him. "I'm Doctor John Sullivan, a member of the West Philadelphia Historical Society."

"Larry Griffith, city building inspector. Pleased to meet you."

"What the heck are you doing down here at such a late hour?" asked Sullivan.

"Just trying to get some more data before they implode the building," said Griffith. "I came in through the south entrance." He looked back at the bookcase. "I've been trying to make some sense out of some abnormal readings. I stopped coming down here during the day because I felt unwelcome."

"How so?"

"The foreman. A brute named Rocco. He told me to stay out of his way."

"Well I noticed a series of cameras strung up in strategic locations on my way down," said Sullivan. "So they still know you are here."

"That's standard protocol for a demo project," said the inspector. "Doesn't bother me. In fact, cameras are mandated by city code."

"I see. May I ask what kind of abnormal readings you are picking up, Mr. Griffith?"

"Radon. At least I think radon," said the city worker while staring down at his detector. "This is our newest machine and the readings are off the charts. It seems that the focal point of the spike is behind that old bookshelf. I was trying to shimmy my way around it."

"Focal point?"

"Yea, the levels are high throughout the basement, but as you approach this area the sensor just starts flashing 'DANGER'. Especially near the corner of the foundation, behind that case. I'm trying to see if something is behind that bookcase."

"Maybe I can help," said Sullivan, now completely interested in the worker's concern. "You do know the bodies of two men were never found down here, despite an exhaustive search."

"Sure I do," said Griffith. "That's why I thought you were a ghost."

"There are no such things as ghosts, Mr. Griffith."

The two men walked back through Dr. Schmidt's main office toward the bookshelf, which extended from the floor to the ceiling. The right-side corner of the case was a bit off its base, exposing clear concrete beneath. To the right of the bookcase was an ornate alcove, known to be the favorite reading room of Dr. Schmidt.

"I was able to move it just slightly before you arrived."

"Are you sure about this?" asked Sullivan as he sized up the situation.

"I was just following the sensor. It went crazy near the shelves."

Both men forcefully pushed the bookcase toward the center of the room, away from the concrete wall of the north edifice. Their combined effort capsized the case, sending it crashing down upon the floor. Behind the case was a solid concrete wall.

"Hmm," said Sullivan. "Dead end."

"Chirp, chirp, chirp!" screamed the sensor in Griffith's left hand. The alarm escalated as he held the device against the foundation.

"Something is in or behind this wall," said Griffith. "Something odd I might add."

Sullivan and the city worker began to cautiously inspect the old cinder wall, which was wet with condensation. A trickle of water seeping down from the ceiling disappeared into a long, broad crack along the wall, near the floor.

"Peculiar," said the inspector. "The water is running easily through that seam."

Griffith raised his foot and forcefully kicked the wall, causing it to collapse inward. The old stone crumpled down onto the floor of a narrow corridor.

"I've been down here a few times before and thought the basement ended here," said Sullivan as he squatted down to peer through the hole. "I've even reviewed the blueprints and Schmidt's office marked the northernmost extent of the construct."

"Uh-oh," said the inspector shining his light into the space. "I hope we don't find any skeletons back here."

Griffith continued to kick in the wall and eventually opened up a narrow crawlspace, which emptied into a walkway. Both men crawled through the opening. The area inside was dark, dank and void of any material contents. Thick spider webs littered the hidden chamber.

"Yikes," said the inspector.

"A hidden walkway," said Sullivan as he stood up, his head nearly touching the ceiling. To his left was a dead end, prompting the duo to turn right.

"It looks like it arches around this wall of marble," said Griffith. "At least I think it is marble." He ran his hand across the smooth, cool stone.

"That's granite," replied Sullivan as he stroked the wall to his right. "Next to the bookshelf was the alcove in the doctor's study. This must be its back wall." He peered upwards to see the wall stretch over twenty feet high. "It's absolutely massive."

Slowly, the duo began to walk down the passageway, their route hugging the slow curvature of the wall. A mouse scurried across their path.

Look!" said Griffith while shining his light up toward the wall. "An inscription."

Dr. Sullivan immediately recognized some wording, engraved into the stone in an exact manner. He wiped the wall clean with his hand while blowing across the etching, freeing it of cobwebs. The wording sat at eye level.

"The Used Key is Always Light...–R.S." stated Griffith. His light scanned above and below the wording, searching for completion of the sentence.

"R.S?" asked Sullivan. "Who is R.S.?"

"I have no idea."

The duo carefully inspected the remainder of the wall, which was void of any other phrasing.

"Chirp, chirp, chirp," continued the sensor.

"This whole walkway is hot," said Griffith while staring down at his machine. "Even hotter when I bring it closer to the granite."

"Dead end ahead," said Sullivan as he approached the wall's terminus. The granite abruptly merged into an old cinder wall, in exact fashion to the opposite end. The doctor got down on his buttocks and kicked out the old wall, sending it tumbling down on the opposite side. They exited back into the main basement area, now to the left of Zachary Schmidt's reading room.

Griffith continued to inspect the area with his sensor, which continued to beep in a crazed fashion near the stonework.

"It's definitely the granite," said Sullivan while looking upward. "On this side of the wall it appears to only reach the ceiling, but on the opposite side it's at least two stories high."

"The floor. Look at the floor," said the inspector.

On the floor, directly in front of the granite wall, was a star shaped design with a singular stone set in the center. The stone measured six feet from corner to corner. A large eye was etched into the block's midsection. The ceiling above was slightly conical, it's apex directly parallel with the alcove's granite wall. The floor inlay was perfectly positioned to the center of the granite arch.

"Look at my sensor," said Griffith as he stepped onto the granite slab. "It stopped chirping." While talking he swept a layer of grime and debris off the stone block.

"Fascinating."

Sullivan pulled out his cell phone and began to take some photographs of the chamber and star configuration. He stood on the granite slab and took two overhead shots of the ceiling construct. While doing so the building inspector continued to scan the room. They found no other passageways.

"We've got to preserve this," said Sullivan with a broad grin. "At least the granite wall itself. It's utterly magnificent. At a minimum it needs to be relocated prior to the implosion."

"'The Used Key is Always Light'. What does that mean?"

"Schmidt's key," said Sullivan. "It surely had something to do with his key."

"Whose key?"

"Dr. Schmidt, the physician who worked down here. He always wore a key around his neck," said Sullivan. "He called it the 'key to the future.'"

"The doctor who disappeared?" asked Griffith with wide eyes. "He wore a key around his neck?"

"Yes," said Sullivan with a shake of his head. He looked slowly up at the wall. "Dr. Zachary Schmidt."

"You're starting to freak me out," said Griffith with a shake of his body. "I'm starting to think their bodies are somewhere down here, behind one of these old walls. Let's get the..."

Just then a rat scurried out from behind the wall, frightening both men. It squealed as it ran.

"O.K., that's a wrap!" said Griffith while throwing both of his arms upward. "I just filled my pants. Let's get the hell out of here."

"Agree," said Sullivan. "But tomorrow we've got to get back down here. What we've found tonight is of significance and must be explained before this old building comes down."

"I agree," said Griffith. "But there's one major problem."

"What's that?"

"The Pagano Destruction Company. Have you ever dealt with them before?"

"No."

"Consider yourself lucky. They don't believe rules apply to their decision process. The company has some crazy pull downtown at City Hall too." Griffith looked around. "But this is something big... we just can't ignore it. Right?"

"Absolutely," replied the doctor. "You push from your end, and I'll push from mine. I've got to take another look at those blueprints. We're certainly onto something here, Larry."

Both men shook hands and made their way out to the desk of Reggie Washington, who was enjoying a late-night movie. After discussing their findings with the watchman, Inspector Griffith departed.

"Oh Doc, I almost forgot," said Washington. "Over the years when I made the rounds through the Franklin, I would occasionally find some knickknacks of interest. You know... a cuff link, penny, or tie clip. I've thrown them all into this old bin," said Washington while hoisting a tin canister onto his desk. He shook the can for audible effect. "You can look through it if you like?"

"That would be great," said Sullivan with a smile. He took the canister. "I'll be sure to return it to you. Thanks, Reggie. Good night."

"Goodnight, Dr. Sullivan."

Once home the doctor quietly looked into his mother's bedroom. Mrs. Sullivan was fast asleep with Moses at her side. The front window was open several inches allowing some fresh air in. The cat slowly lifted its head to acknowledge his presence. A note taped to the door from Nurse Ella said all was well, and the Pugs won.

The doctor went downstairs to his study to try and make sense of the recent events. He first pulled up some blueprints of the Franklin basement on his computer, searching for the hidden corridor. No such walkway existed. Next, he pulled out his camcorder battery to place it into a charger attached to a wall outlet. Once the battery locked into the charger the device immediately read "Fully Charged." Peculiar, he thought. Next he went to upload his cell phone photos, noticing the two shots taken atop the granite block were not saved.

"What the hell is going on?" he asked himself. Technology was never his forte.

Lastly, he stared at the yellow tin canister given to him by Reggie Washington. It read 'Weldon Babyland Mix Hard

Candy' and was peppered with dents and rust spots. The old can's lid was round shaped and held tight by a snug inset design. A straight edge screwdriver was necessary to pop off the top. The doctor dumped the contents onto his desk, unloading a smorgasbord of Franklin Wing souvenirs.

There were buttons of all shapes and sizes and a few round pieces from a game of checkers. A foreign coin with a hole in the center was intertwined with a pin promoting Franklin D. Roosevelt for President, the democrat's photo included. In the middle of the hoard appeared a shoehorn along with a small vial of Vaporole antidote. Various religious medals displayed the Sacred Heart of Jesus along with two medallions, one of a pig and the other a naval anchor. Ubiquitous to the lot were long lost keys, displaying their places of origin to include Chicago, IL and The Acme Lock Co. Yet, as Dr. Sullivan sifted through the stockpile, one peculiar key caught his attention–an old skeleton key with a peculiar cut that he had seen before. The smooth yet pitted surface signified antiquity to the lever lock, yet it was incomplete. Missing was the upper one half of the circumscribed circle top, nowhere to be found in the heap. Sullivan carefully lifted up the passkey and held it beneath his desk lamp. He brought a magnifying glass to the key noting some peculiar symbols stamped onto the metal shaft, along with the initials 'R.S.'. The physician immediately knew what he had recovered. It was the skeleton key that hung from the neck of Dr. Zachary Schmidt–the physician who mysteriously disappeared in the Franklin Wing nearly forty years ago. Just then, a city bus rumbled past his home, rattling the aged windows in a peculiar fashion.

CHAPTER FIVE
AIDAN

"Uncle John! Uncle John!" yelled the five-year old as he ran through the apartment. A set of round glasses dominated his face. "I knew it was you!"

"How did you know, Aidan? Did Daddy tell you?"

"No," said the child now in his uncle's arms. "I can tell by the way you knock on the door."

"It's our secret knock," said John Sullivan with a hug. "Don't tell anyone." He held the hug a bit longer than usual.

"I won't," said the child, his eyes looking through the thick lenses and his breathing labored.

"Where's your father?"

"In here," came the reply from the kitchen, just around the corner.

"Smells good," said Sullivan. "What's for dinner?"

"Five-alarm chili," said George Sullivan while stirring the contents of a large pot. "Dad's old recipe. As you know... it speaks for itself."

"If that's the case, Dad bragged about it all the time," laughed the doctor now looking at a finger painting on the refrigerator. "Wow, who's the artist?"

"I am," replied Aidan proudly. He flicked the back of his hand across a nose full of mucous. "It's a flower. I made it for Grandma."

"And a beautiful one at that. Did you make it at school?"

"Yes."

"Do you like school?"

"Yes, especially Miss Gamble. She's my teacher."

"I know all about Miss Gamble," said John with a glance at his older brother.

"Daddy said you and Miss Gamble are going on a date. Is that true?"

"Not exactly," answered the doctor. "At least no one told me about a date. George, do you know anything about a date?"

"Hey Aidan, it's six o'clock. Time for your show!" countered George Sullivan. Slowly he returned a lid to the pot of chili and turned toward his brother. He appeared hesitant to make eye contact.

"The Junior Jujitsu Squirrels, ready to fly!" shouted the youngster as he darted out of the kitchen in the direction of a television set.

A silent sense of unease occurred in the room. Several seconds passed before the elder Sullivan spoke.

"Well, I know the answer... but tell me anyway," said George Sullivan to his younger brother. "I'm sure it's still positive." While speaking he held a drying towel in his hand, running each finger through the cloth. A look of resignation consumed his face. "Did the additional testing confirm the diagnosis, John? Yes or no?"

"I'm sorry George... but yes, it did," replied Dr. Sullivan with a somber tone. "The results were unequivocal. I went over them in detail with Dr. Kim this morning."

"So... no other testing necessary?" asked Aidan's dad. "That's it?"

"No, there isn't, George. The diagnosis is absolute. Aidan has the x-variant. Every test confirmed it."

"Just my luck," bemoaned George Sullivan as he stared over his brother's shoulder, at his son. "First his mom, now him."

"I'm so sorry."

"One kid out of five... normally I'd take those odds," said the elder Sullivan, now taking a seat on a kitchen chair. He shook his head and stared downward.

"I know it's the worst-case scenario," continued the physician. "But with current treatment regimens, his life expectancy..."

"How much time, John?"

"Fifteen to twenty years," replied the physician while trying to sound upbeat. "With modern medicine, who knows... hopefully much longer. According to Dr. Kim, there are some exciting breakthroughs in treatment for the disease coming out of Europe."

"So right after college, right?" Aidan's dad rapidly blinked his eyes, holding back some tears. "Why even go to college?" He flicked his wrists forward in disgust.

"George, George – we've had this discussion before. Let's take it a day at a time brother, you and me. We'll get through it together."

"It just doesn't seem fair."

"Don't you remember Karen's dying words?"

"No."

"Well I do," said the doctor sternly. "She gave you some marching orders regarding Aidan. 'Enjoy Aidan's journey... no matter what'. Remember that, George?" He pointed his finger at his brother. "She knew he could be a carrier, just like her younger brother. Be thankful you're here... for Karen and Aidan's sake."

"Maybe I remember her saying that. I don't know. It's been two long years now. Everything in life is coming off the tracks. First Karen, now this, and don't forget about Mom... hanging on the brink."

"You let me take care of Mom," stated the doctor. "And together we'll take care of Aidan. Understand?"

"Do I have a choice?"

"No."

"So there's your answer."

Doctor Sullivan paused, acutely aware of his nephew's diagnosis. He suffered from a rare genetic entity called Polycystic Global Demyelination Syndrome, or PGD for short. The diagnosis was made when he was an infant, but testing for the dreaded x-variant only began at age five. Two prior tests had come back markedly positive, so the news although devastating, wasn't entirely unexpected. The disease was a random genetic mutation only seen in males with a variable clinical presentation. Twenty percent of those affected by the disorder carried an x-variant which when present, signified a grim prognosis. On average, Aidan Sullivan would make it to his twenty-first birthday. Shortly thereafter, the disease process would extinguish his life.

Both men spoke no further until dinner hit the table. The silence allowed each brother to gather some composure.

"Thank you Jesus for the dinner before us," said Aidan with his hands held together and eyes closed tight. "Thank you for Daddy and Uncle John... and tell Mommy that I love her... Amen."

"Amen," said the brothers.

"Daddy, am I going to be farting later today?" asked Aidan while blowing some steam off the chili. "From the beans?"

"All Sullivan men fart after eating Grandpa's five-alarm chili."

"It's called flatus," said the doctor. "That's the medical term for farting. Commit that to memory Aidan. F-l-a-t-u-s."

"Flatus?" replied the child. "That's a funny word."

"Oh no, don't start the memory game, John. Not tonight."

"A child's brain is like a sponge, George. Aidan is capable of absorbing and storing data at an astonishing rate. I would highly encourage at his age a structured approach..."

"Miss Gamble calls it 'passing gas,'" interrupted Aidan, now looking behind his uncle at the Jujitsu Squirrels on T.V. "'Excuse me, I passed gas, is what we have to say.'"

"How's Nurse Adams doing, John?" asked the older brother. "Any progress on a second date?"

"She is doing fine... and no. There has been no progress on a second date. Thank you for your concern. Your interest in my personal life is commendable."

"That's what big brothers are for, John. By the way, you're invited to Aidan's parent-teacher conference next week. I'm sure Ms. Gamble would love to see you again. She's quite a catch if you ask me."

"Funny, I don't remember asking you," replied the doctor as he finished off the first bowl of chili. "And my memory is pretty good."

The family enjoyed dinner together, a Thursday night tradition in the West Philadelphia apartment for the past two years. Their conversation tried to center on the positive life and times of a five-year old boy. Near the end of the meal the doctor updated his brother on his research for the Historical Society.

"We came across a piece of granite about two stories high," said the younger Sullivan. As he spoke the doctor projected his arms overhead and gazed toward the ceiling. "It's situated in old Doc Schmidt's reading room... somehow we have to preserve that piece of wall. Behind the granite was a crawlspace and inscription. A city inspector and I found it late last night after we kicked in some bricks. He mentioned something about radon levels being off the charts. Well anyway, an etching on the back wall read..."

"And how do you expect to do that, John?" interrupted the older brother. "Rent a bulldozer and a crane? That office is four or five stories underground. It would take a year to remove that wall in a safe manner. You're talking about a massive undertaking." George Sullivan knew of his brother's love for artifact and history, which at times bordered on fanaticism. "Where are you going to put this massive hunk of stone, John?" Sarcasm exuded from his voice. "In your backyard?"

"I'm sure one of the local museums in town would be..."

"Give it up, John. Take some photos and let it crumble."

John Sullivan stared back at his brother, aware of his current state of mind. He cautiously continued. "I'm just saying George, there's something special about that whole area. It's a shame they're going to implode it."

"John, listen to yourself. That building is a safety hazard. It's falling apart. They're doing West Philadelphia a favor by razing it."

"I understand, but..."

"Rip!" blasted the sound from underneath Aidan's slightly raised left buttock, the blast of bowel gas ricocheting off the wooden chair. His eyes popped wide open as his left hand fanned rapidly back and forth in front of his face.

"Excuse me! I passed flatus."

"My boy!" shouted Aidan's father. "Spoken like a true Sullivan!"

"That was your grandpa talking," laughed the doctor. "I recognize that voice anywhere!"

Levity filled the room, the child's expulsion segueing the discussion away from the Franklin Wing demo. Over the next thirty minutes the trio laughed and joked their way through a second round of five-alarm chili. After dessert, the doctor bid farewell.

"Good night, Aidan," said Dr. Sullivan. "I'm going to see Grandma now. I'll tell her about the flower."

"Tell her I love her," said Aidan. "I hope the Pugs won."

"Me too. Good night, George. Keep the faith."

"I will, see you next week... and thanks for being there all the time. We'll get through this together."

The walk home took Dr. Sullivan past the PGH campus, the western sky lit red by the setting sun. Another hot June day gripped the city with no end to the humidity in sight. Despite the hour, a beehive of activity swarmed around the PGH main lobby, with patients and hospital personnel weaving through each other in a haphazard fashion. Two blocks ahead sat the Franklin Wing, cordoned off with scaffolding and protected walkways. While passing by Sullivan pictured Zachary Schmidt racing down that very street with a police officer in chase, his hospital gown flapping in the breeze. He recalled the sentry's description of Schmidt's carefree expression and a wink of the eye. What a character thought Sullivan, but how did he lose the key, and where did he go? He had to have an expert look at that key. Two blocks past the aging edifice, his cell phone rang out.

"Hi Ella, what's going on?" asked Sullivan.

"Mom took a bad spell," wailed the home caretaker. She sounded distraught. "Right after the seventh inning stretch, she mumbled something about no good lefties in the bullpen and rolled her eyes back. Then, she went out cold!"

"Is she responsive?"

"She's breathing... has a shoddy pulse. Oh Dr. Sullivan, she doesn't look good."

"Listen Ella, get a damp washcloth and place it..."

"I called 911!" shouted the nurse. "Oh, there they are, out front already. They're outside already, Dr. Sullivan! I've got to go and open the door... Moses, look out! Oh that cat is gonna kill me some day!"

"Reeerrrr," screeched the cat.

"Ella! Ella! Listen to me. Mom doesn't want to go back to the hospital anymore! Do not let them take her out of the house!"

"Dr. Sullivan. They're here with the stretcher!"

Sullivan picked up his pace while hearing the commotion over the phone. Nurse Ella quickly gave the paramedics a concise history of his mother's condition as they proceeded up the stairwell and into the front bedroom. He next heard a paramedic say, "B.P. 80 over 50."

"Ella, Ella! Listen to me!" shouted Sullivan now in a trot with the phone to his ear.

"That's right," said Ella to the paramedics. "The Philadelphia General. Her son is a doctor there."

"West Philly Unit Six to the PGH E.R.... we've got an unresponsive eighty-four-year-old woman in route to the PGH, she has a history of lung carcinoma and hypertension, a patient of Dr. Brown's. Pulse is faint at sixty-eight with a blood pressure of..."

"Dr. Sullivan, she's headed to the E.R., at the Philadelphia General!"

"Yes, I heard that Ella," said Sullivan, now stopping in his tracks, a bit short of breath. He turned around and headed back toward the hospital. "I'll meet her in the E.R."

"Oh Dr. Sullivan, she doesn't look well! Oh, get out of the way crazy cat, before you get run over!"

"Reeerrrr!"

While running back toward the medical center an ambulance with flashing lights sped past the doctor. He could see through the rear window a paramedic moving frantically while positioning an overhead intravenous bag. By the time Sullivan arrived at the E.R. his mother had already been rushed inside. He found her in one of the main exam rooms with a flurry of personnel surrounding her supine body.

"B.P. is 80 over 40!" shouted the triage nurse over the clamor. "Keep that I.V. wide open. Does anybody have a list of her medications?"

"I do," interjected Sullivan as he worked his way through the medical team. "She's my mother."

"John, what's going on here?" asked the E.R. attending upon entering the room. While approaching the patient he pulled out a stethoscope from his white coat.

"I don't know," replied Sullivan while placing his index finger on her radial pulse. "The home nurse said she just passed out. No fall or anything like that... has been battling lung CA for a while." He looked at his mother, her skin a bit more ashen than usual. "Mom wake up. It's John. Open your eyes!"

The emergency room physician placed the stethoscope on Mrs. Sullivan's chest, then slowly moved the instrument across her bony frame. "What's her code status?" asked the E.R. doctor while popping the listening device out of his ears.

"D.N.R.," replied Sullivan. "Do not resuscitate... comfort care only. I'm her medical proxy."

"She's a D.N.R.!" shouted the E.R. doctor to the staff. "D.N.R.!"

The medical team immediately dispersed, leaving Sullivan alone with a singular nurse in the room.

"Wow, that was quick," said Sullivan. He raised both arms in the air with palms to the sky. "Did a fire alarm just go off?"

"Do you still want the I.V. running?" asked the nurse.

"Sure I do," snapped Sullivan in a bit of disgust. "I'm not going to just let her die. Keep the fluids running... just no mechanical ventilation. She's a do not resuscitate... not a do not care for."

"John," mumbled Mrs. Sullivan. While speaking she kept her eyes closed. "John... where am I?"

"You're in the Philadelphia General E.R., Mom. You passed out during the game." Sullivan rubbed his mother's hand. The overhead monitor signaled an improving set of vital signs. "You're doing fine, maybe just a bit dehydrated. What did you have for dinner?"

The nurse left the room, leaving the two alone.

"Did the Pugs win?" asked Martha Sullivan.

"I don't know, Mom. Are you having any pain?"

"What happened to 'no more hospital visits'? Why did you bring me back here? I want to die at home."

"I know Mom, but Ella panicked and called 911."

The patient slowly shook her head back and forth. After a minute she opened her eyes and reached her hand forward, the action prompting her son to lean downward.

"John…"

"Aidan says hello, Mom. We just had Dad's five-alarm chili together. He drew you a flower."

"John, listen to your dying mother…"

"Yes, Mom?"

"Let me die in peace. Can you promise me that?"

"But Mom…"

"Please, let me die in peace."

CHAPTER SIX
THE BARBER OF SILVERWOOD

Seth Barber loved his job. After graduating from college with an English degree, his family warned him not to become a writer–so he became a newspaper reporter. Conformity was never his forte. After five years of service at the *Philadelphia Chronicle* he recently received a well-deserved promotion to Associate Editor. His weekly print column read average at best, yet the bulk of his readership dwelled on the world wide web, where he excelled as the notorious "Barber of Silverwood." The moniker paid tribute to both his surname and the fact that he lived above a barbershop in a run-down flat on Silverwood Street, across from Pretzel Park in the Manayunk section of town. There, his true talent as a writer developed over the midnight hour with a bottle of vodka and a much older roommate named Selena. The Barber's daily blog carried the highest internet traffic of any *Philadelphia Chronicle* writer.

"Is Mr. Pagano expecting you?" asked Stephanie with a look of confusion. She was standing behind her desk, staring at the young reporter. "I don't see your name on his schedule." While talking she glanced down at a blank desk calendar. The smell of fresh nail polish permeated the air.

"No, not really," replied Seth Barber. "I was hoping by chance to have a few words with him. It's in regard to the Franklin Wing demolition scheduled for July 5th." A crumbled paper in his hand had the name Pagano Destruction scribbled on it, the note given to him by his senior editor earlier in the day. He couldn't help staring at the secretary's racy outfit, the only highlight of an otherwise mundane morning. The stub of an ink pen protruded from the back of her hairdo.

"Oh," said Stephanie with hesitation. "You're not with the police department or anything like that? Are you?"

"No, no," laughed Barber with a shake of a hand. "I'm a reporter for the *Philadelphia Chronicle*, trying to put together an article regarding the Franklin building. You can tell Mr. Pagano it will only take a few minutes. I would really appreciate it."

"Alright," said Stephanie as she stepped away from her desk. "What's your name again?" While speaking she stared down at a business card with his name on it.

"Seth Barber, from the *Philadelphia Chronicle* ah... and your name is?"

"It's Stephanie, pronounced just like it sounds," replied the secretary with a grin. She sized up the reporter from head to toe, liking what she saw – a lean frame set at six-foot tall, held together by a tight pair of jeans and T-shirt. "I'll see if Mr. Pagano is available." She turned and walked down a hallway into the CEO's office.

"Who?" barked Winky Pagano. "I'm not expecting anyone."

"Barber. A Mr. Seth Barber." She handed him the business card.

"And he's from the newspaper?"

"Yes. The *Chronicle*."

"Tell him to get lost," growled Pagano, turning his attention back to the sport's page. "We're not interested. That paper is a rag."

"He wants to talk to you about the Franklin building," said Stephanie, holding her position. "Seems real official."

"WHAT?" asked the CEO. "Who sent him? Did he mention anyone's name?"

"No."

"Probably some environmental wacko trying to save a robin's nest. Tell him to shove off."

"He's writing an article on the July 5th demolition."

"Barber, Barber. I don't know anybody named Barber." He stared at the name card.

"He's kind of cute."

"Oh, well that settles it!" shouted the CEO with his hands raised into the air. "He's cute! Why didn't you say so in the first place, Stephanie? Well then, show him right in! Maybe you can start working for him when I get a new secretary!"

"Or maybe I'll get a brand new boss," retorted the secretary in anger. "Somebody who appreciates me!" She turned to walk away.

"Go right ahead," growled the company boss. "Be my guest! Come to think of it, I'm not exactly sure what the hell you exactly do around here!"

"That's it! Friday night nookie is cancelled!"

"Ah Steph... I'm only joking!"

While waiting the CEO of Pagano Destruction folded up the newspaper and placed it on the side of his desk. Something deep down inside irked him about the Franklin project. There were already too many delays. Earlier in the day he received a phone call from the company's major creditor, asking why two payments were overdue. Another work stoppage would push the project deeper into the financial red. A picture of his father appeared in his mind as he listened to a sweet-talking secretary in approach.

"Right this way, Mr. Barber," said Stephanie with an accentuated gyration of her body. "Mr. Pagano is more than happy to speak with you." She chomped her gum as the reporter slid by, sizing up his behind.

"Mr. Pagano," said Barber with an extended hand. "Thank you for the time. It's a pleasure to meet you."

"Ah yes," said Pagano with a handshake. "A pleasure to meet you, Mr. Barber. Do sit down. What brings you here... that old Franklin building?"

"Yes sir," replied Barber. "My editor asked me to put together an article on the wing, which as you know, is full of history. It will be a two-part series, sir. I'm a bit under the gun on this one... you know, the timing and all."

"Ah yes," said Pagano with a wave of his hand. "But you're in the wrong office, young man. I'm not a historian. My company is solely responsible for one job, and that is to safely implode and level that building, which in my opinion, should have been done a decade ago."

"Yes sir, but..."

"The Pagano Destruction Company has been quietly serving the Philadelphia area for over sixty years, young man." While talking the boss proudly chewed on an unlit cigar. "We cleared the site for the West Philly convention center, which was a monumental task."

"Understood. But about the Franklin Wing, to my understanding it dates back to the late 1700's..."

"My grandfather started the firm and passed it down to my dad. The Pagano's have destruction in their blood, if you know what I mean." The chieftain chuckled while rocking back and forth in his chair.

"Uh... not exactly, Mr. Pagano. Have you ever heard of a Dr. Zachary Schmidt from back in the 1970s? He had an office in the Franklin basement."

"We are the premier demo team in the Delaware Valley. No project is too big or too small. Hell, we've had a run on Catholic churches recently, been blowing them up one after another." Pagano made a quick sign of the cross with his right hand. "Bad for the brethren... but good for the Pagano."

"Right," replied Barber followed by a pause, recognizing a company promo pitch in progress from the owner.

Over the next five minutes the destruction kingpin pontificated upon the need for progress. He spoke of public safety and city ordinances along with the need to provide good paying jobs. Sprinkled into the monologue was the fact that none of his workers had been maimed or killed on the job site for over two years, a streak he hoped to continue. "Well, I hope that helps your story," said Pagano. "You can certainly mention our firm in the article, but otherwise we like to keep a low profile... so don't go too heavy on us. Alright?" Pagano rose from his seat. "Thank you for the interest in our firm, young man. I love your newspaper. Have a wonderful day."

"But Mr. Pagano, do you know anything about the history of the Franklin Wing? Or is it just another set of bricks about to tumble?"

"Only that the building is a safety hazard and at risk for collapse," growled Pagano. He didn't appreciate the follow-up question from the young reporter. "It's infested with rats and mold and a threat to the surrounding hospital environment. Do you know how hazardous mold is to your health?"

"No sir."

"I hear some vagrants occasionally live there, especially in the winter months. It's probably a crack house with needles strewn all over the basement! The place is an eyesore to the West Philadelphia community, young man." His eye began to twitch. "That's all I need to know about that blemish on the PGH campus."

"Yes, it is an old building. But I hear that two bodies are rumored to be..."

"On the morning of July 5th, we'll be doing the community a favor. Trust me." Pagano inhaled deeply. "Have you ever seen a building collapse in on itself like a house of cards, Mr.

Barber? It's a thing of beauty when done correctly. Make sure you're there to witness my craft."

"What about the radon levels?"

"Who the hell sent you here?" barked the CEO, now walking around his desk in a threatening manner. "The EPA? Because if they did, we've danced this dance before."

"My editor, sir."

"But who got your editor involved?" snapped Pagano. "We've been blowing up buildings for decades and this is the first time a newspaper has come knocking on our door. Why? What's so important about this particular shit hole?"

"I believe my editor got a call from some Historical Society in West Philadelphia. They requested we look into the matter. They voiced concerns about the remains of Dr. Schmidt and some off the chart radon levels. Will the radon still be elevated after the implosion?"

"That's it!" shouted Pagano his face turning red. "This interview is over! We have a judge's order to proceed forward with this demolition. There will be absolutely no more delays! I'm not going to waste another breath talking about some old geezers trying to save a building." The CEO proceeded to walk back towards his chair. "Stephanie, get the hell in here!"

"But... Mr. Pagano, I need to hear your side of the story... for a balanced article that is."

"Stick it up your ass! How's that for balance? Don't you dare mention our company name in your third-rate newspaper... or else I'll sue you for slander!"

"Actually, that would be libel..."

"Yes, Mr. Pagano?" asked Stephanie with an attitude. "How can I help you?" While talking she ran a rasp across her manicured nails.

"Stephanie, please show mister, ah... mister..."

"Barber, my name is Barber."

"Mr. Barber to the door," implored Pagano. A tetanic contraction took hold of his right eye. He continued to shout as the reporter left the room. "An orthopedic center of excellence is going to rise like a phoenix from the ashes of the Franklin Wing... in order to provide care to thousands of baby boomers in the area. *That* young man... is why the Franklin will fall! So help me God!"

"Right this way," said Stephanie with a broad smile. "Don't worry, he likes to yell."

"I love your perfume, what's the name of it?" asked Barber as his body brushed the secretary's shoulder in the tight corridor.

"Stephanie! Get me Uncle Frank and Louie on the phone. Now!"

"Wait right here," ordered the assistant with a roll of her eyes. "I'll be right back." She disappeared back into the CEO's headquarters.

Seth Barber sat down in a cramped waiting area consisting of two chairs and brown paneled walls. After several minutes he stood to look at some framed pictures littered haphazardly over the walls. Each snapshot consisted of a group of men in hard hats, situated in front of a run down facade. Ubiquitous to the collage was the frame of a massive man with a protruding forehead, hairy forearms and massive biceps. Across the Neanderthal's orange hat ran a piece of masking tape with the word "ROCCO," scribbled on it.

"It's called *Get a Room*," said Stephanie after reappearing. She picked up her purse, leaned forward and opened her mouth above a garbage can on the floor. A piece of bright orange gum fell from her gaped orifice and pinged the can on impact.

"Get a room?"

"Yea, the name of the perfume... *Get a Room*. I got it on sale in the bargain basement at Wanamaker's." The secretary checked her watch while walking towards the exit. The timepiece read noon. "Lunch time. Where do you want to eat?"

"Excuse me?

"I said... where do you want to eat? I hate eating lunch alone."

"Oh, of course," said the pleasantly amused Barber. "How much time do you have for lunch?" He inhaled her scent while holding the front door open.

"Officially... forty minutes," said Stephanie as she stepped out into the bright sunshine. "But technically... I don't have to be back until around... oh, three o'clock." She put on a pair of black sunglasses that accentuated her lips and began to walk down the sidewalk. "How about Chinese... I'm in the mood for some General Tso."

"But what about Mr. Pagano? Doesn't he need you?"

"Nah, right after lunch he takes a long nap. I'm mad at him anyway. He's being a jerk."

"I see."

"So, it's my treat... or should I say, Pagano Destruction Company's treat." She grinned while glancing at the reporter, her eyes hidden behind the dark lens. "You're cute, did anyone every tell you that?"

The newly acquainted Philadelphians enjoyed a lunch buffet at a popular neighborhood eatery. She, a thirty-eight-year old divorcee and current mistress of Tommy Pagano Jr. and he, a carefree beat writer with a penchant for vodka and older women. Stephanie loved her job and proudly reported holding the position for five years, currently the longevity record for a secretary at Pagano Destruction. Seth disclosed the fact that he lived with a woman in order to "share rent" and "make ends meet." His disclosure had no impact on the conversation. Within fifty minutes their business luncheon spilled into happy hour at a local bar down the street. There the reporter learned that Stephanie never had any children and hated her marriage surname that she strangely kept.

"Peacock. That's my legal name."

"Peacock?" replied Seth with a grin. "If you don't like it, why did you keep it?"

"It's a double entendre," she claimed. "At least I think."

In return, the reporter disclosed his hidden obsession to binge play videos and attend gaming conferences. Together they shared vodka in various shapes and forms, albeit the end result the same – legal intoxication in the state of Pennsylvania. The alcohol pulled their bodies together like a magnet.

"I love your stench," declared Barber.

A spirited discussion concerning the *Get a Room* scent led to an emergent taxicab ride downtown. She entered the hotel first, the lobby staff familiar with her perky frame.

"Ms. Peacock, is it Friday already?" asked a tall, well-dressed attendant standing behind a desk.

"No, DeSean... but YOLO," replied Stephanie with a beam. The attendant handed her a room swipe card. "Thanks, DeSean."

The rapidly developing story continued twenty minutes later when Seth Barber entered the penthouse suite. Full disclosure occurred in a matter of minutes, the exposé playing out high above the city skyline. It was during the main thrust of the interview that the author caught a direct visual of Ms. Peacock's rear torso, where a tattoo sat midline to her sacrum stating: "Danger–Destruction Zone." Despite the ominous wording, the notorious Barber of Silverwood completed the interview, in signature fashion.

CHAPTER SEVEN
THE SULLIVAN GANG

"Mrs. Appleton, can you still recall the earliest moment in your childhood?" asked Dr. Sullivan. He was seated in the day room of the Alzheimer's floor, with three of his patients present. Family members sat among the group, adjacent to their loved one.

"Sure, I can," said Appleton. "I was running outside, and my dog Penny was on the porch. It was a bright sunny day."

"And...." said Sullivan with a glance at chief resident Garcia. "What were you running outside to see?"

"Hmmm. I can't seem to remember," replied the patient.

"Think, Gertrude," urged Sullivan. "Up in the sky. Your mother called you out to see it."

"Oh yes, a canary. My mother had a bird feeder out back and the most beautiful goldfinches would come in the evening. She called her favorite one, Miss Carolina."

John Sullivan glanced at Gertrude Appleton's niece, seated at the side of her aunt.

"She's right," said the niece proudly. "She always talked about Miss Carolina when I was small. Every yellow finch in the yard seemed to be Miss Carolina."

"Bravo!" said Sullivan with a clap of his hands. The whole group began clapping for Gertrude. "What a great memory."

"Thank you, doctor," said the patient with a smile.

"Can you remember anything else from that day?"

"Sure," said the patient. "An airplane flew right over the house and the pilot waved at me."

"Who was with you?"

"My mother, of course. The whole neighborhood came out to see it. Oh, I can still smell the roses from mother's garden."

"Very nice," said Sullivan. "Now Gertrude, I'd like you to tell us what you did after the plane disappeared."

"Absolutely," said the patient in a matter of fact tone. "I watched the cat eat Miss Carolina." She shook her head sadly.

A collective moan emanated from the group.

"The cat ate Carolina?"

"Yes, as soon as the plane flew by, she jumped from the porch rail and latched onto that canary. Oh, that little bird let out such a sad chirp."

"What was the cat's name?"

"Midnight," said Gertrude. "Dad named it that. She was a fat, nasty black one... always hissing at me." The patient looked up toward the ceiling and paused, as if allowing her circuits to recalibrate. "Actually no, wait a minute... she didn't really eat Miss Carolina, but she tried, until mother hit her on the head with a broom. That's right, the cat screeched, and the bird flew away."

A round of applause broke out in appreciation of a happy ending to the story, from decades ago.

"Why thank you, Mrs. Appleton. Thank you for sharing such a wonderful memory with your family," said the medical director.

"You're welcome, Dr. Sullivan."

"Now everyone, I'd like to introduce to the Sullivan Gang our newest floor member," announced Sullivan. "Her name is Grace Jones, and she comes to us from Elderwood Manor. She was an assisted living resident at the Manor for the past several months and her family thought a stay on our floor would be beneficial."

A light round of applause followed the introduction. Seated next to Grace Jones was a thin girl named Monique, who was a senior in high school. She still had on her school uniform.

"Prior to our session, I asked her niece Monique if she would be willing to tell us a thing or two about her great aunt, and she gladly agreed. So, everyone I'd like you to meet Monique."

Monique stood up and ran her hands nervously down her skirt. A crimson bow complemented her black hair. She cleared her throat before speaking.

"Aunt Gracie is sixty-five years old," said Monique. "She was the youngest child in a family of seven, and the only remaining member of her family who is still alive. Aunt Gracie was the younger sister of my grandmother, who passed nearly five years ago."

While Monique spoke, Ms. Jones just stared forward, a blank look on her face. She moved her lower jaw up and down out of habit.

Sullivan leaned toward Dr. Garcia as the history continued. "She's the one I told you about, Olivia... carries the diagnosis of post-traumatic amnesia for decades. Physically she is fine, yet her mentation is disabling. All of her scans are completely normal."

"Aunt Gracie cannot recall anything about her childhood," continued Monique. "At times she can remember her wedding day, but other than that, her memory is pretty poor. It has been that way ever since I've known her."

"Does she remember you, Monique?" asked Doctor Garcia. "When you walk into her room, does she recognize you?"

"Oh sure," replied Monique. "She always recalls my name and believe it or not – my birthday. Every year when I visit

64

her on October 27th, she sings Happy Birthday and gives me a card with a five-dollar bill taped inside."

"Fascinating," said Sullivan. "Her long-term memory is seemingly void, yet her immediate recall appears somewhat intact. It's certainly a reversal of the norm. Anything else, Monique?"

"Yes, there is one more thing," said the young woman. "Aunt Gracie likes to sing the same song over and over. Well, not really sing, but kind of hum the lyrics, with a few words thrown in. It's the same tune, over and over."

"What song?" asked an elderly family member in the group. "I used to teach voice in college many years ago."

"I don't know. I always ask her, but she never answers. Grandma told me she wrote the song herself."

Doctor Sullivan stood up and walked toward Mrs. Jones. She was a slight woman with straight hair to the mid neck level. A flat, dark mole dominated the left side of her forehead. While looking forward she furled the skin above her eyebrows, as if in deep thought. She made no eye contact with the physician.

"Gracie, welcome to your new family, better known as the Sullivan Gang. I'm Doctor John Sullivan." He raised a hand toward Gertrude Appleton. "This is Mrs. Appleton and to your right is Mr. Brownstone." He pointed to a massive man sitting in a wheelchair, with a full crop of grey hair, cut high and tight. "We call him Tank, that was his football nickname."

"Put me in coach," laughed Tank Brownstone. "Watch out for the flea flicker." A mock scowl ran across his weathered face.

"Tank played professional football for years. He was just able to recall a tackle he made in the 1951 Championship Game across the street in Franklin Field. Are you a sports fan?" asked Sullivan

Grace Jones didn't respond.

"Your great niece, Monique, told us all about you. May I ask you a question?" The physician paused.

Silence.

Monique rubbed her great aunt's hand, trying to generate an answer.

"Grace Jones, can you recall the very first memory in your life?"

No answer.

"How about the names of your parents?"

Nothing.

"She seems a bit nervous," said Monique. "I can tell."

"Yes, perhaps a bit too overwhelming," responded Sullivan. "Maybe we should…"

Grace Jones suddenly began to sing a little tune. It was a short burst of notes, repeated in a quick repetitive fashion. "Tada, tee-da… Tada, tee-de." As the newest member of the group delivered the ditty, she walked her index finger up and down in the air. "L-O-V-E… forever, just you and me."

"That's it!" shouted Monique. "That's her song!"

"Our voice expert," said Sullivan quickly with a point to the teacher. "Name that tune!"

"Hmmm, not exactly familiar with that one," replied the voice coach. "Had a little Duke Ellington vibe to it, but not one I can immediately recall."

Despite demands for an encore performance, Grace Jones would not deliver the notes again. She failed to answer any more of Sullivan's questions.

"I tell you what Monique," said the group leader. "When she sings the tune again, can you record it on your cell phone?"

"Sure," said Monique.

"That way, once recorded, we can ask the computer what the name of the song is. What a wonderful world of technology we live in."

"Right," said Monique. "I never thought of that, Dr. Sullivan. Good idea."

"By next week, we'll have named that tune," said the group leader. "Along with a little help from our cell phones of course."

Laughter broke out among the group, including an unexpected smile across Grace's face. The exercise ended with all members receiving a "Sullivan Gang" sticker on their chest, signifying participation in the session. Dr. Sullivan and Chief Resident Garcia strolled back to the nursing station.

"Ran a bit over on that one," said Sullivan.

"Mrs. Appleton is starting to break through," said Garcia. "I'm glad her family member showed up."

"Yes. I've got a good feeling about her. In due time we are going to unleash a flood of memories in her mind. Miss Carolina and Midnight, what a neat little story."

"I liked the part about smelling her mother's roses."

"Of all the senses, smell is the most powerful memory tool," stated Sullivan. "I can still remember my mother's cabbage soup simmering on Sunday morning."

As the duo entered the nursing station Doctor Sullivan visually scanned the area. As usual the station was nearly abandoned with one elderly male nurse e-charting some data. Dr. Garcia retrieved her backpack from a lunchroom and said goodbye.

"Tony, did Nurse Adams leave already?"

"Yes," said the nurse. "You just missed her. Anything I can help you with?"

"No. No," said Sullivan. "I just had a question for her."

"I can leave her a message if you want," said the nurse.

"No. I'm O.K., Tony. It was a personal matter I wanted to discuss with her."

"How's Mom?" asked the nurse.

"Stable. She took a little spell and we had to bunk her into the hospital. It looks like dehydration, but Dr. Gelberman is running some tests."

"Tell her I said hello and remember, I'm available for private duty."

"Thanks, Tony. I'll keep you in mind."

The doctor began a somber walk toward the elevator, a bit disappointed that Nurse Adams had already left. His brother's prodding had triggered a sense of urgency within him, but the invitation for a follow-up dinner date would have to wait. While walking past Grace Jones' room, he heard the floor's newest member humming her happy tune. Waiting for the elevator at the end of the hall was Monique.

"Do you hear it?"

"Yes," said Sullivan to the high school student.

"She will sing that tune over and over. It's kind of sweet."

"I agree. A very pleasant song."

Their conversation continued as the elevator descended to the ground floor.

"How long was she married, Monique? Did she have any children?"

"I'm not sure. Grandma told me her marriage was brief, after which she 'stopped living.' Those were Grandma's words. She didn't have any children."

"How many other family members are in the area?"

"None. That's the problem. Once Grandma passed, I became her sole caretaker. When I turned eighteen, I became the Power of Attorney for her estate. She has no other family."

"Well, Grandma would be very proud. You handle yourself well."

"Thank you doctor, but I'm worried about leaving for college next year. Who is going to keep an eye on her?"

"We'll figure it out together, Monique," said Sullivan as they exited onto the main floor. "Trust me. Let me know if you want the social work department to get involved. O.K.?"

"I will Dr. Sullivan. Thank you for inviting me to group session. I've got a good feeling already. Good night."

"Good night, Monique."

While walking through the hospital lobby Sullivan hummed the recently learned tune, whispering the final words – "L-O-V-E... forever, just you and me." The words uplifted his spirits.

"John," called out a voice from behind. "John!"

Turning around, Sullivan came face-to-face with the Philadelphia General Hospital's CEO, Ralph Covington.

"Ralph, good evening," replied Sullivan. "You're here late."

"John, I never go home," responded the CEO. He wore a flashy three-piece suit with a purple handkerchief protruding from his jacket. The smell of cologne exuded from his rotund frame. "Do you have a minute?"

"Sure. What's up, Ralph?"

Before speaking, the longstanding CEO led Sullivan to the side, maintaining a hand on his shoulder.

"Exciting times," said the CEO, his blazing white porcelain teeth in full view. "Exciting times, John."

Sullivan sensed angst. Over the years he learned to mistrust Covington, his modus operandi driven by the almighty dollar. The hospital's marketing mantra of "compassionate health care" sat nowhere in his moral fiber.

"Are you getting everything you need out of the old Franklin Wing?" asked the CEO. While speaking he nodded to another physician passing by. "I hear there's still a lot of junk down there. I hope you didn't find any bodies."

"Ah, well actually I've come upon a rather amazing..."

"I'm glad they're allowing you access to the building, John. You know I went to bat for you." Covington stared down at his cell phone, smiling at an incoming text message. "I had to give the ultimate clearance for access."

Sullivan fell silent, well aware of the facts. The CEO had wanted the Franklin Wing down for years.

"John, as you know, the upper two floors of the Franklin Building are still being used... believe it or not, by our billing department." Covington continued to smile while setting up the bad news, a learned trait from snaking his way up the company food chain. "We're going to need some new space for the billing crew. Without collections, there is no Philadelphia General," chuckled the health care leader. "You know that. Right old friend?" He now patted Sullivan's shoulder.

"I'm aware of that."

"John, how is it going up on the Alzheimer's floor? You've been up there now for five years."

"Well Ralph, we're making some great strides via group session. I'm confident that our unique approach toward Alzheimer's will ultimately recalibrate the geriatrician's treatment of the disease, which reintegrates our patients back into a family setting. That's the key, Ralph... reestablishing the family network. Hence, the Sullivan Gang."

"John, the delivery of health care is rapidly evolving. Even I can't believe the dramatic changes that have occurred over the past two to three years. I'm sure you've seen it yourself. Hospitals being bought and sold every week... bitter rivals joining forces... and even insurance companies merging. Hell, everyone is running for cover, John. The ground beneath us is constantly moving. National health care is on the horizon."

Sullivan again went silent, allowing the directive to let out.

"John, the hospital board of trustees is concerned about your billing numbers," said Covington, his smile suddenly gone. "They've been pretty anemic, my friend. I know we touched upon this last year during your performance review. Do you want to go upstairs and take a look at the numbers?"

"No, I do not. Gains on the Alzheimer's floor are not measured in dollars. I'm confident that my method will prove fruitful in the care of patients with Alzheimer's."

"I know that, but the chief financial officer doesn't." The CEO paused and looked over his shoulder. He whispered, "John, we're losing money on your Alzheimer's floor. It's that simple, a lot of money to be exact. The Medicare dollar isn't paying for your care. You're running hard in the red, doctor."

"Ralph, you hired me to develop an Alzheimer's program here at the PGH. Over the past five years I've been trying my damn best to accomplish that goal. Now, I must say, your administration has not been exactly helpful in my pursuits. Remember our conversation last year about a marketing program?"

"Have you written any scientific articles, John?" interrupted Covington. "I realize full professorship is still fifteen years away but being a leader in your academic field is key to securing such a coveted position."

"Well," mumbled Sullivan in defense. "I'm just starting to gather good data and plan on presenting our findings at the next meeting in…"

"John, what am I supposed to tell the board? Help me out here. You're losing money every quarter and not producing anything academically. I'm under the gun… *the hospital* is under the gun. We're just trying to keep the ship afloat here." Covington glanced at his cell phone while speaking. "God forbid we sell out to another hospital." He slowly looked back up. "Hell, then I'll be out of a job. We can't let that happen."

Before Sullivan could respond, the CEO closed the open space in their conversation.

"John, I'm going to be blunt. The hospital board of trustees has made the decision to close down the Alzheimer's wing. I'm sorry my friend, but I wanted to tell you in person. The billing department needs a new home once the Franklin comes down." The CEO continued to pat the physician's shoulder. "I'm sure you understand. You must have sensed it coming?"

"I respectfully disagree with your decision process," blurted back Sullivan. "You cannot turn your back on my patients! Over five million people currently live with Alzheimer's disease and by the year 2050, the number is projected to rise to nearly fourteen million! Listen to me, Ralph... Alzheimer's is the sixth leading cause of death in the United States! I welcome you to come up and witness the amazing work we are doing. I'm absolutely convinced that my group method works. I implore you and the board to reconsider..."

"Start making plans," interrupted Covington. "The patients need to be farmed out. I'll notify the social workers tomorrow. Maybe there's some room over at our nursing facility, but only if the major insurers pay for it." The CEO paused as his porcelain smile again returned. "John, I'm here to help you. A few years from now you'll come to understand our decision process. Trust me. It's just that I have a better vantage point to see all the moving parts."

Sullivan didn't respond, not appreciating the "farmed out" comment.

"I'm very sorry, John."

"Listen to me Ralph. You're making a big mistake. I demand a meeting with the Board of Trustees! Alzheimer's disease is rapidly turning into a national epidemic. If you close down my wing, the lives of so many patients and their families will be irrevocably harmed by..."

"Of course, we're going to keep you on staff, John," interrupted Covington. He glanced back down at his cell phone, further infuriating Sullivan. "We'll abide by your employment contract. But I'm going to have to insist you drop down into the hospitalist pool. They're moaning for some more night shift coverage. You're trained in internal medicine, right?"

"What about your promise, Ralph?" snapped Sullivan. "Remember? You promised me a long term, compassionate environment to help better understand and cultivate a breakthrough in the care of Alzheimer's disease."

"Well, I'm afraid the world has changed rapidly," shot back the CEO. "It's a bitter pill physicians are being forced to swallow each and every day. I'm sorry, John." He began to walk away but turned back. "Now orthopedics... that's a money maker, John. That new joint center replacing the Franklin Wing is going to be a cash cow. We take in about $35,000 per joint replacement, even more if we discharge the patient straight home. How about we get you involved in that, John? How does that sound? We can have you clear the patients preoperatively for their hip and knee replacements. Think about it. I'll run it by Dr. Pagano... you do know he's going to be the department chair?"

Sullivan turned and walked away in silent anger, refusing to listen anymore. He heard enough from the corporate stooge.

"One month! You've got one month, John!" shouted the CEO. "The social work team will be up there tomorrow to get the ball rolling. Trust me on this one, John! You'll thank me some day."

The geriatrician bolted out a side entrance into the streets of Philadelphia. While walking home an inner ire brewed in his soul. How dare they close *his* wing... *his* patients, being "farmed out" to make more money! How dare they!

"Squish," slipped his right foot on a steamy load of fresh dog manure parked on the sidewalk. He nearly fell to the ground.

"Ah, crap," bemoaned Sullivan while looking down at his shoe. He scuffed his foot repeatedly in anger, on the grass between the sidewalk and the curb.

CHAPTER EIGHT
UNCLE FRANK

"What's the emergency?" asked Mayor Chubb as he strolled into his office. "I had to cancel my tee time out on the Main Line. For Christ's sake, it's a beautiful day outside." The mayor's stomach woefully protruded over the waistline of tan golf pants. Sweat marks stained the armpits of his white collared shirt. He tossed a set of keys onto a desk.

"We've got a problem over in West Philly," replied Attorney Pompano. "The Franklin Wing project." Pompano sat in an oversized armchair in the mayor's office, looking out onto Market Street, where some children were playing in a water fountain.

"What Franklin project?" asked Chubb. "I don't even know what you're talking about, Louie."

"The old Franklin Wing up on the PGH campus. It's set for demo on July 5th. You helped our firm secure the project."

"Oh yea. Thanks for the summer digs at the shore, but didn't that deal go down some time ago?"

"Yes, but there's been a ton of delays. We even had to get the judge involved."

"So, what's the holdup now?"

"Elevated radon levels," bemoaned Pompano. "One of your building inspectors keeps registering markedly high levels, and somehow a writer down at the *Chronicle* caught wind of the readings. Sounds like he might try to make some noise."

"Radon?" barked the mayor. "The city sits on a goddamn radon belt, Lou." The civic leader plopped down into an oversized faux leather chair that moaned from the impact. "Every home has radon, even mine. I had to put some sort of a fan in the basement. Hell, if you ask me, I don't even think radon exists."

"Well, it's real," said Pompano with a shift in his seat. "At least I think so."

"How about a bag full of cash?" asked Chubb. "Did you try that?"

"It didn't work," replied Pompano with a check of his watch. "Where's Winky? He's the one who set up this meeting."

"Here I am," growled Tommy Pagano Jr. as he bolted into the room. "I'm a race car engine running in the red, Louie!" The CEO of Pagano Destruction shook the mayor's hand. "Thanks for coming, Chet."

"No problem."

Winky began to pace the room liked a caged tiger. "I'm losing money by the hour!" snarled Pagano while chomping on a cigar. "The creditors are starting to call, I've got equipment and workers sitting around, and now some punk strolls into my office asking about elevated radon levels." He looked at Attorney Pompano. "Louie, where did I go wrong? I'm just trying to make an honest living here."

"Everything will be alright," said Pompano with a soothing hand gesture. "We'll get that building down on July 5th, trust me."

"*You're* losing money?" asked Mayor Chubb incredulously. "How is that possible? I've gift wrapped every church demolition in the Delaware Valley to your firm."

"There are no more churches to blow up!" shot back Pagano while making a quick sign of the cross. "Jesus, Mary and Joseph... pray for us."

Two portly, middle-aged men suddenly walked into the room, both wearing polyester pants and ill-fitting short-sleeved shirts. They stood on each side of the entrance. Neither man spoke but their appearance prompted Pompano and the mayor to immediately stand up. Behind them walked in six-foot, three-inch Francesco Anthony Russo, wearing a crisp, cotton sport coat and tie. A light blue fedora hat with a yellow feather adorned his head. Two additional bodyguards trailed Russo, both well past their physical prime.

"Louie, Chet... Winky," said Russo with gusto. His lean frame towered over everyone else in the room. "Where's the judge? Is he coming?" Handshakes were exchanged.

"No, Mr. Russo," replied Pompano with reverence. "He's in session now... but he sends his regards."

"I see." Russo strolled over to a coat rack and hung up his hat. A long nose anchored a weathered face that was framed by a grey hair comb-over. At age sixty-eight, the well-known businessman maintained a fit frame. He poured himself a cup of black coffee. A set of cufflinks glimmered in the sun. "What's going on boys? Why the emergency?"

"The Franklin Wing project up at the PGH," replied Pompano. "There's a fly in the ointment."

"I hate flies," said Uncle Frank as he sat down. Everyone else in the room took a seat. "What kind of flies? Big flies or small flies?"

"Small, but pesky," replied Pompano. "It's just that we're getting close to our deadline."

"The Pagano Orthopedic Institute?" asked Russo. "That's what we're calling it... right Tommy?" He winked at the demo boss. "For Christ's sake, Tommy. Your son is going to run the place. Smile!"

"Thank you very much, Uncle Frank," replied Tommy Pagano in a tone of respect. "The Pagano family thanks you for helping out with the name… we are forever grateful."

"Vincent is a good boy," declared Russo. "Always has been." The businessman slowly blew some steam away from his coffee cup. "It kind of has a nice ring to it – The Pagano Orthopedic Institute."

"The problem at hand is a city worker who keeps reporting elevated radon levels," continued Pompano. "Despite the usual offering, he continues to make noise."

"Who's your man on the project?" asked Russo to Mayor Chubb. "A rookie?"

The mayor shuffled through some papers on his desk while donning reading glasses. "Let's see here… the Franklin project. One moment, please. It's Larry… Larry Griffith." He took off his glasses. "Larry's been with the city for sometime now. He's no rookie."

"Any red flags on Mr. Larry Griffith?" asked Frank Russo.

"Not to my recall. He's kind of an even keel type of guy."

"Well, I suggest you get him off the project tomorrow," shot back Uncle Frank. "Tell him it's an administrative decision."

"Easy enough," replied the mayor.

"Replace him with my man, Freddie Freeman," instructed Russo. "Fred's a cash whore. He can be counted on."

"But didn't Freeman triple his fee when we tumbled St. Rocco's Church?" asked Pagano. "Don't you remember, when we came across those bones in the basement?"

"Who cares," quipped Uncle Frank. "The city paid for it, right Chet?"

"How the hell do I know," laughed the mayor. "I'm out of here in a year. This city is running so hard in the red it doesn't even matter anymore. Let the next poor bastard worry about the budget."

A lighthearted chuckle rolled through the room.

"Louie," said Frank Russo. "Hire an independent expert to get down there and register some normal radon readings, just in case."

"Right," replied the long-time consigliore.

"And get the readings over to the judge ASAP... understand?"

"Yes, sir."

"Alright," said Russo confidently. "Problem number one solved." He took a slow sip of coffee. "So, to my recall, all the decision makers in this Franklin demo have a significant financial uptick on the flip side. Isn't that right?" thought Russo out loud.

No one answered while the entrepreneur counted the fingers on his right hand.

"Let's see... there's me, the investors, Pagano Destruction, the fine mayor sitting before us and even Ralph Covington, the CEO up at the PGH." He looked up. "Who am I missing... oh yea, a few of the senior PGH board of trustees members."

"The judge... don't forget the judge," added Attorney Pompano.

"Right. So that's a pretty tight circle my friends," said Uncle Frank. "Everyone involved in the decision to drop that hospital has a skin in the game." Russo took another slow sip of coffee. "So, what am I missing here – unless someone from Washington is reaching into the pot?"

"Some punk reporter from the *Chronicle*," blurted Winky Pagano. "A pretty boy who strolled into my office asking a lot of questions about radon." The destruction boss's right eye fluttered. "The Historical Society tipped him off."

"The Historical Society has been legally neutered," shot back Pompano. "The judge made sure of that."

"So the only fly left is this reporter from the *Chronicle*?" asked Uncle Frank. "If I'm reading everyone correctly?"

"Right," replied Pompano. "I looked the kid up, he's from North Philly, an associate editor at the *Chronicle*. He's been with them for about five years."

"He wanted *our* side of the story," cut in Pagano. "Something about his article needing to be balanced."

"The *Chronicle*, hmmm... that can be a little tricky," warned Frank Russo with a pointed index finger. "Back in the day, they were in our pocket, but now there's no guarantee. Too many writers crawling over each other, trying to make a name for themselves."

"What's his name?" asked the mayor. "I can have our P.R. man check him out."

"Barber," replied Pompano. "Seth Barber."

"Anything else on Mr. Seth Barber?" asked Uncle Frank.

"He lives over in Manayunk, near Pretzel Park... rents a place over a barber shop."

"Married? Kids, anything like that?"

"Not to my knowledge," replied the attorney. "I've checked out all of his social media sites."

"LIFT," interjected Mayor Chubb with a goofy smile. "Someone told me that's a good mnemonic to remember today's key social sites. It stands for LinkedIn, Instagram, Facebook and Twitter. Pretty catchy, eh? Have you checked all of his *LIFT* sites, Attorney Pompano?"

"Well, actually..."

"Here's my mnemonic for those sites," cut in Uncle Frank. *HORSESHIT!* How's that?"

The four goons in the room chuckled along with Tommy Pagano.

"I'm assuming you're off the grid, Mr. Russo?" asked Pompano respectfully. Like any good attorney, he knew the answer before asking the question.

"Absolutely," laughed Russo. "I communicate the old-fashioned way, Lou. I look a man in the eye and tell him what

I think. If there's a problem, we talk it out. If not... well then, we step outside and settle the matter. It gets the job done."

"Sounds efficient," replied Pompano.

"Why make it so complicated, right?" chuckled the kingpin.

"Exactly," replied Pompano. "But to answer the mayor's question, I did check out his so-called LIFT sites, and there's not much there. Just a bunch of photos of him drinking booze in some beat up apartment, with a ferret and older woman... who looks half in the bag all the time."

"So a lightweight," said Russo. "Probably doesn't even know what's he's sticking his nose into. Right?"

"Absolutely," answered the attorney.

"Well, let me see," said Russo. "One of the senior editors down at the *Chronicle* owes me a bit of a favor. I'll give him a call tomorrow morning."

"We're on a tight time frame here," interjected Pompano respectfully. "Any noise in the system at this point can derail the project."

"I can't take any more delays!" shouted Winky. "My father appeared to me in a dream last night! He warned me not to repeat his mistakes!" The CEO looked at the ceiling and made a sign of the cross.

"Gentlemen," interjected Russo. "You disappoint me." He stood up to retrieve his hat. "After what we've been through over the years... hell, this is a chip shot."

"Oh yea," cut in Pompano. "I almost forgot. This Seth Barber kid goes by a weird moniker on the internet."

"What's that?"

"He calls himself the notorious Barber of Silverwood," answered Pompano with a cocked eye.

Everyone in the room laughed upon hearing the name.

"Well," chuckled Russo while donning his cap. "The notorious Barber of Silverwood is about to get a crew cut." He donned his hat and strolled towards the door. "The question is... how close of a shave does he want?"

"Thank you, Uncle Frank."

"Prego. Ciao, ciao," said Russo with a tip of his hat.

CHAPTER NINE
TESTING 1-2-3

"I want to go home," growled Martha Sullivan with a stubborn scowl. "I feel fine." She sat upright in the hospital bed with her arms crossed.

"That's not my decision," replied her son as he re-arranged a dinner tray at her side. "We still have to hear from Dr. Gelberman."

"Dr. Gelberman is a good man... Dad always liked him."

"You need to eat more, Mom. Look at all this food being wasted."

"You eat it," snapped back Mrs. Sullivan. "Or take it home for Moses." She took a slow, thoughtful breath. "How's my little precious?"

"Moses is perfectly fine. Do you want me to turn on the game?"

"No, it's on a rain delay."

John Sullivan sat down at his mother's side. Three days had passed since her hospital admission, with no discharge in sight. She clinically looked much better after being rehydrated, however her prognosis remained unchanged. She was in an ornery mood that evening.

"I'm ready for the hole in the ground," said his mother. "Put me on your father's left-hand side. That's the way we slept together in bed."

"Mom, I'm not going to start talking about that."

"Your uncle Leo is buried two plots over, to his right. Keep me away from him."

"Mom, please."

"He never liked me. I still remember the day your father brought me home to meet your grandparents. Uncle Leo didn't think I was good enough for the Sullivan clan. Hah! Look what happened to him. That old booze hound."

Into the room walked Dr. Daniel Gelberman, chairman of the Department of Oncology at the PGH. A set of hunched shoulders slowly propelled his short, stocky, sixty-year old body forward, as if the weight of the world bore down on his frame. A thick, grey beard and glasses covered his rosy face.

"Martha, John… good evening," said Gelberman. "How's my favorite patient?"

"I want out," replied Martha.

"She's getting feisty," said Sullivan. "Which is a good sign."

"A good sign indeed," added Gelberman. The physician took a seat next to his patient's bed. He smiled warmly. "How's your appetite, Martha?"

"Fine," replied the patient. "My appetite is fine. I'm peeing fine and this morning, I had a good bowel movement. So, all the pipes are working."

"You're still a bit anemic," stated the oncologist in a respectful tone. "Despite two units of blood." He nodded his head while maintaining eye contact with Mrs. Sullivan. "Something is still going on inside that body of yours."

"It's called cancer and time to go home," replied Martha. "That's what's going on inside my body."

Gelberman smiled at the response, but his demeanor soon turned serious. "Martha, I just looked over your scans from this morning with the radiology team…"

"Give it to me straight," shot back Mrs. Sullivan. "Don't sugar coat it. We've known each other way too long."

Gelberman paused while looking toward his colleague. "John, have you seen the scans?"

Sullivan slowly nodded his head in the positive.

"Martha, there are a few more spots near your liver and a new one now... believe it or not, in your brain." He paused. "I'm very sorry to tell you that."

Silence.

"Up until this point we've been able to keep the cancer in check with the sequential rounds of chemotherapy. I'm actually a bit surprised by the intracranial lesion, which..."

"How much longer do I have?" interrupted Martha Sullivan. "To live, that is."

"Well, that depends on what we do next."

"What are our options?" asked Dr. Sullivan.

"We have a few," said the oncologist. "There are stronger medications we can try. A colleague of mine at Johns Hopkins recently reported good success with a new combination of chemotherapeutics, including Adriamycin and..."

"Hospice," said Mrs. Sullivan.

"Excuse me?"

"Enough already. I want home hospice. We've given it our best Dr. Gelberman. But it's time." Slowly she shook her head. "My husband is waiting for me."

"Hospice is certainly an option," said the elderly physician.

"Are you sure, Mom? Don't you think we should get George's input on this? He's always involved in the decision process."

"You can, but my mind is made up. I can't go on like this. This is no way to live." The dying patient looked at her doctor. "Quite frankly Dr. Gelberman, I'm not sure if the cancer is killing me... or the treatment. Either way... it's time."

The medical oncologist remained respectfully silent, knowing beyond a doubt, the cancer was the culprit.

"I only have one request, Dr. Gelberman."

"What's that, Martha?"

"Just keep me comfortable at the end. Alright?"

"I will. I certainly will."

"Dan, I'd like to talk to my brother about the final decision," interjected Dr. Sullivan.

"Understood," replied the oncologist.

"I don't see the point," said Martha Sullivan. "Especially since I'm the patient."

"Mrs. Sullivan, I recommend you give it another day or two. If hospice is your ultimate decision, I'll fully respect that," said the medical doctor while standing up.

"Well…"

"Come on, Mom. I agree with Dr. Gelberman. Let's discuss it with George."

"Fine," said the patient. "But my mind isn't going to change." She defiantly crossed her hands back over her chest.

"Thanks, Dan," said Sullivan. "We'll make a final decision over the next day or two. Good night."

"You're welcome," said the oncologist as he exited the room. "I'll talk to you in the morning."

After thirty more minutes of frank discussion, Dr. John Sullivan kissed his mother good-bye. She held firm on her hospice decision.

"Good night, Mom."

"I know where you're going," said Mrs. Sullivan. "Stay out of that basement, John. You're looking for trouble."

"Good night, Mom."

Sullivan walked through the Philadelphia General Hospital, which occupied four city blocks. His destination was indeed the Franklin Wing, where Reggie was standing guard. While walking, the doctor sang his new favorite tune.

"L-O-V-E… that's love… just you and me."

"Hey Doc," said Reggie. "Got your stuff right here." Reggie reached behind his desk and lifted up the doctor's camcorder, now on a tripod. "Is it charged?"

"You bet," answered Sullivan with a smile. "Reggie, thanks for watching it and thanks for allowing me access to that wonderful collection of artifacts from the Franklin. Do you mind if I hold onto it for a while? I want to show the Historical Society some of the contents."

"Yea, sure Doc. Keep it as long as you want. Just promise me if anything is worth a million dollars in there, that we split it. Ah-right?"

"It's a deal, Reggie."

"Hey Doc," said the watchman before Sullivan walked away. "Be careful down there." Before Sullivan could respond he added, "I know. I know... there are no such things as ghosts."

The subbasement, as usual, was deathly quiet. Sullivan made his way to Dr. Schmidt's office and immediately noticed that the crawlspace to the hidden walkway was smashed wide open. The floor of the reading room was covered with hunks of concrete and cinder blocks, making visualization of the star design difficult. Some additional lighting was added to the area, and a sensor sat atop some neatly stacked bricks, flashing a small red light every thirty seconds. A tag hanging from the device read 'The Office of the Philadelphia Building Inspector. Do Not Remove Under Penalty of Law'.

Sullivan carefully walked around the debris to rig up his camcorder. He set the camera and tripod facing the alcove, thankful for the additional light. Next, he focused the lens on several concrete blocks littering the granite slab in the mid-section of the star. Once satisfied he returned to the granite slab and pushed away the cinder blocks, surprised as to their weight. After clearing his voice, he stood on the block and stared back at the camera. He took a remote control from his pocket and pointed it at the camera. After pressing the

'Record' button Sullivan said loudly, "Testing 1-2-3. Testing 1-2-3. How now, brown cow. This is a test." He paused the video. A review of the tape noted the angle, lighting and sound to be acceptable. Satisfied with the test, he returned to the granite slab.

"Hello, this is Dr. John Sullivan from the West Philadelphia Historical Society. Today's date is June 15[th,] 2020 and I am reporting to you from the subbasement of the Philadelphia General Hospital's Franklin Wing. I'm in the former office of Dr. Zachary Schmidt, who as you know, disappeared about forty years ago in this very building. I am standing in the middle of Dr. Schmidt's reading room, near the northern foundation wall. Behind me is a massive curved wall of granite, which serves as the room's architectural centerpiece. Recently we discovered a short, narrow passageway on the opposite side of this granite facade. Later in the video, we will explore this corridor and some interesting engraving found on the wall's backside."

The doctor paused to look around and then overhead before speaking again. He felt a subtle vibration in the room.

"The reading room I'm standing in is remarkably stark and was known to be Dr. Zachary Schmidt's favorite study area. Just outside the alcove, to the right and left were a series of large oaken bookshelves, which at one point in time, held the personal library collection of Dr. Schmidt. What's peculiar about this room, besides the majestic wall of granite behind me, is the floor. I am standing upon a most distinctive, large star configuration embossed into the floor itself. It is a grand design etched into the concrete, replete with colorful tiles. At the center of the star is a singular granite block with the symbol of an eye upon it. Later video will show you this inlay pattern. Above me is a conical ceiling whose point coincides exactly to the center of the granite block, measuring about twenty feet in height."

Sullivan paused to gather his thoughts. He again felt an ever so slight rumble beneath his feet. A dumpster truck on street level he thought. Some dust drifted down from the ceiling.

"This room however is not the only significant discovery we've stumbled upon during this project. I've recently had the privilege of recovering the actual key that Dr. Schmidt wore around his neck. It was contained within a hodgepodge of artifacts collected from the Franklin Wing by Security Guard Reginald Washington, whose recollection of July 4, 1976 will be included in this video."

The doctor dug into his right front pant's pocket to reach for the key. As he pulled it out the rumble beneath him grew. A heavy low hum began to fill the room. Some gravel on the floor gently shook.

"Whoa," said Sullivan. "I'm going to keep the camera running here but pause a bit on the oral presentation. As you can see, some seismic activity is ongoing. I'm going to assume it's from street activity above, since temblors are rare in this geographic area." He paused and looked overhead. "The walls in this section of the facility are over two hundred years old, so if the activity continues, I'm going to be off screen quite quickly."

The doctor slowly stepped off the granite slab and toward the room exit. The rumbling eased. After a few minutes he returned to the room's center.

"Very good. O.K." said Sullivan with some relief. "As I was saying, in my right hand is the very key worn around the neck of Dr. Schmidt. The key itself is estimated to be over two hundred years old and will be undergoing further analysis by several members of the society with expertise in antique keys."

A slow, roll of thunder was heard outside.

"The key itself was worn 24/7 around the neck of Dr. Schmidt and secured to his body with a ring of tungsten steel." The physician held up the key to his neckline while continuing to speak. "It was rumored there was no latch on the steel necklace, but as you can see a portion of the key's bow has been broken. This theoretically could have caused the trinket to slip off its steel chain. When this occurred I cannot say, but I will point out that the last known photograph of Dr. Schmidt, taken on the psychiatry floor of the PGH just days before his disappearance, showed the key to be secure around his neck."

The doctor began to bring the key away from his neckline, but it touched upon his collar, causing it to fall to the floor. A fierce rumble shook the basement, causing Sullivan to panic. He quickly reached down to pick up the skeleton key, and ran towards the room's perimeter, in fear of a ceiling collapse. The tremor ceased.

"Interesting," said the physician. He waited for several more minutes before cautiously approaching the granite slab again. Once back atop the eye, he turned toward the camera.

"We seem to be having a series of small earthquakes," said Sullivan to the lens. "I should be getting out of here but I've noticed the rumbling to halt when I step away from the granite. Why... I do not know."

The physician held the key high into the air, and nothing happened. He held it out in front of his frame while rotating 360 degrees, and nothing happened. He then stooped down and the tremble returned, only to stop when he stood erect.

"What the heck is going on here?"

Again he squatted toward the floor and the rumble returned, prompting him to stand up and stare forward.

"Something odd is occurring," said Sullivan to the camcorder. "It seems that whenever this old key comes close to the granite slab, it sets off a rumble." He paused in a pensive fashion. "Obviously I'm concerned that if the tremors become more violent, a cave in may occur. So, I'm going to proceed with caution here."

Slowly, Dr. John Sullivan lowered his frame toward the floor. It seemed like he was able to control the intensity of the quake, by lowering or elevating the key. While doing so he felt a gravitational pull, as if the granite slab was drawing the key downward. Instinctively he stood back up and looked square into the camera.

"It appears that there is some sort of reaction going on between the granite and the key," said Sullivan. "At least I believe this stone is granite. Perhaps I'll take a chunk to the geology department here on campus to have it analyzed." He shook his head and looked at the old key. "A most peculiar series of events. I must admit."

The physician turned away from the camera to face the wall, his eyes scanning the structure. A layer of thick grime and dust covered the edifice. The newly strung construction lights cast an eerie reflection off the stone, and while doing so, exposed a faint hint of color change – directly in the center of the wall. While still standing on the stone floor slab, Sullivan was able to lean forward and touch the main wall of granite. He slowly wiped away the grit, exposing a short oval piece of marble, about five inches long and two inches high. Dirt plugged the middle of the marble inset.

"What do we have here?" mumbled Sullivan to himself, the video still recording. "A piece of non-granite, situated directly in the absolute center of the wall." He ran his fingers firmly across the oval, realizing an irregular depression existed beneath the film of crud. With his index fingernail he began to unplug the cavity, releasing morsels of solidified dirt. He blew forcefully into the stone notch, causing some residue to flash back into his eyes. Leaning back from the wall the physician wiped his eyes and refocused. He stared back at the wall and much to his surprise, viewed the symbol of a skeleton key, cut into the stone. "Uh-oh," said Sullivan as he stroked his fingers over the depression. The indentation was perfectly level and matched the silhouette of Schmidt's key.

Stepping backwards he returned to the camera and zoomed in onto the stone pattern. Next, he quickly returned to his position. While pointing towards the marble stone, he began to speak loudly.

"I've discovered a carved-out area of stone, which appears to be a perfect slot for Dr. Schmidt's key. Perhaps it was a resting place for his personal treasure. This newly found recess is not a keyhole, since it's carved to accept the key on its side, as if you were placing it on a tabletop." He continued to inspect the slot. "I will say… the stone recess is absolutely inviting me to place Dr. Schmidt's key inside." Sullivan paused, while looking over the entire wall before him. "And so I shall, perhaps returning the turnkey to its original resting place. Here we go." He took a confident, deep breath.

The physician slowly raised and placed the skeleton key into the center of the inlay, prompting a tremendous roar to fill the room.

"Crack!" went the sound of thunder, followed by a flash of brilliant light and high-pitched zoom.

The noise prompted the physician to scream. He tried to run but his feet were incapable of motion. It seemed as if the granite wall grabbed his hand, and the stone floor captured his feet. His body was rendered immobile.

"Crack!"

He grasped the key as an inescapable gravitational pull seized his body, followed by another tremendous flash of light. A thunderous roar pierced his cranium followed by brilliant sparkling lights and the sense of speed – tremendous speed. He screamed aloud but there was no sound. No perception of direction existed, only acceleration. He tried to open his eyes but the force would not permit. A high pitched whine was followed by absolute darkness. Then… silence and speed.

Sometime later he awoke in a dark room, his forehead bloodied, lying prone on a marble floor. The last thing he remembered was feeling the skeleton key, clenched inside his right hand.

CHAPTER TEN
THE BASEBALL STITCH

"Three more weeks!" shouted Rocco while walking through the Franklin basement. His voice echoed through the complex despite the sound of machinery in the distance. "Three more weeks and this shack will drop like a house of cards!" An army of workers diligently moved around him.

"Did you find any more hidden chambers?" asked newly appointed City Inspector Freddie Freeman. He chewed on a toothpick while speaking.

"Nah," said Rocco. "I took a good look around. There's only city bedrock behind that wall."

"Didn't I work with Pagano Destruction on the cathedral implosion in Norristown?" asked Freeman. He was a cynical appearing middle-aged male with a permanent frown on his face, balanced by a forehead full of ridges. A set of thin arms and legs caused his rotund belly to teeter back and forth with every step.

"Yea. You did," replied Rocco. "That was a few years back. I remember all the parishioners protesting on the perimeter. What the heck was the name of that old church we blew up? God, I loved the way that dome collapsed in on itself."

"It was Saint Rocco's," said the inspector in an incredulous tone. "How can't you remember that?"

"Oh, that's right," said the foreman as he sidestepped a workman drilling a borehole in the foundation. "They spelled it differently though, at least I think."

"What did you ever do with those ornate crucifixes we found in the crawlspace?" ask Freeman. "They were probably worth a pretty penny."

"Ah… ah, I donated them to charity," mumbled Rocco with a look of guilt. "Why? Who wants to know?"

"No one does, Rock," laughed Freeman while patting the foreman on the back. "No one. Just asking a question."

The duo turned the corner into Dr. Schmidt's reading alcove, to see Inspector Larry Griffith, staring at his sensor equipment.

"Someone said we had an earthquake last night," quipped Freeman.

"My sensor!" screamed Griffith in dismay. "What happened to it?" He reached down to pick up the sensor he had carefully set on the stack of bricks. It appeared to have been struck by a sledgehammer several times. Several pieces were strewn across the floor. "Oh my God! It's completely destroyed."

"A sneeze can bring these old walls down," said Rocco, ignoring the presence of Griffith. "Any rumble, and you'll see me and the team scurry out of here like a bunch of rats."

"Must have fallen, Larry," said Freeman to his underling. "Probably from the quake. You should have secured it better."

Griffith glared angrily at Rocco. A few workers behind him snickered. One actually had a sledgehammer in his hand.

"Is this the area?" asked Freeman. "The source of the radon levels?"

"Yes. This is the epicenter," moaned Griffith.

"What were the readings?"

"I sent you every set of the readings!" snapped Griffith. "Didn't you review them?"

"Sure I did," replied Freeman. "Were the levels repeated? That's standard operational protocol."

"Yes, they were... multiple times! I sent those results too."

"Listen you two," snarled Rocco. "No more delays. My boss isn't going to tolerate any more delays, or I lose my job. Understand?"

"Ah, excuse me," said Griffith. "I'm just doing my job as a city..."

"No more delays!" screamed Rocco with a step toward the inspector. He clenched his right fist in anger.

"Rock, come on now, we've been down this path before," said Freeman. He patted the brute on his shoulder. "And we've always finished on time. Right?"

"Yea. But something bugs me about this job," growled Rocco. "This old building is a hazard to my crew. It should have been razed years ago." The foreman stroked his biceps before continuing. "And just like I predicted, one of those Historical Society screwballs got hurt down here!"

"What?" asked Griffith. "When? Where?"

"Right there," answered Rocco. He pointed to the eye inlay on the floor. "One of my workers found some of his belongings this morning, then we heard he was admitted to the hospital late last night."

"Who was it?" asked Griffith with concern. He knew of Sullivan's plans to record a video presentation the prior evening.

"How the hell do I know!" barked Rocco.

"Oh no," replied Griffith. He began to quickly gather the remnants of his sensor. "It must be Dr. Sullivan."

"I just can't take it anymore!" screamed Rocco. "Someone is going to get killed down here."

"Listen Rock, calm down. Let me look at the data," said Inspector Freeman. "I'm sure this can all be explained somehow. There's radon in all these old basements. We can work this out together." Freeman winked at the destruction foreman. "Larry's off the project as of this morning... I'm the new city inspector on the case."

"We have to get another machine down here," interrupted Griffith. "These levels are outrageous and have to be accounted for."

"Larry, Larry you're overreacting," said Freeman with a raise of his hand. He took the toothpick out of his mouth. "I'm in charge here now, per the mayor. I've worked with Pagano Destruction before, so there is a level of comfort between us."

"I agree," said Rock.

"With all due respect sir, I don't think the mayor..."

"Larry. You're off the job," said Freeman sharply. "Understood? Gather up your machine and head out."

"Sir, I've been working on this project ever since its..."

"It's over Larry," snapped Freeman. "Period. Any questions... ask Mayor Chubb. It was his decision. Now get out of here and get downtown. I'm putting you on the Fillmore project."

Larry Griffith didn't respond. He turned around and left the group in anger, his mangled sensor in hand.

"Great! Thank you, Fred," said Rocco. "The boss will be happy you're on site. Did you drive over here today?"

"Why yes I did, Rock."

"Where are you parked?"

"I'm on the first floor of the main hospital parking lot."

"A Hummer. Do you still drive that big Hummer?"

"Yes I do... good memory Rock. A bright yellow one with a license plate reading 'Inspect 1'." The chief inspector paused with a smile. "The front passenger door is open."

"Great," said Rock with a firm handshake extended toward Freeman. "See you on demo day my friend."

"It's my pleasure, Rock. Thanks for the invitation. Say hello to Mr. Pagano."

"Let's move it people!" shouted Rocco into the air with a grin on his face. "Three weeks to D-day! Drill, baby drill!" His voice echoed through the hall.

At that very moment, in the Jefferson wing of the PGH complex, George Sullivan sat next to his mother, waiting for Dr. Gelberman to arrive on morning rounds.

"Where's John when you need him?" asked Mrs. Sullivan, her breathing labored. "It's unlike him not to be here." A clear plastic oxygen tube ran into her nostrils.

"Must be busy with a patient," replied her son.

"My obituary is in the second drawer of my dresser," continued Mrs. Sullivan. "I wrote it about a month ago." She smiled in a devilish way. "I listed Moses as one of my surviving family members."

"Mom..."

"Don't ignore the inevitable, George. I'm going to die soon, despite the efforts of your brother. He thinks I'm immortal."

"John is only trying to help." He checked his watch. He tried to contact his brother last night and this morning, to no avail. It was uncharacteristic of him not to be present.

My favorite blue outfit is also in the dresser. Make sure the undertaker doesn't wrinkle it all up. I ironed it last week. Put a picture of your father in the coffin."

"Mom, I'm not going to start talking about that."

Dr. Gelberman walked into the room.

"Good morning, George. Good morning, Martha." He took a seat at the bedside. "Have we come to a decision?"

"Well, Dr. Gelberman," started George. "I'd really like to get my brother's input..."

"Hospice," blurted Mrs. Sullivan. "That's my decision, and I'm the patient. So please, send me home. I'm tired and I've got a cat to take care of."

The oncologist respectfully nodded to the patient. "I fully respect your decision, Martha." He looked at George. "George, are you in agreement with Mom's decision?"

"Yes," came the painful reply. "She's as stubborn as an old army mule." He patted his mother's hand. "But I'd still like to get John's approval."

"Can you answer me one question?" asked the patient.

"Sure, Mrs. Sullivan."

"How much longer do I have?" She pointed an arthritic finger at Gelberman. "Give it to me straight."

The physician paused while trying to measure his response. Despite his years of experience, the answer never came easy.

"The way I feel right now…I'd guess about a month," stated Mrs. Sullivan. "Probably until around the all-star game."

"Excuse me?" asked Gelberman.

"The Major League All-Star Game," continued Mrs. Sullivan. "The mid-summer classic. Aren't you a fan?"

"No. I'm not a big sport's fan," said the physician with a smile, sensing a diversion.

"Oh, I'm sorry to hear that."

"Mom's loved baseball ever since she was a child," said George.

"Dad took me to Shibe Park when I was five," reminisced the patient. "Up in North Philly, on 20th and Lehigh Street. I can still smell the popcorn and see the flags flying above the outfield wall." She looked Gelberman in the eye. "I once caught a foul ball there. It ricocheted off a few people in front of me and landed right in my lap!"

"Very nice. Do you still have the ball?" asked the doctor.

"Sure I do. It's at home. But I can't remember who hit it?"

"Unfortunately, there was no video replay back then," laughed George.

The physician paused, allowing his patient to continue.

"I played a pretty mean short stop back in the day," proclaimed Martha with a fake toss of a ball across the room. "Could hit better than most of the boys."

"Not me. I had a chicken arm," quipped Gelberman. "I played one year of little league and they stood me out in right field. I remember the gnats swarming around my head all game. The following year, my parents signed me up for violin lessons, thus ending my athletic career."

"Do you still play the violin?" asked the patient.

"Yes. I actually do," beamed Gelberman.

"Well then, kudos to your parents for steering you in the right direction."

"You're right. Thank you, Martha. I never looked at it that way." The medical doctor stood up. "I'll start the process for home hospice. You'll be hearing from the nursing service and social work team. Now Martha, hospice doesn't mean we are going to stop caring for you. I'm always a phone call away."

"I understand. Thank you, doctor."

"Very good," replied Gelberman. "If all goes well, then perhaps you'll be able to go home tomorrow morning. How does that sound?"

"Marvelous."

"George, a moment of your time?" said Gelberman as he stepped away. "A nonmedical issue."

"Sure," replied George. He stood and walked out of the room with the doctor.

"It's time, George. I'm sure you recognize that," said Gelberman.

"Yes. I do. But that doesn't make it any easier. Especially with Dad gone."

"She's an amazing person. You're both lucky to have had her for so long."

"Absolutely."

"Now," hesitated Gelberman. "Has anyone informed you of your brother's admission to the hospital last night?"

"No," came the concerned reply. "What happened? John was admitted to the hospital?"

"Yes, sometime early this morning. They think he may have had a seizure on his way to work."

"Is he alright?"

"Yes. He's fine. He's down in the ICU. I just happened to see him there on rounds. He's a bit groggy, but certainly stable."

"A seizure! John's a healthy man."

"They're thinking a seizure," clarified Gelberman with a raised hand. "Someone can pass out from a multitude of conditions."

"The ICU? What floor is that on?"

"Third. The main elevators will get you there."

"Thank you, Dr. Gelberman. And thank you for taking such good care of my mother."

"You're very welcome."

After saying goodbye to his mother, and not informing her of John's plight, the elder Sullivan headed toward the ICU.

"Room six," said a clerk in the unit reception area. "Last room down the hall."

George Sullivan hurried around a corner in the direction of room six, his heart pounding. Upon entering the room, he came face to face with his brother, sitting up in bed and staring forward. There were bruises on his forearms and a sutured laceration above his left eyebrow. Intravenous lines ran normal saline solution into his veins, as overhead screens monitored his vital signs.

"George, good to see you," said the doctor nonchalantly. "What brings you here?"

"What brings *me* here?" asked the brother. "What the hell happened, John? Did you pass out?"

"I can't remember," answered the patient. "Everyone keeps asking me what happened, but honestly, I don't know."

"What do you remember?"

"Going down to the Franklin Wing last night," came the reply. "I talked to Reggie and set up my video recorder."

"And... then what?"

"I woke up this morning in the ICU, connected to all these monitors."

"That's it? You don't remember anything else? How long were you down there?"

"Honestly, I don't know. But obviously I fell, hitting my head. Maybe a piece of ceiling fell on top of me? Was there an earthquake in the area last night? Why do I remember the floor rumbling?"

"No, John. There wasn't an earthquake. I told you to stay out of that basement."

At that moment, Dr. Francis Lee walked in, the attending physician involved in the case. He was a senior member of the medical staff and a trusted colleague of Sullivan. Lee explained to the Sullivan brothers his ongoing diagnoses of syncope of unknown origin, along with a concussion. The treating physician recommended a cardiac echogram and another twenty-four hours of ICU monitoring.

"We'll repeat the CT scan of your cranium tomorrow morning," said Lee. "Just to make sure there is no bleed."

"Sounds good," said Sullivan. "I agree with your recommendations. How were my cardiac enzymes?"

"Your blood work is good," said Lee. "You didn't have a heart attack, John. How's your head?" While speaking he stared at the suture repair on his right forehead.

"Sore. I've got a bit of a headache too. I must have tripped and fallen."

Dr. Lee leaned in closer to the patient, now peering down a set of glasses perched on his nose. "Peculiar," he said.

"What?"

"Your suture repair job, John. It's kind of old school. It's a running baseball stitch. I haven't seen a stitch like that since back in my intern days. That's how they used to close a wound when sutures were made out of cat gut."

"Really?" said Sullivan while reaching up to feel the suture line. It was about two centimeters long and covered with some Neosporin ointment. "It's still a bit numb."

"Must have been an older physician in the ER," said George. "Whoever it was, he or she did a nice job. If anything, it's an improvement."

"I agree," chuckled Dr. Lee. "Except for one point, Mr. Sullivan."

"What's that?"

"Your brother wasn't treated in the ER," continued the ICU attending, now folding up his glasses and placing them in his lab coat. "At least to my knowledge. He was a direct admit to the ICU."

"Well then, who stitched me up?" asked Dr. Sullivan.

"I'll look into it, John," said Lee. "Maybe a med student or resident somewhere along the way. Who knows, the PGH is crawling with students, eager to whip a couple of stitches into an unsuspecting patient's skull. Remember, it's a training hospital. See you tomorrow morning. Get some rest."

"That's peculiar," said John Sullivan as he looked at his brother.

"I'll say," said George. "I thought they just put glue on lacerations nowadays. What the hell is cat gut?"

"George," said John Sullivan to his brother. "Can you do me a big favor?"

"Sure," said his brother, realizing it wasn't a good time to discuss their mother's situation.

"Is there a video camera anywhere in this room?"

"What do you mean?"

"A camera. My old video recorder with the tripod, I had it running last night when I fell, or got hit in the head. It should have captured the whole event on tape." While talking he gazed around the cramped confines of the unit room.

"No," said George as he stood up and circled about. "Not that I can see."

"Can you make sure they find it," said the patient with a look of concern. "It's imperative."

"Sure, John. But who... make sure who finds it?"

"The construction company running the demolition," said Sullivan while again stroking his forehead. "The Pagano Destruction Company. They must have it."

"Sure. I'll call them this afternoon. Anything else?"

"Yes, can you hand me that personal bag over there, with my clothes sticking out?"

"Sure."

The physician fumbled through the bag, which contained his clothing from last night and a wallet. After dumping out the contents he looked up in utter dismay.

"It's missing," said John Sullivan to his brother.

"What's missing?"

"The key. I've lost the key!"

·   ·   ·

That night, Mrs. Martha Sullivan had a most peculiar dream. At her bedside stood the silhouette of a tall man, with the Philadelphia skyline shimmering behind his slender frame. He stood motionless for some time, his shoulders rising up and down with each breath. The stranger then reached his arm over the bed rail and touched her hand, the contact generating a spark. On his face sat a familiar grin. Despite the years she was able to immediately recognize the visitor. He slowly bent forward and whispered.

"Hello Martha. It's so good to see you again."

CHAPTER ELEVEN
A VISITOR IN THE NIGHT

"You lost the key?" shouted the old timer from the rear of the room. On the screen was a picture of the keepsake, being shown to the Historical Society. They were gathered for a rare morning meeting in the upstairs room of Attorney Mills' home. "How is that possible?"

"Who gave it to you?" asked Attorney Mills.

"The night watchman," replied Sullivan. "Reginald Washington."

"The sentry on guard the night Dr. Schmidt vanished?"

"Yes," answered Sullivan. "Over the years he collected small artifacts scattered throughout the old wing. He can't recall exactly where he picked up the key."

"That key is well over 200 years old," said the old timer. "It's worth a pretty penny. That's a darn shame."

"Listen everyone," said Sullivan as he clicked up onto the screen a photo of the granite wall. "I've stumbled onto something big here, *really* big." Over the next few minutes he succinctly reviewed the etching on the rear of the wall, along with the front key recess. "I vaguely remember placing the key into the granite slot."

"The used key is always light?" pondered Mills aloud. "What in the world does that mean?"

"That makes no sense," chimed in another member of the group.

"And who is R.S.?" asked Mills. His face looked at Sullivan, yet his eyes veered off to the ceiling in a peculiar fashion.

"I have no idea," replied Sullivan.

"Wait a minute everyone," said Mills as he stood up. He pointed at Sullivan. "Wait one minute! John. What was the name of Zachary Schmidt's uncle again?" He snapped his fingers repeatedly as if trying to recall. "It was a Germanic descent... Richard von something."

"Rickard von Steiger!" answered Sullivan rapidly. "That's it! R.S. was Rickard von Steiger!"

"Bingo!" said Mills while grinning in a celebratory fashion. He pointed to his cranium while scanning the crowd. "The memory banks are still working."

"Wait another twenty years," shouted the backroom veteran. "You won't even remember where the bathroom is!"

Laughter broke out from the crowd as the president took his seat.

"So, von Steiger obviously knew about the key," continued Sullivan. "That's amazing! We're starting to put some pieces together. I just can't believe I lost it!"

"But the saying? What does that mean? The used key is always light." Mills shook his head in thought.

"I don't know, but we'll figure it out," replied Sullivan in a confident tone. "But step one is preserving that wall."

"John, it will take months to relocate a wall, and a ton of money," said the man with the walrus mustache. "We're just a few weeks away from demolition."

"You can't recall anything after putting the key into the slot, John?" asked Attorney Mills. "Maybe one of the construction workers found the key."

"No, I can't recall anything else," replied the physician, still with a slight headache. He was discharged from the hospital yesterday, after all his tests came back negative. "But I plan on stopping by at Pagano Destruction later today to recover my camcorder. Everything must have been captured on film. Perhaps they have the key?"

"Don't count on them being helpful," cautioned Mills. "Their attorney won't answer any more of my phone calls. Nothing's going to stop this implosion."

"Maybe the radon levels will slow the project up," said the walrus man. "You've got to keep in touch with the inspector's office, John."

"I plan on calling him too," said Sullivan. "But his own equipment was destroyed by the work crew in that basement. Quite frankly, the destruction company has turned the Franklin Wing into a hostile environment."

"We've got a judge's order to be down there," growled Mills, his dander now up. "I've got the papers in my office! If need be, I'll call in a good litigator I know from Scranton." The attorney was now standing and waving his arms in the air, his face turning red. "I'll turn this whole thing into a legal fistfight!"

"Yea! Right!" shouted the members. "Save the wall! Save the wall!" came the chant.

"The video!" shouted the old timer from the rear. With cane in hand he hobbled to the front of the room. "You have to recover that video, John. Understand?"

"Absolutely," replied Sullivan.

"The video is our new key," said the elder with his cane pointed towards Sullivan. "We need to know what the hell happened when you put that key into the wall! Something happened, for heaven's sake, you ended up in the hospital! Look at the scar on your head. Maybe one of their goons hit you! So, get down there right now and ask Pagano Destruction and their puppet judge to produce the video."

"Or else I'll turn this into a donnybrook!" howled Mills. "A legal brouhaha."

"Where's the video? Where's the video?" rang the chorus.

"Great work, John," said Mills with an extended hand-shake.

"Thank you, Fred."

Attorney Mills raised his hands in an attempt to calm the mob. "Gentlemen, I thank you all for coming out this morning to discuss John's concerns. We've made great strides! In honor of the first ever emergency meeting of the West Philadelphia Historical Society, I'd like to treat everyone for breakfast, over at Shep's House of Pancakes!"

"Hurrah!"

"It's senior citizen Tuesday at Shep's... until eleven o'clock," declared the walrus man with a glance at the wall clock. "We've got twenty minutes to get over there for the discount!"

"Well then, what are we waiting for?" howled Mills. "Let's go!" He bolted toward the stairwell with his hungry constituents in tow.

"Save the wall! Save the wall!" continued the cry as the group of elders gimped out onto Baltimore Avenue.

John Sullivan passed on the offer and headed over to the PGH to visit his mother. She was scheduled for home discharge that afternoon having responded favorably to an electrolyte and fluid regime. Upon entering the room, he found her in a despondent state of mind.

"I'm starting to see things at night, John," whispered his mother. "She was staring at the television in front of her, watching baseball highlights.

"Mom, it's not uncommon for elderly patients to become a bit disoriented in the hospital. You're out of your normal environment. Did they give you a sleeping pill last night?"

"Who knows what I'm getting in this place. You wrote my orders, didn't you? I just take what they give me."

"It's called Sundown Syndrome, Mom, and commonly occurs around twilight. It's a benign condition. You've had it before. Remember when you saw the devil visit you?"

"This is different, John. What I'm seeing at night is real."

"Tell me what you are seeing."

She didn't respond, but just continued to look at the television screen.

"Did Dad visit you again?"

"Your father was a good man, John," said Mrs. Sullivan. "A hard-working man. If it wasn't for that darn war... that ruined everything."

"He was part of the greatest generation."

"Oh, did he suffer at the end." Mrs. Sullivan turned off the television set and stared out the window. "Don't let me suffer like that, John."

"I won't."

"John, will you promise me something?"

"Sure."

"Promise me that this is my last hospital admission. If I take ill again, let the good Lord take me."

"Mom, let's take it a day..."

"No, John! Promise me this is my last hospital admission. It's time and I have no regrets. Please, promise to let me die. I'm tired of trying to live. Your father is calling me."

"So, Dad *did* appear to you last night?"

"Maybe," came the meek reply.

The physician stared back at his mother. Ever since she was diagnosed with cancer three years ago, their lives were never the same. It was a miracle she was still alive, a tribute to the PGH medical staff and their VIP service. Physically he knew she was nearing the end, yet mentally she was sharp, making the process more difficult.

"John, let me die in peace. Promise to never readmit me to the hospital. Listen to me, I'm your mother."

He paused.

"John Thomas Sullivan, this if your mother speaking! I'm the woman who brought you into this world. The one who wiped your…"

"I promise, Mom," replied the physician with a wave of his hands. "I promise."

"Promise me what?"

"I promise never to have you readmitted to the hospital. O.K?"

"Yes. Thank you. Now let's stop at the Acme on the way home. I want to get Moses some ground beef. How's my little precious doing?"

"Wonderful," responded the son, happy to finally see a smile on her face.

"Dr. Sullivan, you wanted to talk to me?" interrupted a hospital employee as she poked her head into the room.

"Yes. Yes. Thank you, Katie," said Sullivan, while walking outside the room to talk to the Admission Office manager.

"Well, did you find out anything?" asked Sullivan to the administrator.

"It was an older man who brought you to the hospital, Dr. Sullivan. He claimed to be your neighbor?"

"Really?" asked the doctor. "What time did he bring me in?"

"Oh, at about 4 a.m., with your head bandaged."

"What did he say? I mean, where did he find me?"

"He told the clerk you wandered back home after falling near the hospital. He was concerned about your state of mind and thought it best to bring you in."

"To the Admission's Office? Why not the E.R.?"

"Don't know, but he told the clerk you needed to be admitted to the intensive care unit, for a concussion. So, she paged the hospitalist on call… they gave the orders for the admission. Apparently you were pretty groggy."

"Interesting," said Sullivan, thinking he may have wandered home after a fall. But why hadn't any of his neighbors spoken to him since? "Anything else Katie, did the clerk on duty say anything else?"

"No, not really," said the manager. "Except for the fact that he was very polite and spoke with authority. After being assured of your pending admission, he left the office."

"Did she get his name? Did he leave any info? A phone number perhaps? Anything?"

"Nope." The manager peered into the room. "How's Mom?"

"Good, very good. She's heading home now," replied Sullivan. "Thank you for asking, Katie. We were just about to leave. Thank you for the information."

"My pleasure Dr. Sullivan. Give me a call if I can help you with anything else."

Sullivan turned back into the room.

"Oh, Dr. Sullivan," said Katie as she stepped back into the room. "One more thing. The clerk said the man was quite dashing, in an old-fashioned type of way."

"Dashing? What do you mean by dashing?"

"Well, he was wearing some sort of a cape around his shoulders and a big bow tie. Even had one of those old-fashioned handlebar mustaches." The manager smiled as if picturing the man. "She made it sound like he was a real ladies' man. Even told her she had a bright future." She grinned. "You don't hear that type of talk nowadays."

Sullivan stared back at the administrator in disbelief. "Did he have a key around his neck?"

"A key? No. The clerk said a bow tie, Doctor Sullivan, a big, flashy bow tie. There was no key. Why would he be wearing a key around his neck?"

Sullivan turned back into the room, speechless.

"Let's go," said his mother. "First pitch is at 7 P.M." She stared at her son. "What's the matter, John? It looks like you've seen a ghost."

"There are no such things as ghosts, Mother," mumbled the doctor. He began to wheel her out of the room. "There are no such things as ghosts."

Later that night, after putting his mother to bed, John Sullivan sat in his study. As a man of science, he was attempting to process the information at hand in a rational manner. The Pagano Destruction Company denied any knowledge of a video recorder, or the presence of a key. A discussion with several neighbors failed to tab any one of them as the Good Samaritan. In short time, there were too many questions and not enough answers. Yet time was running out, and once the Franklin Wing was imploded, all would be lost under a pile of rubble – forever.

That night the physician had a most peculiar dream. He was at the side of his mother's deathbed, having just spoken his final words of gratitude. There were no more hospital admissions and she was at peace, ready to take a final breath. Then, through the door of her bedroom, walked in Dr. Zachary Schmidt with a fedora hat in his hand. His appearance was that of an old-time doctor making a house call. Calmly he walked into the room to assess the situation and sat on the edge of the bed, nodding to his medical colleague. He pulled out a stethoscope from a black medical bag and placed it onto his patient's chest, carefully listening to her lung sounds. While looking down at a watch, he grasped her wrist to calculate a heart rate. Afterwards, he placed the back of his hand onto her forehead to gauge her temperature. The situation brought concern across the elder doctor's face. His patient was in critical condition. Calmly he paused to generate a plan. From his bag he lifted a syringe full of a deep red liquid. After uncapping the needle, he held the vial up toward the light and lightly pushed the plunger, venting a few air bubbles. He then brought the syringe downward and drove the sharp tip into the patient's upper arm, delivering the antidote. Within seconds the blue eyes of Martha Sullivan opened and she reached forward to hug her savior. The old-time physician had rescued her from an eternal resting place. She leaned back and went to speak...

"Knock, knock, knock!"

The dream. Who was knocking in his dream?

The knocking continued.

John Sullivan opened his own eyes, only to hear the rapping noise again. Someone was knocking at his front door. Looking to the left his clock read midnight.

The knocking turned into a repetitive bang. It was a rapid sound, as if in haste.

He put on some slippers and hustled down the stairwell. While peering out a side window he pictured the silhouette of a man, raising his hand to hit the door again. With his right hand he swung open the door, shocked to see the unannounced guest.

"Doctor Sullivan, he's back!" cried Reggie Washington, with a crazed look on his face. "He's back! Oh my God, I saw him with my own eyes!" The sentry was trembling, having just traversed several blocks.

"Who? Who's back Reggie?"

"Zachary Schmidt! Dr. Zachary Schmidt!"

CHAPTER TWELVE
WORD FROM ABOVE

"Seth, a moment of your time," directed the managing editor as he peered into the reporter's cubicle. "My office." He turned and walked away.

"Uh-oh. Seth's been a bad boy," quipped the reporter sitting in the adjacent desk. "He's going to the principal's office to get detention."

Seth ignored the wisecrack and slowly walked down an aisle past his co-workers. His head pounded with each step forward, a byproduct of yet another night of debauchery with Stephanie Peacock. In the corner office loomed the silhouette of his boss staring out a window. Behind him stood the thirty-seven-foot statue of William Penn perched atop city hall, the eyes of the city's founding father peering directly into the upper floor of the *Philadelphia Chronicle's* main office. It was a sunny morning in Philadelphia.

"Seth, good morning. Have a seat," said the editor while turning to face Barber. "Close the door behind you."

"Sure, Mr. Patrick," replied Seth as he shut the door. He took a seat opposite the editor's desk. "What's up?"

"How's the Franklin Wing story coming along?"

"Great, Mr. Patrick. To tell you the truth, I didn't think much of the assignment, but it's turning into an interesting story."

"How so?" asked Patrick as he plopped his sixty-three-year-old frame into a chair. He wore a white shirt and blue tie, the color combination rarely altered since securing the managerial position fifteen years ago. His chair let out a creaky moan as he leaned backward.

"Well as you know, the Franklin Wing is set to be razed on July 5th by a construction firm called Pagano Destruction."

"Did you head over to their office like I told you so?"

"Absolutely, Mr. Patrick. I spoke to their boss, a Mr. Thomas Pagano, Jr."

"And?"

"Quite the curmudgeon," laughed Seth. "He started with a company pitch that somehow morphed into a threat to sue our third-rate newspaper. It all happened in about a five-minute span. He basically tossed me out of his office."

"I see," replied Patrick as he slowly rocked back and forth in his chair. "Anything else?"

"Well," continued Barber a bit concerned about the morose look on his boss' face. "Yesterday I spoke to Mr. Pagano's son, a Dr. Vince Pagano. He's an orthopedic surgeon over at the Philadelphia General."

"How did that go?"

"Great. Apparently the new hospital wing is going to be called the Pagano Orthopedic Institute, a one-stop center for joint replacement surgery. It sounds pretty darn impressive. Dr. Pagano is going to be the medical center director."

The editor bobbed his head up and down in a methodical fashion. He reached forward and slightly adjusted the position of a paperweight on his desk.

"Later today I've got an interview set up with a Mr. Larry Griffith. He's a city inspector involved in the destruction. To my understanding, he's been registering some astronomical radon readings in the basement of the Franklin."

The editor stopped fidgeting and made direct eye contact with his underling.

"And tomorrow, I'm meeting with an Attorney Mills. He's president of the West Philadelphia…"

"Seth, I'm going to be blunt," interrupted Patrick. "I've received word from above about a necessary change in direction of the Franklin article."

"What do you mean?"

"It means that I'll be taking over the project… starting today."

"What!" retorted Barber. "That's crazy! This is *my* story."

"Sorry, Seth. They'll be other great stories in your career. Trust me." He continued to adjust the paperweight while talking. "I've decided to team you up with Leo Pinetti."

"Pinetti!"

"Yea. He's struggling to finish a story on who exactly has the best cheesesteaks in Philadelphia. Unfortunately, Leo's been pounding down the greasy concoctions on a nightly basis and ended up in the Philadelphia General E.R. with a gallbladder attack."

"I'm sorry sir. But I'm not giving up the Franklin story."

"Your other option is an article on the comeback of Schmidt's beer," continued Patrick. "They're planning to open a brewery in the Queen Village section of town. Hell, you might get a few free cases of booze out of the deal."

"Mr. Patrick. With all due respect, I request to remain on the Franklin project. I've recently made significant headway with one of the employees over at Pagano Destruction."

"What do you mean by *headway*?" asked Patrick.

"I'd prefer not to say."

"It doesn't matter. You're off the case." The editor sat back down and began to look at some papers on his desk. "Leave the door open on the way out."

"Then I quit."

"Listen, Seth. You need to cool your jets," said Patrick in a fatherly tone. "I appreciate your youthful enthusiasm, but you're going to have to learn what the phrase "word from above" means in this business." He leaned back and paused as if choosing his next words carefully. "It means that the story you're digging into is a bit deeper than meets the eye." He cocked an eyebrow. "Understand?"

"No. I don't," answered Barber with a stare down.

"Let me put it this way. A few powerbrokers in the City of Brotherly Love are getting concerned about any further delays in the razing of that building, including the ownership of the *Philadelphia Chronicle*. Can you understand that? People are losing some serious money, Seth."

"I'm just reporting the facts."

"Which may further delay the demolition, thus angering the powers that be."

"So. Isn't that our job… to create a balanced article and generate public discussion? Isn't that what the motto engraved above our front door suggests? 'Expect the best… read the best'."

Patrick sighed and smiled.

"What's so funny?" asked Barber. "Am I missing something here?"

"No. It's just that you remind me of me… about forty years ago."

Barber didn't respond.

"Seth, being a reporter in a major city is a dangerous job," continued Patrick. While speaking he rolled up the sleeve on his left arm. "See this?" He pointed to a longitudinal scar on the outer side of his forearm. "When I was your age my editor told me to step down from a story regarding some dead bodies found down near the Naval Yard."

"And?"

"I didn't listen. I was young and cocky. So, I continued to stick my nose where it didn't belong." He pulled the sleeve back down over the scar and slowly buttoned it. "So, one night, when I came home, two goons knocked the living crap out of me. The orthopedic surgeon called my shattered forearm a nightstick fracture, because I raised it in self- defense to thwart the blows from a steel pipe raining down on me." He tried to rotate his hand to the ceiling, but his forearm wouldn't allow. "I lost some palm up motion from the event, which makes getting change at the supermarket a bitch." He smiled at Seth. "There's still a plate and seven screws inside that arm, a souvenir from my youthful days of indiscretion." Patrick leaned forward. "Seth, what I'm trying to say is, don't repeat my mistake. Understand? You need to stand down from the Franklin story. Give Pinetti a call. They'll be other great stories down the line."

Seth got up to walk out.

"Seth. It's not my decision! Trust me. Stay away from the Franklin Wing and Pagano Destruction… if you know what's good for you."

Seth stormed back to his cubicle. He angrily shut down his computer, gathered a few personal items and walked out of the office. The reporter then crossed the street, entered City Hall and took an elevator up to the fifth floor. He entered the Department of City Inspections.

"May I help you?" asked a male receptionist.

"Yes. Hi. I'm a bit early," said Barber, still trying to calm his ire. "I have an eleven o'clock appointment with a Mr. Larry Griffith."

"Yes. I see that. But you're an hour and a half early," came the polite retort. "You're certainly welcome to take a seat." He pointed to a row of chairs against a wall.

"I'll see him now," came the voice of a man peering his head out of a smaller office to the rear right of the room. He waved his arm. "Come on in, Mr. Barber."

Seth navigated his way past a series of boxes filled with city records, the aged office cramped for space. He extended his hand while approaching Griffith.

"Seth Barber here. Thank you for seeing me, Mr. Griffith."

"A pleasure. C'mon in. Please, have a seat."

Griffith's office was a shoebox, being no more than ten by twenty feet in size. A shelf permanently attached to the wall served as his desk, which separated two folding chairs. Surrounding the workstation rose files of city projects dating back to the 1980s, their brown folders held tight by rubber bands, stacked precariously atop one another.

"Wow. You've got a ton of records in here," said Barber as he looked upward. "You better hope there's never an earthquake, because you'll be buried alive."

"I've certainly collected a hell of a lot of data over my career," answered the inspector. "Each one of these files represents my input on a building project, either in the beginning or the end." He grinned and scanned the room. "They're like my children."

"Cool," replied Seth. "Sounds like you love your job."

"I do… most of the time."

"Me too," said Barber. "Which brings me to the Franklin project."

"Well, you can save your breath," countered the inspector. "I've unfortunately been relieved of my duties in West Philadelphia."

"You're not involved in the Franklin destruction anymore?"

"No. I was unceremoniously canned this week." A grimace ran across his face. "Word from above."

"I hate that phrase," said Barber.

"Me too. But that's life in the beautiful city we call Philadelphia. I've learned over time not to spit into the wind. It kind of stings."

"Can you still talk to me about the high gas readings you were picking up in the hospital basement?"

"Technically, no," replied Griffith. "I'm sorry Mr. Barber, but I can't give comment to the *Chronicle*. My head would roll."

"Oh." Barber paused to consider his options. "What if I told you I quit?"

"Quit what?"

"The *Chronicle*... my boring job. Would you be able to talk to me then, as a concerned citizen of Philadelphia?"

The city inspector sat silent for several seconds, mulling the option. "Hmmm, that's an interesting question." He tapped his fingers on the cluttered desk. "You quit your job at the *Chronicle*?"

"Yea, about twenty minutes ago. I'm onto something here and they're not going to silence me."

"How do you suppose you're going to get out the message?"

"The internet. I've got about 60,000 followers in the greater Philadelphia area. My readers are loyal."

"I like your bluster, young man. I wish I had it, but age unfortunately tempers one's enthusiasm."

"Screw the system," continued Barber. "Something bizarre is going on up in West Philadelphia. You know it... and I know it. So, don't you think the people of Philadelphia should know it? Because Mr. Griffith, if we don't say anything now, no one will." He emphatically pointed a finger to the ground. "They're going to build a state-of-the-art hospital over the mother lode of toxic gases. Everyone in that hospital is going to be unknowingly fried on a daily basis by insane levels of radon. Can you live with that on your conscious?"

"Well, if you put it that way, then no," came the prompt reply. "It's hard to argue against sounding the alarm." He took a deep breath. "If we don't sound the alarm now then hell, we'll probably be the scapegoat in the future… when the truth is uncovered."

"Exactly," shot back Barber, sensing a breakthrough. "The powers that be will blame us for not bringing the elevated levels to their pompous attention."

Griffith leaned back in his chair and placed both hands over his mildly obese abdomen. He rapidly flickered his index and long finger up and down while attempting to render a decision.

"Who took your job?" asked Barber.

"A senior inspector named Freddie Freeman."

"He's probably on the take. Right? That name even sounds slippery."

Griffith nodded his head in the affirmative but didn't speak. He looked over Barber's shoulder to assure no other employees were in earshot. Barber sensed his angst and closed the door. The reporter leaned closer.

"I say the hell with Freddie Freeman and the hell with the powers that be." He pointed his finger at Griffith's chest. "Let's blow the roof off this project before it's too late." He reached out a hand. "We've got an obligation to the people of this city." He grinned. "What do you say, Mr. Griffith. Are you in?"

Griffith only paused momentarily before answering. "What the hell! I'm in," came the firm reply with an even firmer handshake. "I'm going with my heart on this one, young man." He stood up while still grasping the reporter's hand. "We just can't stand by. It would be unethical."

"Let's make some noise," proclaimed Barber. He pulled Griffith forward to initiate a chest bump. "I'll be in touch," quipped Barber. "The Barber of Silverwood will come a call-ing."

"Excuse me," said Griffith. "The Barber of what?"

"Silverwood. I'm the Barber of Silverwood. That's my Twitter handle. What's your social media name?"

"My name? Larry Griffith is my name."

"You don't even know what I'm talking about, but let me work on that, Larry Griffith. I'll come up with a good handle for my trusted source. You can count on me."

Griffith smiled and said, "Damn the torpedoes, full steam ahead!"

"Torpedoes? Who said anything about torpedoes? Were you in the navy?"

Griffith laughed. "It appears that we're going to be learning a lot from each other, Seth."

"True that, Larry. Peace out."

Seth Barber walked out of City Hall and sent a text to Stephanie. Thirty minutes later she pulled up in a company van, the vehicle peppered with dents, mud and the Pagano Destruction logo.

"Thanks, Stephanie," said Barber as he hopped into the front seat. "I quit my job, let's get some lunch."

"Where at?"

"There's a sub shop near my apartment in Manayunk. It's buy one, get one free day. My treat. Do you mind driving there?"

"Sure. I'm on my hour lunch break, from eleven to three."

"Nice ride. Where's your car?"

"In the shop with a busted tire. So, I get to use the company van. It's kind of a perk."

As the vehicle sped onto the Schuylkill Expressway, Seth peered back into the rear compartment of the transport. A hodgepodge of construction equipment wildly tossed back and forth as the driver darted into the passing lane.

"You've got a lot of junk back there," quipped Barber. "It looks like everything except the kitchen sink." He chuckled. "Oh wait, there is a kitchen sink."

"What the f..." shouted Peacock with a lean onto the horn. She sped past a vehicle trying to change lanes. The car in front of the van slowed down, prompting the secretary to hit the brakes.

"LOOK OUT!"

The van skidded to a stop, the deceleration rocketing some of the destruction equipment forward. Into Seth's lap landed a crowbar, two empty beer cans and a video camera, attached to a tripod.

"Take it easy," declared Seth with a hand on the dashboard. "You're going to kill both of us. Slow down." He pushed the equipment off his frame and in doing so, dislodged the camcorder from the tripod. The video recorder fell to the floor.

"What?" countered Stephanie innocently. "I didn't hit anyone. No harm, no foul." The van started to move forward. "That idiot in front of me was trying to be a Good Samaritan. Doesn't he know he's on the Schuylkill? The guy must be from out of town."

Seth picked up the video device and flipped open its LCD screen, prompting the machine to turn on.

"What's on video?" asked Seth. "Nookie night with Winky?"

"Hah. You wish."

Seth reversed the video and hit the play button, his action generating an image of Dr. Sullivan talking into the camera. The physician's voice came to life.

"Today's date is June 15th, 2020 and I am reporting to you from the subbasement of the Philadelphia General Hospital's Franklin Wing. I'm in the former office of Dr. Zachary Schmidt, who as you know disappeared about forty years ago in this very building."

"What the hell," stammered Barber. "Whose recorder is this?"

"Beats me," answered Stephanie. "What exit do I take?"

"Manayunk," answered Seth as he continued to gaze at the screen.

"*What's peculiar about this room, besides the majestic wall of granite behind me, is the floor,*" sounded Sullivan's voice. "*I am standing upon a most distinctive, large star configuration embossed into the floor itself.*"

"This dude is in the Franklin Wing," said Barber. "Somewhere in the basement. Does he work for the demo company?"

"Let me see," said Stephanie with a glance toward her passenger.

Seth raised the viewing screen to show her Sullivan's face.

"Nah. He doesn't work for Pagano. I've never seen him before."

"*This room however is not the only significant discovery we've stumbled upon during this project. I've recently had the privilege of recovering the actual key that Dr. Schmidt wore around his neck.*"

"A key. What's he talking about Steph?"

"No idea." She blew the horn again and accelerated the van, darting past a slow-moving vehicle.

Over the next several minutes the ex-reporter for the *Chronicle* intently scrutinized the video presentation of Dr. Sullivan.

"Sounds boring," quipped the driver.

"*I've discovered a carved-out area of stone, which appears to be a perfect slot for Dr. Schmidt's key,*" declared Sullivan. "*Perhaps it was a resting place for his personal treasure.*"

"Right or left?" asked Stephanie as she sped down an off ramp.

"Right," answered Seth without looking up. "Just follow the train tracks overhead."

"*This newly found stone recess is absolutely inviting me to place the key of Dr. Zachary Schmidt inside.*"

As the van drove over a road of cobblestone, the Barber of Silverwood tried to hold steady the recording device. He intently watched Dr. Sullivan reach forward to place the key into the granite slot.

"And so I shall, perhaps returning the turnkey to its original resting place. Here we go."

"What in god's name is he doing?"

"Crack!"

"Holy mother!" yelled Barber as he watched the physician vanish behind a brilliant flash of light. "He disappeared!"

"Right or left?" asked Stephanie. "I'm getting hungry."

Barber peered out the front window. "Left and then a right down that alley." He pointed to a massive cathedral just over some rooftops. "The sub shop is next to that church."

As the vehicle roared down a narrow lane, Barber intently stared at the screen. "I don't believe what I just saw! The dude vanished into thin air." He hit the fast forward button to speed the tape while they waited at a red light.

"There's a spot," said Stephanie. She pulled up to some parked cars and K-turned the van into a tight slot, crashing into the front bumper of the rear vehicle. "How about that park job?"

"Holy crap! He just reappeared with another man!" exclaimed Barber. "Look!" He reversed the film and held the camcorder screen in front of Peacock. "See? Right there, they appear out of nowhere!"

"Cool. I dig the old timer with the mustache." She got out of the van and closed the driver door. "Let's go, Seth."

Seth watched the mustached man help his friend gimp out of view to the right of the camera. A large rat scurried behind. The passenger door to the van swung wide open.

"He's bleeding from the forehead," stated Barber.

"I'm starving!" pleaded Stephanie as she held the door open. "C'mon, Seth. Look at it later."

Barber flipped closed the camcorder and tucked it between the front passenger seats. He hopped out of the van and put his arm around Stephanie.

"What are you hungry for?" asked the unemployed writer.

"I need something Italian... with prosciutto and Genoa salami, and provolone cheese. What about you?"

"I'm going with a cheesesteak. This place has the best. See the sign? It says right there... *Best Cheesesteaks in Philadelphia.*"

Over the next forty minutes, Seth and Stephanie enjoyed their fare with a bottle of beer. During the luncheon, a local vagrant opened the driver side of the van and swiped the camcorder, along with a load of construction equipment. He immediately took the stolen goods to a local pawnshop, scoring five hundred dollars to help sate his addiction to opiate narcotics.

CHAPTER THIRTEEN
INGRID

"There!" shouted Reggie Washington as he pointed at the screen. "That's him, Dr. Schmidt!"

"Freeze it," said Sullivan. He stood next to Washington inside a cramped Philadelphia General Hospital security office. The doctor leaned closer to the screen. "Can you zoom in, Teddy?" They were watching some video footage captured by a security camera perched above Reggie's guard station, just outside the Franklin Wing.

"Nah," replied the medical campus policeman, a longtime friend of Washington. "I'm sure you can, but I don't know how." He repeatedly clicked on a computer mouse, to no avail.

The trio stared down at an outdated monitor, projecting a somewhat grainy image of a slight man dressed in a cape and bowtie, strolling nonchalantly up to Reggie's security point. The time on the screen read 2330 hours.

"Let it run," requested Sullivan.

The figure stepped up to Reggie and bowed in regal fashion, as if he were the ringmaster of a traveling circus. He then extended a handshake.

"He bowed to me! Can you believe it," exclaimed Reggie. "Holy smokes! Just like in the old days. Dr. Schmidt always bowed to me. I'm glad you captured this on film. The ghost of Zachary Schmidt!"

The video showed Reggie shaking the visitor's hand and then stepping backward in disbelief, while putting both hands on his forehead.

"I nearly passed out!" quipped Washington.

"Was his hand cold?" asked Teddy.

"No."

"Let me get my bearings here," stated Sullivan as he pointed to the screen. He cocked his head sideways. "So… he was coming out of the Franklin Wing? Is that correct?"

"It appears so," answered the policeman. While answering he scanned some other monitors. "This is our first camera outside the demolition zone, all the other cameras inside the Franklin basement are controlled by the destruction company. You may want to cross check with their security team regarding any other visual of the suspect."

The film projected both men exchanging some words and then the mystery guest patting Reggie on the back in reassuring fashion. He turned and walked away.

"Stop it there!" snapped Sullivan. He leaned closer to the screen. "What in the world?" He looked at a close up of the unidentified intruder's face.

"I told you so," boasted Washington. "That's him. After he left, I ran to your house. I had to tell someone."

The hospital sentry kept replaying a clip of the stranger walking directly under the camera. The man on film looked up at the security cam while walking by and grinned. "That's your best face shot," said Teddy. He paused the tape. "Nice mustache."

"That's him," said Washington. "No doubt."

"I fully agree that it appears to be Dr. Schmidt," stated Sullivan. He stood erect and stroked a hand across his chin. "Except for one major problem." He pulled out his cell phone and took a snapshot of the screen.

"What's that?"

"He hasn't aged," came the impassive response. "So it cannot be Zachary Schmidt. That's an absolutism."

"But I saw him, Dr. Sullivan. I know what I saw."

"Reggie, he vanished in 1976! That's over forty years ago," retorted Sullivan. "Schmidt was forty-six years old when he disappeared."

"So, he should be in his late eighties by now," added the policeman as he squinted at the screen. "That guy's not in his eighties."

"I agree," said Sullivan. "He was born in 1930, so that would make him at least eighty-nine years old." He patted Reggie on the back. "Sorry, Reg. The guy in that video looks like he's about fifty."

"Well then, who was it?"

"That remains to be determined," replied Sullivan as he checked his watch. "Teddy, how long is that video kept on record?"

"All surveillance video concerning the PGH is kept for thirty days," replied the sentry.

"Then what happens to it?"

"If it's not saved, the system just records over it."

"Alright," replied Sullivan, as he stood erect. "So, we have some time. It just can't be Dr. Schmidt. I'm sorry, Reggie... not unless he discovered the fountain of youth."

"I know what I saw. Maybe ghosts don't age like we do?"

"I'll agree that something very strange is going on here," followed up Sullivan. "And I intend to get to the bottom of it." He headed out of the cramped office. "Thanks, Ted. Thanks, Reggie. I've got to go."

Sullivan hurried his way across the hospital grounds and through the university campus. At the corner of 42nd and Sansom Street he turned right and walked halfway down the block, stopping in front of a stately brownstone residence. He pushed open a black iron gate and approached the front door. The physician rechecked the address written on a piece of paper while grasping a bronze doorknocker shaped in the form of a lion's head. He gave the door three loud raps. A cat scurried out from a hedgerow to his right. Five seconds later, the door opened slowly.

"Mrs. Ingrid Hoffman?" asked Sullivan.

"Yes. I am Mrs. Hoffman," came the formal reply in a tone that suggested a Germanic descent. She wore a white long sleeve blouse with a buttoned collar held together by a circular brooch. A blue skirt ran to ankle length just above a set of sturdy, black shoes. Her height equaled that of Sullivan, yet her frame stood a bit more robust. A set of glasses anchored a rectangular shaped face capped with grey hair.

"Dr. John Sullivan, from the Philadelphia General. I spoke to you earlier today over the phone."

"Yes, of course. Dr. Sullivan. Do come in. I am Ingrid Hoffman." She firmly shook his hand. "Welcome to my home."

She led Sullivan into a foyer surrounded by walls of heavy oak carved in an ornate pattern. Across the floor ran a series of granite tiles with symmetric inlays of black, square stones. From the wooden ceiling dropped a single chandelier and to Sullivan's right stood an end table with a bowl and two candles on top, set beneath a massive mirror. Flanking the mirror hung the antique portraits of two men, symmetrically set to please the eye.

"Thank you," replied Sullivan as he scanned the vestibule. "You have a beautiful home."

"Please. Come sit down." She walked Sullivan down a hallway and turned to the right, leading him into a room facing the street. A series of cuckoo clocks in the house simultaneously sounded off three times, their cries echoing in the solitude of the house.

"Oh my, what a fantastic sitting room," commented Sullivan as he entered the chamber. A white marble fireplace anchored the room as did yet another ornate mirror above the mantle. The entire construct was surrounded by detailed stone masonry including the face of two young women sculpted into each side of the pit. Four single candle holders ran across the mantle, each perfectly spaced in relation to the other. A large floral bouquet sat directly in front of the fire screen. Two large sofas sat to each side of the fireplace, as did a set of leather chairs.

"Please, have a seat," said Ingrid while pointing to the sofa. She sat opposite to her guest. "May I offer you a cup of tea?"

"No, thank you," answered Sullivan. "It's an honor and a pleasure to meet you."

"The pleasure is all mine. Now, how can I help you? You want to know something about my father?"

The cold bluntness of Ingrid Hoffman's personality somehow put Sullivan at ease. She exuded exactness, as did her home.

"Yes, if you don't mind. I'm chairing a committee for the West Philadelphia Historical Society and we're trying to capture as much history as possible regarding your father and his workings within the Philadelphia General's Franklin Wing. As you may well know, the Franklin Wing is going to be razed in two weeks."

"My father was Rickard von Steiger. He was born in Stuttgart, Germany in 1900, the youngest of eleven children." She spoke without hesitation. "At age ten he attended boarding school and eventually graduated from the University of Berlin with a degree in physics. He next attended Swiss Polytechnic in Zurich where he met my mother, Anna." She pointed to a portrait over her head and a tad to the left. "That is my mother."

"She's beautiful," remarked Sullivan.

"They married in 1929 just after father returned to Germany to accept a position in the Physics Department at the university. Then in 1933 they fled Europe and came to America."

"1933, I see."

"A terrible time."

"Yes."

"I can still hear my father citing the events of that year... a new Chancellor, the Reichstag fire, an Enabling Act, the formation of a Gestapo, trade unions banned, 25,000 books burned, the withdrawal from the League of Nations and a madman ranting about a geopolitical principle called lebensraum."

Sullivan remained silent.

"Along with his colleagues, he sensed what was about to happen. The new government approached him to help build a weapon of mass destruction."

"So he fled?"

"Hastily, in the middle of the night, with my mother and his young nephew, Zachary. He had no time to say goodbye to his own parents and siblings. He grabbed only a few personal items." She looked at the floor. "He never saw his parents again."

"I'm very sorry."

A car horn outside penetrated the stillness of the room.

"But he loved his life here at the University of Pennsylvania," continued Ingrid. "He adored Philadelphia. It all worked out in the end... I suppose." She smiled. "So, here we are. What else do you want to know? It's been a long time since someone came asking about father."

"He accomplished so much in such a short time," added Sullivan. "Having a building named on campus is quite an accomplishment."

"He loved physics, so it was never a job for father. He always told me he never worked a day in his life."

"So true," added Sullivan. "So, what do you remember about his love for physics, specifically in relation to the

Franklin Wing? To my understanding he carried out most of his experiments in its basement."

"I was young when he perished in 1962," came the reply. "Eleven years old to be exact. I only remember Professor Rickard von Steiger as a father, as opposed to a scientist. I cannot comment on his workstation."

"I understand."

She stood up and walked across the room, her first few steps with a slight limp. "He was a kind and loving man." She opened a glass cabinet and reached toward the lower shelf. "From the eyes of a young child, there could be no better... as I suspect most fathers are to their daughters."

Sullivan smiled as he scanned the photo of Ingrid's mother, which appeared to be peering directly back at him. A cat from another room meowed twice.

"Father was always tinkering and teaching, even to his children. He championed independent thought."

"And you had one other sister?"

"Yes. Ursula. She was three years older than me. Ursula died two years ago from lymphoma. She lived in Los Angeles."

"I'm sorry."

She walked over to Sullivan and sat beside him on the couch. "Here is an album containing some photos of his office and laboratory." She sat the book on her lap and carefully opened it. "Mother put it together after his death. There are no photographs from Germany."

Inside was a collection of approximately thirty photographs of von Steiger, most of them head shots from the college yearbook. They were set in chronological order from 1933 through 1962. Only near the end of the collection did a single photo show von Steiger in the Franklin Wing basement.

"Here he is in the laboratory." She pointed to her father wearing a white coat pointing to a mechanical contraption. Beside him stood a younger student with a smile. "1961," said Ingrid. "One year before his death. That is my cousin Zachary next to him."

Sullivan leaned nearer the photograph, which captured a moment in time, shared by an uncle and his nephew. The snapshot represented one of the few photos ever taken in the hospital basement during von Steiger's time. Behind the duo stood the curved edge of a granite wall.

"It must have been taken in the future office of Dr. Schmidt. That large granite wall is going to be destroyed in the implosion."

"Look at how happy they are," commented Ingrid.

"Do you mind if I take a cell phone shot of this picture?" asked Sullivan. "It captures the essence of your father and the basement itself."

"No. I do not mind."

Sullivan took out his cell phone and took a photograph of the image. "Cell phones. What would we do without them?"

"Can I help you with anything else?" asked Ingrid. "I'm sorry, but outside of that single photograph, I have no other memory or stories to tell you about my father as a physicist, except that he died in an experimental explosion. I am sure you are aware of that event. Otherwise, his professional accolades are well documented in the Physics Department on campus."

"Yes. I've been there already. They have a wonderful display in his honor. A very accomplished man."

Ingrid smiled in appreciation. She stood up and carefully returned the album to the cabinet. She then took her seat opposite Sullivan.

"Mrs. Hoffman, does the saying, "the used key is always light", mean anything to you?"

She paused in thought. "No. It is meaningless to me."

"That exact wording is etched on the back of the granite wall seen in the photograph you just showed me. The initials 'R.S.' stand next to the wording on the wall.

"R.S.? Perhaps it was spoken by my father?"

"Yes. That's what I was thinking, too. But, it has no meaning to you?"

"No. I do not recall my parents speaking such a line."

"Did your father every speak of a special key?"

"No," laughed Ingrid. "But my cousin, Zachary… he did!" She began to laugh loudly. "Oh, what a man."

"Dr. Zachary Schmidt. Correct?"

"Yes. He is the student in the picture. Zachary worked in the Franklin Wing for years before the establishment tried to squelch his foresight."

"So I understand."

"Dr. Schmidt lived in this very home for some time," quipped Ingrid while raising her hands overhead. "He helped care for mother before she passed in 1973."

"He was your cousin?"

"Yes. But more like a father to me, as was my father to him."

"What can you tell me about Zachary Schmidt?"

She laughed again. "Where to begin describing Dr. Zachary Schmidt is difficult. He was a brilliant and complex man." Her tone ran upbeat and proud. "An absolute Renaissance man by anyone's standard."

"Please, tell me more."

For the next fifteen minutes, Ingrid Hoffman spoke in reverence in regard to Zachary Schmidt. She described an energetic man of integrity, intelligence and intrigue. An educator never comfortable with the accepted norm of the day, always challenging accepted standards in a brazen fashion. Similar to his uncle, he possessed an insatiable thirst for knowledge.

"Amazing," said Sullivan after the synopsis. "The avant-garde of his time."

"Oh, and that key he wore around his neck!" She laughed loudly. "Always bragging about it being the key to the future.

He had it welded to his neck by a blacksmith down in Kennett Square. It never came off."

"So, I understand," chuckled Sullivan, the delight of his host now infectious. He allowed a few seconds to pass as Ingrid wiped some tears of joy from her eyes. "Did he ever say where it came from?"

"That crazy key?"

"Yes."

"An old friend," replied Ingrid with right and left hand air quotes. "It came from an 'old friend'. That's all he told everyone. Who the friend was... I have no idea."

"Did he ever speak of anyone else with the initials R.S., or of a used key being light?"

"No. Not that I can recall."

"Mrs. Hoffman, when was the last time you ever saw your cousin before he disappeared?"

"Hmmm. Let me see." She looked over Sullivan's shoulder in thought. "July 2nd, 1976. I visited him on the Psychiatric wing of the Philadelphia General. He looked so gaunt in that hospital gown."

"Was he distressed?"

"Surprisingly... no. He mentioned pending plans for a lobotomy procedure, but it didn't seem to concern him. He told me not to worry." She sighed.

"Mrs. Hoffman, what do you think happened to him on July 4th when he ran into the Franklin Wing and seemingly disappeared into thin air? I mean, I've researched this event over and over. I've spoken to just about everyone with first-hand knowledge of the event and shockingly, no one seems to know." He locked a sympathetic gaze into her eyes. "How can a man just vanish without a trace?"

"At first I was convinced that somehow he made it outside the hospital, perhaps via an unknown exit. But over the following two or three years, he never contacted me, which is unlike Zachary. So, I'm convinced that something went awry that night, inside the basement of the Franklin, perhaps between Zachary and the policeman. Over time I began to believe that both he and the young police officer were killed and the details were somehow covered up. How else can one explain such a bizarre occurrence?"

"Fascinating," came Sullivan's reply. "I never looked at a conspiracy or cover-up angle."

The cuckoo clocks chirped four o'clock.

"Oh my goodness, it's been an hour already," said Sullivan as he stood up. "I've run past my promised twenty minutes of your time. It is time for me to bid farewell."

"The pleasure has been all mine," countered Ingrid as she walked Sullivan back to the front door. "Thank you for your interest in my father and cousin." She pointed at the two portraits in the entrance foyer. "Here, stand between Rickard and Zachary, I'll take your picture."

"No, Mrs. Hoffman. I couldn't."

"I insist, doctor. They would both be proud of your efforts. I can assure you of that."

Sullivan grinned and handed her his cell phone. He straightened his hair and looked back at the portraits of both men, positioning his body between the two.

"Smile."

"Snap," went the phone. She handed him back the cell.

"Please, keep in touch, Dr. Sullivan," stated Ingrid as she opened the door. "If I find anything else of interest, I'll surely notify you."

"That would be fantastic. Thank you, Mrs. Hoffman. Thank you very much for your time." Sullivan shook her hand and stepped outside.

After locking the door, the last living offspring of Professor Rickard von Steiger walked down the hallway and into the kitchen. A slim tabby cat shot past her and bolted upstairs in crazed fashion.

"That was interesting," said Ingrid. "He seems like a nice man."

"I fully agree," said the man in the corner with a handle-bar mustache. He put down the *Philadelphia Chronicle* and brought a freshly baked slice of apple strudel to his mouth. "I am here solely because of his noble pursuits." He took a bite of the pastry. "Mmmm. I missed your strudel, Ingrid."

"You look so thin, Zachary. Why is that?"

"I was homesick," came the reply in jest.

Ingrid laughed and slowly poured some hot water into a teacup. She took a seat opposite the doctor and smiled.

"I still can't believe it is you," said Ingrid. "My life now has meaning again. I knew that somehow, someway... you would return."

"Here I am," boasted Dr. Zachary Schmidt. "I told you not to worry about anything. Didn't I?" He took another bite of strudel. "So, Ingrid, please tell me what's happened over the past forty years. I already know... but tell me anyway."

CHAPTER FOURTEEN
GROUND ZERO

"This is where we control the demolition," boasted Winky Pagano as he led the reporter into a trailer parked in the middle of an abandoned lot. The compartment sat unhitched and perched atop a series of concrete blocks. "There's the miserable house of cards about to crumble," laughed Pagano. While speaking he pointed out a window along the side of the trailer. Across the street stood the Franklin Wing. Pagano pointed to a folding table set in front of the window, littered with computer screens and keyboards. A mangled series of wires ran beneath the table and into a large, white PVC pipe piercing the trailer floor. "My control team sits here." He pointed to several folding chairs pushed beneath the table. "You are now at Ground Zero, Mr. Patrick."

"Interesting," replied Pat Patrick. "It all looks so high tech."

"Pagano Destruction is on the cutting edge when it comes to the controlled demolition industry," continued the company CEO. "Dropping a building nowadays is a fine art that combines technology, innovation and experience." He took an unlit cigar out of his mouth. "No one in the greater Philadelphia area has more experience in razing a building, than the Pagano team." He looked at the only other person in the trailer, a morbidly obese, bespectacled man wearing a hardhat and safety vest. "Isn't that right, Bart?"

"Absolutely," came the reply from the head engineer of Pagano Destruction. His high-pitched voice failed to match the breadth of his frame.

"What's your background, Mr. Little?" asked Patrick while looking at the worker's nametag, which read 'B.B. Little'. "If you don't mind me asking?"

"I have a B.S. in biology," came the reply from the Pagano employee. His head nervously bobbed side-to-side during the response and he looked upward, as if expecting the ceiling to collapse.

"We call him Big Bart Little," cut in Pagano with a laugh. "He's the smartest banana in the bunch. Bart's been with us for years. He cut his teeth back in 1994, with the Sears Merchandise Center implosion up in North Philly. We stole him from the competition."

"50,000 people showed up for that demolition," proclaimed Bart Little. "We dropped that baby in about seven seconds." He pointed to a scar above his right eye. "See this scar? A flying boulder hit me in the head at a distance of 200 yards. I had to be hospitalized for three weeks."

"He's the best," added Pagano with an eager chomp on his cigar. "Big Bart Little knows his stuff."

"I see," replied Patrick. "That's quite a badge of honor, Mr. Little. So... how long have you two gentlemen been imploding buildings?"

"I'm a third generation destroyer," replied Pagano. "Grandpa Pagano started the business."

"I've been doing it for nearly thirty years," answered Little. "Been working with Mr. Pagano since 1995."

"But the word 'implosion' is a bit misleading," continued Pagano with a professorial wave of his stubby hand.

"How so?"

"Tell him, Bart."

"Well, I don't want to get too technical," started Bart Little. "But an implosion involves the difference between inward or outward forces, that when properly manipulated, cause a structure to collapse inward."

"So, isn't that what you're doing?" asked the *Chronicle* editor.

"No," came the quick response from the demo expert. "No forces are applied in perpendicular fashion to the walls. We simply negate crucial supports inside the building, which doesn't allow the construct to support its own weight."

"I see," said the reporter.

"Then we leave it up to my most trusted employee," chimed in Pagano with a reassuring grin. "Someone who always shows up on time, is reliable, and works for free."

"Your most trusted employee?" asked Patrick with a quizzical look across his face. "That works for free? Who might that be, Mr. Pagano?"

"Gravity," chuckled Pagano. "Gravity is what will bring that old building down to the ground."

"Exactly," added Little. "Gravity is undefeated in the demo business. We blow the lower floors first and then the laws of gravity take hold."

"Interesting," said the reporter as he turned his gaze back across the street. "So what do you use… dynamite?"

"We use dynamite for the concrete," replied Pagano. "Bore holes are drilled throughout the building and the dynamite sends a powerful shock that pulverizes the concrete."

"What about the steel?"

"I'm going to defer to Bart on that one," replied Pagano. "He's the college grad."

"RDX is used on steel," answered the biologist. "It's a more efficient, higher velocity explosive that was developed just after World War II, when they had to raze bombed out cities en masse. An RDX explosion travels at about 26,000 feet per second, which in essence, will cut a steel beam in half."

"Dynamite and RDX," mumbled Patrick into a hand held Dictaphone. "RDX cuts the steel... developed after World War II. Most trusted employee is gravity." He went to place the recorder back into his pocket but then brought it back to his mouth saying, "Big Bart Little, hit in the head with a boulder at 200 yards... Sears demolition, 1994."

"Our detonators are all electrical," continued Bart. He pointed to a large red button contained beneath a piece of glass on the main table. "That button sets the process in motion. It's triggers an electrical lead line which runs directly to each set charge in the building. The current heats the detonator end, which is surrounded by explosives."

"That in turn triggers the primer charge on each pile of dynamite," chimed in Pagano. "Which sets off the main explosives." He pointed at the red button. "Once that button is hit, there's no stopping the explosion."

"We call it 'Mr. Rubble' for obvious reasons," smirked Bart. "Once that button is hit the whole place blows in exactly 120 seconds."

"Why the delay?"

"Federal regulations," answered Pagano. "Mr. Rubble triggers a warning alarm consisting of five long blasts from a grid of sirens inside the complex. Then in exactly two minutes... kaboom!" He wiggled his fingers into the air. "Rubble, rubble... everywhere."

"How do you control the sequence of explosions?"

"We put delay mechanisms on each blasting cap," answered Little. "So we can accurately dictate the sequence of explosions."

"How do you know how much dynamite and RDX to use?" asked the reporter.

"Experience," came the quick reply from Pagano. "We're walking a fine line, Mr. Patrick. You don't want to get embarrassed by not dropping the building, but on the other hand, we need to avoid showering West Philadelphia with gobs of concrete."

"We usually just blow out a few windows from the surrounding buildings," added Little. "But that's about it."

"Nice," said Patrick as he stared out the window. He mumbled a few more lines into the Dictaphone. "Where do you guys go to school to learn this stuff?"

"The school of hard knocks," laughed Pagano. He nodded his head up and down as if reminiscing old times.

"On the job training," added Little. "That's the only way. Colleges don't offer a major in demolition."

"It's a generational thing," added Pagano. "My grandfather taught my father, who then taught me." He bobbed his head up and down. "As a side note, we've been experiencing a recent run on Catholic churches, which from an aesthetic standpoint is a thing of beauty." He raised his hands upward. "When that steeple drops down, dead center into a mushroom cloud of dust..."

Just then the door to the trailer ripped open and in stormed Rocco, wearing a T-shirt and hardhat.

"They're back!" screamed Rocco as he bull rushed toward the computer screens. He pushed past all three men and started manhandling the main keyboard. "I'm going to kill one of them! So help me God."

"Who, Rock? *Who's* back?" asked Pagano. "Take it easy on that keyboard."

"The historical society nut jobs!" howled Rocco as he pounded the computer mouse up and down, imploring the machine to speed up. "C'mon, c'mon!" The plastic mouse shattered in his muscular hand.

"Rock, settle down!" implored Pagano. "You're destroying the computer. Bart, help him out."

The science officer wobbled his frame past Rocco, their combined mass pushing both Pagano and Patrick in a backwards direction. Bart grabbed a mouse from another pad and moved it in a slow, circular pattern, his actions bringing the screen to life.

"Camera three," growled Rocco. He pointed at one of a series of security camera icons in view. "There they are! It's like a convention down there!"

Bart double clicked on camera three, his command enlarging the live stream of events playing out in the Franklin basement. There, standing just in front of the granite wall stood seven men, three of which were recognizable to the viewing team.

"That's the doctor who's always creeping around down there!" howled Rocco. "He's the ringleader. Remember?" He looked at Pagano. "He's the lunatic who ended up in the hospital with a head injury."

On the screen, Dr. Sullivan stood in front of the troop, pointing majestically to the curved wall behind him. He then called attention to the security camera, prompting every member of the team to look directly into the camera lens.

"And there's that city inspector thrown off the job by Freddie Freeman," continued Rocco. "What's he doing back down there? He's the one yakking about elevated radon levels!"

"Oh no," mumbled Pat Patrick as he leaned closer to the screen. He took a pair of reading glasses out of his front pocket and put them on, leaning closer. "I don't believe what I'm seeing... that's the Barber of Silverwood."

"What?" snarled Rocco with a glare toward Patrick. "Who the hell are you... and what are you doing here?"

"That's the young punk who came to my office," snapped Tommy Pagano with a pointed finger at the screen. "He's a real smart ass."

"Seth Barber is his name," blurted out Patrick. "He no longer works for the *Chronicle*. He just quit. I told him to stay clear of the Franklin building."

"Is he a member of that freaking history society?" roared Rocco with a lean toward Patrick. He didn't allow any time for a response. "Because if he isn't, that dude is trespassing on private property!"

"No. No, he's not," answered Patrick. "At least not to my knowledge. He's an ex-reporter for my newspaper."

"Ahh!" screamed Rocco as he sprinted to the right, crashing into a file cabinet and toppling it over. "I've had it with these idiots stumbling around in that basement. What the hell are they looking for? I can't take it anymore!"

"Rock, take it easy," said Bart with a set of raised, short stubby hands. "Did you take your medications this morning?"

"That's it!" screamed Rocco. He took two quick steps to the left and smashed his forearm into the trailer door, causing it to nearly unhinge. He burst into the outdoor sunlight without saying another word.

Big Bart Little grabbed a red phone sitting on the control desk. He brought the receiver quickly to his mouth. "Security to the Franklin basement! Security to the Franklin basement! Red alert! Rocco is inbound to the Franklin basement. I repeat… Rocco is inbound to the Franklin basement. Protect the civilians!"

The trio watched the foreman sprint across the dirt patch that separated the trailer from the Franklin. In the process, he body checked a portable toilet and capsized its frame, spewing out a worker with his pants half down into a wave of human excrement.

"He was an All-American down at Tulsa Tech," announced Tommy Pagano proudly. "A real life Tarpon. He played for Coach Buford B. Hayes on their national championship team. The coach said nobody hit harder than the Rock."

Patrick stared incredulously at the CEO. "Where's he going? What's he going to do?"

"He's going to knock the living shit out of that little twerp," answered Pagano. "Rock's pretty good at that kind of stuff. That kid deserves what he's about to get. He has no right to be down in that basement."

"Are you kidding me?" shot back Patrick. "He'll kill Seth! Maybe you should just call the police."

"Hopefully security will intercept him," whined Bart. "I can only pray." He turned a look of concern toward his boss.

"That little snot nosed brat needs a kick in the can," railed Pagano. "Rock will teach him some manners."

The trio continued to watch Dr. Sullivan address the party in animated fashion. He led them over to the granite wall and ran his hand across it."

"I was a consultant for the Veterans Stadium demolition in 2004," boasted Little. "We dropped the venerable Vet in about 62 seconds... in circular fashion." He ran an index finger around a tight circle. "I swiped a row of seats from the 700 section before it dropped." He pointed his index finger at Patrick and whispered. "I've got the seats at home in my garage. People tell me they're worth a ton of money."

Pat Patrick didn't respond as he monitored the screen, anticipating Rocco's entrance. Pagano nervously stood at his side, rocking up and down on his toes. Forty seconds later, and from the right side of the screen, the hulking frame of the Pagano Destruction foreman appeared, on a direct bull rush toward Seth Barber.

"Holy hell," whispered Patrick in horror. "Where's your security team?"

"Ouch," winced Bart as the trio witnessed Rocco lower his shoulder into the slight frame of the unsuspecting Barber, the impact causing both men to tumble across the concrete floor.

"Somebody stop him!" implored Patrick.

As Rocco stood up, some security guards rushed to his side, clamping onto his burly forearms. The frame of Seth

Barber lay motionless on the ground as Rocco struggled to break free.

"Oh, the coach would be proud of that hit," laughed Pagano. "Bart, send Coach Hayes a clip of that tackle! I saw some snot flying out of that kid's nose."

"What?" shouted Patrick. "Do you think this is some kind of a joke? He just assailed that man." He pointed to the screen. "Seth isn't moving! Call an ambulance!"

"No," snarled back Pagano. "This isn't a joke, Mr. Patrick." He turned his head to the right and spit on the trailer floor. "That building is ready to collapse and the general public has been cordoned off by the letter of the law! Your reporter has placed his life, and the lives of all of my workers at risk, with his reckless act of trespassing. We've already set some bore holes with dynamite!" He looked at Bart. "Call the Philadelphia Police. I want that punk arrested and prosecuted to the fullest extent of the law."

"Right-O, chief," answered Little as he pulled out a cell phone.

"Oh my god!" howled Patrick as he continued to stare down at the screen. "Somebody just slugged your strong man!" He leaned in closer. "Is that a man… or a walrus?"

Chaos erupted in the basement of the Franklin Wing, where the walrus man just took liberty in delivering a cheap shot across the jaw of the restrained foreman. The elderly member of the Historical Society shook his right hand back and forth after delivering the blow, prompting Rocco to swing his right arm forward in an attempt to retaliate. His action hoisted an already attached security guard high into the air. The Historical Society brethren quickly positioned themselves in a protective stance between the two combatants.

"That man just assaulted one of my workers!" bellowed Pagano. He shoved Patrick aside, tossed down his cigar, and bolted out the trailer door. "We got a donnybrook in the basement. I'll kill that turd! All hands on deck! Bart, sound the general alarm!"

"I don't believe what I'm seeing," muttered Patrick. "These are grown men going at each other." He watched Pagano storm across the vacant lot, imploring the capsized toilet man to join him. "What kind of an outfit are you running here?"

"I just work here," replied Bart as he took a stale donut out of a cardboard box. "I'm not an investor, or anything like that." He took a chomp out of the confectionary treat and held up the other half in Patrick's direction. "Want a bite?"

CHAPTER FIFTEEN
THE TWIN PARADOX

"Grandma, it smells in here," moaned Aidan as he wiped the back of his hand across a mucous plugged nose. "What smells so bad?"

"Never you mind," replied Martha Sullivan. "Look at where I'm hanging your painting." She pressed down onto the scotch tape holding the child's finger painting to the wall. "Isn't that pretty?"

"Daddy said you like flowers."

"I love flowers," replied Martha with an unsteady step backwards.

"Does Moses like flowers?"

"Of course. What kind of cat doesn't like flowers? Now, be a good boy and help Grandma over to that chair." She pointed her cane to a reclining chair next to her bed. "Hurry now."

The seven-year-old hustled over to his grandmother's side and carefully helped her across the room. She lowered her sickly frame into the chair, letting out a moan.

"What's the matter, Grandma?"

She ran her hand through Aidan's hair and smiled. "Nothing's the matter with Grandma. I'm just tired."

"Are you going to die?"

"No. But I am getting ready to go visit Grandpa up in heaven."

"Where's heaven?"

"Up in the sky," came the firm reply. "In the clouds."

"Will you see Mommy? She's in heaven."

"Of course, I will."

"Tell her I love her."

"I will."

"Will you miss me?" asked the child.

"Absolutely." She reached out and hugged the boy. "But remember, I'll always be in your heart." She tapped an arthritic index finger on the child's chest. "So, you'll never be alone. I'll always be with you."

"Is Grandpa in your heart?" While speaking he looked at a framed photograph of his grandfather at the bedside, dressed in military garb. "Is that why this heart is next to Grandpa's picture?"

"Yes. But that's a special medal called the Purple Heart," proclaimed Mrs. Sullivan. "Your grandfather was a war hero… in Vietnam."

"Where's that?"

"The other side of the world." She stroked the medal gently, its ribbon covered with dust. "He was so proud of this award."

"Is that Grandpa on the medal?"

"No," came the reply. "That's General George Washington. He was our nation's…"

"First president!" came the quick line from the preschooler. "George Washington chopped down a cherry tree. He taught us to never tell a lie."

"Very good," said Mrs. Sullivan. "Did they teach you that in school?"

"Yes. Miss Gamble told us. She's going on a date with Uncle John."

"Oh *really*? That's news to me." She pointed to a blanket across the room. "Fetch me that afghan."

The child obliged and helped cover up his grandmother.

"Grandpa was wounded in the war," proclaimed Mrs. Sullivan. "Someone shot him in the hip. He was darn lucky to make it back alive."

"Did it hurt?"

"Yes. But he was tough... a United States Marine." The front door downstairs opened and then closed. "I think I hear your Uncle John."

"Hurray! Dinner is here," shouted the boy.

"Mom, I'm home," declared Dr. Sullivan from below. "Gyro time."

"Open up that folding table," ordered the octogenarian with a wave of her cane. "Where's Moses?"

"Under your bed," said Aidan as he struggled to unfold a wooden side table next to his grandmother.

"Hello everybody," said Dr. Sullivan as he entered the bedroom. The cat immediately crept out from beneath the bed, stretched and yawned. "How was your day together?"

"Who's Miss Gamble?" asked Martha to her son.

"Who wants some macaroni and cheese, soup and a gyro?"

"Mac and cheese!" shouted Aidan.

John set the gyro down on the ground for Moses and handed his mother the soup, with a piece of crusty bread. He pulled out a salad from the grocery bag and took a seat. "What did you two do all day?"

"Grandpa got shot in the war," spouted out Aidan. "He got a medal in the shape of a heart." Sullivan's nephew pointed to the photograph.

"That's right, Aidan. That's called the Purple Heart and it's given to soldiers wounded while serving their country."

"Why is it purple? Why isn't it red?"

"I'll let Grandma answer that one."

"It was George Washington's favorite color," came the savvy response. "How's your mac and cheese?"

"Good." Aidan turned his attention back to dinner. "It's better than Grandpa's chili. I pass gas after that."

"Flatus, Aidan," said his uncle. "F-L-A-T-U-S."

An old rotary phone next to Mrs. Sullivan rang, the harsh metallic din scaring the cat. Moses bolted out of the room as Mrs. Sullivan ignored the call.

"Grandma needs a cell phone," quipped Aidan. "So I can text her."

"It's probably just another marketing scam," growled Martha. "Somebody calling to tell me the IRS is investigating my tax return and they need my personal information. Don't answer it."

"Never give out your social security number," said John.

The phone continued to ring.

"Alright, alright," cried out Martha. She picked up the receiver. "Hello." She stared forward intently. "No, this is his mother." The cat slowly returned to its dinner plate. "What's your name again?" She shook her head. "I don't know anyone named Ingrid." She looked at her son. "John, do you know anyone named Ingrid?"

"No," replied the doctor. A few seconds went by. "What a minute. Don't hang up! What's her last name?"

"Hoffman," came the reply from his mother, her left hand over the mouthpiece. "She sounds upset and keeps talking about a cousin."

The physician bolted across the room and grabbed the phone. "Hello, this is Dr. Sullivan." He listened intently with a gaze out the window. "Yes, sure… right now? No problem. I should be able to make it." He checked his watch and quickly looked at his mother. "Mom, can you watch Aidan for another hour or so?"

"The Pugs are on in twenty minutes." She looked at her grandson. "Are you a Brookside Pugs fan?"

"Yes," replied the boy.

"Then I can watch him," answered Martha with a grin.

"Very good, Mrs. Hoffman. I'll be over in about twenty minutes or so. Thank you. Sure, it's no problem." He hung up the phone.

"Who's Ingrid?" asked Mrs. Sullivan. "Miss Gamble's competition?"

"Hmm. That's peculiar," said John with a cocked eyebrow.

"What's peculiar?" asked his mother. "Who's Mrs. Hoffman?"

"Ingrid Hoffman is the last surviving offspring of Dr. Rickard von Steiger," replied Sullivan. He waited for his mother to recognize the name, but she didn't flinch. "She's also a first cousin to Dr. Zachary Schmidt."

Her mother immediately recognized the Schmidt name and without moving her body, directed a wary gaze upon her son. "I told you he wouldn't let that building be destroyed." Her voice cracked as if a shiver ran through her vocal cords. She pulled the afghan a bit higher up onto her chest. "The spirit of Dr. Schmidt is alive and well, John… and it resides inside that building. Trust me when I say the old Franklin Wing is haunted."

"There are no such things as ghosts," replied the medical doctor as he wrapped up his half-eaten dinner. "Trust me when I say that, Mom. I'm a man of science."

"But I knew Zachary Schmidt," came the quick retort with a pointed finger. "He promised to come back!"

"So, what are you saying, Mom? He all of a sudden reappears… forty years after vanishing from sight? Is that what you're telling me? The ghost of Zachary Schmidt came back to help save that run down building. Where's he been for the past four decades?"

His mother didn't respond as a look of scorn ran across her face. She tightened her lips.

"What kind of a promise are you talking about? He made a promise?"

She refused to continue the conversation and glared forward in defiance.

"I'll be back in about an hour, Aidan," said John. He stooped down to kiss his nephew on the head. "Take care of Granny. She's afraid of ghosts."

"So am I," said the child. He got up and ran over to his grandmother's side.

The physician stepped over the recumbent cat and walked out. Twenty minutes later, he was again led into the parlor of Ingrid Hoffman's home. Sullivan took a seat on the sofa, opposite his host.

"Thank you for coming over on such short notice," said Mrs. Hoffman. "I have somewhat of a favor to ask of you."

"A favor? What kind of a favor?"

"Yes, well… this is all going to sound a bit absurd to you, Dr. Sullivan," continued Hoffman. For the first time in their short relationship, she broke eye contact with Sullivan. "I never thought I would ever be discussing such a matter with anyone outside of the family," stammered Hoffman. "I don't know where to start."

"Why did you mention a cousin over the phone?"

"I… it's very difficult for me to say."

"Are you aware that some surveillance video from the Philadelphia General Hospital recorded someone in the Franklin Wing with facial features resembling that of the late Dr. Schmidt?" He paused but there was no response. "Do you have a relative in town, say in his late forties or earlier fifties?"

"Dr. Sullivan, I'm about to tell you something that will permanently alter the course of your life, in quite a dramatic fashion." She reestablished eye contact.

"In a good way or bad way?"

"Both."

"I see."

"But, before I proceed, you must be willing to accept such an undeniable consequence." She paused. "Your personal life and medical career... will never be the same."

"So, are you asking my permission to continue?"

"Absolutely. If we continue this conversation, you'll never be the same person again."

"And how did I get involved in this discussion?"

"Your zealous pursuit of the past in regard to the Franklin Wing and Dr. Schmidt. That's what brought us together on such short notice."

Sullivan's heart began to rapidly pound in anticipation. He thought he heard a faint cough from the rear of the first-floor dwelling, but the synchronized cry of every cuckoo clock in the house muffled the sound. Deep in his heart, he needed to hear the news. He waited for the clocks to go silent.

"Go ahead. I consent."

"Are you sure?"

"Absolutely."

"Do you believe in the existence of time travel?" asked Mrs. Hoffman.

"Ah, well... I can't say I've given it much thought." He furrowed his eyebrows in an attempt to generate a meaningful response. "I mean, outside of a few novels and movies, my knowledge of the topic..."

"Time does not flow at a constant rate," continued Hoffman. "Time flows at different rates in different places."

"I did sign up for a quantum physics class in college, but it was filled," recalled Sullivan. "I ended up taking a cooking class, which in hindsight, probably served me better."

"Time is relative." She stared at her silent host. "Hence, Einstein's Theory of Relativity. Are you familiar with that concept, Dr. Sullivan?"

"Somewhat."

"Are you aware that my father was a close personal friend of Mr. Einstein? They were colleagues in Germany and worked in the same laboratory."

"Yes. Yes, I am aware of that."

"The General Theory of Relativity states that time is linked, or related, to both matter and space."

"Yes."

"Therefore, the dimensions of time, space, and matter constitute what we call... a continuum."

Sullivan held up his hands. "Mrs. Hoffman, with all due respect, where are we headed with this conversation? I mean, what does my involvement with the Franklin Wing have to do with Albert Einstein's General Theory of Relativity?"

"Dr. Sullivan, my cousin disappeared into thin air over forty years ago. Did you ever wonder how a man could just vanish from sight... without leaving a trace?"

"I've given it great thought. It's inexplicable."

"There's only one explanation," came the retort. "That is, if you believe in the existence of time travel."

"Uh-oh," quipped Sullivan. He stared coldly at his host. "You're not suggesting..."

"That's right, Dr. Sullivan. Once you entertain the possibility, it all starts to make perfect sense. Think about it. How else can someone just disappear from the planet earth?"

Sullivan looked down to consider the plausibility of such an occurrence, which although bizarre, could certainly explain everything. He looked back up. "Mrs. Hoffman, you're not trying to tell me that Dr. Zachary Schmidt was a..."

"Time traveler," cut in Hoffman. She nodded her head slowly up and down. "Yes... that's exactly what I am telling you. Dr. Zachary Schmidt was a time traveler." She paused for several seconds, allowing the magnitude of her statement to set in. "I know it sounds crazy but trust me when I say it's true." She smiled as if spreading out the winning hand in a poker game. "My cousin, the eccentric Zachary Schmidt, escaped prosecution on July 4th, 1976, by stepping into a time portal. In doing so, he successfully eluding his captors and their draconian plan to proceed with a state mandated lobotomy the following day."

Sullivan remained speechless. It made sense but couldn't be true. In his mind, time travel was science fiction, the cliché plot for works of science fiction.

"Both my father and cousin were keenly aware of the portal's existence. Each man, throughout their career, benefitted from their ability to travel into the future. A remarkable perk, if you think about it... the ability to take a peek around the corner of life. Yet over time, the tunnel cut both ways. You see, Dr. Sullivan..."

Sullivan stood up and put both hands on his head. "Stop! You're starting to freak me out a bit." He took two steps to the right and turned back to face the host. "You're asking me, a man a science, to accept the notion that man can travel backward in time?"

"Forward. Only forward travel is possible."

"Backward or forward... it doesn't matter! It can't be true. It's never been done." He scanned the room. "Are there cameras in here? Am I being punked?"

"I'm unfamiliar with that term."

"Oh, this is just too bizarre," stated Sullivan. "A bit too surreal for me." He looked back at Hoffman. "Mrs. Hoffman, I appreciate your confidence in providing me with this information, but I'm going to need time to digest your proposal. What you're asking me to believe is a bit far-fetched, and to be quite honest..."

The sound of a man coughing came from the rear of the home.

"Does someone live with you?" asked Sullivan with a quizzical glance toward the foyer.

"No."

"Well then... who may I ask, is in your home now?"

A smile slowly appeared on her face. "A visitor from the future."

"No. Don't even suggest it," warned Sullivan. Sweat began to run down the middle of his spine. For some reason he mumbled, "There are no such things as ghosts."

"He's no ghost," came the calm response. "The man on the hospital surveillance video was indeed my cousin. I'm sure the hospital sentry notified you of their recent reunion. Zachary always admired Mr. Washington and it brought him great joy to rekindle their friendship."

"The man on the video was no older than sixty," shot back Sullivan. "Your cousin should be in his late eighties. How can you explain that?"

"The twin paradox," came the answer.

"Excuse me?"

"Einstein made it clear that there is no such thing as 'time' in the singular. Time passes differently for different observers, depending on their motion. The twin paradox is an extension of his theory of special relativity."

"But what does it have to do with twins?"

"Let's say you have two identical twins," stated Hoffman. "One makes a journey in a high-speed rocket into outer space, and the other stays on earth."

"Alright."

"When the traveling twin returns home, will they be the same age?"

"I suppose," guessed Sullivan. "Or maybe not. I don't know."

"The twin who remained on earth will have aged much more," came the answer.

"How so?"

"There is no symmetry between the spacetime path of each twin," answered Ingrid with a smile. "The traveling twin's trajectory involved two different inertial frames, one for the outbound route and the other for the inbound return. Acceleration and gravity also play a significant role."

"You seem to have tremendous knowledge on this topic," said Sullivan. "How so?"

"My father was a brilliant physicist," came the proud reply. "He taught his nephew and two daughters well, even at our young age."

"So why me?" asked Sullivan. "Why are you suddenly divulging the existence of this so-called time tunnel to Dr. John Sullivan? What makes me so special?"

"Because you brought him back, doctor. Zachary Schmidt was trapped in the future for the past forty years, until you stepped into the picture."

Sullivan lifted an eyebrow. "I brought him back?"

"Yes."

"And how exactly did I do this, without my knowledge?"

"The key. You found the key."

"That skeleton key? The one that Reggie Washington had buried in a can of oddities from the Franklin?"

"Absolutely. That key triggers the opening of the time tunnel. The slot in the granite wall is set exactly to the portal's opening. Once the key is set into the slot, the worm hole opens and the laws of physics take control." She smiled warmly. "I know this is crazy, doctor. But, it's all true."

"Dr. Schmidt wore that key around his neck."

"Yes. And unfortunately, on the night of July 4th, 1976... immediately after activating the tunnel, the young police officer crashed into Dr. Schmidt. His actions broke the key at its bow, sending the bulk of the skeleton key onto the floor of the Franklin."

"And the remaining stump of the key stayed on the necklace?"

"Exactly. It was perfect timing, Dr. Sullivan. The latchkey stayed behind... but the two men transported forward."

"Interesting."

Unfortunately, the nub of key remaining on Dr. Schmidt's necklace wasn't enough to reactivate the time tunnel on the other side of the tunnel. So sadly, Dr. Schmidt and the police officer had no ticket to return home. Without that old key..."

"They were trapped in the future?"

"Yes."

"Things are starting to make too much sense," said Sullivan in a rapid tone. "You're really starting to scare me now."

"Fortunately, Mr. Washington found the key. But unfortunately, he stored it away for the next four decades." She smiled. "Until you came into the picture. Dr. Sullivan, let me make this clear–it was you who delivered the key back to Dr. Schmidt."

Sullivan stood speechless.

"You delivered him back to our time."

"But..."

"Do you remember placing that key into the slot?"

"Yes," stammered Sullivan. "There was a tremendous flash of light and crack of thunder."

"Do you remember the sound of silence and acceleration?"

"Yes. But I don't remember much more. Except for waking up the next day in a hospital."

"You traveled forward in time, doctor."

Sullivan didn't reply.

"You sustained a concussion in the transport. Take a guess who put those stitches into your head?"

Sullivan reached up and ran a hand across his healing head wound. He recalled the old-fashioned 'baseball' stitch described to close the gash.

Mrs. Hoffman stood up. "Dr. Sullivan, would you like to meet my cousin... Dr. Zachary Schmidt? He wants to thank you."

"He has the key?" stuttered Sullivan as he steadied himself on a wing chair. The room began to spin.

"Yes. It's back around his neck… safe and secure." She took hold of Sullivan's arm and led him into the foyer. They took a right at the stairwell and walked past the kitchen.

"But the favor?" asked Sullivan as he plodded forward. "What's the favor?"

"He needs your help," came the reply. "You need to go back into the future… to save his life."

CHAPTER SIXTEEN
THE VOLUNTEER

"OH... MY... GOD!" stammered Sullivan as he turned the corner into a rear bedroom. "I do not believe my eyes!" He brought both hands forward to cover his nose and mouth. "It's impossible."

Dr. Schmidt lay supine on a sofa with a blanket covering his slight body. He appeared frail, except for radiant energy emanating from a set of blazing blue eyes. His mustache was unchanged from photographs of old, and his grin, unmistakable. The smell of pipe tobacco permeated the airspace and to his right, a fire crackled inside a stone hearth.

"Ah, Dr. John Sullivan," replied Schmidt. "An honor and a privilege to make your formal acquaintance." He held out his right hand. "Please excuse me for not getting up. I'm a tad fatigued at the moment."

Sullivan reached out to shake the physician's hand, anticipating it to be ice cold, but it was warm and firm. Schmidt flashed a set of pearly white teeth beneath his trademark mustache and held the grip for several seconds.

"Dr. Zachary Schmidt here... a fellow physician on staff at the Philadelphia General. Sorry I've missed the last one hundred or so medical staff meetings... I've been away."

"Am I dreaming?" asked Sullivan as he gawked down at Schmidt. "Is this all true?" He looked back at Ingrid.

"It's true, young man," answered Schmidt. "Everything that Ingrid told you is the absolute truth. You indeed traveled forward in time and liberated me. For that, I shall always be grateful."

"You're welcome," mumbled Sullivan. "I'm sorry, but I don't remember our initial meeting."

"Nothing to be sorry about," countered Schmidt. "You incurred a concussion with that head laceration, so I'm sure a bit of amnesia came into play. After suturing up your head, I transported you back to the Philadelphia General Hospital for immediate care."

"Thank you."

"Please, take a seat," said Schmidt as he pointed to a chair. "Stay for a while. We have lots to talk about."

Before Sullivan could respond, Ingrid slid a chair across the room and placed it next to Schmidt's head. She helped Sullivan sit down.

"I'll make some tea," said Ingrid as she left the room.

A cat jumped up onto Schmidt's body and slowly curled up into a ball near his stomach.

"That's Riley," quipped Schmidt as he patted the cat. "She's named after our nation's 52nd president." He elevated an eyebrow and grinned. "A most resolute and distinguished woman from our state of Pennsylvania… the city of Scranton to be exact."

"It's back around your neck," said Sullivan with a pointed finger. "The skeleton key. I thought I lost it."

"Quite the opposite… you returned the key to its rightful owner. You fortunately held tight when your body was sucked into the portal, but you forgot to tuck your body into a forward roll. That was a nasty head wound I had to stitch up. You hit your head on my office desk, in the basement of the Pagano Orthopedic Institute."

"Wow. I'm afraid to ask, but what year did I show up in?"

"2065," answered Schmidt with a cough. "Excuse me." He appeared short of breath. "The time tunnel terminus is set to 2065."

"But your age? How old are you? You look too young."

"Chronologically, I'm forty-nine years old."

"How? How is that possible?"

"The twin paradox and witch hazel," came the quirky reply. "I use witch hazel on my face every night... it gently tones and cleanses." While speaking, the physician ran the back of his hand across his cheek.

"Witch hazel?"

"Yes, but more so the twin paradox. Professor Einstein and Uncle Rickard were absolutely correct in so much that time *is* relative. Speed plays a crucial role in the rate at which we experience time."

"I see... at least I think so."

"Time passes more slowly the closer you approach the unbreakable cosmic speed limit we call the speed of light. The hands of a clock inside a speeding rocket move more slowly than those of a stationary clock."

"But the speed of light is unobtainable, at least by human means," stated Sullivan. "That much I know."

"I don't want to overwhelm you but suffice it to say that as postulated by the Einstein-Rosen Bridge, wormholes do exist!"

"So let me understand... there's a so-called wormhole in the Franklin basement?"

"Absolutely. A wormhole is a structure linking discordant points in spacetime. Try to visualize it as a tunnel with two ends, each at separate points in spacetime."

"And time passes differently at each end of the tunnel?"

"Exactly!"

"So, what's the aging ratio?" asked Sullivan. "I mean, how does time pass by for someone in 2065 versus the present?" He pointed to the floor. "Here, right now, in West Philadelphia."

"Twenty to one," came the answer. "So even though I vanished over forty years ago... I've only aged about two years since then."

"Wow! That's absolutely unbelievable."

"Pretty neat stuff," said Schmidt. "It still amazes me, too."

Sullivan shook his head as if trying to recalibrate. "I can't believe this, but it makes sense." He pointed at Schmidt. "You, the key, vanishing from sight... but what's going on right now?" came the concerned question. "You appear quite infirmed."

"Your clinical prowess is keen," countered Schmidt. "Hence my request to have this chat with you."

Ingrid returned with two teacups and a pot of steeping tea. She placed the tray on a small coffee table in front of Schmidt.

"Some East Frisian tea for my Zachary," stated Ingrid proudly. "Cream is in the cup. I'll leave you two gentlemen alone." She turned and walked away. "Call if you need anything."

"Thank you my dear, Ingrid," spoke Schmidt. He slowly reached out a trembling arm and lifted the pot, filling each cup nearly to the brim. "Have you ever been to East Frisia?" asked Schmidt.

"No. No I haven't," answered Sullivan. "Thank you."

"A lovely area of Germany, located about four hours northwest of Berlin, by automobile that is." He poured just a touch of cream into the brew. "The area is flat, just like the Netherlands to the west. There my good friend, is where the best tea in the world is blended... East Frisian tea." A grin of satisfaction came across his face as he lifted the warm tea to his mouth. Slowly he blew across the steamy beverage.

Sullivan took a sip of the hearty brew. "A very robust taste."

"The teas come from northern India," quipped Schmidt. "But the blend, is classic East Frisia."

A full minute of silence passed by.

"I suffer from upper medullary asymmetry," stated Schmidt in a matter of fact fashion.

"I'm unfamiliar with that malady," said Sullivan.

"It's about to be discovered at the University of Leiden in three years," stated Schmidt. "A rather lethal disease that took hold of my frame years ago. If it weren't for the time tunnel, I would have certainly succumbed by now."

"How so?"

"In 2045, researchers discovered a treatment for the disease via genome sequencing. It's not a cure, but treatment protocols halt the progressing of the disease, allowing an affected individual to carry on a normal and productive life." He took a sip of tea. "Modern medicine... amazing."

"I'll say so. You're talking about treatment for a disease that hasn't even been discovered."

"I require intravenous administration of targeting agents every two weeks. Each treatment takes about thirty minutes and keeps me fit as a fiddle."

"So, we need to get you back home as soon as possible... for your infusion," stated Sullivan. "That's obvious."

"That was my initial plan, but it seems the disease has progressed in an uncharacteristically brisk manner since my arrival. It makes perfect sense if you think about it." He reached for a sugar coated cookie and took a bite. "You see, even though I've only been back for three days on my 2065 time schedule, my body is sensing it as well over two months." He coughed and chuckled. "So in reality, I've missed four treatment sessions and as predicted, my nervous system is on the fritz." He looked at Sullivan in a concerned fashion. "Dr. Sullivan, simple stated... I'm too weak to travel."

"Meaning?"

"If I don't receive treatment soon, my ability to sponta-neously breath will cease to exist. I'll need to be admitted to the PGH and put on a ventilator, to survive a disease that has yet to be discovered." He took another sip of tea. "A rather nasty conundrum, if you think about it."

"So, you'll never come off the breathing machine?"

"Correct. It's quite the quandary. I've dubbed the con-dition 'time travel jet lag'." He grinned. "Do you like that term?"

"Yes," smiled Sullivan, already enthralled by Schmidt's persona.

"Time travel jet lag. Hah, I do like that. A tad oxymoron-ic."

"So what's plan B?" asked Sullivan. "How do we get you well?"

"I need a volunteer," responded Schmidt in a direct tone. "To travel forward to 2065, receive an intravenous dose of medication, and promptly return it to this exact residence."

"Oh no, you're not going to ask me to…"

"You seem to be a man of high moral character, Dr. Sullivan. And yes, I am… asking you to return to the future. You see… my life depends on it."

Sullivan's face went blank, as he pondered the request.

"I will say that time travel is relatively safe," added Schmidt. "I've traveled through the tunnel well over a hun-dred times in my career." He dabbed his mouth with a napkin and pushed away the empty teacup. "A bump on the noggin here and there, but that's about it." He took a slow and labo-rious breath. "Unfortunately, no material goods larger than a skeleton key can safely traverse the tunnel, hence the need to instill the medicine into your veins for a safe return. If agreeable, you'll be considered a pioneer in travel medicine." He grinned.

"And then what happens? When I return?"

"A direct transfusion into my veins, here in Ingrid's home." He raised his hands in the air and looked around. "We've no other choice, my dear friend. As you can imagine, time is of the essence."

"But your blood type?"

"Type AB," countered Schmidt. "The universal recipient. So, I can receive a transfusion from anyone. A bit of lady luck there."

"How much time are you talking about?" asked Sullivan. "If you can estimate?"

"About twenty days... in 2020 time. I'm a definite goner in three weeks, and that's stated within a reasonable degree of medical certainty."

"So I've only got about twenty four hours of 2065 time to turn this around? Is that accurate?"

"Yes," replied Schmidt while counting on his fingers. "If my math is correct."

"And you think I can do that?" asked Sullivan in an incredulous tone. "Just pop into the future, walk into a hospital, get a transfusion and transport back through some sort of a wormhole?" He waited for a rebuttal, but Schmidt just continued to smile. "I'm not even sure I can get back into the Franklin Wing," added Sullivan. "It's like a war zone down there."

"Ah, Mr. Washington will certainly aid us in our endeavors," followed up Schmidt. "And I've a man on the opposite end of the tunnel who can always be counted on. Allister is his name, a wonderful chap from the north of England."

Sullivan felt himself suddenly overwhelmed by the request, which he knew in his heart, could not be denied. A man's life was at stake.

"So doctor, I ask you, will you please travel to the future to pick up my temporizing antidote for this horrid disease?"

"Yes! I'll do it." A rush of adrenaline shot through his arteries.

"Bravo!" shouted Schmidt with both hands clasped above his head. He looked toward the kitchen and shouted, "Ingrid, he said 'yes'!"

"Wunderbar!" came the return cry.

"Wonderful," said Schmidt with a wide smile. "That means wonderful. She tends to speak more and more German as time goes by."

"It's common for the aging to resort back to their native tongue," quipped Sullivan. "English at times is a second language on my Alzheimer's floor."

"Ah, Aloysius Alzheimer, a fine German physician who Uncle Rickard actually had the privilege to call his one-time mentor."

"Your uncle knew Dr. Alzheimer?"

"Absolutely. Uncle Rickard was just a young student at the University when they met. It was near Dr. Alzheimer's final years on staff. Let me see now, what University was that?" He snapped his fingers a few times in an attempt to recall the school's name.

"The Freidrich-Wilhelm University," shouted Ingrid from the kitchen. "He taught at the Psychiatric clinic there."

"Ah yes! Thank you, Ingrid." Schmidt leaned toward Sullivan and whispered. "Her hearing however, is still quite good."

"I heard that!" shouted Ingrid.

The two physicians chuckled as the cat stood up, slowly stretched its body, and curled back into a ball.

"One perk of your pending travels shall be the ability to familiarize yourself with the advancements made in the treatment of Alzheimer's disease," stated Schmidt. "I can assure you of that." He rolled one arm of his mustache between a thumb and index finger. "I'm sure you'll be quite pleased with the progress made over the next four decades."

Sullivan was flabbergasted by the possibility.

"You'll someday be called a 'forward thinker' in your field of expertise," added Schmidt. "That's a guarantee."

"Unbelievable."

"Now, let's get down to brass tacks," continued Schmidt with a few taps of his index finger on the table. "You'll have Mr. Washington slightly divert the security camera located in my old office. On the other side of the tunnel you'll immediately befriend Allister, who per my charge, always stands vigilant in my absence. Once you explain my plight to Allister, I'm confident he'll coordinate your medical care and movements up to and including a safe return to the Franklin. He's quite the efficient fellow."

Over the next thirty minutes, the two physicians plotted out their plan of action, which would trigger over the next several hours. After sealing the deal with a handshake and a round of warm apple tarts, Sullivan stood up to take leave.

"Thank you, Dr. Schmidt," stated Sullivan. "And thank you, Ingrid, for reaching out to me."

"It's been an absolute pleasure meeting you," answered Schmidt. He abruptly stopped speaking and smiled.

"What?" asked Sullivan. "What are you smiling about?"

"Aren't you forgetting something?"

"No. I don't believe so," replied Sullivan. He hand checked his pockets. "I've no cell phone."

"The portal," said Schmidt with a grin. "You have to activate the portal." He pointed to the skeleton key around his neck.

"Oh, right," shot back Sullivan. "The key! How can I travel to the future without the key?"

Schmidt slowly reached both hands behind his neck and popped opened the clasp holding the passkey.

"Listen to me," continued Sullivan. "I'm talking about traveling to the future like it's an every day event."

"Ingrid bought me a new chain," said Schmidt as he handed the key to Sullivan. "She said I have to keep up with the times."

"But you're from the future," laughed Sullivan. "You're well ahead of the times."

"Exactly!"

They all burst into laughter.

"Take care of that key, doctor," commanded Schmidt. "If you lose it... there is no Plan C. Keep it locked around your neck, you can lean forward to place it into the granite slot."

"I won't lose it," promised Sullivan. He locked the chain around his neck and tucked the key behind his shirt. "Good night, Mrs. Hoffman." He bowed. "Good night, Dr. Schmidt."

Sullivan departed the Hoffman residence and hurried back home, his mind a mishmash of thoughts. He spotted the ambulance parked in front of his Spruce Street address about a block away, the hazard lights of the transport blinking in a slow, rhythmic fashion. Much to his horror, two attendants were slowly transporting a body covered by a sheet down the front steps, into the rear of the vehicle. The sight of the gurney prompted Sullivan to sprint forward. By the time he arrived, one of the EMTs slammed the rear door shut.

"PGH... this is EMT Nine, inbound with a recently deceased," spoke the emergency provider into a radio receiver clipped to his shoulder.

"What's going on here?" gasped Sullivan. "What happened?" He looked into the rear of the vehicle, only to notice a motionless frame. Looking upward he spotted the terrified face of Aidan peeking out from behind a window curtain.

"*EMT Nine, PGH E.R. is currently on divert status,*" crackled the radio. "*Recommend redirect to the morgue for pronouncement. Over.*"

"And you are?" asked the medical provider.

"John!" came a shout from atop the concrete steps.

Sullivan looked up to see his childhood friend and neighbor, Pete Peterson.

"Perch! What's going on?" asked Sullivan.

"It's Mom," came the sad reply. "*My* Mom."

Sullivan immediately felt a sense of relief. He looked back at the EMT saying, "I'm sorry… my mistake." He turned and slowly walked up the shared steps that lead to parallel sidewalks separating the two homesteads. He reached out and shook Peterson's hand.

"I call her twice a day," said Peterson. "This morning she was fine, but she didn't answer this evening. So I hustled over here."

Sullivan didn't try to finish the story, well aware of the obvious outcome. Mrs. Peterson, like his mother, was also suffering terminally from a malignancy. She lived alone and would not allow any further treatment or hospice care. Her final wish was to die peacefully at home.

"She didn't answer the phone, so I ran over."

"And…?" asked Sullivan.

"She was gone, John." He wiped tears from his eyes. "Sitting in her favorite chair with that television blaring."

"Are you sure she's…"

"She was cold and blue, John." He paused to gather some composure. "The medics couldn't even lay her flat. She had no heartbeat."

"I'm very sorry, Perch," said Sullivan with a hand placed on his friend's shoulder. "She's at peace now, with Donny. I'm very sorry."

"I knew it was coming. But I really didn't get to say goodbye to her. If you can believe that."

"You took good care of her, Perch… right to the end. That's what really matters. Knowing that you cared for her each and every day. She wanted to pass at home."

His friend took a deep breath and exhaled. "Well, I've got to get down to the hospital." He looked back at the opened front door of his home.

"Get going," ordered Sullivan. "I'll close up the house." He reached out and held his neighbor's shoulders. "I'm here if you need me."

"Thanks, John," replied Perch. He took a few steps away but turned back. "They took good care of us," said Peterson with a nostalgic look. "We grew up in a great neighborhood, John."

"The best," responded Sullivan. "The absolute best." He looked up to now see his mother's face in the window, looking down upon the two.

"Thanks again, John," said Perch as he walked away.

Sullivan shut down the old Peterson homestead, taking one final walk through the dwelling. He practically lived next door as a child, the two side entrances facing each other and only twenty feet apart.

"Mom, Aidan... I'm back," hollered the physician as he entered his own home. "Sorry I'm late." He went upstairs and entered the front bedroom.

"Is Grandma's friend dead?" asked Aidan.

"I don't know," came the measured reply. "She's going to the hospital. Pack your bags up, Aidan. Time to go home."

"They go in threes," came the morbid pronouncement from Martha Sullivan. "First Mr. Grimes, and now Aggie. Mom always said... 'When the Lord comes a calling, he takes three'."

"Say goodnight to Aiden, Mom," countered Sullivan. "I hope the Pugs won."

His mother didn't respond.

"They got killed," blurted Aidan as he swung a gym bag over his shoulder. "The manager can't coach his way out of a paper bag and these young players don't know how to bunt."

Sullivan smiled as he patted his nephew on the back. "You're starting to talk baseball like Granny," said the doctor as he left the room. "You're certainly learning from the best."

Later that night, after tucking his mother into bed, Dr. John Sullivan set his alarm clock for three o'clock in the morning. As he dozed off into a fitful sleep he stroked the skeleton key around his neck, appreciating some irregular etching on the passport. He heard a voice in the back of his head softly whisper… "You should have asked him about R.S."

CHAPTER SEVENTEEN
VINCENT ROMEO

"To my son!" shouted Winky Pagano with a glass of champagne thrust into the air. "Dr. Vincent Romeo Pagano... future president of the Pagano Orthopedic Institute!"

"Hear! Hear!" came the reply from the intimate crowd gathered inside the gates of the posh country club. "To Vincent!"

Vince Pagano took a sip of alcohol and sauntered his way to the podium. He wore a sleek, black tuxedo that held tight to an athletic body. He smiled, adjusted the microphone, and gave a wave to a local television crew to his right. Red and white balloons anchored each side of the makeshift tribune. A banner overhead the stage announced: *"Montgomery County's Most Eligible Physician."*

"Thank you very much," said Vince. "Thank you." He glanced at his father and graciously bowed. "I'd like to thank the *Philadelphia Chronicle* for bestowing this honorary title upon me." He looked at Pat Patrick sitting in the first row. "It's truly an honor to be recognized by the *Chronicle*'s society board and their staff. But I fully understand the moniker of 'most eligible physician' means more than just being unwed. To me, it signifies an opportunity to positively impact the lives of countless individuals throughout the..."

As he continued to speak, his father beamed with pride. Without a doubt, Vincent was his favorite son, a blend of his mother's looks and the devilish Pagano charm. To his right sat Vince's mother, having driven back from the Jersey shore earlier in the day. She patted her husband's thigh as their son continued to address the crowd, her hand leathered and tan from a lifelong addiction to the sun.

"So, it gives me great pleasure to announce a donation of ten thousand dollars from Pagano Destruction to the West Philadelphia Women and Children's Center," continued Vince. "Like my father always said, a Pagano not only destroys... but helps others to enjoy."

As another round of applause rose from the gathering, Winky scanned the crowd in search of Stephanie. It was certainly uncharacteristic of her to miss a gathering at the Main Line club, especially with Vincent involved. The CEO's concubine was nowhere to be seen, despite her promise to attend.

"So thank you once again for this honor, I look forward to a bright and productive future together," finished Vincent. "Together we can make a difference throughout the greater Philadelphia area." He gave a thumbs up and stepped down from the podium into the adoring crowd of patrons.

"My Vincent," proclaimed his mother with a kiss. "We're so proud of you." While talking she wiped some lipstick off the doctor's cheek with her finger.

"Thanks, Mom. Thanks, Dad," replied the surgeon. He firmly shook his father's hand.

"My boy!" shouted Pagano with a grin. "Congratulations."

"Nice speech," said a young woman appearing at the eligible bachelor's side. She stood tall and confident in a stylish black dress, her dark hair complementing the outfit.

"Thanks, Jordan," said the man of the hour.

Jordan McCarthy put her left hand around Vince's torso and gave a firm squeeze. She was the odds-on favorite to dethrone *Montgomery County's Most Eligible Physician*, having been his significant other for just over two years. The couple met during Vincent's orthopedic residency, she being a critical care nurse at the Philadelphia General.

"Jordan, you look stunning tonight," stated Mrs. Pagano. "I love your necklace." The Pagano's adored their potential future daughter-in-law, a refined product from a wealthy Main Line family.

"So do you, Mrs. Pagano. That dress is absolutely divine."

Uncle Frank broke into the circle with an extended handshake. "Vincent, congratulations," quipped the family patriarch. Behind him walked two of his watchmen, flashing their gaudy 1970's lounge attire. "I couldn't be more proud of you. We expect great things from the Pagano Institute."

"Thank you, Uncle Frank," replied Vince. "Thank you for all your help."

Uncle Frank turned toward Jordan and smiled.

"Uncle Frank, I'd like you to meet Jordan McCarthy," said Vince proudly. "She's a critical care nurse at the Philadelphia General."

"A pleasure to make your acquaintance, Ms. McCarthy," spoke Uncle Frank with an extended handshake. "I've heard so many wonderful things about you."

Just then, a slight commotion broke out behind Uncle Frank's security detail, prompting everyone to turn around. There, standing in the middle of a double doorway, stood the teetering frame of Stephanie Peacock. She held a half empty bottle of liquor in her extended left arm and flashed a fiery look in her eyes. The secretary took a few unsteady steps forward and a tad to the right, prompting the two henchmen to reach out.

"Get your dirty paws off me!" cried Stephanie, her hair a mess across the front of her face. She swung the bottle wildly at one of the bodyguards, barely missing his midsection.

"Here, here!" shouted the manager of the club as he pranced into the fray. "What's going on here?" He was a slight man, about the size of Peacock, with a slick, well-cropped head of hair. "Young lady, I must insist that you..."

"In here!" shouted Stephanie with a wave and look behind. "I told you they'd all be here... in their cozy little lodge."

Seth Barber stepped defiantly into the club's main chamber, his right eye blackened and a cast on his left wrist. He held a rolled up scroll of paper in his right hand.

"Seth!" shouted Pat Patrick. "What the hell are you doing here?"

"Attention everyone!" shouted Barber. "I've in my hand a petition, signed by over one thousand concerned Philadelphians online, demanding that the Franklin Wing destruction be put on hold!" He waved the papers over his head.

"You little piss pot," growled Winky. He stepped forward to squelch the infidel, but Vince latched onto his forearm.

"The Franklin contains a majestic wall of granite that must be saved!" continued Barber. He looked to his left to see the television crew aiming their camera in his direction. "Along with the West Philadelphia Historical Society and a cohort of my brethren, we demand an immediate forum to voice our concerns."

The two bodyguards aggressively moved forward in the direction of Barber.

"Tony! Gus!" snapped Frank Russo.

The hired hands looked back at their boss, who quickly walked away, his action prompting them to follow suit. The trio vanished in a matter of seconds.

"I've seen the ghost of Zachary Schmidt appearing in the basement of the Franklin Wing," continued Barber. "A man who mysteriously disappeared from the face of the earth some forty years ago!"

"How dare you!" squeaked the club manager. "This is a private gathering!"

The inebriated body of Stephanie Peacock suddenly listed to the right, as if the left side of her brain spontaneously infarcted. She catapulted head first into a majestic pyramid of champagne glasses, each filled to the brim and softly overflowing with expensive bubbly. The artistic display collapsed onto her fallen frame. "Crash!" shattered the glass all across the floor, drenching the secretary's prone body with a tidal wave of effervescence. She let out a guttural moan but did not move.

"Stephie!" cried Winky with a step in her direction. Vince now latched both hands onto his father's forearm, in order to preserve his mother's honor.

"My champagne waterfall!" screamed the manager. "Oh heavens!"

Several attendants rushed to the fallen woman's side, brushing shards of glass from her backside. They rolled her supine while gently patting her cheek. The Pagano Destruction employee was out cold.

"You hooligan!" howled the club manager at Barber. "Get out of here this very instant." He began to rapidly slap Seth's arm and chest. "I'm calling the police! Look what you've done to my tower! You brute!"

"Visit my website!" shouted Barber into the television camera. "*The Barber of Silverwood.com* for everything you need to know about the ghost of Dr. Schmidt. Save the wall!" He thrust his cast boldly into the air. "Save the wall!"

A cadre of more formidable club attendants swarmed around Seth, their combined action squelching his call to action. The rabble-rouser was forcefully led into another room and fifteen minutes later, an EMT squad carefully lifted the alcohol soaked body of Miss Peacock onto a gurney. As her body rolled away, the shocked crowd began to disperse.

"What the hell just happened?" asked Vince. "Who was that maniac?"

"A former employee at the *Chronicle*," babbled Mr. Patrick. "Trust me. There will be some serious repercussions on our behalf."

"Dad, what was Stephanie doing?" asked Vince. "She was tanked!"

Winky Pagano stood silent, his right eyelid in a feverish twitch. An inner ire began to churn within his soul, having been publically betrayed by his mistress.

"Your father's in shock," spoke Mrs. Pagano with a barely perceivable tad of sarcasm. "His son's big night was ruined by his secretary." She ran a hand across her husband's reddened face. "Isn't that right, dear? There, there. You'll be just fine. Let's get you home."

"I'm so very sorry," exclaimed the club manager. "I'd like to offer our deepest apologies to the entire Pagano family."

"It's not your fault," said Vince.

"We weren't expecting anything so utterly distasteful to occur," whined the manager. "How those two delinquents got past the front gate is beyond me. There will certainly be an investigation, I can assure you of that!" He turned to the mound of glass on the floor. "Oh, my gorgeous spire. Look what they've done." Without saying another word he stooped down and began picking up fragments of glass.

"Mr. Pagano," butted in one of the news reporters with an extended microphone into the CEO's face. "What was that man talking about? Who is Dr. Schmidt and what wall is he trying to save?" His coworker aimed a video camera into the face of the destruction don.

"He has no comment," said Vincent politely. He put his hand around his father's shoulder and began to lead him away. "No comment. Isn't that right, Dad?"

Winky didn't answer.

"Mr. Pagano, a comment please," begged the reporter as he trailed the exiting entourage. "Where is this Franklin Wing? What about this so-called ghost?" The family circle closed tighter around their distraught leader. "Mr. Pagano... do you believe in ghosts?"

Mr. and Mrs. Pagano exited the club shortly after, their ride back to South Philadelphia uncharacteristically mute. It wasn't until their vehicle took the South Street exit of the Schuylkill Expressway that Mrs. Pagano spoke.

"I think I'll head back down to the shore tomorrow morning."

Ten blocks later, Winky pointed to a corner intersection, prompting his wife to stop. He got out from the passenger side of the vehicle.

"Drive safe," was his parting line.

Tommy Pagano Jr. waddled into his favorite watering hole and took a seat at the bar. Without speaking the bartender plopped a shot and a beer in front of his long-time customer. He proceeded to drink in hellacious fashion for two hours, until the barkeep pointed to an overhead television screen.

"Hey Tommy, you're on the ten o'clock news!" blurted the bartender with a laugh. "Ghosts? What the hell are they talking about?" Some drunken denizens of the pub began to cackle. "Tommy, why didn't you say anything? Hell, it looks like *you* saw a ghost!"

Pagano unleashed a loathsome string of profanity as he watched the cocky face of Seth Barber shouting at the camera. Beneath Barber ran a chyron stating: *"Local newsman leads effort to save wall in Philadelphia General's old Franklin Wing... Claims to have video evidence of physician who vanished there on nation's bicentennial."* Behind him stood the beautiful and enticing Stephanie, until she inexplicably dove out of sight. At the end of the news clip, Pagano stood up, exited the tavern and walked three blocks south. There he entered a low level gentleman's club and deposited his body on a stool next to a round table with a bowl of stale pretzels. The family elder pulled out a wad of cash from his front pocket and raised his hand high into the air. He subsequently drank himself into oblivion, surrounded by dancing women. Near the end of consciousness, they all looked like his Stephanie.

Just a few blocks away, another male Pagano was in the process of making a personal statement of his own. Vincent Pagano stared into the brown eyes of Jordan McCarthy and adored everything about her, the skyline of Philadelphia framing her beautiful face. The two had just completed dinner high atop a downtown terrace owned by Uncle Frank. Vince took a sip of port wine while listening to a violinist playing Vivaldi, from somewhere inside.

"That was absolutely delicious," declared Jordan with a napkin dab of her lips. "Thanks for the birthday treat." She looked over Vince's shoulder. "I love the way the clock on city hall lights up just a tad orange."

"Well, happy birthday. I wanted to make it a special evening. Sorry it started out a bit bizarre."

"You did make it special." She reached across the table and squeezed his hand. "My very own… most eligible physician."

"The cook is Uncle Frank's personal chef," countered Vince. "He runs a French restaurant downtown."

"My compliments to the chef."

"Indeed."

"Tell me more about Uncle Frank."

"Let's talk about you," countered Vince. "You're thirty-two years old today. Can you believe it?"

"Is he some type of underground kingpin? He looks and acts like one."

"Thirty-two is the new twenty-two. That's what they're saying nowadays."

"I mean, who are those guys hanging out with him all the time?" She grinned. "Spokespersons for the polyester cabal?"

Vince burst out laughing. He loved her sarcastic humor.

"I mean really. Plaid pants and white shoes? Someone needs to introduce them to the color wheel."

"Tony and Gus grew up in his neighborhood. Bloodlines run deep in South Philly. You know that."

"What type of work did Uncle Frank do?" She held out her glass for some more port. "And why does everyone call him, Uncle Frank?"

"Never you mind," answered Vince. "How does it feel to be so old?"

"A lot younger than you... you old fart!"

"Were you born a smart ass, or did it develop over time?"

"Hah, hah?"

"Listen," said Vince with authority. He stood up and rubbed both hands together. "Today's your birthday. So let's get the party going. Time for the presentation of the gifts."

"That's a weird saying." The port wine was starting to take hold of her mindset. "Presentation of the gifts... are we on a game show?"

"That was my dad's line on our birthdays. Good stuff."

"Your poor father," mumbled Jordan as she watched Vince walk away. "Betrayed by his own secretary." She looked over the terrace rail at William Penn, high atop city hall. "Vince, is anything going on between your father and Ms. Peacock?"

Vince disappeared into the penthouse apartment and proudly returned with a stack of carefully wrapped presents. One by one, he began to shower Jordan with a rainstorm of gifts, each bringing joy to her heart.

"What's this?" asked Jordan while fondling the final gift, a black box measuring about three by four inches in size. A single red bow held the lid tight.

"A new car!" shouted Vince.

She shook the box near her ear.

"Careful," said Vince with two extended hands. "It's fragile."

"Oh, really?" She bobbed the gift up and down, gauging its weight.

"You'll never guess," added Vince nervously. "Go ahead… try and guess. The box is deceiving. It's not what you think."

She stopped moving and looked deep into his eyes. He didn't flinch.

"Let's hear it," said Vince in a stone cold fashion. "What's your guess?"

"Nah, you wouldn't believe what I'm thinking." Her hands trembled as she slowly pulled the bow loose. "Not from the most eligible physician in the city," came the whisper. She opened the lid in hopeful anticipation.

"Surprise!"

"A dog biscuit?" She held a brown dog biscuit in the air. "Really, Vince. A dog biscuit?"

"It's a dog biscuit!" yelled Vince. "What can you possibly do with a dog biscuit?"

"Vince. Why are you shouting?"

Nothing happened.

"A dog biscuit!" yelled Vince again, now looking toward the terrace door.

Jordan took a nip of the biscuit. "Blah. Tastes like stale cardboard."

"What could you possibly do with a dog biscuit?" shouted Vince again in a loud tone.

"Are you O.K., Vince?" She looked over her shoulder. "Is someone else here? You're scaring the neighbors."

Nothing happened.

The physician stood up, turned around, held both hands to his mouth and hollered. "A dog biscuit!" He waved in the direction of the door. "For Pete's sake… NOW! Open the door!"

The sliding door to the penthouse slightly opened and out rushed a plump, yellow Labrador retriever puppy with a red collar. At first the dog appeared confused, but it spotted Vince and Jordan and began a clumsy dash in their direction.

"Vince!" shouted Jordan. "It's a puppy!"

The dog's butt got ahead of its frame causing it to tumble forward. The canine rolled and eventually recovered, continuing a charge in the direction of her new owners. A set of flapping ears framed a jet-black nose.

"Vince!" screamed Jordan as she dropped to her knees. The puppy ran into her extended arms. "Oh, she's beautiful." She cradled the pooch as it began to wildly lick her face. "Oh, her breath smells like a puppy."

The dog whimpered as its tail frantically wagged.

"I thought the apartment was getting a bit lonely," thought Vince. "You always said you wanted a dog."

"It's ours?"

"Yes, if you want her," replied Vince. "I mean we can always..."

"Of course I want her!" said Jordan as she dropped onto her back. The dog wiggled and rolled atop her chest. "Oh, you're so adorable! Look at your little red collar. Her nose is so cute!"

"I've always wanted a dog of my own," continued Vince. "Ever since I've been a kid... but my brother was allergic to fur."

"Vince! What's this?"

"Maybe we can call her, Barnyard. It sounds silly, but I've always wanted to name a dog..."

"Oh my god," stammered Jordan as she rose to her feet with the puppy in her arms. She slowly looked up at Vincent as if suddenly in a trance.

"What? You don't like that name? Barnyard? It's negotiable."

Tears began to well up in Jordan's eyes as she reached back down to the dog's collar. She slowly slid an attached ring from beneath the dog's neck to the top of its nape. A massive chunk of diamond set in a traditional pattern, twinkled in the twilight. The most eligible physician in Montgomery County dropped down onto one knee.

"Jordan Ally McCarthy," said the surgeon. He reached up and held her trembling hand. "Please make me the happiest man in the world."

Jordan began to cry.

"Will you marry me?"

Jordan squeezed the dog tight as she ran her index finger over the engagement ring. The few seconds that passed seemed like an eternity to Vince. She looked back down at him with a set of dazed eyes.

"Will you marry me?" asked Vince again, unsure if she actually heard the first request.

"YES! Yes! I'll marry you!" came the emotional reply. "I heard you the first time." She stood in shock. "I'll marry you! Yes! Yes! Yes!"

"Whew!" He stood up and pulled his fiancée and their new puppy into his arms. "I got a little worried there for a second."

"Oh Vince… it's gorgeous." She kissed him. "The puppy and the ring. I can't believe it! What a surprise!"

"You paused a bit there, Jordan. My heart skipped a beat."

"There was no pause," countered Jordan emphatically. "No pause at all. I love you, Vincent."

They hugged each other and strolled over to an outdoor sofa to sit down, the city of Philadelphia in full view. Vince slid the ring onto Jordan's finger. The puppy immediately fell asleep on Jordan's lap.

"Vince, before we go any further," stated Jordan. "We are *not* naming her Barnyard."

CHAPTER EIGHTEEN
THE CARDINAL RULES

"Ouch," winced Dr. Sullivan as his head hit off the desk of Zachary Schmidt. The impact caused his body to recoil backwards onto the floor. Bright lights beamed into his eyes until the silhouette of a man appeared. "Oh, that *really* hurt," continued Sullivan while rubbing his forehead.

"I've got to relocate that bloody desk," declared the man.

"Allister?" asked Sullivan. "Is your name, Allister Brooks?"

"At your service," answered the Brit with an extended arm. He helped Sullivan stand. "Easy now, take a few slow, steady breaths. You've just traveled through time." He wiped some grit off Sullivan's trousers. "Not an everyday occurrence."

Sullivan looked around at the cramped office, his eyes locking onto a wall calendar. It was June, but the year incredibly read... 2065.

"I made it." He quickly reached to his neck and felt the key. "*We* made it."

"Indeed," came the confirmation from Mr. Brooks. "But where's Dr. Schmidt?" He looked around the room as if to spot his body. "Didn't he transport with you?"

"No. Do you mind if I sit down?" asked Sullivan. "I'm a bit woozy."

"Surely." The host quickly slid a chair forward to help the physician sit down. "The speed of light will do that to a man. A spot of tea, perhaps?"

The magnitude of the moment overtook Sullivan as he dropped his head into his hands. "I can't believe what just happened." He looked around. "Is it really 2065 and am I inside the Pagano Orthopedic Institute?"

"Yes… and sadly, yes," answered Brooks. "The Pagano is a rather dreadful edifice that we still call home." He looked around. "You know, with the time portal situated here, it's kind of tough to relocate. Impossible, one might add." A concerned look came over his face. "Ahem. Yes. Perhaps once you've gathered your senses, you can you tell me exactly where Dr. Schmidt is? I'm actually fearful to learn of his whereabouts. The man's a bit of a rapscallion, you know… always talking about unfinished business back in time."

During the next fifteen minutes, and over an obligatory cup of tea, Sullivan summarized Dr. Schmidt's dilemma.

"Quite the quandary," quipped Brooks. "I must say, the 'time travel jet lag' caption is quite catchy." He finished off his tea. "Classic Zachary."

"You're aware of his medical condition?"

"Absolutely," came the reply. "My husband is the physician who administers his targeting agents. He's an Immunology professor at the University."

"Well then you certainly know that time is of the essence," stated Sullivan. He stood up and put a hand on his aching back. "Does your husband know about the time tunnel?"

"No. Only Zachary and I are aware of the portal. It's one of his cardinal rules of time travel."

"Cardinal rules? What cardinal rules?"

"The cardinal rules of Zachary Schmidt. He likes to coin terms and make lists, if you haven't noticed yet. One of the cardinal rules of the portal is stealth. To declare its presence is tantamount to its destruction."

"You haven't told your husband?"

"No, I have not. It's been difficult. But we've only known each other for a touch over three years now. We're newly-weds. Perhaps someday, I'll tune him in."

"How did you find out about it?"

"You need a co-pilot to safely traverse time," came the answer. "Zachary had his uncle, Rickard. I worked alongside both of them in the laboratory, so naturally, I came on board when Dr. von Steiger perished."

"I see."

"I was already situated in the future on July 4th, 1976." He checked his watch. "That was about three or forty years ago… depending on your vantage point." A pang of sadness overtook his otherwise upbeat persona.

"And back in time?" asked Sullivan. "Did you leave some-one back in time?"

Brooks' silence answered the question. He put on a tan bowler hat and patted the top of the cover firmly. "Away we go, Dr. Sullivan. Dr. Gordon Hayhurst has an office a few blocks south of here. Are you strong enough to travel?"

"Absolutely," replied Sullivan. "Thanks for the tea."

The duo exited the Pagano Institute onto 34th Street, the usual hustle and bustle of the city on display. Looking up, Sullivan immediately spotted the massive logo of the Pagano Orthopedic Institute, its lettering aesthetically too large in comparison to the building itself. The sun glared off the building's gaudy facade.

"I still can't believe it," mumbled Sullivan.

"Believe it. Welcome to 2065."

"Whoa," said Sullivan as he stopped dead in his tracks. "Where are the drivers?" He pointed to several fast-moving cars and trucks on the street, their driver seats empty.

"There are no drivers," came the reply. "Driverless tech-nology has long taken over the roadways."

"There aren't a lot of accidents?" The duo began to walk forward again, Sullivan a bit cautious as a driverless truck backed into a parking slot.

"Absolutely not," came the reply. "Operator error has been completely eradicated from the thoroughfares. It's a win-win situation, except for the plaintiff lawyers." He chuckled. "They lost their goose that laid the golden egg. No more fender benders." Brooks grabbed Sullivan's forearm and directed him across Spruce Street. "But they made up for their losses with..."

"Whish," shot a mechanical drone directly over Sullivan's head. The delivery device rapidly rose and disappeared over the roof of a building.

"Drones," laughed Brooks with a pointed finger overhead.

Sullivan looked up to see at least thirty or forty of the whirly birds in the sky, crosshatching the airspace between each building.

"Every once in a while, a pedestrian gets whacked in the noggin with a drone," said Brooks. "It bloody hurts. But even that's becoming more of a rarity."

"There are so many new buildings," stated Sullivan. He pointed to the skyline. "They're all massive."

"The population has exponentially grown over the past forty years," added Brooks. "So overhead space is now at a premium. Buildings nowadays are multipurpose." He pointed to a prominent skyscraper just ahead, at least seventy stories high, wedged between two hospital wings. "Take Pinetti Plaza, named after a Pulitzer Prize winning writer from North Philadelphia. It holds luxury apartments, a K-12 school system, retail stores, a supermarket, the children's hospital and believe it or not, the university's new basketball arena."

"What! That's where the Palestra used to be!" blurted Sullivan. "And where's Franklin football field?" He pointed down Spruce Street in the direction of the Schuylkill River, the iconic brick venue nowhere in sight. "It's missing!"

"Gone. Nobody plays football anymore. Too dangerous."

A sleek looking elevated train rocketed overhead.

"An el train?" spouted Sullivan. He craned overhead to catch a glimpse of the fast-moving transit, covered with shiny, reflective tiles. "That's new, and there's no graffiti on it!"

"Completely eco-friendly, too. Those are all solar panels on the outside of the train. I'm happy to report that we've made great progress in reversing climate change."

"What about all the underground subways... the Market-Frankford line?"

"Bike paths," answered Allister. "A rather beautiful scene down below. You'd think you're in Amsterdam. The entire subway system was converted about thirty years ago for bikes and recreation. The college students love it, especially in the winter."

Sullivan shook his head in amazement. "What's with all the cameras?" He pointed to a grid of video cams above an intersection. "Big brother watching?"

"No. Big data gathering," replied Allister. "Every inch of Philadelphia is under constant surveillance."

A slow moving and colorful robot passed by, its flat cargo bay filled with packages. "Pardon me," spoke the machine. "I'm making another on time delivery for your now profitable, United States Postal Service. Have a fantastic day."

"Drones, robots, artificial intelligence and green vehicles are commonplace," spouted Brooks with a pointed finger to a moving line of electronic cars. "The City of Brotherly Love is now a 'smart city', being efficiently run by the Internet of Things. Or the 'IoT' for short."

"The Internet of Things?"

"Yes, the Internet of Things."

"Which is?"

"The chap who coined the phrase defined it as the tipping point in time when more things or objects connect to the internet than people." The two men continued their walk down Spruce Street, their destination a block ahead.

"And that tipping point has occurred?"

"Yes. I'd say about thirty-five years ago, and it's still tipping. The so-called 'things to people' ratio tracks the growth of the IoT, which last year set another record at 10.5. Amazing."

"Interesting. So, what are these so-called 'things' that make up the IoT?"

"Car dash cams, home automation, wearable technology, sensor networks, computers, traffic lights and lamp posts. You name the product and it probably has a recording device inside." Brooks pointed to a large gateway at the base of the Pinetti complex. "There's our entrance."

"So they all record information and dump it on a cloud?"

"Yes. Smart cities use the real time data to improve transportation efficiency, balance power grids and monitor energy usage. It can track the environment, manage utilities, control supply chains and improve the cleanliness of our waterways." He stopped walking and looked at Sullivan. "Simply put, the city of Philadelphia is on autonomous control, for the betterment of us all."

Sullivan didn't respond but stared forward in amazement, his mouth agape.

"What?" asked Brooks. "You look aghast."

"Where are they?" asked Sullivan with a pointed finger.

"Where are what?"

"The cell phones?" came the reply. "Why isn't everyone walking around staring down at a phone?"

"Hah!" laughed Brooks. "Cell phones! A rather discourteous appliance of the past."

Sullivan held his palms up to the sky. "They're gone?"

"Indeed they are, a rather nasty environmental nightmare to boot."

"So, what replaced them? Something had to replace them."

Brooks looked directly into Sullivan's eyes. "Here's a clue. Your name is Dr. John Joseph Sullivan, born in Philadelphia in 1977, the brother to an older sibling named, George. You attended St. Joseph's Preparatory School and continued your schooling and medical training at the University of Pennsylvania. Currently you reside on the 43rd block of Spruce Street and specialize in the field of Geriatrics."

"Common knowledge," countered Sullivan.

"Your favorite color is green, you're the current president of the West Philadelphia Historical Society and you registered as an Independent in the last ten presidential elections." Brooks smiled. "Pistachio is your favorite ice cream, you're quite ambidextrous and in your free time, enjoy poetry."

"How do you know that?"

Brooks pointed an index finger to his eye. "The internet of things… feeding information to my smart lens."

Sullivan paused in an attempt to assimilate the suggestion.

"It's all on my contact lens," blurted Brooks. He slapped Sullivan on the shoulder and began walking forward. "Everything is in my eye."

"Are you kidding me?"

"No sir. Everyone is wearing a so-called smart lens. It took a bit getting used to, at least to my generation, but kids nowadays are born with a chip in their eyes. It's shocking what they can do with a couple of winks."

"So… the internet is in your eye?"

"Indeed it is. Web sites, stock quotes, incoming messages, outgoing texts and social media sites… even those annoying pickup truck commercials, all claiming to be the best in class. It's all in my eye, including a facial recognition of anyone standing directly in front of me."

"Wow. Now you're blowing me away."

"Once the chip identifies your face, a landslide of personal data shows up on my screen." He smiled. "I know more about you, than you know, Dr. Sullivan. Even your shoe size, a ten... double-E."

Sullivan stopped and grabbed Brooks' arm just outside the Pinetti complex. "If that's the case then tell me... am I currently married?" He spoke in a tone that dared Brooks to answer. "Now, in the year 2065?"

"Yes."

Sullivan's eyes grew large. "And my wife's first name is?"

Brooks shook his head in the negative. "Another cardinal rule, my friend," came the reply. "Another cardinal rule."

"Which is?"

"Do not delve too deep into the future, especially your personal life. It will utterly ruin the past."

"Karen Adams, is it Nurse Adams? Or perhaps, a Miss Gloria Gamble?"

"Come along," said Brooks. "Let's stay on point. We've got to get that medicine back to Zachary." He led Sullivan into the doors of Pinetti Plaza.

"Please... just tell me her first name. I beg of you."

A chaotic scene played out inside the vast lobby, as a swarm of people filtered by. Grade school children darted past medical personnel surrounded by senior citizens pushing grocery carts. Young couples walked their dogs through a Central Park like setting. Several members of a basketball team ran through the crowd, obviously late for practice. An occasional bike darted down a side ramp, disappearing into the subterranean underground. A hodgepodge of food eateries flanked the northern wall of the plaza. The combined din was deafening as Brooks steered Sullivan toward a long row of elevators. They stepped inside.

"Floor fifty, please," said Brooks to a young schoolgirl. She pressed the button.

On floor six the student got off. On floor twenty, an elderly attending physician wearing a long white lab coat got on, with a group of medical residents and students in tow. The scene brought a smile to Sullivan's face, the time-honored tradition of medical rounds still in place. The crunch of the crowd pushed Sullivan and Brooks to the back of the transit.

As the elevator rose, a resident looked at her attending and smiled. She whispered, "I'm actually thinking of going into geriatrics." The medical trainee paused. "It's between that and pediatrics."

"Geriatrics is a wonderful field," replied the elderly physician. "You just have to look for the little things. Be patient. That's the key to becoming a good geriatrician."

Sullivan immediately recognized his own advice and more importantly, the voice. His heart began to beat wildly as he attempted to peer over the crowd.

"My favorite mentor once told me his mantra for geriatrics," quipped the attending in sage fashion. "He called it the 3R's."

"Which is?"

"Respect, Renew and Rejuvenate." The doors to the transit opened and the medical herd disembarked. "His name was Dr. John Sullivan."

"From the Sullivan Institute?" asked the resident.

"Yes."

Sullivan went to step forward, but Allister held him back. As the elevator doors began to close, the attending physician turned nonchalantly to her left and looked back at the two men. A bemused look of distant recognition shot across her face. The black lettering on her white lab coat read: *Olivia Garcia, MD.* Beneath the name ran: *Chairwoman, Department of Geriatrics.* In an instant, the elevator doors shut close.

"Oh my god," muttered Sullivan. "That's my chief resident! I know her."

"No. That *was* your chief resident, John."

"But…"

"Cardinal rule, John. Thou shall not speak from the past."

"But I knew her. She recognized me. What if she said 'hello'?"

"Never identify yourself as John Sullivan from the past. Just mumble something about 'mistaken identity' and move along."

"But, what if I see myself? What if I turn a corner and run smack into Dr. John Sullivan?"

The elevator doors opened to the fiftieth floor.

"Play the doppelganger card," answered Brooks as he stepped out.

"Doppelganger?"

"Yes. Zachary taught me the word... German origin of course. It's defined as 'an apparition or double of a living person'."

"So, a clone?"

"Exactly. There are eleven billion people on earth, John... everyone has a double walking around out there."

The elevator emptied into an open lobby, the flat cut lettering on the wall proclaiming the Philadelphia General Department of Immunology. Brooks directed Sullivan to take a seat in the waiting area.

"I'll be right back," said Brooks. He walked through an unmarked door while waving at a receptionist.

Sullivan took a seat, surprised to see the waiting room of the future basically unchanged. He reached to his right and picked up a computer tablet, the screen immediately coming to life. The feature article read: *Dr. Gordon Hayhurst of the Philadelphia General*. A subtitle proclaimed: *Pioneers Breakthrough in the Treatment of Lung Cancer*. A picture of the physician stood proudly beneath the headline, the Department of Immunology logo over his right shoulder. Sullivan dove into the article that described the intravenous administration of a targeting agent specifically designed to incapacitate lung cancer cells. Hayhurst was widely credited with developing the crucial tweak to a long line of precursor drugs, the end product a single dose of genetically altered immunoglobulin, considered to be the greatest breakthrough in modern medicine over the past fifty years. Clinical trials at the Philadelphia General boasted a greater than 90% survival rate for those stricken by the previously lethal carcinoma. Treatment involved a single four-hour intravenous dosage, with few side effects. The column declared Hayhurst the frontrunner for next year's Nobel Prize in Medicine.

"Can it be?" whispered Sullivan to himself.

The door behind him opened and out rocketed Allister, with a look of painful resignation. "Let's go," snapped Brooks as he hustled out of the department. "Hurry." He looked back as if expecting trouble. Brooks spoke no more until the two men exited Pinetti Plaza, their pace brisk and in the direction of the Pagano Institute.

"Gordon can be quite the prig," growled Brooks. "One of his ugly spots. A stickler for rules and regulations."

"What happened?" stammered Sullivan as he tried to keep up with his host. "I can't get the transfusion?"

"He won't administer the drug to anyone other than Dr. Zachary Schmidt."

"Nor would I," countered Sullivan.

"He correctly pointed out that Zachary has missed his last several treatments, expressing concern over such inadmissible behavior."

"And?"

"He angrily pointed to some unused intravenous bags filled with his medication, both about to expire."

"So?"

"So, when he stepped out of the room to answer a call, I swiped one of the bags." He grinned and pulled a one liter I.V. bag out from beneath his shirt.

"Are you kidding me?"

"A man's life it at stake," barked Brooks. "Zachary's life!"

"You stole the medication!"

"A bit of a harsh description," countered Brooks. "I prefer to consider it a life-saving transfer of care." He grinned. "Let's just call today the official birth of time travel medicine. Hah! Zachary is going to love that play on words!"

"So, I can just take the bag back with me? Right?"

"Wrong," declared Brooks as he navigated his way across Spruce Street. "Cardinal rule. You can't carry any objects larger than a key through the tunnel."

"Why not?"

"Too risky. Even a blunt object at the speed of light becomes a lethal projectile. That's why Zachary wants it in your veins."

"But where are we going to do that?"

"Zachary's office," answered Brooks as he led Sullivan into the Pagano lobby. "Zachary keeps it well stocked. We'll pop an I.V. into your vein and be done with it."

The two men worked their way through the lobby and into an elevator, the only other occupant a burly hospital security guard. The doors closed and Brooks hit the button for the basement level. He nodded to the sentry.

Brooks looked back at Sullivan with a smile. "We're going to make it, old chap."

A sense of extreme accomplishment overtook Sullivan's heart. In a short period of time, he got an amazing peek into the future and the article on Dr. Hayhurst piqued his interest. He thought of his mother and began to slowly hum a tune, while reciting the words in his head... 'L-O-V-E... forever, just you and me'."

"What did you say?" asked the guard as he turned sharply toward Sullivan.

"I didn't say anything," came the defensive reply.

"You just sang a song," growled the guard with a pointed finger. "What song was that?"

"I'm not sure," stammered Sullivan. "I... I don't know the name of it."

"Where did you hear it?" demanded the sentry. "*Tell me!*"

"It's alright, Randall. He's with me," cut in Brooks. "A visiting professor."

"What's your name?" asked the law officer with an aggressive step forward. "Where's your visitor tag?" He scanned Sullivan's nape and quickly glanced back at Brooks.

"Ah, ah… Dr. John Sullivan," came the muted reply. "I'm on staff at the Philadelphia General."

"He said you were a visiting professor!" countered the sentry.

The elevator pinged and the door opened. Brooks spotted the guard eyeballing the necklace around Sullivan's neck. The top of the skeleton key was visible at the bottom of the chain, its lower outline in full silhouette beneath Sullivan's shirt. He tried to step between the two, but it was too late.

"The key!" blurted the hospital sentinel. He lunged forward and pulled Sullivan's collar apart. "The key! You have the key!" The guard shoved Sullivan into the wall. "Give that to me!"

"Let me go," whined Sullivan as the brute pushed him out of the elevator into the basement. "You're hurting me!"

"Randall!" hollered Brooks with a feeble attempt to ward off the assault. "He just arrived. I can explain!"

Randall Jones drove Sullivan into the ground and began to forcefully wrench the trinket off his neck.

"You're choking me!" garbled Sullivan. "You're choking me! I can't breathe."

"The key! The key!" shouted the sentry. "Give me the key!"

CHAPTER NINETEEN
UTTER BLISS

"Where in the world is John?" asked Attorney Fred Mills. "It's not like him to miss a meeting." He stood in front of the Historical Society on the second floor of his estate. "Wally, did you speak to his brother?"

"No," answered the Walrus Man. He stood up and turned to face his brethren. "But I did speak to his mother. She claims he left town on very short notice to attend a meeting."

"When will he be back?"

"She didn't know."

"Peculiar," countered Mills. "He didn't mention anything to me. By the way, how's Mrs. Sullivan coming along?"

"She's hanging in there," replied Wally in a reassuring tone. "A bit upset about the Brookside Pugs' middle relief pitchers, but otherwise fine."

"It's unlike John to leave the greater Philadelphia area," added Mills. "Especially with his mother being ill."

"Ping his cell phone," yelled the old timer from the rear.

"What exactly does that mean, Burt?"

"I have no idea, but I saw it on a crime show last night on television… caught the guy out in Vegas, having a good time with his secretary."

Some light laughter rolled through the group.

"Does anyone in here actually own a cell phone?" asked Mills.

A smattering of negatives rose from the crowd.

"I didn't think so," said the society president.

"Fred, no one here is below the age of sixty-five," declared Burt. "John's the spring chicken in the group."

"And he's flown the coop," squeaked the thin man in a sweater. "At the worst possible time."

"Alright," said Mills with a calm wave of a hand. "I'm sure John has good reason for being absent. That wall down in the Franklin means the world to him. We all know that."

"So, what's our plan?" asked Wally. "Where do we go from here?"

"Well, I've got some good news," boasted Mills. "My lawyer friend up in Scranton is very well connected in Washington. He's graciously agreed to draft a request demanding a judicial injunction to halt the Franklin Wing demolition."

"I thought we lost that battle?"

"We lost that battle to the corrupt local regime," came the reply from Mills. "But we're taking the fight to the next level… the federal judicial system." He took a deep breath and twanged the chest straps of his suspenders. "Sometimes, it's not what you know, gentlemen… but who you know. To my understanding, the legal request is going to be a slam dunk. It's going to be electronically filed in the District of Columbia tomorrow morning."

"Your buddy in Scranton better hurry," said Burt. "We're under the two-week mark."

"Secondly, in oh… about five minutes," continued Mills while checking his watch, "Seth Barber will be arriving to update us on his progress in coordinating a rally in West Philadelphia, to protest the destruction of the Franklin. As you know, Mr. Barber has a large following on the internet, his words capable of mobilizing equally minded activists of his ilk. He's anticipating a robust turnout."

"A rally? Who came up with that idea?"

"Mr. Barber," replied Mills. "He's done it before for other local causes."

"That was a darn good stunt he pulled out at that fancy-schmancy country club," interjected Burt. "It aired on the six o'clock news again last night. What's with this video evidence he claims to have of that guy who disappeared back in 1976?"

The doorbell downstairs rang.

"Well, that's probably the self-proclaimed Barber of Silverwood," said Mills with a nervous bob up and down on his toes. "How exciting! He'll gladly answer all of our questions." The society president walked downstairs to let the guest speaker in.

Over the next twenty minutes, Barber updated the club on his progress, noting that the country club caper had already paid off big time. He spoke in a manic tone.

"I've been contacted by several newspapers outside of the Philadelphia area," commented Barber. "All asking for my side of the story. We're getting some tremendous traction along the northeastern corridor."

"What about the *Chronicle*?" asked Mills. "Have they approached you?"

"No. Once I resigned, they cut ties with me."

"How about Pagano Destruction? Have they reached out?"

"Absolutely not," laughed Barber. "I don't expect to hear from them. If you want my personal opinion, that company is just a bunch of buffoons and brutes, blowing up buildings in a reasonably unsafe manner. Quite frankly, I'm surprised they're all still alive."

"So explain to me again this readership that you have," cut in Wally. "It's over the internet? People from the internet are going to demonstrate?"

"I blog under the pen name of the Barber of Silverwood," answered Barber. "It's a millennial thing. Nobody my age picks up a print paper anymore. We all roam the internet into the wee hours of the morning, trying to sate our short attention spans."

"And that's legal?" asked Mills. "Pontificating on any topic under an alias, immune to the standards of journalism?"

"Absolutely," came the response. "You can put up just about anything on the internet nowadays, thanks to the First Amendment. Now, I certainly developed a large following while writing for the *Chronicle*. That, I'll admit. But I will say, my readers are loyal."

"So, what do you blog about?" asked the man with the squeaky voice.

"The demand for social responsibility and clarification of who stands for what," came the reply.

"What the hell does that mean?" barked Burt from the rear guard. "I don't know what you just said." He gawked at his colleagues. "Did anybody understand that answer? Was it in some sort of secret code, young man?"

"No, sir," countered Barber. "Through my writings I try…"

"Does anybody know the name of the secret code used by the Nazis in World War II?" followed up Burt with a shake of his hickory stick.

"The Enigma Code," came the answer from the second row. "Too easy, Burt."

"Oh yea… well who broke the Enigma Code?" shot back Burt. He scanned the room, but no one replied. "Hah, you should all be ashamed of yourself."

"Alan Turing," answered Barber. "He broke the code, Burt."

Burt cocked an eyebrow at the youngster, a bit of a wise-acre in his mind. "That is correct, Mr. Barber. Perhaps, I underestimated you and your generation." The army veteran appeared to be flustered by the accurate response. "Now Mr. Barber, let's take it up a notch. Can you please tell us how Mr. Turing died?"

"Gentlemen," said President Mills. "Let's try to stay on course here. We've got our own mission to accomplish."

Barber remained silent.

"I didn't think you'd get that one," moaned Burt with a smirk. "I'll consider your first response a lucky guess."

"Alan Turing died after eating an apple laced with cyanide," countered Barber. "After being sentenced and subjected to a chemical castration by his own government, simply because of his sexual orientation."

The correct answer instantly stifled Burt.

"Wow," said Wally. "How do you know that?"

"So, his draconian sentence was similar to Dr. Zachary Schmidt," stated Mills. "Remember, Schmidt was headed for a state mandated lobotomy... before he vanished."

"That's a very interesting parallel," added Barber.

"So what exactly do you blog about?" cut back Burt in an attempt to redirect the discourse. "I didn't understand your answer the first time."

"I talk about the value of culture," answered Barber. "My commentaries dovetail into the need for diversity and inclusion along with the concept of ideas above things. These are critically important topics to men and women of my genre."

The room went silent as each man tried to digest the statement.

"For example," continued Barber. "Take my former job at the *Chronicle*. It was a disgraceful microcosm of how company culture can completely ignore the concept of work-life balance. Without engagement and purpose..."

"Ding-dong," rang the downstairs doorbell.

"Thank god," proclaimed Burt. "Saved by the bell."

"I wonder who that can be?" asked Mills with a stroke of his chin. "I wasn't expecting anyone else and all members are accounted for.... except for John."

"Maybe it's that ghost of Zachary Schmidt," scoffed Burt.

"That may be the news team," stated Barber.

"What news team?"

"Oh, I thought I told you," answered Seth. "I invited the KYX Investigative Team to do a story on the Historical Society and the Franklin Wing. I didn't mention that?"

"Ahem, no you didn't," replied Mills.

"Ding-dong."

"Is there a problem with that?" asked Barber.

"No. No," hesitated Mills. "But there is a protocol... I believe." He looked at the group. "Isn't there a form to fill out in regard to a member bringing a guest?"

"Are you talking about Bliss Bradshaw?" asked Wally in an excited tone. "The self-proclaimed spearhead of the KYX field team?"

"Absolutely!" answered Barber. "The one and only, Bliss Bradshaw. He used to date my mother."

"I see," stammered Mills. "And the purpose of inviting Mr. Bradshaw is?"

"To blow this story into the stratosphere," said Barber. "We've got to keep our positive juju going, and Bliss Bradshaw is the man to do it. Everybody knows him in Philadelphia. He agreed to do a story on the Franklin."

"Yes. I believe I've heard of him," said Mills with a glance upward. "But, perhaps a vote is in order. We have to respect protocol."

"Let him in," said Wally. "I'd love to meet Bliss."

"What's the problem?" shouted another member.

"Hell, it's a circus already," snarled Burt. "Why not let in another clown?"

Mills rolled his head to the left and right, as if empowered by the positive comments. "Any objection to letting a Mr. Bliss Bradshaw into the meeting?"

"No!" came the unified response.

"Alright then," followed up Mills. "Let's go admit Bliss." He excitedly walked downstairs with Barber at his side, to let in the well-known, local rabble-rouser. President Mills opened the door.

"Good evening! Bliss Bradshaw here, from the KYX Investigative Team!" spouted the reporter. Behind him stood a young woman staring at a cell phone and a man with a camera atop his shoulder. He reached to shake Mill's hand, the whiteness of his porcelain teeth forcing the club president to slightly squint. "If you've been hurt... let Bliss dig the dirt!" Bradshaw's head bobbed to the right and left while delivering his shakeup team's mantra.

"Yes... ah welcome," said Mills with a handshake. "Attorney Fred Mills here."

"Seth, so good to see you," said Bliss as he pushed past Mills, the investigative team in tow. "Let's light this candle, I've got to get over to the casino to emcee a celebrity roast."

"Great seeing you, Bliss. You look fantastic."

"I just got back from L.A.," said Bradshaw with an arm over Barber's upper back. "How's Mom?"

"Super."

"Tell her the Bliss-master says hello. I've been meaning to call her."

"Thanks for coming by," said Mills, now trailing from the rear. He followed the group up the steps. "It's an honor to have you here."

"Never fear... the Bliss-ter is here!" shouted the investigative journalist as he swaggered into the upstairs meeting room. His hair was thick for a man his age, dyed blonde and waved up front. He wore a pair of mauve trousers that strangely complemented a salmon stripped seersucker jacket. An audacious pink tie and polka dot handkerchief completed the ensemble.

"Mr. Bradshaw, thank you for supporting our cause," said Wally with an extended hand. "My wife adores you."

"You're a lucky man to be married to a woman with such impeccable taste," quipped Bliss. "What's her name?"

"Mildred."

Bradshaw's attaché immediately held out an 8 x 12 inch headshot of the local celebrity, his photo-shopped eyes an icy shade of blue. While autographing the keepsake, he scanned the room. "I'll stand here," he said to his female co-worker. He jutted forward a jaw. "How's the lighting?" He thrust the photograph in Wally's direction.

"Great," said Morgan. She pulled out a cosmetic case from her purse and began to apply some rouge to the reporter's cheeks.

"The West Philadelphia Historical Society has been in existence for more than seventy-five years... at this very location on Baltimore Avenue," boasted Mills. "The society was founded by my father, a prominent Philadelphian and attorney specializing in..."

"Stop," said Bradshaw with a raised hand. "Don't clog my brain with details." He looked at Barber. "Seth. Give me the top five talking points." He snapped his fingers rapidly while checking his teeth in a compact case mirror. "Talk to me!"

"The old Franklin Wing on the Philadelphia General campus is about to be razed. It contains a massive granite wall in the basement with a peculiar engraving. A medical doctor named Dr. Schmidt and a city policeman mysteriously vanished near the wall back in 1976. The case to date remains unsolved."

"Morgan, are you getting all this?" asked Bradshaw.

"Absolutely," replied his assistant as she scribbled each talking point down separately onto a series of large flash cards.

"Recent surveillance video shows a man with similar facial features to Dr. Zachary Schmidt," continued Barber. "Perhaps a ruse to segue into a ghost story? Some say the Franklin is haunted."

"And, Seth?" asked Bradshaw while straightening his tie. "The most important thing? You forgot the most important thing."

"Excuse me?" asked Seth, a bit confused.

"Who's the villain in the story?" followed up Bliss with a rapid forward roll on his finger. "The bad guy... our sacrificial lamb?"

"Oh, right," replied Barber. "Pagano Destruction. A family owned company that implodes buildings in the greater Philadelphia area. They've set July 5th as the drop date for the implosion... and we're trying to delay it."

"In order to save the wall?" asked Bliss.

"Absolutely."

"Alright. I think I have it," stated Bliss as he cleared his throat. "Old Franklin Wing ready to drop, a granite wall with a mysterious engraving, an unsolved missing person event coupled with a recent ghost sighting and our pigeon... Pagano Destruction." He looked around the room. "I'll need just two interviewees. Any volunteers?"

"I'm the president," shouted Mills with a step forward.

"Alright," said Morgan. "You'll go first."

"And I'm the vice president," added Wally.

"That's two," said Bliss. "Listen to my questions and keep the answers tight." He pointed at the Walrus Man. "Make your wife proud... understand?"

"Yes sir."

"What about me?" objected Burt. "I'm the club treasurer and most senior member of the group! I landed on Omaha beach on Tuesday, June the sixth, 1944... at exactly 1053 hours, underneath a firestorm..."

"Testing 1-2-3... testing 1-2-3," said Bliss into a handheld microphone. He looked at the cameraman.

"Wait a sec," interrupted Morgan as she stepped up to Bliss. "Your handkerchief." She nervously adjusted the prop in his upper suit pocket.

"Make sure it's a flat fold," directed Bradshaw.

"Perfect," said Morgan as she stepped back and held up the first flash card.

"Everyone else, gather behind me," ordered Bliss. The club members hustled behind his frame. "I only do one take! That's how the Bliss-ter rolls." He pointed over his shoulder. "Make sure they see the large map on the wall. I dig that map."

"Roger," said the videographer. "I'll need the guy with the cane to move a tad to his right." He waited a few seconds while peering into his eyepiece. "Good. We've got it." He held up a hand. "And 3-2-1... action." He pointed a finger at Bliss.

"This is yours truly, Bliss Bradshaw and the KYX Investigative Team coming to you live from the meeting house of the West Philadelphia Historical Society... good evening to all of our loyal viewers across the Delaware Valley!" His voice was firm and authoritative as he peered into the camera. As he spoke, his flashy smile somehow stayed in full view, a skill taking years to hone. "We've been summoned by these fine men standing behind me, many of them military veterans, to look into their gritty battle with the powers that be... to preserve a granite wall of invaluable historical significance, deep inside the bowels of the Philadelphia General's old Franklin Wing."

As he continued to embellish the details, the members of the historical society jostled for position behind their newly chosen mouthpiece. Each man craned forward, with an occasional glance at a small monitor to the left. A few of them silently lipped the flash cards being held up by Morgan.

"Their valiant efforts have been thwarted at every turn by the Pagano Destruction Company," continued Bliss. The Pagano name generated a series of grumbles behind the professional agitator. "Their noble fight for historical preservation of this newly discovered Philadelphia landmark was nearly extinguished... until they summoned the KYX team."

He reached out in the direction of Attorney Mills. "Now let's hear from the Historical Society's president and vice president, two men in charge of this honorable crusade."

Over the next ten minutes, Bliss Bradshaw spun an intricate web of intrigue, vilifying the Pagano Destruction team and glorifying the Historical Society's struggle for justice. He spoke of Dr. Zachary Schmidt and video evidence of his ghost reappearing in the Franklin Wing to thwart the pending demolition. He riled as to how a case involving two men vanishing into thin air forty years ago, could somehow remain egregiously unsolved to the current date. Near the end of his rant of hyperboles, a chant emerged from the old guard.

"Save the wall! Save the wall!"

"Sadly to date, our efforts to contact Pagano Destruction, have gone unanswered," finished up Bliss.

"SAVE THE WALL! SAVE THE WALL!"

"This is Bliss Bradshaw signing off from the hallowed halls of the West Philadelphia Historical Society and remember... if you've been hurt, let Bliss dig the dirt. Good night, Philadelphia." He gave a trademark wink of the eye into the camera.

"And cut!" shouted the cameraman. "That's a rap. Perfect!"

An avalanche of praise rained down upon the local celebrity, his performance by far the most exciting moment in club history. He signed a few more photographs and took a picture with Burt in front of the American flag, thanking him for his service. Then, as quickly as he arrived, the Bliss-master departed, amid a round of cheers.

"Godspeed, my historical friends!" shouted the showman as he was whisked away to his next performance venue across town. "Save the wall!"

"Bliss! Bliss! Bliss!"

Seth Barber arrived home several hours later, full of bluster and newfound vigor. He parked his car beneath an elevated rail line, along the southeast edge of Pretzel Park, in the

Manayunk section of town. He stopped at a liquor store to pick up a bottle of vodka and began a pensive walk through the park en route to his Silverwood flat. The light from a passing train eerily lit up the small village green, which due to the late hour, stood desolate. He opened the bottle of spirits and took a hearty slug. Halfway through the park he noticed two men standing just ahead, their midsections disproportionate in relation to their limbs. One of the men wore a porkpie hat.

"Seth Barber?" shouted one of the figures. "Are you Seth Barber?"

"Yea," snapped back Barber. "Who wants to know?" He took another sip of bravado. From behind he heard the sound of footsteps on gravel. The two men began a slow approach toward him. "Hey," laughed Barber. "It's the two fat bastards from the country club. Welcome to my..."

The first strike came from behind, the blow of the nightstick landing behind Barber's right knee, prompting his leg to buckle. He struggled to stand erect but a second blow across his upper thorax returned him to the pavement. He glanced up to see the third strike, a fierce right-handed cross from the man wearing the porkpie prop. The impact broke Seth's jaw and jettisoned the bottle of booze out of his left hand. He let out a tremendous wail but the din of a westbound train muffled his cry for help. The four goons began to repetitively kick his prone torso amid a hailstorm of profanity. The last thing the Barber of Silverwood remembered was his body being hoisted up and driven head first into the park's iconic structure, a large metallic pretzel perched atop an ornate Roman column. The impact generated a dull thud that resonated through his head.

CHAPTER TWENTY
BLOOD BROTHERS

"Uh-oh," whispered Dr. Schmidt, his voice dim and weak. "Ingrid, this can't be good."

Ingrid reached out and held his left hand as it protruded from beneath the afghan. The coolness of his extremity concerned her deeply. "Be strong, Zachary. Be strong." She covered his hand.

"Save the wall! Save the wall!" came the chant from the television set perched in front of Schmidt. *"Sadly, to date, our efforts to contact Pagano Destruction, have gone unanswered."* The camera slowly zoomed in on Bliss Bradshaw's face, his youthful appearance a tribute to his well-known plastic surgeon. *"Save the wall! Save the wall!"* The spearhead of the KYX Investigative team paused before delivering his trademark goodbye. *"This is Bliss Bradshaw signing off from the hallowed halls of the West Philadelphia Historical Society and remember... if you've been hurt, let Bliss dig the dirt. Good night, Philadelphia."*

"There! He always winks," commented Ingrid excitedly. "Did you see it?"

"Yes, my dear. Oh, how absolutely dreadful. They're drawing attention to the time portal. Dr. Sullivan will never make it back in time. I'm going to perish amid the mass hysteria."

"Have faith, Zachary."

"It's been a week already," bemoaned Schmidt. He took a few slow, labored inspirations. "I'm afraid I haven't much time."

The clocks in the house all chimed eight o'clock as a look of dismay overtook the physician's face. He clicked off the television and slowly stroked the cat at his side. Several moments of silence followed, the serenity shattered by a series of wild bangs on the front door. Ingrid stood up, straightened her skirt, and walked briskly into the foyer.

"Who can that be?" asked Ingrid.

"Perhaps it's Mr. Bliss Bradshaw," quipped the doctor.

"Open up!" came the cry from outside. "Open the door!"

She opened the door, immediately viewing the crazed face of Randall Jones. Behind him stood Dr. Sullivan with a look of forlorn.

"Where is he?" asked Jones as he rushed past Ingrid. "Is he still here?"

"I pray he's still alive," said Sullivan in an apologetic tone. "Hello, Mrs. Hoffman. Sorry I'm late. We ran into a stumbling block." He pointed at Randall's back.

"He's still alive," proclaimed Mrs. Hoffman while closing the door. "Did you get the infusion? Please tell me you did."

"Randall! What are you doing here?" asked an astonished Dr. Schmidt. "What's going on? How did you get involved in this mess?"

"How long have you been transporting people back and forth?" shouted Officer Jones. "You had the key all along! Why didn't you tell me?" He went to grab Schmidt but was taken aback by his frailty.

Schmidt slowly sat up and proceeded to respectfully recount the series of recent events, including the sudden appearance of Dr. Sullivan with the long, lost key. The details of his story corroborated with that of Allister Brooks, thus calming Randall's ire.

"That's the truth," finished Schmidt. "You have to believe me, Randall. I would never lie to anyone, especially you. I hope you understand."

"I believe you," came the response from the sentry. "That's exactly what Mr. Brooks told me. But it's 2020, Dr. Schmidt. The year is 2020!" Randall held both hands to his head. "I can't believe it! I want to be back in 1976."

"Randall, I'm sorry," stated Schmidt in a comforting tone. "The tunnel returns a traveler back to their entry point to include the additional passage of time. Which in your case, is greater than forty years."

"I know. I know. You've explained it a million times."

"Ingrid, please… a cup of tea for our weary travelers," requested Schmidt. "Gentlemen, do sit down." He looked at Sullivan and grinned. "Doctor, welcome back. What do you think of the future?"

"Thank goodness you're still alive," said Sullivan. He nervously approached the patient. "I thought we'd be too late."

"Well. I hope you have the antidote."

"Yes. I have it," answered Sullivan. "Thanks to Allister. He stole it from the medical clinic!"

"Oh, my Allister. The man's incorrigible," laughed Schmidt.

"But he warned me that I've only four hours to deliver the targeting agents into your veins, before it loses all potency," continued Sullivan. "And, I'm not sure how the tunnel affected that timetable."

"So, let's have a go at it," stated Schmidt with a new sense of purpose. "We've no time to lose." He forced his frame into a more upright position, prompting the cat to dart away.

"But how? How are we going to accomplish that?" asked Sullivan. He scanned the room. "There's no transfusion equipment in here."

"Doctor, what are they teaching you in medical school nowadays?" spouted Schmidt. "The PGH faculty should be ashamed of themselves!" He raised his feeble arms. "We have everything we need, right here in Ingrid's parlor."

Sullivan remained silent.

"The Father of Medicine himself, better known as Hippocrates, laid the foundation for what is about to occur."

"Oh, no," interrupted Randall. "Here we go again."

"What?" asked Sullivan.

"His tone of voice," replied Randall. "We're in for a lecture."

"The earliest transfusions known to man centered upon the four humors of Hippocrates," stated Schmidt. "Our medical patriarch felt that all illness was the result of an imbalance among those four humors."

"The four humors? I vaguely remember a lecture…"

"Blood, phlegm, yellow bile and of course… black bile." He chuckled before continuing, "And believe it or not, Hippocrates considered lust and arrogance risk factors capable of generating an overabundance of blood." He laughed heartily. "Can you imagine? If true, that would be the leading cause of death in today's society!" His laugh was infectious and brought some levity to the ongoing crisis. "Arrogance and lust… we'd have an epidemic!"

"Tea for our guests!" announced Ingrid with a serving tray in her hands. "And some windmill cookies."

"So, the practice of blood-letting and direct blood transfusions came into vogue to balance a patient's humors," continued Schmidt. "A rather standard procedure in an old-time doctor's repertoire."

Ingrid placed a steamy cup of tea in front of the speaker. He paused to carefully add a splash of milk into the brew. Sullivan stood amazed at his steely composure in the face of death.

"Of course, the seminal moment of direct blood transfusion occurred around 1908 or 1909, if my memory serves me correctly, in New York City." He took a slow sip of tea.

"When a well-known local surgeon stood helpless, watching his one-week old daughter, bleed to death." He looked up at Sullivan. "The poor child had been hemorrhaging from every orifice since birth. The situation was dire."

"So, he did a direct blood transfusion?"

"Yes. He had no other choice," replied Schmidt in a matter of fact tone. "She was bleeding to death."

"And it worked?"

"I believe the father's name was Lambert," continued Schmidt. "His colleague, a vascular surgeon named Carrel, performed the procedure. Dr. Carrel received the Nobel Prize a few years later."

"But did it work?" asked Sullivan. "Did they save the infant?"

"Yes. Dr. Carrel sutured the father's radial artery directly from his wrist to a vein in the child's leg. And, it was all performed without any local anesthesia, mind you. Immediately after receiving the blood from her father, the child's skin pinked up and the bleeding stopped." He shook his head in amazement. "It was later presumed to be a Vitamin K deficiency, which was rapidly reversed by the transfusion." He took another sip of tea.

"That's an amazing story."

"Indeed. Dr. Carrel returned to New York City to surprise the child on her 21st birthday. How tremendously fitting that he showed up." He took a bite of cookie. "I wish I could have been there."

"A heartwarming story," said Sullivan. "But how does that help us?"

"How does it help us?" repeated Schmidt incredulously. "Dr. Sullivan, the historical transfusion that I just described, occurred in the dining room of Dr. Lambert's own home... not in a hospital setting." He stood up and raised his arms high into the air. "So, let's recreate that historical moment, here... today, over one hundred years later, in the sitting room of Mrs. Ingrid Hoffman!" Schmidt's bodily gesture mimicked that of a carnival showman, pitching a bottle of his magical elixir. "Let's remake history!"

Sullivan mumbled one word, "How?"

"Me, you and gravity," came the upbeat reply. He slowly took off his sweater and rolled up a sleeve. "The process only requires donor-recipient proximity and quickness, to deter clotting." He glanced at Ingrid. "Ingrid, please fetch me your sewing case."

"What?" shouted Sullivan. "Are you crazy!"

"He's crazy," chimed in Randall. "Trust me. The man is crazy."

Ingrid reached behind the sofa and lifted up an old wooden sewing case. She proudly carried the ornate box to the other side of the settee.

Before Sullivan could object any further, Schmidt grabbed a cardboard box from beneath the sofa. He put it on the coffee table and opened the top. "Of course, I must confess that I've ordered a few things over the internet, in preparation for today's event," chuckled Schmidt. "Believe it or not, it took a whole two days for this apparatus to arrive." He lifted some intravenous tubing out from the box, along with several 14-gauge intravenous needles. "How horribly inefficient," mumbled Schmidt while untangling the tubing. "A big brown truck spewing toxic fumes consumed a quarter tank of fossil fuel just to get it here."

"Drones," said Randall. "Put your money in drones."

"Dr. Sullivan, would you be kind enough to come over here and place an intravenous line into my median cubital vein?" He began to open and close his fist, the maneuver dilating the subcutaneous vessel situated in the flexor crease of his right elbow.

Ingrid opened her sewing kit to produce a long elastic band about one inch wide. She wrapped it tightly around

Schmidt's upper arm, the makeshift tourniquet helping to further engorge the vein.

"You can't miss that one," joked Schmidt as he tapped the plump vein. "Ingrid, would you be kind enough to fetch me the rubbing alcohol from the medicine cabinet. We must abide by aseptic standards."

"Yes, Zachary."

"I don't want to put any pressure on you Dr. Sullivan," quipped Schmidt. "But a first-year medical student could hit that vein."

After cleansing the skin with alcohol, Dr. Sullivan expertly placed an intravenous catheter into the cubital vein of Dr. Schmidt. He then secured a plastic cap over the catheter's hub. "There," said Sullivan with a sense of accomplishment. He looked up at Schmidt. "Now, what about me? Where do we put my catheter?"

"One of two choices," came the reply. "Option one is your median cephalic vein and we let gravity do the trick. You'll have to stand high above me throughout the process. However, the risk of blood clotting is quite high. Ingrid would have to use her knitting needles to continuously roll the tubing."

"And option two?"

"Into your radial artery at the wrist," said Schmidt with a wince. "A bit more painful, but the pulsatile beat from your artery will certainly create a most favorable pressure gradient. The beat of your heart will surely deliver..."

"Use my artery," stated Sullivan without hesitation. "Let's make this work." He stepped up to Schmidt, extending his forearm. "Your life depends on it."

Ingrid prepped Sullivan's wrist with alcohol along the palm side. No tourniquet was required. Schmidt reached forward and felt Sullivan's pulse with his index and long finger.

"Strong pulse," said Dr. Schmidt. "I can tell you're a fit young man." He raised the sheathed needle in his hand. "Do you exercise regularly? How's your salt intake?"

"Do it," said Sullivan. He closed his eyes. "Just do it." The pain of the needle tip penetrating the arterial wall was intense, as if stung by an angry hornet, but the geriatrician held firm. He didn't move a muscle.

"Bulls-eye," said Schmidt. "Ingrid, tape it directly to the skin. Wow, what a pulse. It's been a while since I've put in an A-line. Reminds me of my intern days back at the PGH."

Sullivan opened his eyes to see pulsating streams of bright red blood surging out of the arterial line. Dr. Schmidt quickly connected the intravenous tubing to the arterial feed, the action sending a rush of blood through the short tubing, directly into Schmidt's vein.

"No signs of clotting," stated Schmidt as he watched his colleague's blood surge directly into his arm. He grinned with a sense of accomplishment.

"We did it!" shouted Sullivan. "It's working!"

"Indeed," said Schmidt. "We've recreated the magical moment that saved a young child's life over a century ago." He looked up at Sullivan. "But now it's my life being saved! Thank you, doctor."

"You're welcome," replied Sullivan. "I can't believe it! It works."

"Never doubt the laws of physics."

"I've seen enough," interrupted Randall with a look of horror. He turned his gaze away and sat down. "Do you know what this makes you two?"

"What?"

"Blood brothers," came the answer. "You two are blood."

"The absolute definition of blood brothers," added Schmidt.

"How much is enough?" asked Sullivan. "When do we stop?"

"I'd give it about twenty minutes," came the estimate. "Or whenever you pass out... whichever comes first. I just need enough targeting agents to get me upright and back into that tunnel. After that, my time travel days are officially over."

"I concur," stated Sullivan.

The transfusion ended twenty minutes later, when Schmidt's arm began to engorge, and Sullivan's face turned a pale shade of grey. Both catheters were pulled and pressure was applied to each participant's site of entry.

"I'd hold pressure over that artery for a solid fifteen minutes," stated Schmidt to his colleague. "I'd say you've donated about a unit and a half of blood." He stood up and took a deep breath. "I feel better already!"

"You should," said Sullivan. "I just filled up your tank."

"That's it," spouted Randall. "You two are creeping me out." He looked at Ingrid. "Mrs. Hoffman, may I take a rest somewhere? I've technically been up for a few years. I'm exhausted."

"The guest room!" shouted Ingrid with a spry jump to her feet. "I will prepare it."

"We insist that you stay with us," added Schmidt to the former Philadelphia policeman. "Until we transport back."

"I'll stay," said Randall as he followed the host down a corridor. "But I'm not going back, Dr. Schmidt. Not in a million years. Sorry." He lumbered down the hallway. "And by the way... I have the key."

The two physicians sat quietly in the room, the methodical tick of the clocks soothing their souls. Ingrid returned with some orange juice for Dr. Sullivan and she pulled out an old phonographic record. The audible scratch of the needle on the spinning disc added to the serenity. The hostess dimmed some lights.

"Ah," whispered Schmidt. "J.S. Bach, from the town of Eisenach." He closed his eyes as the music filled the room. "Time for the thinking game."

"Zachary prefers Bach, but not me," stated Ingrid with conviction. She took a chair opposite the two men. "Johannes Brahms is my favorite German composer. A citizen of Hamburg." She closed her eyes.

Sullivan sensed a spirited discussion about to occur.

"Hah!" spouted off Schmidt with his eyes still shut. "A bit too academic if you ask me… Brahms that is."

"Shame on you, Zachary. Johannes was a master of counterpoint and he held firm to Germanic tradition." She waited for a rebuttal, but there was none. "A touch of romantic motif is exactly what Bach lacked."

"Ingrid. You're upsetting our guest. It's thinking time," stated Schmidt. "The thinking game."

A sense of calmness overtook Sullivan in a manner he had not experienced in years, the music creating a buffer of solitude. For the next several minutes he either fell asleep or reached nirvana, the end result being the same… that of an idyllic place. He dreamt of playing catch with his father in the back yard, the smell of his new baseball glove, leathery and fresh.

"How does it feel?" shouted his dad from across the yard. He just delivered his trademark underarm fastball.

"A little stiff," came the reply as the ball audibly popped into the mitt.

"We'll oil it later," came the advice from his father. "And tie a shoestring around it with a ball inside. That's an old trick."

"Thanks, Dad."

"John. What are you thinking?" asked Schmidt, his mind also in a tranquil state.

"What did you say, Dad?"

"I said, what are you thinking, John? We're playing the thinking game."

"He's dreaming," said Ingrid.

Sullivan opened his eyes and looked around the room, slowly blinking his eyes in order to recalibrate. "I'm sorry. Did someone just ask me a question?"

"Yes," said Schmidt. "I asked you a question. What are you thinking about right now… at this very moment?" Both he and Ingrid kept their eyes closed.

"What am I thinking?" said Sullivan. "I'm thinking about who was the first owner of that skeleton key hanging around Randall's neck? You know, the one with the initials 'R.S.' embossed directly on it. That's what I'm thinking. Perhaps someone in the room can tell me?"

Ingrid opened her eyes to peer at her nephew, but Schmidt didn't flinch. The music continued for another minute.

"That's a very old key, John," declared Schmidt. "I'm sure you know that. It dates back hundreds of years."

"I know that, but who is R.S.? Your uncle?"

"No. Another person with those initials owned the key, well before Uncle Rickard."

"And his full name?"

No response.

"Was he or she aware of the time portal?"

"Perhaps."

"Did they etch that saying into the granite wall?"

"Maybe."

"Why won't you just tell me his or her name?"

"Zachary has to make a game out of everything," interjected Ingrid. "Remember, we're still playing his famous thinking game. He's not going to divulge the answer without forcing you into thought."

"Uncle Rickard taught me the thinking game," retorted Schmidt proudly. "I firmly believe it provides a mental edge to those who participate."

Sullivan just stared at the two, their faces serene and their bodies motionless. "How about a hint?" asked Sullivan. "Do the rules of the game allow a hint?"

Zachary opened his eyes and slowly turned toward Dr. Sullivan. "You want a hint?"

"Absolutely."

"Alright. I'll give you a hint." He closed his eyes and looked forward. "Have you heard of the Declaration of Independence?"

"Ah, yes. I am aware of that announcement," came the reply in jest.

"The historical document signed in the City of Brotherly Love by the Second Continental Congress on July 4th, 1776?"

"Yes. That's the one I'm familiar with," said Sullivan. "Why? Is there another one?"

"No."

"So? What's the hint?"

"The Declaration was signed in the Assembly Room of Independence Hall, in downtown Philadelphia. Have you ever been there?"

"Not since my eighth-grade class trip. But I remember it well. It was a bit hot and musty."

"Do you know how many people signed that document... the Declaration of Independence?"

"No. Is this a quiz?"

"A total of fifty-six signatures graced the proclamation."

"Is that the hint?"

"No. Here's the hint." He reopened his eyes and looked directly toward Sullivan in a coy manner. "R.S. was one of those fifty-six men who signed the Declaration of Independence." He turned his gaze forward. "How's that for a hint?"

"Too easy!" blurted out Ingrid. "You're slipping, Zachary. A child in grade school can figure that out."

"The key is that old?" asked Sullivan. "Wow!"

"Now, to be fair, I will say that more than one man with the initials R.S. signed the document." He grinned. "There's the twist in the clue. It's your job to figure out which one."

"I can only think of Thomas Jefferson and John Hancock," said Sullivan.

"Nope. Not R.S.," said Schmidt. "You've cut it down to fifty-four. Congratulations. You're on the right track. Keep thinking."

Sullivan laughed. There was indeed something mystical and charming to the man whose life he just saved. He certainly was from another place and time.

The shrill of a cell phone shattered the stillness of the Hoffman homestead. Sullivan pulled the cell out of his pocket to see an incoming call from his brother. He answered the call.

"John! Where the hell have you been?" railed George Sullivan.

"Ah, didn't Mom tell you?" stammered Dr. Sullivan. "I had a conference..."

"Why haven't you been answering my calls?"

"Ah, you see... the battery on my phone went dead and I can't seem..."

"John, I don't know where you are, but you better get back into town soon. Mom has taken a horrible turn for the worse."

"What? Oh no!" He stood up. "Is she alive?"

"Barely. Get home now, John! This very instant... if you want to say good-bye."

CHAPTER TWENTY-ONE
THE PROPHECY

The first thing Sullivan noticed while sprinting up Spruce Street was a 'For Sale' sign in front of Perch Peterson's home. He looked up to see the light on in his mother's front bedroom, the silhouette of his brother at a standstill. He prayed he made it in time. Just inside the front door, he ran into Nurse Ella.

"Oh, Dr. Sullivan. She doesn't look well," blurted Ella as she carried a load of soiled linen on the way to the basement.

"Is she alive?"

"Yes… but unresponsive." Moses rocketed out from beneath a chair. "You old crazy cat!" hollered the nurse.

He took the stairs three at a time and bolted into the front bedroom. There, sitting on the side of the bed, was a hospice nurse. George Sullivan stood to his mother's right.

"Faint and shoddy," said the nurse with her hand on the patient's pulse. She wrapped a blood pressure cuff around Mrs. Sullivan's right arm and pulled out a stethoscope.

"What's happening?" said John. His mother was ashen white and gaunt, her respirations irregular and shallow. Her eyes were closed and her mouth open.

George Sullivan just shook his head in the negative while staring at his brother. They waited for the nurse to speak.

"Eighty-five over fifty", stated the nurse. She took a deep breath and looked at Martha's two sons. "Well?"

"Well what?" snapped John. "What's going on, Janice?"

"She stopped eating," said his brother. "Stopped drinking. She hasn't gotten out of bed in four days. She lost consciousness today."

The doctor approached the bedside saying, "Mom. It's John. Open your eyes." She didn't respond. "Mom! Open your eyes!" He rubbed her sternum with his knuckles, the maneuver eliciting no response. He put a hand on her dry cheek. "She's dehydrated." He looked over his shoulder to see Nurse Ella return. "Has she been urinating?"

"Her diapers have been pretty dry," replied the caretaker. "It doesn't surprise me. She's hasn't been drinking at all... been giving her food to the cat."

Sullivan looked back at his mom. "Mom. Wake up! The Pugs are on. It's the seventh inning stretch. Time to stand up."

She didn't respond.

"I stopped over to see her last night," said George.

"Did she recognize you?"

"Yes, barely. She told me to let her die." He paused. "She wants to go, John."

"What about an I.V.?" asked the physician. "She's dry as a bone. Let's get her hydrated."

The hospice nurse didn't immediately respond and took a deep breath. "Dr. Sullivan, we're at the doorstep. An intravenous line is just going to delay the inevitable. When I saw her earlier this week, she begged me for no more heroic measures."

Before Sullivan could respond, Nurse Ella chimed in. "She told me the same thing, too."

"A liter of normal saline solution is *not* a heroic measure," retorted the doctor. "It's the humane thing to do. We can't just let her shrivel up like a potato chip." He looked at his brother. "George, talk to me."

"It's your call, John. You're the health care proxy. I'll abide by your decision."

"Put in an I.V.," ordered the doctor in a stern tone. "It's not like we're giving her antibiotics or cardiac vasopressors. We can't let her die this way!"

The nursing team quickly responded to the medical power of attorney. Within two minutes, an intravenous line was dripping normal saline solution into her vein.

"Open it wide up," said Sullivan. "How many liters do we have here?"

"Five," said the hospice worker. "That should do it for the night." She checked her watch. "I've got another family across town asking for me. Do you mind if I leave you two alone with Mom?"

"That's fine. Thank you, Janice," said John in a slightly apologetic tone. "We appreciate all you've done. It's just that, it's my mother, and..."

"Dr. Sullivan... George, I completely understand. This is your one and only mother. You've both taken excellent care of her so far. You have to be comfortable with her last few days. That much I know," stated the nurse. "I respect your decision."

"Thank you, Janice."

"Good night, Ella," said the caretaker as she left. "Thanks for your help."

Ella completed her duties and left the two brothers alone, on opposite sides of their dying mother. Moses wandered into the room and hopped up onto the bed.

"Who gets the cat?" quipped John as he stroked his mother's hand.

"You get the cat. I've got Aiden."

The number 42 bus rumbled down Spruce Street, it's tonnage rattling the aged windows of the family estate. Downstairs the parakeet could be heard chirping.

"The Peterson house is for sale," said George.

"Yea. I saw the sign."

"Perch just took a few of his mom's personal things. Everything else went to the Salvation Army."

"Wow. That was fast."

"I'm at peace," said George. "I said my good-byes last night. I had a strange feeling it would be our last conversation together." He blinked his eyes rapidly. "She was a good mom."

"The best."

"She wanted me to tell you… that she loved you," said George. "Just in case you didn't make it back in time."

"Anything else?"

"That she was proud of everything you've accomplished in life."

John Sullivan didn't ask any more questions. He choked up as tears began to roll down his cheeks.

"You took fantastic care of her, John. In the end, that's what matters."

"I suppose," came the weak reply.

"What? You think we could have done more?"

"No… I mean it's inevitable." He wiped away the tears. "She can't go on forever. Dad went in a flash, but watching Mom fade away hasn't been easy. Her mind was sharp."

"I agree, but she's ready."

"I know." He took a deep breath. "It's just that I had this crazy dream the other night. That at this very moment, an old-time doctor that she worked with at the Philadelphia General would waltz into the room with his black bag and deliver a life-saving antidote." He frowned. "Old Doc Schmidt was his name." He let out a heavy sigh. "Good old Zachary."

"What did you say?"

"I said… good old Zachary. That was the doctor's first name. He worked with Mom back in the day."

"John, Mom mumbled the word "Zachary" last night. Just before losing consciousness," said his brother.

Dr. Sullivan froze.

"In fact, she asked for Zachary. That's strange. I just thought she was, you know… kind of out of it."

"What? What did she exactly say?"

"She mumbled 'where's Zachary?' and then said something about 'knowing you would always return'."

"Oh my god," said Dr. Sullivan. He looked at his mother and then his brother. "I don't believe it… the dream and now you're telling me this."

"Who's Zachary?"

"An amazing medical doctor who used to live in the basement of the Franklin Wing. Zachary Schmidt. He worked with Mom for years. Remember? He disappeared on July 4th, 1976… in the Franklin Wing."

"Oh no," shouted his brother with a set of raised hands. "Don't go there, John. Not the Franklin Wing. Not tonight!"

"George! Don't you see? It's a prophecy."

"John, I don't know where you've been, or what you've been doing. But I've heard enough." He began to walk away from the bed. "Do not drag Mom into your obsession with that building." He put his hands on his head. "Listen to what you're saying! A prophecy? Are you insane? Mom's dying!"

A crazed look of conviction appeared across the doctor's face. "No, George. I disagree. Mom is exhorting me to act. Don't you see? I can't let her down. Not now. Not at this moment."

"What? You're going to dial up a doctor who's been missing for forty years? Is that it, John? Maybe he still has his beeper on? Listen to yourself! *Have you gone mad?*"

"Where's Aidan?"

"Asleep, down the hall. Why?"

"So, you can stay with Mom?"

"Of course I can stay with Mom. We moved in last night, expecting the worst. John, are you alright? I mean is there anything you need to talk to me about? You look a bit ragged."

"George, this will all make perfect sense in due time, but I have to leave... immediately."

"How can you leave with Mom ready to die? You're the health care proxy."

"Promise me one thing. Keep hydrating her." He pointed at the I.V. bag. "Don't stop the fluids! Once she gets hydrated, she'll perk up. Trust me."

"But John..."

"Keep the fluid running, George. Giving someone food and water is the definition of comfort care." He reached forward and put both his hands on his brother's shoulders. "Understand?"

"No. I don't understand. She's going to die."

The doctor turned and sat down close to his mother. He gently stroked her forehead. "Mom. It's John. I want you to stay strong. George is going to keep the fluids running." He waited for a few seconds. "I love you very much. Thank you for taking care of me." He gave her a long hug. "I'm going to see if Zachary can help. O.K.?"

She didn't respond.

"I'll be back as soon as I can," said Sullivan as he began to dash out of the room. "It may be a day or two."

"John! John! Are you crazy?"

Sullivan stopped short of leaving and turned back. "George, one more thing. Can you please Google anyone who signed the Declaration of Independence with the initials R.S., and then try to connect them to Philadelphia and the..."

"The Franklin Wing, John? Is that what you're asking me to do... connect them to the Franklin Wing?"

"Yes! Thanks," shouted Sullivan as he turned and ran away. "Keep her hydrated, George."

Sullivan sprinted back to the Hoffman house and rapped on the door. Dr. Schmidt answered.

"Good evening, John. I knew you would be back."

"You visited her in the hospital. Right?"

"Who?"

"My mother."

"Yes, I did," came the calm reply. "After dropping you off at the admission's office with a head injury, the secretary told me that your mother was an inpatient. Apparently, she was a friend of the family. So naturally, I made rounds on Martha that evening. You're aware that I am the primary care physician for the Sullivan family." He put his hand on John's shoulder. "I circumcised your older brother."

Mrs. Hoffman appeared behind her nephew with a proud smile.

"As your mother's primary care provider, I had an obligation to check on her status. So yes, I visited her that night."

Sullivan couldn't believe what he was hearing.

"It felt so good to make rounds again in the Philadelphia General. I felt like a resident again, grinding out another night of call. Ah, the good old days."

"She's dying from lung cancer."

"I know… and that's why you're back. You want to save her."

"Perhaps, but I…"

"Martha wants to die. She told me so."

"Was she happy to see you?"

"Elated. It was like an old Franklin Wing reunion. She was still sharp as a tack. Mom was a fantastic nurse. Oh, we talked for hours."

"Go get the key from Randall."

"I've got it already," said Schmidt. He reached beneath his shirt and delivered the skeleton key. "Randy's out stone cold. He's never going back."

"Can you travel now?"

"I have to," said Schmidt with a heavy heart. "I've gotten a bit of energy from the transfusion, but not a lot. I'm afraid my time on this side of the tunnel is limited. So, I'm glad you've returned. It's best I take leave now, before it's too late." He briefly looked back at Ingrid before continuing. "John, can you give me a minute or two to say goodbye to Ingrid?"

"Sure," answered Sullivan as the door closed. A minute later a car pulled up in front of the house with its flashers blinking. The driver stared impatiently at Sullivan.

"Godspeed," said Schmidt as the door reopened. "Until we meet again." He hugged Ingrid one last time.

"Farewell, my dear Zachary," came the stoic reply from Ingrid. "Thank you for the visit... gute reise."

"That's German for 'have a nice trip'," explained Schmidt as he walked away. "Ah, my driver has arrived!"

"He's waiting for you?" asked Sullivan.

"Sure. I called an Uber," quipped Schmidt. "Get with the times, John."

"I'm a bit confused with the concept of time.

"How many more days before the implosion?" asked Schmidt as he slid into the rear of the vehicle, somewhat short of breath. "You have to be careful to make it back in time."

"Ten days in 2020 time," came the nervous reply. He slammed the door. "I can be back in no later than nine days, which puts me on July 4th."

"That gives you about eight hours in 2065," said Schmidt. "You can't dilly-dally, John. Promise me that."

"I promise."

The ride to the Franklin Wing was brief, yet it was apparent that Dr. Schmidt's physicality was in a rapid decline.

"We better hurry," said Sullivan as he helped the doctor out of the car. Dr. Schmidt's respirations and ability to ambulate were suddenly impaired.

"Perhaps Mr. Washington can be of assistance," said Schmidt as he put his arm around Sullivan's shoulder. "Reginald has been on guard faithfully, since 1974... a remarkable young man." Schmidt let out a moan. "Oh, doctor. I'm afraid the targeting agents are wearing off." They paused for several seconds before continuing forward.

Reggie Washington was indeed manning his post at that very moment, his reaction euphoric upon seeing the two physicians.

"Dr. Schmidt! Dr. Sullivan! What are you two doing here?" asked the sentry. His enthusiasm turned to concern as he watched Dr. Schmidt struggle with each step. "What's wrong?" He grabbed a wheelchair and steered it behind Schmidt, helping to lower his frame into the seat. "Are you alright, Dr. Schmidt?"

"Yes. Yes. I'm perfectly fine, Reginald. How's Mrs. Washington?"

"She's well."

"Did she try that turmeric that I recommended for her rheumatism? Did it help?"

"She did, doctor. And it did help. Thank you for the advice."

"Remember, two teaspoons after breakfast and dinner," followed up Schmidt with a pointed finger in the air. "And have her rub some witch hazel on that sore knee. Witch hazel is a magical elixir."

"Reggie, we've got to get Dr. Schmidt back into the Franklin basement immediately, before it's too late."

"Roger," said Washington without question. He began to push the transport forward.

"What in the hell is going on here?" came a stern voice from behind. "John. What are you doing?"

The trio looked back to see Dr. Vince Pagano standing several feet away. He wore blue shorts and a short sleeved, seersucker shirt.

"Vince. What brings you out tonight?" stammered Sullivan. He stepped slightly in front of Dr. Schmidt.

"What brings me out? Well, let's say I just got a hysterical phone call from a woman named Stephanie Peacock," replied Pagano as he eyeballed Dr. Schmidt.

"Stephanie Peacock?"

"Yea. She's my dad's personal secretary."

"Oh."

"It seems that Miss Peacock is holding a vigil at the side of Seth Barber's hospital bed."

"Seth! What happened to Mr. Barber?" asked Sullivan.

The conversation was interrupted by a fitful coughing spell from Dr. Schmidt.

"Excuse me," mumbled Schmidt. "The humidity seems to be getting the best of me." He held a hand to his chest and began to wheeze.

"I'm not sure what happened to Mr. Barber," answered Pagano. "He may have fallen. But he has multiple fractures and a broken jaw, yet despite the pain, he keeps mumbling about the Franklin wall. The goddamn wall that everyone is all of a sudden squawking about. Why is that, John? Why is everyone talking about this wall?"

"Ah, I'm not exactly sure," answered Sullivan.

"Well, neither am I. So that's why I've decided to drop by and check things out for myself." Pagano grinned. "Funny meeting you here."

"I see," said Sullivan.

"Stephanie swears she watched a video showing you and another man appear out of nowhere, directly in front of the wall."

"*That's my video*," snapped Sullivan. "Who has it?"

"Someone stole it from her van. It's gone."

"Dr. Sullivan, excuse me... but we best keep moving," implored Reggie. "Dr. Schmidt doesn't look well."

Washington's medical assessment was quite accurate. Dr. Schmidt's face was turning a peculiar shade of blue and his eyes began to flicker backward in an eerie fashion. A rolling tetanic contracture took hold of his right hand.

"Zachary!" shouted John. "Zachary! Take a deep breath!"

Schmidt appeared to recognize his voice but appeared incapable of breaking the fit. He raised his left arm in the air.

"Let's go, Reggie," stated Sullivan.

"Is that the man who appeared out of nowhere with you?" asked Pagano as he began to follow the medevac team forward.

They didn't answer.

"Stop!" shouted Pagano. "Where do you think you're going?"

Sullivan and Washington frantically pushed the convulsing doctor forward, prompting Pagano to jump directly in front of them, ten feet from the Franklin Wing entrance.

"Who is this man?" asked Pagano again. He pointed directly at Schmidt. "And why are you rushing him into an abandoned building?"

"The cardinal rules!" gasped Schmidt.

"What's he talking about, John?" asked the orthopedist. "You're not going in there until I get an answer. Talk to me, John!"

Schmidt began to shake violently.

"That's it, I'm calling 911!" blurted Pagano. He pulled out his cell phone.

"No. Stop!" said Sullivan. "I can explain."

Vince slowly put the phone down to his side. "Start talking. What's so special about this wall, John? The implosion is just ten days away. So if you've got something to say... say it now."

"I'll talk, as long as you allow us to keep moving forward," urged Sullivan. "I've got to get this man inside... or he's going to die."

Pagano mulled his options, realizing that a firestorm was brewing in the press regarding the wall. He needed answers.

Earlier in the day his father expressed morbid angst in regard to the situation at hand, including hints of a federal injunction to shut down the project. Slowly the physician reached into his right front pant pocket and pulled out an I.D. card. He took three steps backward and swiped the card through a security slot. The buzzer rang and the double doors swung wide open.

"Thank you," said Sullivan as he and Reggie pushed their patient forward. "Thank you so very much."

"Start talking," ordered Pagano as he trailed the wheelchair into the dimly lit corridor. "What's going on here?"

"Can I ask you two questions, Vince?" countered Sullivan. "Two very important questions?"

"Sure," came the reply from the surgeon.

"First of all, can you call your fiancé and tell her that you'll be gone for a few days... perhaps on a retreat to a Zen monastery up in the Catskills? You know, kind of off the grid to do a little soul searching?"

"That's a bizarre request, John. What's the second question?"

"Do you believe in the concept of time travel?"

CHAPTER TWENTY-TWO
OPERATION FIRECRACKER

Just across the Schuylkill River the inner circle of the Pagano Destruction team gathered around Mayor Chubb's desk. The lights of Philadelphia outlined the city leader's frame as he nervously rocked back and forth in his chair.

"He's late," moaned the mayor while checking his watch. "My wife is going to kill me if I don't get home in forty minutes. Her mother is in town."

"Uncle Frank is never late," said Attorney Pompano with an extended hand. "The meeting starts when he arrives."

"Who called this meeting?" moaned the mayor.

"I did," came the terse reply from Attorney Pompano.

"Why? What's the emergency?"

"We've got problems with the Franklin."

Tommy Pagano Jr. sat speechless to the right of the mayor's desk, his eye now in a furious flutter. To his left stood Rocco, rubbing his meat hands together as if trying to pulverize a golf ball. His biceps flexed with each turn of a palm. To Tommy's right sat Big Bart Little with a lollipop in his mouth. Next in line was Ralph Covington, the Philadelphia General's chief executive officer. Behind the mayor stood city inspector Freddie Freeman, gawking at the street below.

"Where's the judge?" whimpered Tommy. "Why isn't he here?"

"The judge is over in Italy," replied Pompano. "Lucca to be exact. He rents a home there every summer."

"Lucca is the hometown of Giacomo Puccini," interjected Big Bart in a merry tone. "*O mio babbino caro...*" He began to hum an operatic tune while waving his hands.

"Hey everybody, sorry I'm late," said Pat Patrick as he hustled in. "Did I miss anything?"

"No," said Rocco. "We're waiting for Uncle Frank."

"Uncle Frank... holy crap," laughed Patrick. "His goons really knocked the sawdust out of that Barber kid. I hear he's eating out of a straw."

"Don't ever say that again," interjected Attorney Pompano sternly. He stood up and pointed a finger at the news editor. "How dare you suggest such a thing! The police report clearly indicates that Seth Barber was high on vodka. He slipped and fell in a drunken stupor. He reeked of alcohol in the emergency room."

"Lou, I'm sorry," muttered the *Chronicle* reporter. "I was unaware of that report."

Pompano firmly addressed the crowd. "I suggest that no one in this room mention the name of Seth Barber again. Understood? No one!"

"Yes, sir."

"Who's Seth Barber?" asked Bart Little.

"Shut up, Bart! You stupid idiot," shouted Rocco. "Didn't you just hear what the man said? Don't mention his name."

"No, you shut up!" retorted Bart. "There's no such thing as a stupid question." He defiantly waved his lollipop in Rocco's direction.

Two bodyguards walked in unannounced followed by the lithe frame of Uncle Frank. The local dealmaker had a serious look on his face as he strolled across the room. He placed his hat on a coat rack and poured a cup of coffee. No one spoke until he took a sip of the stale brew.

"Good evening, Uncle Frank," said Pompano. "Thank you for meeting with us on such short notice."

"No problem," said Frank as he walked over to the mayor's desk and side saddled it. He wiped off a piece of lint from his trousers and took a deep breath. "What's going on, gentlemen? What's the problem now?"

"I received a preliminary notification from a federal judge in D.C. attempting to halt the planned July 5th demolition," answered Pompano.

"Which means?" asked Frank.

"If approved by the Washington political machine, an injunction is sure to follow... thus overriding our local court's decision to proceed with the implosion."

"Technically, it's not an implosion," whispered Bart.

Tommy Pagano drove his elbow into the chief science officer's solar plexus, rendering him breathless and speechless.

"Where's the judge?" asked Uncle Frank.

"In Europe," replied the attorney.

"Get him on the phone.... *now!*"

"I've been trying to contact him all day," replied Pompano. "No luck."

"Oh," said Uncle Frank. "Isn't that nice? Well, tell the judge I'm very disappointed in him." He stood up and walked behind the Pagano brain trust, his pace slow and serious.

"Ralph, what's going on up at the Philadelphia General?"

"We're right on course," proclaimed the hospital administrator proudly. "We've cleared our employees out of the Franklin and abided by all of the Pagano team's recommendations. There are no problems on our end. None whatsoever."

"I see. What about this Dr. Sullivan I keep hearing about in the newspaper?"

"An underachiever if you ask me," ratted out the hospital CEO. "I'm in the process of shutting down his Alzheimer's floor. I don't think he can generate much trouble. The guy's a lightweight."

"But he's part of this West Philadelphia Historical Society I keep hearing about," stated Mr. Russo while turning his attention to Pat Patrick. "Pat, how well do you know this Bliss Bradshaw guy?" He brought the coffee cup to his lips and held it there, waiting for a response.

"Bliss is a drama queen," laughed Patrick. "He doesn't have the mental capacity to take a story beyond his opening remarks. The guy's a blowhard. Bliss has a flare for the dramatic but never follows up on a lead. It's too much work. You won't hear from him again."

"Alright," continued Uncle Frank with a glance toward Freddie Freeman. "Fred. What's up with the radon readings?"

"We've got them under control," boasted Freeman. "Larry Griffith keeps sending in elevated levels but I've been successfully countering them with those of my own. We're on top of it."

"His readings don't concern you?"

"No," came Freeman's response. "Larry's a pencil pusher. Nothing will go beyond the reports that he keeps sending up the ladder. He's a company man."

"O.K.," said Frank. "He looked at Tommy Pagano. "Winky, I hate to ask, but what's going on with Stephanie after her swan dive into the champagne waterfall?"

"She's gone A.W.O.L." came the grim reply. "No one's seen her since the country club debacle." He put his head into his hands. "After all I've done for her... she treats me this way!"

"So, let me see if I've got this right," summarized Uncle Frank in a sarcastic tone. "We're being castrated by an underachiever, a drama queen, a pencil pusher and a mistress that's gone haywire." He shook his head. "Is that how I'm reading the situation?"

"Stephanie's your mistress?" whispered Bart to Tommy. The question prompted Winky to stomp on his toes. "Ouch!" whimpered the biologist. "That hurt!"

"It's the collective noise from each party that's starting to add up," stated Pompano. "That stunt from Bliss Bradshaw hurt. All the major news networks have since sent a reporter to town. You mention the word 'ghost' and all the paranormal freaks suddenly come out of the woodwork."

"Mayor Chubb, what's your take on the situation?" asked Uncle Frank. "It's your town, how do we stop the noise in the system?"

"You can't," conceded the mayor. "Every decision I make generates an avalanche of putrid vile from all sectors of society. It's part of being a politician. Hell, you can't please everyone. It didn't take me long to figure that out."

"So, what's your suggestion?"

"Railroad it through," said Chubb as he checked his watch. "Let everybody bitch, it doesn't matter. They're all cretins. Social discord is the currency of choice for everyone with a gripe. As long as we stick together and tow the party line, everything will be fine. That's all that matters." He took in a deep breath of cronyism. "They're all professional whiners. Once that building drops, they'll move on to their next peeve. Trust me... I've been there."

"Well put," followed up Uncle Frank. "I thoroughly agree... except for the federal judge. That my friends, is a problem."

"I've got a few contacts inside the beltway working on the situation," followed up Pompano.

"As do I," said Frank. "But in case we fail, there has to be an alternative plan." He circled back in front of the brigade. "If a federal judge shuts down the project, that building will sit vacant for another two years."

"I agree," added Pompano. "They'll want to extract that wall. I'm starting to hear some buzzwords like 'historical preservation' and 'museum worthy'."

"Pagano Destruction will go bankrupt," whined Winky. "We can't let that happen! We just can't!" He rapidly made the sign of the cross, twice.

"So, what's the alternative?" asked the power broker.

The gathering fell silent for several seconds.

"Why don't we just blow up the wall?" mumbled Rocco.

"Excuse me?" asked Uncle Frank. "What did you just say, Rock?"

"I said, blow up the goddamn wall!" growled the company foreman. "If they stop you from blowing up the building... then just detonate the wall."

Uncle Frank nodded his head up and down while considering the proposal. "An interesting option, Rock."

"Hell, the place is laced with dynamite already, just call it an unfortunate industrial mishap. Accidents do happen."

"Very interesting," continued Uncle Frank. "Winky, what are you thinking? Can we blow the wall?"

"Ah... I mean it sounds too easy," replied the company leader while scratching his head. "But it kind of makes sense... in a crazy way."

"I like it," chimed in Attorney Pompano. "Taking out the wall itself would seemingly solve our problem. Good thinking, Rock."

"You're welcome," said the foreman.

"Wow, there's a first," laughed Big Bart. "Rock doing some thinking."

"Don't make me come over there, Bart!" snapped the Rock. "I'll stuff that lollipop where the sun doesn't shine!"

"Alright everybody," interrupted Pompano. "So, let's just say we go about our business and detonate the building on July 5th, assuming there's no interference from the feds."

"And if there is a federal order?"

"Then we blow the wall to smithereens," declared Uncle Frank. "I like it. I like it a lot."

Tommy Pagano looked at his head science officer to his right. "Bart, is it possible? Can we just blow the lower basement and that stupid wall without toppling the entire house of cards?"

"Are you asking me to stage an accidental explosion in the building to sidestep an order from a federal judge?" asked Little.

"That's exactly what I'm asking you."

"Well," shot back Big Bart. "I've got a bit of an ethical problem with that plan."

"Oh really?" snapped Uncle Frank. "Well how's this for an alternative?" He stepped in front of the scientist. "We'll strap your body to the wall before it blows. That way it will really look like an accident... especially when they find portions of your fat ass over in New Jersey. How's that for an alternative?"

"Sure. It can be done," cowered Big Bart. "Blowing that central section won't drop the entire structure."

"But it will destroy the wall?" asked Pagano.

"Absolutely," answered Bart with newly found zeal. "In fact, I'll concoct a witch's brew of explosives that will pulverize the granite into a thousand little pieces." A crazed look took hold of his eyes as he grinned at Uncle Frank. "How does that sound?"

"It sounds to me like you're a lifesaver," quipped Uncle Frank.

"I've only one request," said Bart.

"What?"

"That you name the covert operation after me... Big Bart Little."

"It was my idea!" protested Rocco. "Screw you! It should be named after me!"

"I'm the chief science officer!" cut back Bart. "Without me, there can be no explosion!"

"But I'm the one setting the dynamite grids!" shouted Rocco. "One false move and I'll be picking my nose with my elbow!"

"Gentlemen, gentlemen!" shouted Uncle Frank. "Take it easy now." He held both hands high. "I appreciate your enthusiasm but we need to stick together. Remember the mayor's advice?"

An icy stare down commenced between the foreman and scientist, neither man willing to surrender their naming rights to the covert operation.

"The most important question," said Pompano. "Is when do we destroy the wall?" He scanned the group. "That is, if it needs to be done?"

"I'd say as close to July 5th as possible," offered Rocco. "That way, the place is already wired to blow."

"I agree," said Winky. "All the charges will already be in place. We can blame the misfire on a circuit malfunction or faulty wire."

"We can throw in the fact that fortunately no one was harmed or killed in the explosion," said Pompano.

"Right," agreed Uncle Frank. "The public likes to hear that no one was injured in a mishap."

"I'll start working on a press release already," said the attorney. "There's going to be a backlash, but we'll be ready."

"I'd say July 4th," suggested Tommy Pagano. "Do it on the Fourth of July. Every office building in the vicinity will be empty. It's a no brainer."

"Mayor Chubb?" asked Uncle Frank. "Any problems with July 4th? Let's say around noon?"

"In West Philadelphia... no," replied the elected official. "Not in the early afternoon. The streets will be desolate."

"Mr. Covington," said Frank. "Anything major going on at the Philadelphia General on that date?"

"No. Not to my knowledge," answered the hospital leader. "The Fourth of July holiday is on a Saturday this year, so the campus will be empty. And remember, we've already made plans to evacuate the surrounding area and adjacent hospital wings as of Friday night, in preparation for a July 5th detonation. So we're all good."

"Well then gentlemen, it looks like we've got an alternative plan," said Uncle Frank. "Now, I strongly suggest that what's been discussed tonight stays within the four corners of this room. Understand?"

"Yes, Uncle Frank."

"I'll take it one step further and personally ask each one of you to keep quiet. Capeesh?"

"Yes, Uncle Frank."

"We're doing this for Tommy and Vince, and the Pagano name," said Frank. He patted Winky firmly on the back. "The Pagano Orthopedic Institute and its legacy will stand tall for years to come! Mark my words." The chieftain strolled over to the coat rack to gather his cover.

"But the name?" asked Big Bart. "We need a code name."

"You want a code name, Big Bart?" asked Uncle Frank with a grin.

"Yes."

"Well here's the code name," said Frank as he donned his cap. "Operation Firecracker... how's that sound, Big Bart?"

"Sounds like a blast!" answered Mr. Little. "A big blast in honor of Independence Day!"

"Stay well my friends. Ciao."

"Goodnight, Uncle Frank."

Operation Firecracker commenced the following day, when a federal injunction landed squarely on top of Attorney Pompano's desk, officially halting the destruction of the Franklin Wing.

CHAPTER TWENTY-THREE
IN LOVING MEMORY

"Ouch!" winced Dr. Sullivan as his head hit again off the desk in the cramped office. "Somebody has got to move that desk!" Next to him recoiled the frail frame of Zachary Schmidt.

"Gentlemen!" shouted Brooks. "Where have you two been? I've been worried to death!"

Zachary raised a weakened arm. "Look out, John!"

The body of Vince Pagano suddenly log rolled between the two, his frame crashing against the wall.

"Holy hell!" screamed Pagano. "What just happened?" He looked around the room in a confused state.

"We have company?" spouted Allister. "You bring a friend home and the place is a mess? Why doesn't anyone tell me when company is coming?" His theatrics vanished while helping to get Zachary up. "My good man, you do not look well!"

"My transfusion got him here," stated Sullivan. "But he's fading fast. We have to get him to Dr. Hayhurst as soon as possible!" He helped Dr. Schmidt stand and walk toward a chair.

"Where am I?" asked Pagano.

"Vince," answered Sullivan. "You're in the Pagano Orthopedic Institute!"

"In the year 2065," added Allister. "Welcome!"

Pagano stood up, speechless.

"I've been patiently awaiting Zachary's arrival," continued Mr. Brooks. "Look!" He held his hand out to an exam table with an intravenous bag hanging beside it. "I've prepared Zachary's medicine, expecting the worst!"

"You stole it again?" asked Sullivan as he helped Schmidt over to the treatment area.

"No. I informed Gordon of the tunnel. I just had to."

"But the Cardinal Rules?"

"Oh," moaned Zachary. "Allister, you are indeed a life saver. He dropped supine onto the table and rolled up a sleeve. "Quickly, my friend... before I expire."

"What's going on here?" asked Pagano as he began to pace the room. "Who are these people?"

"You've traveled through time," answered Sullivan while placing an intravenous line into his colleague's vein. "I told you, the granite wall is a time tunnel portal. That's why we have to try and save it. You've traveled forty-five years forward in time!"

"But..."

"This is Dr. Zachary Schmidt, the man who disappeared without a trace in 1976," continued Sullivan.

"Well technically, John... I did leave an inadvertent clue," muttered Schmidt. "The key. Remember the key?"

"I don't believe it," gasped Pagano. "It just can't be."

"Believe it," said Brooks.

"There," said Sullivan as he opened up the fluid bag. "Run it wide open." The targeting agents began to pour into Schmidt's veins.

"Gordon recommends two treatments, which will take about six hours," stated Allister. "How much time do you have?"

"Six hours... eight hours max," replied Sullivan. "Vince and I have to get back no later than July 4ᵗʰ."

"What are you talking about?" asked Vince while rubbing his neck. "July 4ᵗʰ is about ten days away. You have ten days!"

"The twin paradox," said Sullivan in a matter of fact tone. "You'll understand in due time." He looked at Brooks. "Allister, I have to see your husband. Is he in the office now?"

"Yes. Why? What's the problem?"

"I have a personal favor to ask of him, regarding a dear friend in need... back in time."

"John," whispered Schmidt with reservation. "As your mother's primary care physician, I must remind you of her unambiguous desire to expire peacefully. She's stated that quite clearly to both of us."

"Understood," replied Sullivan, immediately turning his attention back to Allister.

"We must respect her dying wish," continued Schmidt. "The Oath of Hippocrates clearly states ..."

"Can you notify him that I'm on my way over?" asked Sullivan.

"Sure," said Allister. "But I must stay here with Zachary."

"Of course," said Sullivan. "I'll take Vince along. You know, kind of show him the future." He patted Pagano on the back. "Would you like that, Vince?"

"Here," said Brooks. He put a visitor I.D. lanyard around the neck of each man. "This will get you in and out of the Pagano and Pinetti buildings."

"Great," said Sullivan. "C'mon Vince." He checked his watch. "We've only got eight hours to turn this thing around, or else?"

"Or else, what?" asked Vince.

"Or else... we're trapped in the future. At least until the Pagano Institute is rebuilt." He looked at Dr. Schmidt. "Isn't that right? I'm assuming the tunnel remains, even after the implosion. I mean... we're here now... in the future."

"Who knows?" answered Schmidt with his eyes closed. "Who knows? I suggest you don't miss the last train home."

"Get well, Zachary," said Sullivan with a hand on Schmidt's arm. "I'll be back soon."

"Dr. Sullivan," said Zachary. "Wait." He carefully removed the skeleton key from his neck. "Just in case." He handed the key to Sullivan.

"Just in case, what?"

"We don't see each other again. I'm officially retiring from the travel club. I'm getting a bit too old for the speed of light."

"But..."

"It's time to pass the key to a new generation of time travelers."

Sullivan stared at the key in his hand.

"Take care of that key my friend. It's a powerful tool."

Sullivan grinned and placed the antique proudly around his neck. "Thank you, Dr. Schmidt. Thank you very much."

"R.S. is counting on you, too," added Schmidt. "Make him proud."

"Aha!" said Sullivan excitedly. "So, R.S. is a male!"

"Dr. Sullivan, no woman came close to signing the Declaration of Independence," retorted Schmidt in an incredulous tone. "Telling you that R.S. is a male... is the definition of a gimme. Please!"

Sullivan smiled. "Get well, Zachary."

"Godspeed old friend."

As the two physicians stepped outside, Pagano was immediately awestruck by the majesty of the Pagano Orthopedic Institute, the fortress built by his father in homage to his favorite son. "Wow, he wasn't kidding about the size of the sign," laughed Vince while looking upward. "They can see that sign over in Jersey."

"I agree," laughed Sullivan.

"Hey! Where's Franklin Field? What the..."

Twenty minutes later, the duo sat in the office of Dr. Gordon Hayhurst, the immunologist listening attentively to Sullivan's plea.

"So, that's my question," finished up Sullivan. "Can it be done again, realizing my recent success in the case of Dr. Schmidt?"

"Your recent… limited success," followed up Hayhurst while removing a pair of glasses. "Allister just informed me of Zachary's condition. So, although you successfully transported some targeting agents back in time, I must caution you on the efficacy of your proposed plan. Zachary would have died, had he not made it back to 2065."

"I understand," followed up Sullivan.

"You must have realistic expectations, Dr. Sullivan. Your plan, although quite noble, may not work. You have to be willing to accept that distinct possibility."

"I fully realize that… and I accept that risk."

"I mean, the disease can be cured today… here in 2065, but I can't guarantee a cure in 2020." He didn't break eye contact with Sullivan. "And remember, you only have four hours to re-infuse the medication, otherwise it's useless."

"I understand," said Sullivan. "But will you do it?" came the final plea. "For the sake of… "

"Absolutely," said the medical pioneer. "How can I decline helping to save a life from forty years ago?"

"Really?" blurted Sullivan. "So, you'll give me the targeting agents?"

"Why not? If I don't… my wife will take a hissy fit, and we don't want any drama from him. Trust me on that one."

"Thank you, Dr. Hayhurst. I'll forever be grateful."

"Let's go, we haven't much time to lose. Hah, I like that one… no pun intended." The immunologist led John to a treatment room and after placing an intravenous line, began to infuse the targeting agents. The fluid itself was bright yellow, a stark contrast to that of Schmidt's. During the infusion, Sullivan's vein began to tingle.

"It's tingling."

"Very common," said Hayhurst. "Let me know if you feel anything else."

"I will. Thank you, again." Sullivan looked up in awe at Hayhurst. "How does it feel to be the person credited with curing lung cancer?"

"I wouldn't call it a cure," said Hayhurst. "A major breakthrough, yes... but not a cure."

"But, how does it feel?"

"Rewarding. But I'm just one cog in the wheel of research over time, lucky enough to tweak what's been previously discovered by others. That's the key to becoming a so-called genius... improving what's already in front of your eyes."

"I see."

"Otherwise you have to start from square one, and who has the time for that?" Hayhurst laughed again. "Sorry, but I'm still getting use to this 'time is relative' concept."

"How long is this transfusion going to take?" asked Pagano while peering outside a window to street level. "And why doesn't anyone have a cell phone in their hand down there?"

"Four hours," came the reply. "And cell phones were outlawed by Congress years ago."

"What?"

"Yes. They were deemed harmful to the human race... and rightfully so."

"What are you talking about?"

"The dark side of technology," answered Hayhurst. "Like pigeons in a Skinner's box, the human race became addicted to repeatedly tapping the screen on their phones... later discovered to be the most deceptive form of mass marketing."

"Classic variable reward schedule training," added Sullivan. "Wow. It's obvious now in retrospect."

"So, you see, cellular phone providers were knowingly taking advantage of ..."

"I don't know what you two are talking about," retorted Pagano. "I can't live without my cell phone."

"Exactly." Dr. Hayhurst laughed while adjusting the rate of fluid flowing into Sullivan's arm. "But, do feel free to walk around town, Dr. Pagano. I'm sure you'll be quite intrigued, even without a cell phone."

"I'd like that very much. Have any of the roads changed?"

"Absolutely not. The basic grid of the city is unchanged since William Penn's original layout in oh, about 1690."

"Vince," commanded Sullivan. "You have about five hours. You have to be back inside the Pagano lobby no later than five hours from now."

"Roger." He checked his watch.

"Vincent. *Do not* be late," implored Sullivan. "Understand? We don't want to miss the last train out of the station."

"I won't be late. I promise. See you in five hours... in the Pagano lobby." He laughed. "The Pagano lobby... I still can't believe it. Dad would be so proud." He turned and left the room.

"Well doctor, you've got four hours to beef up your knowledge base on Alzheimer's disease," said Hayhurst. He handed Sullivan a sleek looking sheet of clear glass. "Here, I've taken the opportunity to key up some review articles on Alzheimer's to date. I'm sure you'll find progress in our treatment of the disease quite satisfying. I've got to get back to my clinic now. I'll be back to wrap this up in a few hours."

"Thank you, Dr. Hayhurst."

"Oh, and one more thing." He pointed out the window. "See that tall building just to the right of the Philadelphia General."

"Yes."

"It has your name on it." He smiled and walked away.

Sullivan anxiously craned forward to look out the window, the late afternoon sun causing a glare. There in the distance, stood a white building with black lettering near the top right. He squinted to focus upon the wording. There, much to his amazement projected the words: *The Sullivan Institute*. A smaller inscription beneath the heading proclaimed: *Recall Respect Rejuvenate*. A rush of euphoria pulsated through his body as he looked back down onto the information at hand. He had four hours to consume as much information as possible to make his name worthy enough to grace the side of a building.

Over the next several hours Sullivan read article after article that quoted his name. In the year 2065, Dr. John F. Sullivan was widely considered the preeminent scholar and physician in the treatment of Alzheimer's, thanks to his groundbreaking research in the disorder. His fame appeared to have occurred on two separate fronts: the first in regard to the prevention of Alzheimer's and the second, in relation to the treatment of the disease. Prevention spoke of groundbreaking data from a fifteen-year, prospective study headed by Sullivan that unequivocally confirmed the role of salt in the development of the disease's pathognomonic neurofibrillary tangles. Simply put, a person's exposure to a high salt diet over a lifetime created knots of neurons in their brain, thus short-circuiting direct access to their memory banks. The treatment breakthrough discovered by Sullivan involved a 'desalinization' of the human brain, which took advantage of reverse osmosis in a patient intentionally overloaded with an intravascular challenge of distilled water. The intensive process targeted and cleansed a portion of the brain known as the hippocampus, thus reestablishing pathways toward a lifetime of memories. In 2065, Sullivan's desalinization process remained a proven method of treating patients with early signs of Alzheimer's, thus halting their feared progression toward senile dementia.

"Incredible," whispered Sullivan to himself. "Too much salt." Over the final hour of his transfusion, he memorized as much information as possible in regard to his described brain cleanse, a process that would make him both famous and wealthy. In hindsight, it appeared too obvious. He reached up and grasped the key around his neck. Schmidt was right... it was a powerful tool. "But who's R.S.?"

"How's it going?" asked Dr. Hayhurst as he walked back into the room, startling Sullivan. "Got enough info to take home?"

"Yes," answered Sullivan. "I've more than enough information." He paused in amazement as Hayhurst disconnected the intravenous tubing. "I can't believe what I've just... read."

"Discovered... may be a better word," quipped Hayhurst. He helped Sullivan stand up. "I'm looking forward to hearing great things from you in the past, doctor." He laughed a hearty laugh. "Oh, I love this time travel stuff... pun now intended!"

Sullivan handed him back the glass computer. He looked out the window again while saying, "Does that building really have my name on it?"

"Yes, it does. Now take a few slow steps. How do you feel?"

"Good. Real good," came the answer. "What now? I haven't much time." He checked a wall clock. "I'd better get back to the Pagano."

"Not so fast," said Hayhurst. "I just spoke to Zachary. He wants me to take you downstairs to see one more thing... something really special."

"Really special? I doubt anything can trump what I've just read."

"Oh, this may just do the trick," answered Hayhurst with a coy grin. He took off his lab coat and placed it on a rack. "In fact, I've got a feeling this may really blow your mind."

He took a brisk step toward the exit. "Let's go doctor, we'll take the stairs. I'll make it quick."

Several stories below, the physicians walked into the main operating suite of the medical complex. They donned a set of green surgical scrubs and reported to a central desk.

"Operating room seven," said a nurse with a finger pointing down the hall. "Cutie is down there. The room with a crowd."

"Thank you," said Hayhurst. "We'll be brief."

"Cutie?" asked Sullivan.

"Yes. The surgeon's initials are Q.T., so they call him 'Cutie' for short. Everybody loves him."

Hayhurst escorted Dr. Sullivan down the hall to operating room number seven. Through an outer glass window, they were able to make out a surgeon using both hands to operate a series of joysticks and trackballs, his actions projecting on an overhead surgical screen. A group of attentive observers stood directly behind the seated physician.

"Robotic brain surgery," said Hayhurst as he put a surgical mask over his face. He handed John a mask. "Here, put this on. If anyone asks, you're a visiting professor from Los Angeles."

"Roger," mumbled Sullivan from behind his surgical mask. "Why are we going in here?"

Hayhurst didn't respond as the two entered the operating room.

"Here's the final stitch I'm talking about," said the surgeon as he stared into an eyepiece connected to a square box. To his right lay the patient, with a breathing tube and fine instruments penetrating her nostrils and ear canals. "It locks the memory booster in place." He moved his fingertips on the controls, his actions commanding the robot to perfectly place a single suture into a cylindrical metal tube.

"That's directly beneath the hippocampus?" asked a visitor with a strong foreign accent.

"Yes," said the surgeon. "The hippocampus is at twelve o'clock on the screen. That tube is about the size of two or three strands of hair." He paused before continuing. "So, the stimulus from the device fires every two minutes, keeping the neurons above... alive and healthy."

"How many patients have you tried this on?" asked another observer.

"To date... about six hundred." The surgeon kept his eyes in the box as he spoke. "We've recently made it an outpatient procedure."

- "Amazing," added another visitor. "And the results?"

"So far, so good," said the surgeon. "In fact, I performed the procedure on a ninety-four year old about a year ago, and his memory has never been better." He kept working. "There! Once the stitch is placed, the procedure is over." He pushed back from the screen and looked up at the crowd. "We've found that by implanting the nerve stimulator directly beneath the hippocampus, a patient's memory stabilizes in a dramatic fashion." He scanned the crowd with a look of confidence.

"For how many years?"

"Time will tell," came the reply. "Our cohort is about five years out, and the benefits of the implant don't seem to wane over time. I honestly believe this little implant will be a real game changer in the fight against memory loss." He turned his attention back to the control panel and depressed a switch, his actions prompting the surgical probes to withdraw from the patient's cranium.

"Can we wake her up, doc?" asked the anesthesiologist.

John Sullivan stared intently at the surgeon. His eyes appeared familiar, as did the inflection of his voice. However, he couldn't place a name to the face.

"Sure, Ruth. Wake her up," replied the neurosurgeon. "Any other questions? If not, then we can all head downstairs to the surgical simulation lab. There, you can test out the robot for yourself." He took off his mask and smiled at the crowd.

"Thank you, Dr. Sullivan," came a smattering of kudos from the group. "Thank you for allowing us to witness your work."

"Thank you, *Dr. Sullivan*," added Dr. Hayhurst.

"You're welcome," replied the surgeon. "Let's all head downstairs."

John Sullivan froze, his mind suddenly catatonic. A round of gentle applause rose from the crowd. He continued to stare at the young surgeon as he walked by, his movements confident and graceful.

"Thank you again, Dr. Sullivan," said another guest to his right.

"Dr. Sullivan?" whispered Sullivan. "His... his name is Dr. Sullivan?"

Hayhurst steered the stunned body of John Sullivan out of the room, turning him to the left and down the hallway.

"Take a few deep breaths my friend," said Hayhurst as he steadied his guest. "There you go... in and out. Slow and steady. In and out."

"Was... was that my son?" mumbled Sullivan. "They called him... Dr. Sullivan. Isn't that what they called him?"

"Yes, they did, John," answered Hayhurst as they passed the nursing desk.

"Was that my son?"

"No... that *is* your son, John. You should be proud of him. He's the youngest chairman ever elected within the Department of Neurosurgery."

"My son, the chairman of the department?"

"Yes, John. Your son... Quentin T. Sullivan."

"What's his mother's name?" stammered Sullivan as they entered the locker room. "Can you tell me her first name?"

"No. No, I don't know that. Sorry, John."

"Can't anyone please tell me her name?"

Despite his repetitive pleas, the name of Dr. Quentin T. Sullivan's mother was never disclosed. Fifteen minutes later, the duo arrived inside the Pagano Institute lobby, the atrium a hodgepodge of activity.

"Thank you once again, Dr. Hayhurst," said Sullivan. "You don't know how much this means to me. I just can't believe it. I saw my son... the doctor!" He firmly shook the hand of Hayhurst.

"My pleasure," replied Hayhurst. "Where's Dr. Pagano?" His six foot-five-inch frame peered over the crowd. "Ah, there's my Allister."

"Hello, love," said Allister as he approached the two physicians. "How did our Dr. Sullivan do?"

"Mission accomplished. He now has four hours to deliver the antidote back home."

"Well Dr. Sullivan," added Allister. "You're darn lucky it's another direct relative involved in the targeting agent transfer." He checked his watch. "Where's Dr. Pagano? I just saw him in here five minutes ago."

"Excuse me?" asked Sullivan. "What do you mean?"

"About what?"

"About a *direct relative* being involved... and me, being lucky? What do you mean by that statement?"

"The targeting agents that I just administered," answered Dr. Hayhurst. "They key off genetic markers in the bloodstream. So, they're efficacy is quite specific to a patient's bloodline."

"So..."

"You just can't give them to anyone. Forgive me for not bringing this up earlier, but only a family member can receive a transfusion of targeting agents from your veins. Otherwise they simply wouldn't work."

Sullivan gawked at the immunologist.

"But that shouldn't be a problem, right?" continued Hayhurst. "I mean, you're going to give them..."

"But what about Dr. Schmidt?" asked Sullivan. "Why did it work with him?"

"What do you mean?" asked Hayhurst in reply. "I don't understand."

"You're implying that Dr. Schmidt is a direct relative of mine," stated Sullivan. "What makes you think…"

"John!" came a shout from behind. "John!"

The group turned to see Vince Pagano with a wretched look across his face. He latched onto Sullivan's right arm.

"John! Come over here!" He began to rush across the lobby, pulling Sullivan in the process. "We've got to get out of here… *now!*"

"What's wrong, Vince?" asked Sullivan as he followed his distressed colleague. "What's the matter?"

They followed the surgeon through the crowd, to a wall near the main hospital entrance. There, Pagano pointed to a large plaque embossed in black on the wall. A line of gold trim framed the following inscription:

THE PAGANO ORTHOPEDIC INSTITUTE

IN LOVING MEMORY OF
VINCENT ROMEO PAGANO, MD
1978-2020

Dr. Vincent Pagano, surgeon, teacher, friend and son… was tragically killed on July 4[th,] 2020, during the demolition of the Philadelphia General's Franklin Wing. The Pagano Orthopedic Institute was his dream, his vision and now, his legacy.

He will forever be remembered in our hearts.

CHAPTER TWENTY-FOUR
CEO COVINGTON

"Where's Dr. Sullivan?" asked Monique with her arms crossed. "He said he was going to take care of Aunt Gracie." She sat on the side of her aunt's bed with a look of defiance.

"No one seems to know," answered hospital CEO Ralph Covington. Behind him stood two hospital security guards, the taller sentry chomping impatiently on some gum. "Dr. Sullivan is fully aware of our plan to close the Alzheimer's floor," continued Covington. "Your aunt and a Mr. Tank Brownstone are the only two remaining residents." He peered at a piece of paper while pronouncing Brownstone's name.

"Where's Mrs. Appleton?" asked Monique. "She's another member of the Sullivan Gang."

"Sullivan Gang? What do you mean by the Sullivan Gang?"

"Aunt Gracie's family," came the incredulous reply from the high school senior. "Her family... here on the floor. They're called the Sullivan Gang!" She patted her aunt's hand while talking. "It's the only family she has, and now you're trying to take it away." Some tears started to well up in her eyes.

"Dr. Sullivan has given his approval to our plan," said the administrator, his deception veiled beneath a look of concern.

"We've got to close the floor by this evening, for the safety of everyone involved."

"And where is she going… along with Mr. Brownstone?" Over the past several weeks, Monique appreciated a special bond between her aunt and Brownstone.

Covington again looked down at his paper. He had no answer but needed the floor vacated as soon as possible. "The social workers have all that figured out," came the second distortion of the truth. "Trust me when I say your aunt will be in the best of hands." He glanced back at one of the guards with a wheelchair, nodding to him to push forward. "Now, we need to transfer Aunt Gracie. O.K.?"

"No!" said Monique. "She's not leaving until I speak to Dr. Sullivan." She stood upright.

"Now, listen here young lady. I'm in charge of this hospital. Now unfortunately, your aunt's insurance carrier isn't paying for her to stay here anymore. So when that occurs, it leaves us with no choice but to…"

A towering shadow suddenly engulfed the extraction team from behind, as if there was an eclipse of the sun. The squadron turned about to espy the imposing frame of Tank Brownstone standing in the doorway, his girth clogging the doorjamb.

"Whoa," quivered Covington. "Who's that?"

"What's going on here?" growled the former gridiron superstar wearing smiley face pajamas. He took a menacing step into the room.

"Take it easy, Tank," said the senior guard. "Everything is fine." He held up his hands to appease the approaching behemoth.

"What are you doing in her room?"

"They're trying to take away Aunt Gracie," blurted Monique. "Just like Mrs. Appleton. They're taking her away!"

"Nobody is taking away Gracie Jones," growled Brownstone. "*Nobody*. She's staying here… with me!"

"Now listen here, mister," squeaked Covington. "Mrs. Jones is going to be removed from this room now, by order of the hospital administration. Do you understand?" He looked back at Monique. "I've had enough of this nonsense." He motioned for the security team to take action. "Let's go! Move her out."

The taller guard approached Mrs. Jones.

The CEO's directive triggered the former defensive stalwart to rush forward, as if trying to dismember an opposing quarterback. He let out a guttural growl as he lowered a shoulder into the sternum of the gum-smacking sentry.

"Tank!" shouted the shorter guard.

Brownstone leveled the guard, knocking him out on impact. He rolled onto the floor and recoiled upright in a manner that belied his arthritic frame.

"Security alert to the Alzheimer's floor," shouted the upright guard into a shoulder microphone. "Officer down. I repeat… officer down!"

"Help!" screamed Covington. "Someone help!"

"Mr. Brownstone, no!" shouted Monique. "Please stop!"

The Philadelphia sports legend lunged toward Covington, his attempt to further protect Mrs. Jones thwarted by the piercing pain of two taser barbs penetrating his right pectoral muscle.

"AAAH!" shouted Brownstone as 50,000 volts of electricity ripped through his body. He torqued to the right and hit the floor with a tremendous thud, his frame convulsing wildly.

"What's going on in here?" yelled Dr. Olivia Garcia as she ran into the room. "Mr. Brownstone!" She looked at the trembling security guard holding the taser, its uncoiled wires still attached to the target. "Turn it off. You'll kill him!"

"I can't!" came the reply from the guard holding the yellow handgun. "I don't know how!"

The charge from the gun lasted another fifteen seconds, during which time Brownstone's body continued to contort on the floor.

Dr. Garcia ran over to the suddenly listless body of Brownstone, placing her hand on his wrist. Saliva rolled out of his mouth. "He has no pulse!" She looked up at a nurse and waited a few more seconds. "He's gone into cardiac arrest. Call a code!"

"Code blue... Alzheimer's Unit, room 333," cried the hospital operator over the intercom. "Code blue... Alzheimer's Unit, room 333."

A rumble of approaching personnel could be heard in the distance as Dr. Garcia began chest compressions on Tank Brownstone. Within a minute the room was jammed with emergency personnel, tending to the stricken patient.

"Stop! He's a DNR!" shouted Nurse Adams over the din. "Dr. Garcia... Mr. Brownstone is a DNR!"

"WHAT?" came the incredulous cry from the physician. "Are you sure?"

"Absolutely," said Adams. She held the patient's chart high in the air for everyone to see. "Right here... DNR." She pointed to a form signed by Mr. Brownstone's power of attorney. "No mechanical ventilation or heroic measures."

Garcia grimaced and stopped her mechanical compressions. "Stop the code," she said while holding up a hand to prevent an anesthesia resident from placing a breathing tube down Brownstone's trachea.

"You don't want me to intubate him?" asked the eager resident. "He's not breathing."

"We have to abide by their wishes, so yes... stop the code." Everyone in the room went silent as the body of Theodore 'The Tank' Brownstone began to turn a slight shade of blue. He was expiring in front of their eyes.

"Theodore!" bellowed Aunt Gracie. She began to cry. "Wake up!" Tears streamed down her cheeks as her body rocked nervously back and forth. "Wake up... please! Theodore! Don't leave me!"

The behemoth didn't move.

"THEODORE!" screamed Gracie with all her might.

The body of the fallen giant jolted, as if the words from his soul mate shocked his heart into working order. He moaned, rolled to his right and opened his eyes. Reflexively, he tried to stand.

"He heard you," gasped Dr. Garcia. "He heard you!" She put her hands on the patient. "Easy now, Mr. Brownstone, stay down. You've had a bit of a spell." She looked at a fellow resident at his side. "Get these barbs out of his chest!"

"Once he's stable, escort both of them out of here," whined CEO Covington as he straightened out his tie. Three other security guards arrived to aid their fallen comrade. "That man assaulted a hospital employee." He began to walk out of the room.

"They're not going anywhere," cut back Garcia. "Not until we talk to Dr. Sullivan. This is his floor and these are his patients."

"Well, where is Dr. Sullivan?" countered Covington. "He seems to have gone AWOL in everyone's moment of need."

Garcia didn't respond as she continued to monitor Brownstone's pulse. She thought it peculiar that Sullivan had disappeared over the past several days, especially in light of his patients being unceremoniously jettisoned from the hospital. She recalled an odd dream from the prior night, during which time she spotted Sullivan on a crowded elevator, surrounded by strangers.

"He'll be back tomorrow morning," came a voice from behind.

"Who'll be back?" asked Covington. "Dr. Sullivan?" He peered to identify the speaker. "Who said that?"

The body of Reggie Washington slipped in between his two co-workers. "Dr. Sullivan will be back in town, no later than tomorrow afternoon."

"How do you know that?" Covington squinted at his hospital nametag. "Mr. Washington?"

"I just know."

"Where is he? Has he been in touch with you? I mean… his actions are bordering on medical abandonment."

Washington remained silent, abiding by the cardinal rules. He was well aware of the time tunnel, having again slightly diverted an overhead security camera away from the portal just prior to Sullivan and Pagano's recent departure.

"Are you new to our hospital?" queried Covington. "I've never seen you before."

"No sir," answered Washington. "I've been working here since July, 1974."

"In what department?"

"Night watch… over on the Franklin Wing."

"Oh. The Franklin Wing," quipped Covington sarcastically.

"They've cordoned off my post and transferred me to the floor," said Washington. "But believe it or not, today is…"

"Anything else I should know about Dr. Sullivan?" interrupted Covington. "Or his precious Franklin Wing?"

Washington held his tongue.

"I didn't think so," snapped the CEO. He pointed to the lanky security guard now sitting in the wheelchair. "I suggest you get your partner down to the emergency room for some medical care, Mr. Washington." He stepped past the elderly sentry and left the room.

Covington stormed off the floor and down to his office. In his heart he could care less about Gracie Jones or Theodore Brownstone. They were just two of several hundred patients currently housed on the PGH campus. The bigger picture always mattered to the hospital CEO, including his involvement in the Franklin Wing. It was six o'clock on Friday night, July 3rd. He took a deep breath to try and calm his nerves. The clandestine detonation of Dr. Sullivan's granite wall was scheduled for the following day. His phone rang and he picked up the receiver.

"Ralph, all set on your end?" asked Attorney Pompano.

"Yes," came the anxious reply. "I can't wait to get this over with."

"I've got some good news," said the attorney. "Uncle Frank made a few phone calls and guess what?"

"What?"

"You are officially out of the red over at the casino, my friend."

"Really? He cleared my debt?"

"Absolutely. A deal is a deal, Ralph."

"Thank you," exalted Covington. "Thank you so very much!"

"The Franklin demo means a lot to Mr. Russo and his inner circle. He appreciates everything you've done on your side of the bargain... including the board of trustees. We all know there were some other hands trying to get in on the pot."

"It's the least I could do for Mr. Russo," replied Covington. "Please, can you personally thank him for me?"

"Absolutely. That new hospital is going to be a gold mine."

"Will Mr. Russo be here on Sunday for the official implosion?"

"No. No. You've seen the last of Uncle Frank. He avoids the spotlight."

"I see."

"Well, keep it tight my friend," said Pompano. "I just thought you'd like to hear the good news."

"Thank you, Lou. Good night." The CEO hung up the phone and leaned back in his chair. A nasty six month run of bad luck at the local gambling joint dropped him deep into a financial hole, his debt a bargaining chip in the Franklin affair. His name was now magically cleared of all payments owed, and a sense of euphoria overtook his mind. He reached into his lower drawer and pulled out a flask of vodka. After a celebratory toot, he briefly thought of returning to the casino, but felt it best to wait until next week. God forbid his reappearance at the gaming joint suggest any impropriety. His luck was about to change... he just knew it.

Covington fell asleep in his chair until ten o'clock in the evening, when a garbage truck emptying a dumpster at street level roused his soul. He thought it appropriate to take one final walk around the Franklin, to pay further homage to Saint Frank. The administrator took a slow, reflective stroll just outside the fenced off perimeter of the Franklin Wing, his route ending at Reggie Washington's abandoned guard post. All was well on the eve of destruction, until he heard a grating sound coming from behind the double doors leading to the Franklin itself. The Pagano Destruction team had dismantled the door's swipe card entry slot earlier in the day. The grating continued as Covington cautiously approached the darkened gateway. A large DANGER – DO NOT ENTER sticker draped across each entryway. The sound suggested someone or something trying to break open the lock on the opposite side of the door. Just as the CEO went to speak, the thumb latch on the handle jiggled up and down, and the door jarred open.

"Who goes there?" shouted Covington fearfully.

The motion stopped and all went silent. The CEO's heart began to thump loudly in his chest. He looked quickly behind, but no one was there.

"I said, who goes there?" The hospital administrator took a few steps back and pulled out his cell phone. While attempting to access his contact list the door swung open, exposing the silhouette of a singular man, his frame still and slight. The stranger held a crowbar in his right hand. "Yes? Can I help you?" stammered Covington.

The man dropped the crowbar with a loud clank and out of the shadow stepped Reggie Washington. "Wow," said the sentry. "I got locked inside!"

"What are you doing in there?" barked Covington, now recognizing the guard from earlier in the evening. "This area is off limits to all employees!"

"It's my last day of work and I just had to make one more round through the Franklin," answered Washington. "I just needed to say good-bye."

"How dare..."

"I've spent over four decades patrolling this old building, Mr. Covington," proclaimed Washington in a melancholic tone. "I'm going to miss her. I know every piece of brick and mortar inside."

"What were you doing in there?"

"Remembering all the people that passed through the Franklin Wing over time. That's what made it so special." He nodded his head in appreciation. "A lot of good people... my heavens. Where has the time gone?"

"Listen here, man. I forbid you from returning to this area. It's been restricted for the safety of everyone. What makes you think you're so special?"

"What's with all the explosives drilled into the granite wall down in Dr. Schmidt's reading room?"

Covington clammed up and sneered.

"That wasn't there just a few days ago."

"That's none of your business, Mr. Washington," snapped back the CEO. "I suggest..."

"Is someone planning to blow it up?"

"Never you mind."

"Dr. Schmidt loved that wall," continued Washington. "Do you know what's inscribed on the back of it?"

"Give me your badge," demanded Covington with an extended hand. "Consider yourself on paid leave until further notice." He snapped his fingers impatiently. "I want you off the PGH campus immediately." He scowled at the long time employee. "Give it to me!"

"Too late," grinned Washington with a check of his wristwatch. "It's a quarter after eleven. So guess what?" He put his I.D. badge into his front pocket.

Covington didn't answer.

"I retired fifteen minutes ago." He turned to walk away. "Time for Reggie Washington to head home, Mr. Covington. It's been a pleasure working here for the past forty-six years... I honestly mean that. I enjoyed each and every day. Thank you for the opportunity. Good night, sir."

"Give me that badge," howled Covington in pursuit. "Did you touch anything inside there?" He trailed behind the slow moving frame of Washington. "What's so darn special about that wall?"

Washington turned about and faced down the hospital kingpin.

"That's Dr. Schmidt's wall. Dr. Schmidt is a fine man... a good doctor and a real gentleman." He kept direct eye contact with Covington. "That's what we all need around here nowadays," continued Washington. "Some good old fashioned manners and respect for our fellow man. Don't you agree, Mr. Covington? Our world would certainly be a better place."

"You refer to him in the present... as if he were alive," stated Covington. "Why are you talking like that? Dr. Schmidt is dead. Don't tell me you believe in ghosts, Mr. Washington?"

"No," came the firm reply. "I used to, but not anymore."

"I see. Do you think Dr. Schmidt is still alive?"

"Nobody knows for sure. Maybe?"

"Don't be ridiculous. Where's he been living all these years? In there?" He pointed to the Franklin entrance.

"Nobody is living inside that building, Mr. Covington."

"Alright. Now we're getting somewhere." The CEO took a deep breath. "So where's Dr. Sullivan? I think you know where he is. Why don't you tell me?"

"I'm not exactly sure," laughed Washington. He gazed at the walls around him. "He's walking around here somewhere… but where and more importantly… when, I just can't say." A coy grin appeared on his face.

"Have you been drinking on the job, Mr. Washington?"

"No sir. I don't imbibe."

"I see."

The stare down continued before Washington broke eye contact. He extended a handshake to the CEO. "Goodnight, Mr. Covington. It's been a pleasure finally meeting you. I have to get home now, or Mrs. Washington will start worrying."

"Good night, Mr. Washington," replied Covington with a firm handshake. "Thank you for your many years of service. Now, stay the hell out of this hospital. Understood?"

"Yes, sir."

Reginald Washington was welcomed home by his wife and family with a surprise party that included his favorite chocolate cake. A well-deserved celebration followed in honor of a lifetime of hard work and achievement. Unfortunately, the first night of his retirement was unsettled. At one o'clock in the morning, the retiree slunk out of bed and onto the rear fire escape of his apartment complex. There, across the street in bright lights, stood a billboard proclaiming: *If you've been hurt… let Bliss dig the dirt!* Next to the motto rose a one-story high headshot of the bleach blonde agitator, his smile blazing white. Washington pulled out his flip phone and carefully dialed the number on the signboard, directly beneath Mr. Bradshaw's enormous head… 1-800-BLISTER.

Reggie Washington needed to save the wall… for the sake of everyone involved. He held the cellular device to his ear.

"Hello, Bliss Bradshaw…"

CHAPTER TWENTY-FIVE
WINKY'S CALL

"The boss is tired of waiting," snarled the strongman standing in front of Tommy Pagano. "Time's up my friend." The thug sported a receding hairline above a protruding forehead that suggested a passion for anabolic steroids. "I'm just following orders."

"But, but... I can explain," pleaded Winky in a panic. "We've had a bunch of delays."

"Oh really?" The enforcer stroked his left biceps while cracking his neck in a slow, circular fashion. "What kind of delays?"

"Yes. Delays. Well, first of all, elevated radon... crazy high readings, and then this majestic granite wall somebody discovers in the basement. It has an engraving on the back of it... the used key is always light. That's right," blathered Pagano, his life in the balance. "A guy named the Barber of Silverwood suddenly gets involved along with Bliss Bradshaw. You've heard of Bliss, right? Who hasn't heard of him?" Sweat began to roll down his spine. "So, you see... the timetable was thrown back due to circumstances out of my control. Pagano Destruction has been ready for months. You've got to believe me when I say that." His hands began to tremble as the messenger slowly walked behind him. "Oh yea, I almost forgot... a ghost! The Barber saw a ghost on our security video before it was stolen from the van. Stephanie was driving the company vehicle when she left the door unlocked in Manayunk. Someone must have broken in and swiped..."

The sudden snap of a piano wire around Tommy Pagano's neck crushed his vocal cords and ended his beg for forgiveness. He tried to inhale but could not, the high carbon steel shutting down his windpipe in traumatic fashion. His hands reflexively reached backward to stroke the taut, hairy forearms of the assailant gripping the noose. As his body slowly levitated off the chair an enormous pressure built up behind his bulging eyeballs. He voided urine, let out a silent gurgle and strangely realized that his right eyelid stopped twitching. His visual field blackened until he saw the face of his deceased father.

"AAAH!" screamed Pagano as he bolted upright in bed, his body struggling to break free. He gasped for air and reached behind his neck, but no one was there. A cat sleeping to his right lifted its head in silent protest before tucking it back down into the sheets. Pagano rapidly scanned the room. He was alone. A mourning dove on a flat roof adjacent to his bedroom window cooed in a repetitive fashion. It was seven o'clock on Saturday morning, July 4th in the City of Brotherly Love. He quickly made a sign of the cross and got out of bed, his heart pounding wildly in his chest.

"Holy Moses," whispered Pagano as he stared into the bathroom mirror, his reflection tired and gray. He washed his face, brushed his teeth and splashed some aftershave onto his cheeks. While looking up to the ceiling he whispered, "Help me through this day, Dad. Please, help me." The construction kingpin stepped into his trousers and donned a clean, button down shirt. He headed to the kitchen for some toast and coffee. While reading the sports page, the telephone rang.

"Winky, turn on the T.V.," said the garbled voice of Rocco. "We got troubles."

Pagano flipped on the television set to the right of the kitchen table, the relic only tuned to three local channels. There, on the KYZ network flashed the words 'Breaking News'. The camera centered on Bliss Bradshaw interviewing an elderly man, standing in front of the abandoned Franklin Wing. Behind the two walked a throng of people carrying signs. Several of the poster boards screamed, *Save the Wall!*

"That is correct," said Reggie Washington into the camera. "I worked security in the Franklin Wing for over forty years. I know that building better than anyone else."

"And you were on duty the night that Dr. Zachary Schmidt disappeared?" asked Bliss in an exaggerated tone. "Back on July 4th, 1976?"

"Yes. Yes, I was."

"Amazing," commented Bradshaw with a glance at the camera lens. "The alpha and the omega." He paused to accentuate his sage observation. "So, what can you tell us about the current status of Dr. Schmidt's wall, Mr. Washington?"

"It's laced with explosives."

"What?" squawked the Blister. "Our wall? The city of Philadelphia's newfound treasure... the one that a federal judge is trying to protect... is set to blow sky high?"

"Yes. That's what it looked like to me."

"That's outrageous!" howled the professional instigator. "Go on, sir. What else can you tell us?"

As Reggie Washington continued to speak, Winky Pagano's blood pressure reached an all-time high. If the wall didn't blow that day, the Franklin project would surely bog down in a legal quagmire stoked with innumerable delays. His nightmare flashed through his brain, the twang of the piano wire still painfully crisp.

"Now, let's bring in a wonderful, young lady named Monique," said Bliss, his inflection suddenly calm and welcoming. "Hello, young lady. What brings you out here this morning?"

Pagano watched in horror as the high school senior explained the treatment her Aunt Gracie received the day before, at the hands of the hospital CEO. Her voice cracked as she relived the frightful encounter.

"And the hospital administrator involved in this unthinkable act of medical bullying is a Mr. Ralph Covington? Is that your understanding, Monique?"

"Yes."

"The same Ralph Covington who ordered our Mr. Washington out of the hospital last night, in an attempt to squelch his shocking discovery in the Franklin basement?"

"I suppose," came the timid reply.

"And where is Aunt Gracie now?"

"They moved her out in the middle of the night," came the reply through tearful eyes. "I got a phone call this morning that she is somewhere up in North Philly, in a nursing home."

"A nursing home!" squealed Bradshaw with a look up to the sky. "Shame on them!"

The phone rang again, this time Attorney Pompano on the line.

"Wink, get down here quick," ordered the consigliore. "They're protesting out front. There's been a leak in the system! Somebody flipped."

"I'll be right there."

"Uncle Frank is blowing a gasket."

"I said, I'll be right there!" He slammed down the phone and went to turn off the television, until Bliss Bradshaw welcomed his third guest to the microphone.

"Tank! Tank Brownstone!" howled Bradshaw. "Do my eyes deceive me?" He raised his hands in the air as if greeting the prodigal son back home.

The hulking legend lumbered into the picture, his towering frame dwarfing that of Bradshaw. Next to the gridiron superstar stood a sharp dressed man with an impatient scowl.

"The last time I saw you was in Franklin Field, running back that fumble that brought a much needed title to our fair city! A play that still resonates in the heart of so many Philadelphians."

"I got it on the second bounce," proclaimed Brownstone. He raised his hands as if grasping the loose pigskin in his arms. "Took it back sixty-six yards." He struck a pose as if avoiding a tackler.

"And the rest, they say, is history!" tooted Bradshaw. "What an honor. You look fantastic, Tank. And who do we have next to you?"

Brownstone smiled and looked at the man standing next to him, his facial expression posing the same question.

"Attorney Billy B. Rogers," came the brisk reply from the man in the double vested suit. "Always representing the people in need... and today, on behalf of Mr. Theodore Brownstone.... a local legend treated in a most violent and disrespectful manner last night, here in the Philadelphia General Hospital!" A maniacal frown followed the attorney's maniacal comment.

"I see," smiled Bradshaw, appreciating the lawyer's polished syntax. "Can you enlighten our viewing audience on what exactly happened, Attorney Rogers?"

"Certainly," railed the attorney as he reached up to put his hand on his client's shoulder. "Mr. Theodore Brownstone, a.k.a. The Tank. This big old teddy bear standing next to me, was the recipient of an unsolicited charge of 50,000 volts of electricity, delivered into his body via a set of mechanical cables last night, here in the Philadelphia General."

"What?" interjected Bradshaw. "Tank was electrocuted?"

"Electrocuted! Violated! Desecrated! Call it what you want," screamed Rogers. "I'll call it an atrocity, orchestrated and carried out by a goon squad, under the direct orders of the previously mentioned... Mr. Ralph Covington!"

"Unbelievable!"

"Let me make it perfectly clear," roared the plaintiff attorney with a raised index finger. "Teddy Brownstone was targeted and shot, at point blank range, with a taser gun! Zapped! Impaled with razor sharp fishhooks that tore through his skin and sent him into cardiac arrest... while being treated for senile dementia as an inpatient!" Saliva rolled down Roger's chin as he tried to catch his breath. "Outrageous! Salacious! This is a disgrace to the city of Philadelphia and all of humanity on so many different..."

Pagano turned off the television, unwilling to witness any more histrionic stagecraft. He grabbed a piece of toast, walked out the door and hopped into his Rambler parked just outside. As soon as the engine rolled over, the radio feed of KYZ News radio came to life.

"I'm calling out Mayor Chubb to spearhead an immediate investigation into this egregious act of malice perpetrated against my client inside the walls of this city hospital!" ranted Attorney Rogers.

"As am I," agreed Bradshaw over the airwaves. "Thank you, Attorney Rogers. Wow! Now, let's bring in a good friend of mine, Seth Barber. Come on over here, Seth, wheelchair and all! Now ladies and gentlemen, before we begin, I must explain the garbled speech pattern you are about to hear. You see... Mr. Barber was minding his own business one night up in Pretzel Park, when out of nowhere, a gang of middle-aged hoodlums accosted..."

Pagano cut the broadcast, his mind incapable of absorbing any more punishment. The streets of South Philadelphia were desolate on the morning of a national holiday, aiding his speedy transit across the Schuylkill River. As he approached the perimeter fencing of the Franklin Wing, a horde of about one hundred people took notice of his arrival. He carefully turned onto the dirt roadway leading to the front gate.

"*Save the wall! Save the wall!*" shouted the flash mob as they walked beside his slow-moving vehicle. To the right stood Bliss Bradshaw still talking to Barber, the frame of Brownstone at their side. He spotted Stephanie, standing behind the wheelchair, the summer breeze blowing through her hair. Pagano continued forward and pulled up to the trailer across the street from the Franklin. He jumped out of the vehicle and walked into the Ground Zero bunker. A cast of concerned characters met his arrival.

"It had to be Stephanie," snapped Rocco. "I told you she was no good."

"Right. Right," said Attorney Pompano into a cell phone with an extended hand, imploring the crew to be silent. "I completely understand. No. It's not a problem. Thanks. I'll keep you posted." He terminated the call and looked at Pagano. "That was Uncle Frank, he said it's your call, Tommy."

"What do you mean… it's my call?" said Pagano.

"It's your call to detonate the wall."

"Are you serious? Did you see that group of protesters out there? That Bradshaw guy has already mentioned Covington and the mayor. We can't blow the wall now!" He looked at Big Bart Little, sitting in front of a computer, watching a live broadcast of Bliss Bradshaw currently interviewing a man who looked like a walrus. The chief science officer was chewing on a Philadelphia pretzel, coated with yellow mustard, oblivious to the ongoing crisis.

"Turn that off, Bart!" yelled Rocco. "I told you to turn it off an hour ago!"

"Hah… they're talking to the guy that sucker punched you in the mouth," quipped Little. "He must be eighty years old." He started to snicker. "Hell, I can take him."

"Shut up, Bart. I'll stuff that pretzel up your ass," snapped Rocco with an aggressive move toward his co-worker.

"Easy, Rock," ordered Pagano. He stepped in front of the foreman's body. "Sit down." He looked at Chief Science Officer Little. "Bart, turn that crap off. I'm trying to concentrate."

Pompano's cell phone rang again, the city mayor now on the line. The conversation was brief but to the point.

"Mayor Chubb is out," declared Pompano. "He doesn't want any part of Operation Firecracker from this point forward."

"Another chicken shit," blurted Rocco.

"He's going to play dumb and dodge the whole situation."

The door opened and in stormed Ralph Covington. "What the hell is going on out there?" howled the businessman. "Who called that Bradshaw character back again? I thought he was too lazy to follow-up on a story?"

"Stephanie," answered Rocco.

"No. We don't know if it was Stephanie," countered Pagano with a hand across his forehead.

"Well somebody invited that pretty boy back," huffed Covington. "He's out there dragging my name through the mud. I should have listened to my mother and been a dentist."

"Listen, everyone needs to calm down!" implored Pompano. "There's only one decision we have to make here this morning... and only one." He scanned the room to allow some restoration of order. "Now, everybody just take a deep breath. Alright?"

"Blow the wall!" screamed Rocco. He looked around. "Hell, if nobody wants to do it... I'll take the blame." He stood up quickly and approached the red detonation button affectionately known as Mr. Rubble.

"Rock, no!" came a unified scream. "You can't!"

Pompano and Pagano lurched forward to thwart the brute's impulsive plan of attack. He tried to raise the protective glass over Mr. Rubble, but failed to succeed.

"Everybody just cool it!" screamed Pagano. He pushed Rocco across the room. "Stay over there, Rock!"

As Pagano took a seat, a chant could be heard in the distance. "Don't explode! Don't explode!" He tried to think but the sudden drone of an overhead news helicopter began to shake the roof of the trailer. A look of resignation overtook his face.

"We have to abort," said Pagano. "There's no way we can blow it now. Everything is running too hot." He looked up at his comrades. "Abort the mission. Call it off."

"That's pathetic," railed Rocco. "You're letting a bunch of nobodies make the call. Half of those idiots don't even know what they're chanting about!"

Pagano looked at Attorney Pompano for support. In his mind, he could care less about all the noise outside the bunker. Uncle Frank was his principal concern. Pompano held a neutral gaze, unwilling to implicate the name of Mr. Frank Russo in the decision process.

"Hey, what's this?" asked Big Bart with a mouthful of pretzel. He pointed a stub of the local fare at a security camera monitor. "One of the protesters has broken inside the Franklin... down by the wall."

There, on security camera number three, the body of a man could be seen rolling on the ground. He appeared to be tangled in some of the electrical lead lines running to set charges in the granite wall.

"He's ripping out the wires!" howled Rocco. "Holy crap! He's destroying the charge lines!"

The man appeared to struggle in an attempt to get up. Once steadied, he turned about as if to get his bearings.

"A hooligan," screeched Pagano. "How dare they?"

"He'll trigger a charge," whimpered Bart. "Is he nuts? The place will blow sky high!"

The person of interest looked up at the security camera, seemingly aware of its presence. He then looked to his left out of the field of camera view.

"That's Sullivan," said Covington.

"Who?" asked Pompano.

"Dr. John Sullivan. He's been missing for days." He peered closer into the monitor. "Yep. That's him. He belongs to the

Historical Society. He's on the PGH staff. What in god's name is he trying to do?"

"Is this being recorded on video?" asked Pagano in a calm and inquisitive tone. He looked at Bart. "Are we recording this act of terrorism?"

"Absolutely," replied Little. He pointed to a black box on a shelf. "The camera is motion activated, so it's recording right now. See the blinking light? I set it all up."

Pagano's demeanor suddenly changed as he looked toward Attorney Pompano.

"Bart, are you telling us that the man on the screen can accidently set off the explosion?" asked Pompano. "Is that what I'm hearing from you?"

"That is correct," replied the biologist. "I mean, it's hard to do, but certainly possible. He would have to pull a wire hard enough to create..."

"Thank you, Bart," countered Winky Pagano. "I've heard enough." He slowly flipped open the protective glass to expose Mr. Rubble. To his left Pompano directed his cell phone at the security screen, recording the actions of the seemingly crazed intruder, for later playback.

"What are you doing?" asked Bart.

Pagano went to depress Mr. Rubble.

"Are you insane?" cried out Bart as he jumped to his feet. "You can't fire the charge. You'll kill the man!" He went to stop Pagano but Rocco bolted across the room, directly into the science officer's vast midsection. The collision tossed both men to the floor in a thunderous heap of human flesh.

Pagano calmly and firmly depressed Mr. Rubble with a demonic look in his eyes.

"STOP IT!" screamed Bart as he log rolled on the floor and drove a stub of pretzel into Rocco's eye. He belly-flopped toward Mr. Rubble in an attempt to somehow reverse the irreversible command from his employer. The scientist moaned and reached toward the rat's nest of wiring snaking through a white PVC pipe into the trailer floor, but Rocco beat him to the choke point.

"Let it blow!" screamed the foreman as he ripped all the wiring out from beneath Mr. Rubble. "Blow the wall!" Sparks flew into the air as he delivered a hand full of exposed electrical cords overhead. In the distance, the sound of a long siren blast permeated the air.

"Are you crazy?" asked Bart from floor level. "That man is going to be buried alive!"

"Wait a minute!" said Pompano. "There's a second intruder."

Everyone centered their eyes on the monitor, now showing two men motioning wildly at each other.

"What the..." said Pagano.

"Tommy, that looks like..."

"Vince!" screamed Pagano. "Vince! What's he doing down there!" He looked down at the ball of exposed wiring on the floor. "Oh my god! Vince!"

"Abort!" screamed Pompano. "Abort!"

"Stop the explosion!" squealed Rocco as he scooped up the tangled cables and manhandled them back beneath Mr. Rubble. "Stop the explosion. Abort! Abort! Bart, help me!" He haphazardly jammed the wiring into the underbelly of the countertop, hoping for some sort of magical reconnection to occur.

"Vincent!" screamed the surgeon's father.

"Do something!" shouted Pompano.

"Rock, you stupid idiot," barked Bart as he came to his knees. He drove his stubby hands into the electrical disarray. "Yellow has to go to yellow, and black to black."

"Vincent!" screamed Pagano with both arms high in the air. "My Vincent! Get out of there... NOW!"

CHAPTER TWENTY-SIX
DO YOU TRUST ME?

"What the heck," howled Sullivan as his body catapulted directly into the spider web of wires. He was the first person discharged from the time portal. He rolled several times to the right and struggled to get up as Vince rocketed out of the tunnel, his ankle turning violently in the process.

"Ouch!" winced the orthopedic surgeon. "I broke my ankle!" He looked down at a slightly deformed left lower extremity.

"Vince, get up! Get up!" Sullivan looked up at the security camera bearing down on him.

"I'm trying. My ankle! It's broken."

The sickening drone of an air raid siren startled both time travelers, the blast lasting for at least ten seconds.

"What's that noise?" asked Sullivan, now fully erect.

"John, look at the wall!" shouted the surgeon.

Sullivan glanced up to see a honeycomb pattern of circular drill holes peppering the granite edifice, each hole the recipient of a thick, black wire.

"It's rigged with explosives!" continued Pagano.

A second, equally long blow of the siren occurred.

"John, that's a series of warning sirens!" screamed Pagano as he held his ankle with both hands. He grimaced and forced his frame upright. "The place is going to blow in exactly two minutes."

"What!" shouted Sullivan over the blare of the third whistle.

"I've heard it a hundred times. It's a warning to evacuate." Pagano sat back down in pain. "I'm not going to make it, John. Don't you see? This is how I die on July 4th! They've moved up the implosion date." A look of absolute dread covered his face. "I'm going to die."

The fourth siren began to sound.

"We've got to get out of here," proclaimed Sullivan as he kicked the wires away. "I'll carry you. You're not going to die today."

"Are you crazy? You can't even run out of here fast enough! We're both doomed."

The fifth and final alert signal roared through the basement.

"John. Get out of here," ordered Pagano. "Save yourself." He began to whimper. "I'm going to die. We can't change the future. It's impossible."

An eerie silence overcame the basement.

"You're not going to die!" declared Sullivan. "I won't allow it." He grabbed Pagano's upper torso and slid him backwards. "Get back on the portal pad, Vince. I'm sending you back to the future."

An immediate glimmer of hope appeared in Pagano's eyes as he tucked his frame forward. "John, we can *both* make it. The key! Where's the key?" He positioned himself on the center of the embossed eyeball, grimacing in pain. "Hurry! Get on the pad, John."

Sullivan clutched the skeleton key around his neck and forcefully wrenched it off. He handed it to Pagano. "Get out of here, now! I've got to stay. Put the key in the slot, Vince."

"No way. You'll die. I'm not leaving without you."

"Vince, go!"

"I'm not leaving without you." He tossed the key back to Sullivan. "We both go... or we both die." He paused. "I mean it, John. Get on the pad... now!"

Sullivan took firm hold of the key. He swiftly stepped away from the eye grid and slapped the key into its granite slot.

"So long, Vince. I can't go."

A clap of thunder filled the room.

"But John, you'll die!"

A brilliant flash of light lit the basement and Pagano disappeared. Sullivan held tight to the key and bolted from the time portal, back into camera view. He stumbled over a chunk of concrete and quickly righted himself. An internal clock inside his cranium started to count backwards from sixty as he sprinted down a hallway, his progress under constant surveillance from the demo team inside Ground Zero. The escape route was dimly lit and littered with debris. He hit the stairwell at full speed and took a nasty fall on the first step, his internal countdown suddenly at forty. The geriatrician took two steps at a time and hit the ground floor of the PGH complex with twenty seconds to spare. He bolted directly toward the set of steel double doors that would lead him to Reggie Washington's outpost and freedom, but the doors held firm, delivering him back down to the gritty pavement.

"Zero," said a voice in his head as he winced, but there was no explosion. He reached for a crowbar on the ground and gave a mighty whack to the door, the blow flinging the exit wide open. Sullivan rushed forward, his body even with Reggie's post when a horrific blast of energy roared from behind, the force taking hold of his body and tossing it away from the Franklin. He tumbled, rolled and crashed into a distant wall, his body curled and carpeted with flying particles of granite and concrete. The roar lasted for ten more seconds and then everything went silent.

Sullivan opened his eyes and coughed, the air thick with a potpourri of industrial mist. He rapidly blinked his eyes, squinted and carefully moved each of his four extremities. He took several deep breaths. He was alive! Looking backward, a cloud of carnage hovered over a pile of debris, the inner bowels of the Franklin blown wide open. The wall was destroyed.

Sullivan came to his feet. He ran to his right and up a stairwell, exiting the hospital complex on the rear side of the Franklin, opposite the Ground Zero bunker. He fled west, toward home, through the relatively empty streets of Philadelphia. In the distance, approaching sirens could be heard along with a smattering of car alarms, set off by the blast. By the time he reached 43rd Street, his lungs burned and his legs ached. He noticed a 'Sold' sticker stamped on Perch Peterson's 'For Sale' sign. He glanced up to his mother's bedroom and her window was closed. The side door was locked and he began to frantically ring the doorbell. Through a window he spotted a person coming down a stairwell and the door opened. His brother stared him in the eye.

John Sullivan froze and waited for his brother to speak.

"She's gone, John. Mom's dead."

He continued to rapidly inhale and exhale, his lungs screaming for oxygen. He only broke eye contact with his brother when Moses pranced behind him, across the foyer floor.

"She never came back to her senses after you left, despite us running the fluids. She died the next morning, around five o'clock." He reached out to place a hand on the physician's shoulder. "I'm sorry, John."

A peculiar combination of sadness and relief overcame John Sullivan. His mother was dead and finally at peace.

"Is Aidan home?" asked the physician.

His brother stared back. "That's a peculiar question, John. I just told you Mom died, and you want to know about Aidan's whereabouts?"

"George. Do you trust me?"

His brother didn't answer.

"Do you trust me as a brother and a physician?"

"Why, sure... John. What are you getting at?"

"What if I told you... that I have the capability to save Aidan's life?" He pointed to the ground. "Here, right now... today, over the next two hours. Would you believe me, George? Would you trust me?"

"Ah, John... that's kind of a strange set of questions? Are you feeling O.K.? I mean, what are you talking about? You're covered in dirt."

"Would you trust me with his life? Because if you will, I can free him and perhaps our family from that horrible disease... forever."

His older brother took a few seconds to ponder the magnitude of the request. "Mom always said you were different," said George. "Do you know that?"

"No."

"She said you were well... special." He grinned. "Why would she say that, John? Are you some sort of a magic man?"

"No, I'm not."

"A miracle worker?"

"No."

"What's been going on over the past few weeks?"

"A hell of a lot. I will explain it all, but it's going to take too much time."

"Well, how can you save his life, John? Aidan has in incurable genetic disease."

"It's an unbelievable story, but you have to trust me when I tell you... I can do it." He spoke with absolute conviction. "I can make Aidan normal again." He reached out and held his brother's shoulders. That's why I vanished, George. Not for Mom, but for Aidan. I couldn't pass up the opportunity. You have to believe me." He squeezed tight. "Please, let me do it... for Aidan's sake."

Aidan appeared behind his father with his pajamas on. "Daddy, can we have breakfast? Gordon's hungry."

"Sure," said his father. He squatted down and hugged his son. "How was the sleepover?"

"Good. We want pancakes... with chocolate chips."

"You got it," said George. "I'll meet you and Gordon in the kitchen. I'll be right there." He brushed his son's hair aside and sent him upstairs to find his friend. He stood back up. "Alright, John. Let's do it. What have I got to lose? Let's see what makes you so special."

"Thank you! You won't regret it," replied John with a brisk step past his brother. "I'll get things set upstairs. I'm assuming the nursing team left all of the intravenous tubing I requested for Mom?"

"Yes. They haven't been back since the funeral," replied George with a quizzical look. "But, why do you need intravenous tubing?"

"Did a package arrive for me?" asked John with a scan of the room.

"As a matter of fact, yes. Yes it did. It's over there, near the sofa."

John stepped over to retrieve the box. He lifted it to his ear and gave it a subtle shake. "Wonderful. We'll need this."

"What will you need? What's in the box? Did you have this all planned out?"

"You'll see," shouted John as he rocketed up the steps. "Get those kids breakfast, George. After that, we'll recreate the magic that occurred in the living room of Mrs. Ingrid Hoffman, not so long ago!"

"Uncle John. Uncle John!" shouted Aidan as he ran down the stairwell with his pre-school friend.

"Good morning, gentlemen!" replied John. "What a glorious morning it is!"

John Sullivan paused as he entered the front bedroom, fully expecting his Mom to be seated on her bed with Moses.

He said a solemn prayer and carefully tidied up some of her personal belongings. Once settled, he opened the package sent to the house per his instructions by Mrs. Hoffman. It contained a military field blood transfusion kit. Inside were all the tools necessary for a person to emergently transfuse his or her blood into a stricken soldier while in a combat zone. The kit included alcohol pads, a hemostat, sterile gloves, venous constricting bands, intravenous needles and all the necessary anticoagulants to prevent blood from clotting. The physician deftly inserted an intravenous line into his vein and began part one of the process, which involved his blood being drained into a 400-millimeter blood bag. The process took about thirty minutes, during which time breakfast was being served downstairs. After filling the reservoir with his own blood, Sullivan disconnected his intravenous line and placed the bag into a sleek, blue wrap contained within the kit. He hung the transfusion on the arm of a tall floor lamp, via a coat hanger. Next, he prepared the intravenous lines for Aidan. He heard the voice of a parent picking up Aidan's friend.

"They had a great time," said George. "Thanks for letting him sleep over. It meant a lot to Aidan."

"Thanks for having him," said the boy's father. "Did you have a good time, Gordon?"

"You bet. We had chocolate pancakes with the cat."

"Thanks again, George," said the man. "Val sends her condolences to you and the entire family. Your mom was an amazing person."

"Thank you, Rob. We appreciate it. So long, Gordon."

"Good-bye, Mr. Sullivan. Thank you for having me over."

The door closed and George headed upstairs with his son, his steps slow and tentative. Deep in his heart, he trusted his brother.

"Aidan, my man!" shouted John as he entered the room. "Did Dad tell you what's about to happen?"

"Yep," said the child as he jumped up onto a chair next to grandma's bed. You're going to give me some medicine to take care of the family sickness."

"Exactly."

"Will it hurt?"

"Nope." Sullivan pulled out a vial of EMLA cream and placed a dollop of the numbing medicine on Aidan's elbow crease. He waited a few minutes to allow the topical anesthetic to work its magic.

"How's school?" asked the physician.

"I missed two days due to Grandma's funeral. Why weren't you there?"

"I had…"

"Dad said you were away, saving somebody's life."

John looked at his brother in appreciation. "That's right. I'm glad Daddy told you so." He rubbed Aidan's hair. "You know Grandma is looking down on us now? Right?"

"She's in heaven with Mommy and Grandpa. I know that."

"Good. You're a very smart boy. How does your arm feel?" Sullivan gently pinched the child's skin beneath the cream.

"Hah. I don't even feel that."

"Now Aidan, in order to give you the medicine, I have to put a special plastic tube into your arm."

"Go ahead. I've done this before at the hospital." He held out his arm and closed his eyes. "Just tell me when it's done."

Dr. Sullivan expertly placed an access catheter into the child's arm vein. Once secure he took the tubing from the above blue bag and connected it directly to Aidan's intravenous line.

"Done," said the medical doctor.

"Blue is Grandma's favorite color," said Aidan as he opened his eyes and looked upward. "She'd like that bag." He wiped his nose with his opposite forearm. "What's in it?"

"Medicine," said Sullivan. The cat jumped up onto a dresser as if interested in the transaction. "Are you ready, Aidan?"

"Yes!"

"Brother George, are you ready?"

No response.

"I repeat, Brother George," said John in a louder tone. "Are you ready to see your only child cured of a disease that up until this very moment in time, was deemed..."

"Just do it, John! Yes. Yes. I'm ready."

"Alright," said John. "Ready, set and go." He rolled open the stopcock just below the blue bag connected to the hanger, releasing a stream of dark red blood down the clear tubing.

"Is that blood?" shouted Aidan with a look of terror at the approaching fluid.

"Who said anything about blood," quipped the physician. "That's genuine plasma from the vein of a Sullivan, that's been genetically engineered and laced with an anticoagulant to deter the coagulation cascade!"

"It's blood!" howled Aidan as he watched the fluid sneak down the tube into his arm.

"It's nectar from the gods, capable of curing everything from the common cold to Polycystic Global Demyelination Syndrome... or PGD for short!" He raised his hands in theatrical honor of Dr. Schmidt. "Oh evil entity from the beloved family tree, take leave from the house of the Sullivan man!"

"Meow," opined the cat.

"I don't feel a thing," said Aidan in amazement. He looked at his dad. "It doesn't hurt."

"Uncle John said it wouldn't hurt. The question is, will it work?"

"Oh ye of little faith," came the brisk reply. "Of course it will work. Do we have a non-believer among us?" The physician slowed up the rate of transfusion while checking his wristwatch.

"How long is it going to take, John?"

"About an hour. I'm going to run it slow to prevent any reaction."

"Reaction? What type of reaction?"

"Don't you worry, George. Do you have any Tylenol in the house?"

After administering a prophylactic dose of Tylenol, the medical doctor monitored his patient for any signs of a blood transfusion reaction. There were none, and after twenty minutes, Aidan fell fast asleep beneath his grandmother's favorite afghan.

"He's doing fantastic," whispered John to his brother. "He's a real trooper. It's going to work, George. Trust me."

"Where were you, John? Where could you have possibly gone for so long during Mom's demise?"

John Sullivan dropped back into his mother's half-winged chair and proceeded to tell his brother everything: from the moment he met the radon inspector in the Franklin basement, to the moment he and Vince Pagano catapulted back into the explosive grid. He didn't leave out a single detail. Throughout it all, his brother sat silent and seemingly awestruck.

"And that's the absolute truth," finished up the doctor with a tone of relief. "Truly amazing."

"Wow, you make it sound so real," said George. "Especially the part about the U.S. Postal Service being profitable. A command performance indeed. Bravo."

"What? You don't believe me?"

His brother slowly and silently rotated his head in disbelief.

"Turn on the T.V., George. If you don't believe me, maybe Bliss will convince you."

His brother flipped on the television to WKYZ. There, front and center, stood a grim-faced Bliss Bradshaw. Behind him billowed greyish black smoke from the center of the Franklin Wing, its main edifice collapsed inward. As the reporter spoke of an unscheduled explosion and the possible loss of life, a chyron rolling beneath his frame stated:

"Frantic rescue effort in progress for two physicians possibly trapped inside the rubble..."

"So they think you and Dr. Pagano are dead?" asked George. "Don't you think you should tell them?"

"I couldn't delay," answered John. "The antidote is time sensitive. I didn't want it to wear off." He looked caringly at Aidan, fast asleep in the chair. "First things first."

"But what about Dr. Pagano?"

"Vince is safe, albeit on the other side of the tunnel."

George shook his head, everything strangely starting to make sense. "But the tunnel is destroyed."

"I had to tell you, George. I'm sorry, but your life will never be the same. I apologize."

"I understand. At least I'm beginning to think so."

"But, I have to abide by the cardinal rules of time travel."

"Cardinal rules?"

"Yes, according to Zachary Schmidt. Every traveler must have an assigned co-pilot, a trusted wingman... just in case anything goes awry."

"So, I guess I'm your wingman?" asked George.

"Congratulations," grinned his brother. "Welcome to the world of time travel." He reached into his pocket and delivered the skeleton key, dangling it in front of his brother. "Now, if we can only figure out who R.S. is." He brought the key near his eyes. "George, did you look up the signers of the Declaration of Independence?"

George Sullivan's cell phone rang.

"Hello," said George. "Yes, yes... they both had a wonderful time." He paused while shaking his head up and down with a smile. "No problem, I'll have Aidan bring his backpack to school tomorrow." He listened for a few more seconds. "Alright. Thank you, Mrs. Hayhurst. Right... you have a good day, too." He terminated the call.

"What did you just say?" asked John to his brother.

"What?"

"To the caller, what did you just say?"

"Oh, that was Gordon's mom. He left his backpack here. No biggie."

"But her name. What did you say her last name was?"

"Hayhurst. Her last name is Hayhurst. Why do you ask?"

"So her son, Gordon… is Gordon Hayhurst?"

"Right. That's very good, John. You see, Rob and Val Hayhurst had a son named Gordon." He spoke very slowly to emphasize the obvious. "So he goes by the name of Gordon Hayhurst. That's common in these parts… you know for your offspring to take the family name."

"Unbelievable," whispered Dr. Sullivan to himself. He chuckled. "Gordon Hayhurst. Now I know this is going to absolutely work. Fascinating."

"Apparently the kid is a genius."

"Oh, I know," said John. "Trust me. He's a *real* genius."

Just then, a Philadelphia police car pulled up outside the Sullivan homestead. Two officers got out of the vehicle and headed to the side entrance, in search of Dr. John Sullivan.

CHAPTER TWENTY-SEVEN
SIDE BY SIDE

As John Sullivan lay in bed, fireworks lit up the sky over West Philadelphia. He was exhausted yet unable to sleep. Earlier in the day, he told the police the truth, that Vince Pagano approached him as he stood outside of the Franklin Wing, asking multiple questions about the wall. Pagano demanded to see the granite construct, so both men entered the doomed complex together, unaware of any plan to detonate the building ahead of schedule. He made a conscious decision to omit the entire time travel section of the story, out of fear of being committed to an insane asylum. Once inside, they tripped over some wires and became disoriented when the sirens began to blare. Sullivan bolted one way and Pagano the other, each confident in their own route of escape. The two men never saw each other again. Besides the timing of events, his statements to the authorities were indeed, quite factual. The distortion of time didn't bother Sullivan, since time was a man-made entity.

Moses jumped on the bed and circled twice before tucking down at his side. He thought of his mom, almost expecting her to give out a yell while watching the ball game in the adjacent room. "Never count out the Brookside Pugs!" She hoped to watch next week's all-star game, but more importantly, she wanted to die naturally. He recalled Zachary imploring him, as his mother's primary care provider, to respect her final wishes... and let her expire peacefully at home, in her own bed. He respectfully abided by his mother's request. That he was confident of. Just then, a string of firecrackers ripped through the corridor separating the Sullivan and Peterson homesteads, the blast echoing in the night. Sullivan grinned while whispering, "You're welcome, Mom." The cat began to purr when the door to his room cracked open, his brother's head poking inside along with a sliver of light.

"Goodnight, John. Thanks for everything."

"How's he doing?" asked the doctor.

"Fine. Fast asleep. He's had a long day."

"We all have. Good night, George."

"Good job, doc. Mom would be proud of you."

"I know she would. Thanks."

Thirty minutes later the physician stepped out of bed, got dressed and walked outside. As he approached the Philadelphia General Hospital the frequency of fireworks began to wane. It was eleven o'clock at night when he walked through the main entrance of the facility, the lobby still abuzz with activity. His route took him to the Department of Medical Records, a drab confine in the bowels of the PGH basement, staffed by one employee so late at night.

"Can I help you?" asked the bespectacled man behind an old wooden desk. He wiped his nose with a white hanky.

Sullivan held up his I.D. badge. "Dr. John Sullivan here. I need to retrieve some medical records regarding one of my patients."

The man tilted his head back to read the badge. "Go right ahead." He gestured a thumb over his shoulder. "Just key in your password on the computer. Let me know if you need help."

"How far do the electronic records go back?"

"About the mid 1970s," said the man. "Anything prior to that is on microfilm, up in the Cheltenham warehouse."

"Thank you."

Sullivan made his way to a corner cubicle, boxed in by cinder walls painted olive green. After keying in his password credentials, the computer asked him for a name and date of birth to search. He carefully typed in: 'George Sullivan... date of birth – October 31st, 1940'. As the machine began to spin a beach ball on the screen, he thought of his father's favorite birthday saying, "The scariest thing about Halloween, is the number of candles on that cake!" He smiled.

The computer generated a single name that matched the demographic input. It was indeed that of George Sullivan, Sr., and with a trembling hand, the son accessed his deceased father's medical record. Surprisingly, there was only one notation stored within the system, an August 1st office memo from 1974. The letterhead of the report identified the examination to have been performed within the Philadelphia General's Department of Internal Medicine. The history read:

> This 34 year-old white male presents for a second opinion regarding service-connected injuries incurred while serving in Vietnam. Medical care to date has been carried out in the West Philadelphia Veteran's Administration Hospital. Veteran presents for second opinion regarding inability to conceive...

Sullivan's mind scrambled as he rechecked the date of the report. He was born in 1977, three years after the office visit. His older brother was born in 1972. He continued to scroll down on the document.

> No known drug allergies. Medication list included Inderal for high blood pressure and apple cider vinegar for heartburn. Additional history was notable for rare alcohol use and an occasional cigar.

"Rare alcohol use," mumbled Sullivan in disbelief. "C'mon Dad." He fondly remembered running down the basement steps for 'another bottle of Schmidt's beer' on a nightly basis.

> Past surgical history notable for multiple left hip and groin operations while stationed in South Vietnam for penetrating pelvic and groin trauma, to include left sided orchiectomy. Most recent pelvic/bladder reconstruction was two years ago at VA.

Sullivan's heart raced. His parents never went into details regarding the wounds that garnered Dad a Purple Heart, only noting that they changed his life forever. George Sullivan, Sr. was stoic when it came to his military service.

What followed in the record was a sparse examination, documenting multiple well-healed abdomen wounds and surgical scars. His left testicle was listed as "absent" and his right testicle "distorted". The remainder of the examination was unremarkable. The laboratory section of the report made reference to a seminal fluid analysis reporting a sperm count to be "low to absent". The final diagnosis read:

1. Status post penetrating trauma to left hip, groin and pelvis.
2. Status post multiple surgical procedures, to include pelvic wall, bladder and right testicular reconstruction, left orchiectomy.
3. High blood pressure.
4. Infertility.

The record was authored by a chief medical resident, but cosigned by an attending with the initials, Z.S. Below the typed record was a hand-written comment stating: *"Discussed with patient and spouse at length. Had one live born prior to most recent surgery. Recommend boxer shorts only, warm compresses to testicle and no change in coital habits. Discussed the greatest healer of all being 'tincture of*

time'. Will keep them posted of any future breakthroughs....
Zachary Schmidt, MD."

Schmidt's signature, like his persona, was grand. No other medical records existed within the database. He reread the report several times as a puzzling mishmash of possibilities began to roll through his mind. Nothing made sense, especially with the presence of the time tunnel in the equation. He slowly walked out of the hospital and into the hot, humid night, trying to reconcile the facts at hand.

His father was severely wounded in battle, the evidence suggesting a near direct round of ammunition or shrapnel to his groin. It appears he fathered a child with the suggestion of a subsequent reconstructive surgery that rendered him unable to conceive. He was diagnosed with infertility by seminal standards three years prior to his own birth. The question was... what happened between the years 1974 and 1977? Several distinct scenarios existed: some miraculous, some futuristic and some sordid. Did the good Lord above shine upon the young couple and grant them an immaculate conception? Or, perhaps Schmidt transported some sort of miracle cure backward in time? Both were plausible explanations, but neither fully explained Hayhurst's comment on Schmidt needing to be a direct relative in regard to his life saving transfusion. Could the third option be possible, thought Sullivan? No! Never. Not his mother! She was a saint. However... they did work together in close proximity for an extended period of time in the Franklin. Schmidt was rumored to be irresistibly dashing, and from meeting the man, his personality was undeniably vivacious and intoxicating. But she loved... Dad. No. No way. It's impossible! But why did she mumble Zachary's name on her deathbed? He couldn't fathom the possibility, but then again... anything's possible.

"John. What the hell are you doing out here?"

Sullivan looked up to see CEO Covington standing near a security fence near the Franklin Wing. Bright lights lit up the blast zone, a rescue effort still in full force. An army of men and equipment carefully moved hunks of granite from the debris pile, as dogs sniffed through the wreckage.

"Just trying to sort things out," said the bewildered physician. He looked beyond Covington. "Sad."

"If they don't find him by tomorrow morning, it's going to turn into a recovery mission." Covington spit on the ground in disgust. "Now they'll never knock down the Franklin." He glared at Sullivan. "John, what the hell happened in there? I saw you on the security cam. Where did you two come from? It looked to me like you came out of nowhere."

"Why did you close my wing?" snarled Sullivan. He was in no mood to kowtow to Covington. "How dare you!"

"John, you have to understand…"

"Where are Mrs. Appleton and Mrs. Jones? Don't you have any common decency? These are human beings you're dealing with, not numbers on a spreadsheet!"

"Now listen here, John. As CEO, I have to make the hard decisions. So trust me when I say…"

"You're no leader. You're a divider," snapped Sullivan. "I can't believe the way you've treated me… and my patients. How you ever made it to hospital CEO, I'll never know." He turned to walk away.

"So what are you, John?" shouted the CEO. "Running around trying to cure dementia. You're no ball of fire! You haven't generated an academic paper in five years." Covington's anger increased as the physician ignored his comments. "Consider yourself on the hospitalist staff starting tomorrow morning!" howled Covington. "That's right, *tomorrow*. Report to the floor at six o'clock sharp. Don't be late, John… or else."

Sullivan kept walking.

"Recall, respect and ... whatever! Hah! Like that's ever going to make a difference. Give me a break, John. Do you ever wonder why no one else goes into geriatrics? You're wasting your time trying to cure Alzheimer's. It's impossible."

Sullivan turned around and stormed back toward his employer. He stopped three feet away from his face. "I quit," said Sullivan. "Find yourself another geriatrician."

"Now listen to me, John."

"I'm light years ahead of you, Ralph."

"What the hell does that mean?"

"You'll see. Just keep watching."

"Go ahead... quit! See what I care! You won't find a better..."

"I'm going to make a difference in the fight against Alzheimer's... a *big* difference. Mark my words." He stared down his ex-boss, smiled smugly and walked away. "Trust me on that one, Ralph."

"Don't do it, John! Nobody just leaves the Philadelphia General. It's a career ender. We're the big dog on the block, my friend. You'll be sorry."

Sullivan made his way five blocks south, to the historic Ridge Lawn Cemetery, situated for centuries on a set of bucolic knolls overlooking the Schuylkill River. He passed through the dimly lit front gate and turned left, the route to the family plot well established in his mind. One by one, his aunts and uncles ended up in Ridge Lawn, and now... it was Mom's turn. She represented the last piece of the family puzzle. No more plots were available. He immediately spotted the Sullivan headstone and the fresh brown dirt over his mother's final resting place. A lamppost in the distance cast a glimmer of light on the burial mound. He slowly and respectfully approached the grave.

She selected her own headstone, which proclaimed:

MARTHA A. SULLIVAN

JUNE 15, 1942 † JUNE 27, 2020

BELOVED WIFE AND MOTHER

It was perfect, thought Sullivan. To her right a stone declared:

GEORGE W. SULLIVAN

CORPORAL USMC

VIETNAM

OCT. 31, 1940 † MAY 10, 2013

PURPLE HEART

"I'm sorry I missed your funeral, Mom," stated Sullivan. He leaned forward to straighten some wilted roses. "I hear it was a beautiful day." His eyes began to water as he choked up. "Moses is doing well. I still get him a gyro every day... no onions." He paused for several minutes in silence. "The Pugs called up a lefty from Double-A, so their bullpen should be just fine." He reached down again to flip a speck of dirt off the marker. "You can never have enough lefties for the stretch run." He had trouble enunciating anything else. "We all miss you, Mom."

He carefully stepped to his left and walked past his father's headstone to adjust a grave marker. A circular, bronze medallion on the flag holder stated 'Vietnam' on the top with the years '1964-1975' on the bottom. A mixture of military logos symmetrically filled the center of the disc. At its apex flew the Stars and Stripes, proudly honoring one of its true heroes. He straightened the flag post and carefully drove it deeper into the ground.

"There you go Pops," said Sullivan. "Semper Fi." He walked back below both gravesites and saluted.

"Well, this is it. Here you are... side by side for all of eternity." He said a few prayers and made a sign of the cross.

"Goodnight, Mom. Goodnight, Dad." He bowed and stepped backward. "Rest in peace. I love you."

The walk back home remained solemn. John Sullivan fully realized that his life had changed dramatically, in so many different ways. A half block away from home, he noticed a taxicab parked just outside. The car's blinkers were flashing, and the trunk open. A cabbie was setting a series of suitcases on the curb. Behind the luggage stood the frame of a woman, holding a child. As Sullivan approached, she handed the driver his fare before he tipped his cap and drove away.

"Hi," said John. "Can I help you?" It was now one o'clock in the morning. He sensed apprehension. "I live right here," said Sullivan while pointing to his home. "Are you the new neighbors?"

"Yes. Yes, we are."

"Oh great! Hi. I'm John Sullivan. I grew up here... next to the Petersons. They owned the home. Welcome. Let me help you with your bags."

"Why thank you," said the woman, her tone more at ease. She held her child with one arm and picked up a small bag with another. "Our flight was delayed out of London and then by the time we got through customs... oh heavens, we're both exhausted."

"Well then, welcome to Philadelphia," said Sullivan while lugging two heavy suitcases up the steps. "You're from England?"

"Well, originally Nebraska, then London for the past four years."

"What brings you to Philadelphia?"

"Business transfer," came the fatigued response as they reached the door. She fumbled in her purse for the house keys.

"Wait," said Sullivan. He placed the baggage down and stepped back to reach under his own mailbox, delivering a key taped to the underside. "Perch and I... that was the previous owner, Perch Peterson. We both kept a backup key beneath each other's mailbox, just in case." He opened the door.

"Thank you so much…"

"John. It's John Sullivan." He hoisted the luggage toward the entrance.

"Thank you, John."

"And your name is?"

"Oh, I'm sorry, it's Theresa. Theresa Jenkins."

"Wonderful. Pleased to meet you, Theresa." He looked at the little boy, fast asleep in her arms. "And who's the little fella? He's a real cutie."

She grinned. "Quentin is his name, but that's funny you should say that."

"What?" asked Sullivan.

"That you called him a cutie. That's his nickname, at least from me."

"Cutie?"

"Yes. His middle name is Theo. So we call him "Q.T." for short."

A thunderclap went off in Sullivan's brain.

"Get it? Q.T.…. Cutie?"

"I do get it," whispered Sullivan as he looked closely into her blue eyes. Despite the hour and lighting, his new neighbor was undeniably attractive. "And, Mr. Jenkins? When will he be arriving in town?"

"Oh, well. That's another reason for the move." She pulled the child closer. "There is no Mr. Jenkins."

"Oh, I'm sorry," stammered Sullivan. "I just…"

"No, that's fine. It is what it is." She smiled and stiffened her upper lip. "Well, John. It's been an absolute pleasure meeting you. Thank you for your timely help."

"Glad to help. Call me if you need anything."

Just then the child opened its weary eyes and looked around, pointing to a window in the Sullivan home. There on the windowpane sat Moses, striking a perfect pose.

"That's a cat," said the child's mother. "C-A-T. Cat."

The child smiled and tucked his head back into her shoulder.

"Thanks, John. Goodnight."

"Goodnight, Theresa. Goodnight, Quentin. Welcome to the neighborhood. You're going to love it here."

Sullivan's sorrow turned to absolute joy as he closed the door behind him. He quietly worked his way upstairs while watching each room in the Peterson home light up. His heart pounded wildly as he checked on Aidan, the youngster fast asleep. He could not believe his good fortune. Once in bed he thought of Zachary and Vince, so far away in the future. What were they doing? What were they thinking? Would they ever make it back? Could they ever make it back? There just had to be a way. He reached toward the nightstand and picked up the key, feeling its texture in the night.

He just met his future wife and son, Quentin Theo... Q.T.! Zachary must have surely known. That's why he directed Dr. Hayhurst to take him into the operating room. It was a clue from the legendary Zachary Schmidt himself... that old rascal.

"Thanks, Zachary," whispered Sullivan in the night. "Much appreciated." He stroked the initials on the key. "But why can't you tell me who R.S. is?"

CHAPTER TWENTY-EIGHT
R.S.

It was a crisp, sunny September day in the City of Brotherly Love. A crowd of tourists strolled just outside of Independence Hall, taking in all the splendor of the downtown historic district. Horse-drawn carriages trotted along cobblestone streets, past groups of children waiting to catch their first glimpse of the Liberty Bell. In an open field opposite the hall, a military regiment from the revolutionary war reenacted some close order drills.

"It just doesn't make sense," stated George Sullivan. "It's a dead end, John. A conundrum." He chomped on a soft pretzel while sitting next to his brother on a park bench, waiting for Aidan to return from a class trip. Two plump pigeons waddled near their feet.

"Wow. I forgot how absolutely magnificent that document is," stated John. "To read those words in the very room it was signed... hundreds of years ago. What an amazing group of forward thinkers." He stared in awe at Independence Hall in the distance.

"I agree. Our founding fathers certainly had tremendous foresight. Just think about it... their words still set the standard for our daily lives."

Yet, John Sullivan let out a heavy sigh. He allocated the Labor Day weekend to fully investigate the Declaration of Independence and its two signers with the initials R.S. But so far, his on-site research yielded no additional clues regarding the key's original owner.

"So, I don't think it's the guy from Connecticut," said George.

"Roger Sherman?"

"Yea. It's not him."

"I'm not too sure about that, George. He was very well respected by his peers. He served on the committee to draft the Declaration itself."

"But he was quiet. Taciturn. I'd look for someone more flamboyant... like your buddy, Zachary. He doesn't seem like someone holding the key to the future."

"Perhaps. But stealth is one of the cardinal rules."

"What about Richard Stockton, from New Jersey? I like him," said George. "The guy spent a lot of time in Philly."

"He would seem the more obvious choice. But still, where does a key come into play here? Stockton spent years in prison under British rule and died shortly afterward." He looked at his brother. "George, I suggest you scrape some salt off that pretzel. It may cause future memory problems."

"I can't even have some salt on my pretzel? Don't be ridiculous." He took a mighty chomp of the local fare. "You medical doctors can't make up your mind."

"What do you mean?"

"Twenty years ago I couldn't touch an egg and we had bread with every meal."

"So."

"Now my doctor tells me not to touch white bread and eat as many eggs as I want... bacon included!"

"Now, George. Dietary recommendations..."

"Make up your mind!"

John said no more, allowing his brother to finish his doughy snack in peace.

"How's Theresa?"

"Wonderful," answered John with a smile. "We attended the symphony last night. She's a fan of classical music."

"Oh, I'm sorry to hear that. I thought you said she was perfect."

"She is! What luck to have her buy the Peterson home, sight unseen? It's absolute kismet."

George wiped some mustard off his upper lip with a napkin. "How's the new clinic coming along, or should I say, 'The Sullivan Clinic'?"

"Great. It's going to take a while to get established but being independent certainly has its advantages. We're going to remain a day center until we get accreditation for twenty-four hour care. The community support has been outstanding."

"I tip my hat to you, John. You're a man on a mission. And Mrs. Gracie Jones... how's she doing?"

"Excellent. We get her for six hours, seven days a week. She's a new person since her Randall reappeared."

"Now, let me get this straight," continued George. "She and Randall were newlyweds, until he disappeared down the tunnel back in 1976?"

"That's right."

"So she goes into some sort of a catatonic state for forty years, until he magically reappears?"

"Right. She perked up immediately upon seeing him. It was that crazy little song that brought them back together. Dr. Garcia is going to publish a case report on Mrs. Jones. We're going to call it the 'Out of Sight Syndrome'."

"Catchy. And Randall still lives with Zachary's cousin, Ingrid?"

"Yes, they've taken to each other quite well." John leaned back to let the afternoon sun shine upon him. "He visits his wife every day. And most importantly, Monique started college, confident that her Aunt Gracie is in good hands."

"I've got to admit it, John. You're on a roll. Ever since you rocketed out of that tunnel, you're a new man."

"Yes, except for one thing… Vince Pagano." A sense of sadness overcame the physician. "I wrote a lengthy letter to Mr. Pagano, expressing my condolences."

"Have you heard back?"

"No. I can't imagine his grief." He put his head into his hands. "It keeps me up at night, knowing that Vince is still alive. I want to tell him so badly."

"The cardinal rules, John." He patted his brother on the back. "The cardinal rules."

"There just has to be a way to get him back."

"Daddy! Uncle John!" came a shout from behind the two brothers. They turned to see Aidan approaching with a group of classmates, the children dispersing toward their parents at the designated meeting spot.

"There's our miracle child," beamed his father. "Healthy as can be, thanks to his crazy uncle."

"I knew it would work," added John. "With a little help from his friend, Gordon," he whispered.

"I saw Betsy Ross," said Aidan as he jumped into his father's arms. "She sewed the first American flag." He pointed to a sticker of the flag on his shirt.

"How many stars?"

"Thirteen. And those soldiers stayed at Valley Forge." He pointed to the field regiment. "It snowed all the time."

"Did you see the Liberty Bell?"

"Yes. It has a big crack in it," exclaimed the child excitedly.

"They rang it when the war ended." He dropped down from his father's arms and the trio began to walk away. "And I learned that Philadelphia means 'brotherly love'."

"Wow," said his father. "What an informative day."

"But I'm tired," moaned the child. "We walked so far. Can we go home?"

"You bet. Maybe, Uncle John can join us for dinner?"

"No thanks," replied John. "I think I'll just keep wandering around down here," said the doctor. "You know, kind of search for some more clues. Zachary wouldn't just leave me hanging like this."

"What's he talking about, Daddy? Who's Zachary?"

"Never you mind. Say good-bye to Uncle John."

"Good-bye, Uncle John."

The team parted ways and John Sullivan began to amble aimlessly through the historic district. The doctor made his way one block west to the historic area's main visitor center, the venue circled by a caravan of parked tour buses. Once inside, a hodge-podge of interactive activity was on display. Sullivan first watched a weaver in period costume display his trade, followed by a tutorial from a man claiming to be the city's founder himself, William Penn. He next walked by the building's main auditorium where just inside, waves of rolling laughter could be heard. The excitement prompted him to enter the rear of the exhibit hall. There on stage stood an actor in full command of his audience.

"So, here's what we do next," said the speaker wearing a coat, waistcoat and breeches. He looked over a set of bifocal glasses as he continued. "I'll start one of my famous phrases, and then I'll let you finish it. O.K.?"

"Yes. Alright," came the response from the assembly.

"Here we go. Let's start with an easy one. A penny saved..." He raised a hand to his ear.

"Is a penny earned!" came the enthusiastic reply.

"Very good. Very good." He paused. "How about this one? Early to bed and early to rise..."

"Makes a man healthy, wealthy and wise!"

"Honesty is..."

"The best policy!"

"Oh, you're good," said the most famous Philadelphian of all. "How about this one? Time is…"

"Money!"

"How true. Time is indeed money and remember, an egg today is better than a hen tomorrow."

Laughter ensued.

"Last one," quipped the orator. "It's one of my most quoted lines. Are you ready?"

"Yes!"

"Here we go. In the world nothing can be said to be certain, except for two things, that being…"

"Death and taxes!"

"Without a doubt," laughed the speaker. "Uncle Sam and the Grim Reaper, a rather gnarly combination. They'll track you down, no matter where you hide."

Some heartfelt applause followed his remark.

"Here's another game old Benjamin likes to play," said the speaker. He walked back and forth on the stage, his rotund frame balanced by a cane. "Let's see how many of you can recall a place or building in Philadelphia named after me." He quickly held up his hand. "Now don't shout, just raise a hand and I'll point to you… ready, set and go!"

Hands shot up everywhere throughout the venue and one by one, he pointed to an eager responder. An avalanche of answers followed to include: the Ben Franklin Bridge, the Ben Franklin Museum, the Franklin Institute, the Ben Franklin Parkway, Ben Franklin High School, and Franklin Street."

"You forgot one," grinned Ben. "C'mon now, where are our football fans?" He paused and pointed to a man in the third row. "Yes, sir. Help us out."

"Franklin Field."

"Bravo," said Franklin. "I threw a touchdown to Tommy Jefferson in that old stadium, a slant route… against the visiting Redcoats." He dropped pack to throw a pass. "Now, I think we've got them all. Have I forgotten any? Lord, my memory is going!" He scanned the audience. "Yes. A man in the rear... what have I forgotten?"

"The Franklin Wing," shouted Sullivan. "At the Philadelphia General Hospital."

"Ah, yes!" countered Franklin with a set of raised hands. "How could I forget? That was built near my old homestead. Thank you, sir. Shame on me." He wiped his forehead with a white handkerchief. "Now, does anyone have any questions for Mr. Franklin? He pulled out an old timepiece from his vest. "We've only got about ten minutes remaining. I've got a dinner date with John Hancock at seven... and I just love it when he signs the check."

A young boy in the second row raised his hand.

"Yes. Young man. What's your question for Benjamin Franklin?"

"How many brothers and sisters do you have?"

"Great question," said Franklin. "Let me see." He raised up and stared at all ten of his fingers. "Oh heavens, I'm running out of fingers. I had, let me get this right... nine brothers and seven sisters!"

A roar of shock and laughter rose from the crowd, along with some applause.

"That's right," laughed Ben. "There were seventeen little Franklins running around on Milk Street. I was number fifteen. That's what Dad called me, 'number fifteen'. The poor man couldn't remember all our names." He let out a hearty chuckle. "But don't feel bad, I always had a sibling to play with and a ton of hand-me-downs. But the only problem was... we only had one outhouse! Imagine that." He pointed to a young girl in the sixth row.

"Do you like being on the one hundred dollar bill?"

"Absolutely! I'm honored to have my handsome face on the 'C-note'. That infamous mug shot of mine, on the front of the so-called 'Benjamin', was painted by a Frenchman in

Paris... actually, Louis XVI's official portraitist. My only regret is not getting a haircut before that studio session."

A woman in the first row laughed hysterically.

"The one hundred dollar bill is the only denomination to feature a building not located in our nation's capital... which of course is our very own Independence Hall." He smiled. "Yes. The man near the back?"

"Did you create the postal service?"

"No. I created the public library system, but not the U.S. Postal Service. However, I was the first Postmaster General of the United States and I vow that someday, the postal service will again be profitable."

Incredulous laughter broke out in the audience.

"No, really," said Ben. "I promise." He pointed at another member of the crowd.

"What's your favorite Benjamin Franklin saying?"

"Ah, a most glorious question," smiled the founding father. "There are so many witty quips that it is difficult to choose. Let me see..." He held his hand to his chin in thought. "Well, I'm quite fond of... an ounce of prevention is worth a pound of cure." He looked upward. "And of course... he that rises late must trot all day." He continued to think. "And perhaps one that goes... keep your eyes wide open before marriage, half shut afterwards."

Laughter again ripped through the complex.

"But my favorite saying of all... is not one of my most famous. Yet, I believe it rings true to this very day." He nodded his head with firm conviction. "Yes. That's right..."

The audience waited in anticipation.

"My favorite saying of all time is... the used key is always bright."

The words pierced Sullivan's skull like a laser beam. The granite wall, he thought. But that's not exactly it. The inscription on the wall read, "the used key is always light".

"That means to keep working your mind and body, in order to stay shiny and bright," continued Franklin. "Otherwise, like the unused key on the key ring, you'll turn to rust." He pointed a finger to his head. "Pretty good one, eh? Yes, that indeed is my favorite." He grinned. "It makes perfect sense."

An appreciative round of applause followed.

"Did lightning really strike your kite?" asked a young schoolgirl to his right, with bright gold ribbons in her hair.

"Oh, did it ever!" came the emphatic reply. "I remember the day as if it were yesterday. It was June the fifth, in the year 1752." He looked up to the rafters and waved a hand, a look of fear on his face. "A nasty late afternoon storm was rolling in from South Jersey and I took my favorite kite out into a field. No sooner did I tie a skeleton key to the string when a mighty gust of wind drew the kite upward into a swirling, black cloud, and then… *CLAP!* A pitchfork of lightning struck the kite, sending a yellowish blue charge of electricity down the string and into the key!"

"Whoa," came the concerned reply.

"It energized the key and knocked me back onto the ground!" howled Franklin while taking a few dramatic steps backward. "The jolt burned a hole in my sock and rid my body of the gout!"

The kite… a skeleton key thought Sullivan! His heart began to race. But, who's R.S.?

"So in reality I not only invented the lightning rod… I *was* the first lightning rod!" He laughed. "Ah, the good old days."

"So, did you invent electricity?" asked someone.

"No. I credit God with inventing electricity. I did however prove the electrical nature of lightning." He took in a mighty breath of self-accomplishment. "I wrote about the kite experiment in a little pamphlet I used to publish called *Poor Richard's Almanac*," boasted Franklin. "It was a yearly publication, before the internet. Perhaps you've heard of it?"

Some applause followed.

"*Poor Richard's Almanac* was a popular print in the colonies," continued Franklin. "Each issue contained weather forecasts, poems, calendars and the occasional astrological muse, along with a few of my witty proverbs. I also offered the reader a collection of puzzles and games along with some household tips." He smiled fondly. "Kind of like an old fashioned blog, where I could lay it all out there, for public consumption."

"But, who was Poor Richard?" asked someone.

"Another grand question," said Franklin. "Before I reply, does anyone know the answer? Who was Poor Richard?" He scanned the room. "Anyone?"

Silence.

"Well, believe it or not... even back in the day, haters were going to hate... and old Ben Franklin didn't take kindly to criticism. So, like many of the authors of my time, I would occasionally hide my sensitive skin behind a pseudonym, in order to make a point." He looked at some of the school children in the room. "In other words, a pen name." He walked to his right with a hand behind his back. "Oh, I had plenty of them, just to confuse the reader. Let's see, there was Silence Dogood, Mr. Busy Body, Anthony Afterwit, Mrs. Martha Careful, Polly Baker and oh, here's a good one... Benevolus." He broke into laughter. "I love that one. It's grand on so many different levels." He stopped pacing and looked forward into the crowd. "But my most favorite pseudonym of all... was the one I used to author *Poor Richard's Almanac*." He paused and smiled. "And that pen name was... Richard Saunders. So the Poor Richard of *Poor Richard's Almanac* was Richard Saunders... a.k.a. Benjamin Franklin."

Sullivan's visual field went dark as his head began to spin. Richard Saunders! R.S.! The skeleton key was struck by lightning. A used key shines bright! He reached forward to grasp the key around his neck. Ben Franklin! He had Ben Franklin's key!

"And the rest they say, is history," said Franklin with a half bow. As he leaned forward a skeleton key dangled from his neck.

"Is that the key that was struck by lightning?" asked the girl with the gold ribbons.

"Oh this," replied Franklin as he stood erect. He turned the key toward his gaze. "Why yes, it was the one struck by lightning. It's still my favorite… shiny and bright. I call it the key to the future."

Sullivan grasped onto a handrail in order to steady himself. As his body swayed back and forth, he elevated his opposite hand into the air, struggling to make sense of the situation.

"Yes. My Franklin Wing friend in the rear. Go ahead sir… one last question."

The crowd turned about to stare at Sullivan as he tried to enunciate.

"Yes," said the speaker. "Hurry now. Remember, you may delay, but time will not."

"Mr. Franklin," stammered Sullivan. He held firm to the rail. "Sir, did… did you sign the Declaration of Independence?"

"Absolutely!" blurted out Franklin with a raised, fiery fist into the air. "Along with fifty-five other brave Americans, on July 4th, 1776, here… in the great city of Philadelphia. We made a pact to sign it together… so we could all hang together!"

Wild applause erupted from the gathering, in a heartfelt show of patriotic appreciation.

"Never forget the words of your forefathers… we hold these truths to be self-evident," railed Franklin. "That all men are created equal, that they are endowed by their Creator with certain unalienable Rights, that among these are Life, Liberty and the pursuit of Happiness!"

"U.S.A.! U.S.A.!"

Ben Franklin continued to rant, but Sullivan could hear no more. He staggered outside, gasping for air.

CHAPTER TWENTY-NINE
THE FINAL CLUE

"He's been coming here for as long as I can remember," proclaimed the guard to Sullivan. "And I've been around for twenty-seven years." They were standing just outside the Independence Visitor Center, watching Franklin take photos with tourists, including the occasional group selfie. "Lord, they love the man. Just look at all the smiles on their faces."

"He seems to know a ton about Ben Franklin," added Sullivan. "The man spoke inside with such unbelievable conviction."

"He'll stay here until the last tourist leaves," boasted the guard. "Just you wait and see."

"But, what's his real name?"

The sentry looked at Sullivan and hunched his shoulders. "I don't know... Ben Franklin?"

Sullivan waited another thirty minutes before approaching the man. It was nearly sunset as the last tour bus began to pull away. Ben waved good-bye as the transit passed by.

"Excuse me," said Sullivan as he trotted up behind Franklin. "Excuse me, sir."

"Yes," said the man, as he turned backward. "Ah, my Franklin Wing friend." He kept walking but continued to speak. "Thank you for reminding me about the hospital. I'll pay a surprise visit to the children's ward tomorrow morning. I promise."

Sullivan immediately appreciated that the impersonator was indeed quite old. Yet, he kept up a brisk pace with cane in hand.

"Mr. Franklin, my name is Dr. John Sullivan and I belong to the West Philadelphia Historical Society."

"Yes, I've heard of your group. A grand organization."

"Well, I'm not sure if you know it or not. But they're planning to tear down the Franklin Wing."

"What took them so long?" came the quick retort. "They built that ward back in the early 1800s, directly over the foundation of one of my homes." He came to a stop at a street corner, cautiously looking both ways. "It's probably still infested with rats."

A car driving by blew its horn. "Bennie!" came the shout from inside the vehicle. "My brother from another mother!"

Franklin gave an obligatory tip of his hat. "God, I love this town. I was born in Boston… but trust me, Philadelphia is my home."

They walked across the street.

"Mr. Franklin, there is, or should I say was, a grand wall of granite inside that hospital… with a peculiar saying engraved on it," said Sullivan. "It stated…"

"The used key is always light," interrupted Franklin with a laugh.

"Yes. Exactly! But, how did you know that?"

"I lived there! That was my wall, built from stone brought down on a barge from the Granite State." He stopped and looked at Sullivan. "Do you know what colony is nicknamed the Granite State?"

"Vermont?"

"Nope. New Hampshire. Do they teach geography anymore? I mean, kids nowadays with these so-called GPS devices. I'm not sure they know what's on the other side of the Delaware River."

Sullivan smiled, somewhat enthralled by the grandeur of the man. His persona reminded him of Zachary Schmidt. He continued to keep pace at his side.

"I hired a well-known mason to cut my favorite saying into that wall," continued Franklin. "Just before I set off on a trip to France."

"And…"

"Well, he was a fine German man, but spoke limited English. It seems that we miscommunicated a bit on the quote's exact verbiage." He looked at Sullivan. "Remember now, there was no Google translate back then." He chuckled once more. "Oh, you can imagine my consternation when I read that inscription for the first time. Somehow the word 'bright' turned to 'light'."

"The mason made a mistake?"

"Yes."

"Why didn't you have him change it?"

"Impossible! I didn't even mention the error. He was so proud of his work. Did you ever take a close look at that lettering? His handiwork was magnificent and besides, the chap was an honest man… with about ten or twelve children." He smiled. "I gave him a handsome tip of five shillings."

"So that was your wall?"

"Absolutely."

Just then a family with four young children approached the local icon.

"Mr. Franklin," asked the father respectfully. "Can my family take a picture with you?"

"It would be my honor," stated Ben. "Come along here children." He raised his arms to place them around the brood. "What a handsome crew you have here. Welcome to Philadelphia."

The children gathered around and after several photographs, Ben knelt down at their side.

"Are you having a nice visit to the city?" he asked.

"Yes," came the combined reply.

"Always remember to listen to your parents and study hard. Either write something worth reading or do something worth writing."

"Yes, Mr. Franklin."

He grinned. "And if you do poorly on an exam just tell your teacher… I didn't fail the test, I just found 100 ways to do it wrong."

The children started laughing.

"Tell them old Ben Franklin said so." He reached into his pocket and gave each child a shiny penny.

"Look Mommy," declared the youngest girl with glee. "A penny saved is a penny earned!"

Ben slowly rose to his feet and shook the hands of each parent. "You have a marvelous clan here. It was a pleasure meeting you."

"Thank you, Mr. Franklin. Thank you so much."

"Always remember… one today is worth two tomorrows." He doffed his hat, bowed and slowly turned away.

"Who are you?" asked Sullivan in amazement.

"Mr. Benjamin Franklin," came the confident reply.

"No. Your real name?"

"Mr. Benjamin Franklin. I apologize, but I haven't a middle name. Mother said she ran out of options."

Sullivan kept a wary eye on the man's face. He was good at his trade. He glanced down at the key, dangling from his neck.

"Struck by lightning," quipped Franklin. "Knocked my socks off and …"

"Rid your body of the gout… right. So I heard. But why would you call it the key to the future?"

"Because it is." He kept walking. "Time is a man-made entity, Dr. Sullivan. Behind every door is the future."

"Are there any initials on that key?"

"Perhaps." Franklin peered back at Sullivan, apparently intrigued by the question. "Why would you ask such a specific question?"

"I'm trying to figure something out. You see, back in the Franklin Wing, I noticed in the granite wall a rather peculiar slot in the exact shape of…"

Franklin stopped abruptly and turned to Sullivan. "Doctor excuse me. But do you mind if we stop in for a bite to eat? I'm utterly famished." He pointed to an eatery directly behind the physician. "My feet are killing me with these new shoes on, too. You just can't find a good cobbler nowadays. There used to be a fantastic shoemaker over on 13th and Arch, a tall Dutchman. I used to take my Deborah's Sunday best to the man, but he's closed up shop some time ago."

"Sure," answered Sullivan. "I'm hungry, too."

"Marvelous. This little place has the best cheesesteaks in Philadelphia. Trust me when I say that, and I've tasted them all." He placed an arm on Sullivan's back and led him into the establishment.

"Mr. Franklin, good evening," stated a man from behind the counter. "The usual?"

"Good evening, Anthony. How's Mrs. Firenze?"

"She's just fine."

"Wonderful. Yes, I'll have the usual, with a pint of Schmidt's beer."

"Make it two cheesesteaks… and two beers," added Sullivan. They walked over to a side booth, where the two men sat down opposite one another.

Franklin took off his hat.

"Wow, you really do look like the guy on the one hundred dollar bill," stated Sullivan. "Only a tad…"

"Older?" stated Franklin. "Life's tragedy is that we get old too soon and wise too late."

A server placed two draft beers in front of them.

"Ah, I love this place," stated Franklin. "I've been coming here for years." He held up his brew for a toast. "Be at war with your vices, at peace with your neighbors, and let every year find you a better man."

"Cheers," added Sullivan with a clank of their glasses.

"That quote was in the 1755 edition of *Poor Richard's Almanac*," continued Franklin. He placed a napkin on his lap. "Do you know as a child, I only wanted to be a sailor?"

"No."

"Father wouldn't allow it. I had an older brother lost at sea."

"Oh. I'm sorry to hear that." After speaking the condolence, Sullivan took mental pause, reminding himself that he was indeed talking to a skilled thespian.

Two cheesesteaks quickly landed in front of the men.

"I also used to be a vegetarian in my teens," continued Franklin. "Imagine that?" He held up the greasy concoction. "Bon appétit, doctor."

Both men took hearty bites of the local fare, their conversation coming to a halt for several minutes. Throughout the meal an occasional passerby would tap on the window and wave at Ben, prompting him to wink and grin. Despite the interruptions, he consumed his cheesesteak in rapid fashion.

"Wow, you were really hungry," commented Sullivan.

"That was one hell of a cheesesteak," declared Franklin as he dabbed his lips with a napkin. He finished his beer with a gulp.

"And thirsty."

Franklin smiled and paused before speaking. "Doctor, you mentioned something about a slot in my granite wall?"

"Yes," continued Sullivan. "It was in the shape of a skeleton key."

"Did you happen to find the skeleton key?"

Sullivan paused while staring directly into Franklin's slate gray eyes. "Why... did you happen to lose a skeleton key?"

"Is that it around your neck?" asked Benjamin. "The key that is, attached to your necklace?"

Sullivan did not reply.

"Does it have the initials R.S. on it?" asked Franklin. "Because if so, I believe you've found my old key."

"How do you know that?" stammered Sullivan. "*Who* are you?"

"You've asked that question already, dear man. I'm Benjamin Franklin."

Sullivan reached beneath his collar and delivered the key into sight. His hand trembled slightly.

"Heavens," whispered Franklin slowly. He tilted his head back to better focus. "My favorite key! I lost it centuries ago after a contentious card game in the basement."

"A card game?"

"Yes. I had the original man cave up in West Philadelphia. One night, after a few quaffs, John Adams got a bit out of hand after capitulating to my bluff." He smirked. "The pot was grand... he had two pairs and I had absolutely nothing. What followed was a bit of a row. He accused me of dealing from the bottom of the deck." Franklin reached forward to stroke the key. "Somehow in the scuffle, I lost my key." He smiled. "Hello old friend. I thought I'd never see you again."

"So, this is your key?"

"Absolutely," answered Franklin. "The more important question is, Dr. Sullivan... did you place it in the granite key slot?"

Sullivan stared forward. He slowly and distinctly answered, "Yes. That's why I'm here."

A mischievous grin came across Franklin's face. "I see." He nodded in recognition. "So, Dr. Sullivan, let me ask you another question. Are you familiar with the twin paradox?"

"Absolutely."

"Well then, let's say you and I keep walking." Franklin slowly slid his stout frame out of the booth. "I'd like to show you something."

While paying the bill at the counter, Sullivan noticed a framed picture on the back wall. In it stood Franklin with his arm around the owner. The autographed caption read, "Anthony, eat to please thyself... dress to please others." Beneath the caption was Franklin's characteristic signature. Peculiar to Sullivan was the fact that the proprietor, Anthony Firenze appeared thirty years younger, yet Franklin appeared the same age. He glanced back at Franklin.

"The best to Mrs. Firenze," said Franklin. He put on his hat.

"Good night, Mr. Franklin," answered Anthony. "Stay well."

Franklin led Sullivan outside, turning north onto 4th street. His pace was slow and pensive. Dusk was descending upon the city. They walked a half a block before Franklin spoke.

"Do you know what makes Philadelphia so darn special?" asked Franklin.

Sullivan didn't reply.

"The fact that a man can walk around town dressed like Benjamin Franklin and no one would find it peculiar... whether it be 1860, 1960 or 2060. Nowhere else in America can that occur."

"Good evening, Mr. Franklin," said a local denizen as he passed by.

"Good evening, friend," responded the founding father. Several seconds passed. "Do you know that over 20,000 attended my funeral?"

"No."

"It was a beautiful affair. The population of Philadelphia in 1790 was about 28,000. So it was a grand turnout."

Sullivan just stared down at the passing pavement beneath his feet, the rhythmic strike of Franklin's cane marking their forward progress.

"Now, back to the twin paradox," continued Franklin. "May I ask you a hypothetical, doctor?"

"Yes."

"I call it the thinking game. Are you good at mathematics?"

"Sort of."

"Alright now. Let's assume that a man faces his mortality at age eighty-four, in perhaps the year, 1790."

"Yes."

"And a key, blessed with powers from a strike of lightning, gives him the opportunity to transport forward in time to reap the benefits of modern medicine, say in the year, 2065." He looked over at Sullivan. "Are you with me?"

"So, he transports forward... in order to save his life?"

"Yes."

"O.K. I'm with you," said Sullivan.

"With the single caveat that in order to stay alive, he must for the vast majority of his lifetime... remain in the future, where according to the twin paradox, he ages at a much slower rate... say twenty years to one."

Sullivan's heart began to pound as he tried to calculate the possibility.

"Of course, he would be granted the opportunity to occasionally transport back to visit his hometown, that is to say, as local time marches on." Franklin paused to tip his hat to a passing woman. "So here today in the year 2020, how old would that eighty-four-year old man currently be? Keeping in mind, the aging ratio is twenty years to one."

Sullivan mind couldn't calculate fast enough. Over 200 years had passed since 1790. He tried to offer a response, but Franklin spoke first.

"Let me answer the question," continued Franklin. "The lucky chap in the year 2020, with the help of modern medicine... would only be ninety-five years old."

Sullivan's jaw dropped. It was possible!

"Is that your namesake on The Sullivan Institute?" asked Franklin. "Up in West Philadelphia? You know, the tall building with the words... Recall, Respect and Rejuvenate on the facade?"

"Why yes. I believe it is."

"Well then, thank you for caring for me... and thank you for the referral to that young surgeon who implanted a so-called 'memory booster' in my brain. *That*... was godsent. Old Ben's memory was starting to slip before that chip went in." He tapped his forehead as if trying to recall a fact. "What was that young's surgeon's name again? He was a rather handsome lad."

"Quentin?" mumbled Sullivan.

"Yes!" replied Franklin with a snap of his fingers. "Quentin Theo Sullivan. Any relation?"

"Why, yes... or, I mean... I think so."

They continued to walk in silence to the end of the block, turning left on Arch Street.

"Dr. Sullivan, did you ever wonder how one individual could make such a difference in the world?" asked Franklin. "Think about it... the foresight, the wisdom, the inventions and the guidance that fostered the birth of a nation?" He stopped walking just shy of the next intersection. "It's almost like I got a sneak peek around the corner," grinned Franklin. He turned to face Sullivan. "Did that possibility ever cross your mind?"

"So... you *are* Benjamin Franklin," stated Sullivan in awe.

"Yes, in the flesh. The original."

"Oh my god," said Sullivan, a rush of emotions ripping through his frame. "Benjamin Franklin, the founding father of our nation!" His legs became weak and he reached out to grasp a black, cast iron fence to his right. "But, but… why are there two keys?"

"I had a second one in my pocket," said Franklin. "During the kite experiment that is. They both were magically charged… each capable of unlocking the future."

Sullivan looked down to gather his bearings. He took a few deep breaths and stared up into the sky. "Where… where are we?" He glanced to his right to see a graveyard behind the wrought iron fence, next to a church.

"That's Christ Church," stated Franklin proudly. "Founded in 1695 as a condition of William Penn's charter. See that steeple?" He pointed to a majestic white spire rising from the church proper, its apex piercing the darkness of the sky. "I organized a lottery to finance it in 1754. A classic example of Georgian architecture."

Sullivan stood speechless, his mind trying to grasp the magnitude of the moment.

"Do you know the difference between a cemetery and a graveyard, Dr. Sullivan?" He paused a bit. "Remember, the thinking game? We're still playing."

"No. No, I don't."

"A graveyard is always connected to a church, whereas a cemetery is not."

Sullivan stared in astonishment at the man in front of him. He reached out to touch him while mumbling, "Benjamin Franklin."

"Never stop learning, young man," followed up Franklin. "Always remember, when you're finished changing… you're finished." He laughed. "Oh, I've always liked that one."

Sullivan pointed through the iron fence. "Your grave. That's your gravesite." Just inside the fence lay a marble marker, with the etching 'Benjamin and Deborah Franklin, 1790'.

"Indeed it is," came the response. "My eternal resting place, next to Deborah. My dear children, Francis and Sarah are also entombed nearby, along with four other signers of the Declaration of Independence." He made a sign of the cross. "Hallowed ground, indeed."

"Look at all the pennies on top."

"I've often thought of a more majestic tomb," continued Franklin. "But there's beauty in the simplicity of it. I've always considered myself a common man... a Philadelphian through and through. So it's just perfect."

Sullivan paused out of respect. He then turned toward Franklin. "Do you want your key back?"

"No. You keep it." He patted Sullivan on the shoulder. "It may come in handy... in the future."

"Thank you," stammered Sullivan as he grasped the key. "I hope so."

"There's only one thing that still bothers me to this very day," continued Franklin. "One little thing." He stared into the graveyard while speaking.

"What's that?"

"That no one ever figured it out."

"Figured what out?" asked Sullivan.

"That I'm a time traveler," came the reply. "I left everyone such a grand clue. It still amazes me."

"A clue?" asked Sullivan. "Where? Here?" He looked around.

"My epitaph," said Franklin. "See?" He pointed to a bronze marker attached to a stone pillar anchoring the fence. "I wrote it myself. It couldn't be more obvious."

Sullivan turned about to read the inscription:

The Body of
B. Franklin, Printer,
Like the Cover of an old Book,
Its Contents torn out,
And Stript of its Lettering & Gilding,
Lies here. Food for Worms.

But the Work shall not be lost,
For it will as he believ'd
appear once more
In a new and more elegant Edition
Corrected and improved
By the Author.

A flash of light occurred followed by a high-pitched zoom. Sullivan turned around… and Franklin was gone. He next heard the voice of a child walking by with his mother.

"Mommy. That man just disappeared. I saw a ghost!"

"Don't be silly," said the mother. "There are no such things as ghosts. Come along now… we're running out of time."

THE END

ABOUT THE AUTHOR

Dr. Michael Banas completed his undergraduate studies at the University of Scranton. He then attended the University of Pennsylvania School of Medicine followed by an Orthopedic residency at the University of Rochester. His final year of surgical training took him to Los Angeles where he completed a Sports Medicine Fellowship at the Southern California Orthopedic Institute. Dr. Banas currently resides in Dallas, PA with his wife, Theresa. They keep company with Samantha the dog and Milo, the incorrigible cat. Dr. Banas specializes in Orthopedic Surgery and Sports Medicine.

Made in the USA
Columbia, SC
16 September 2021

45556918R10185